TALES OF FEATHERS AND FLAMES

STORIES SET IN THE WORLD OF DIRE

SAYLOR FERGUSON   MARIA PUENCHIR

ALEXANDER BIZZELL   J. F. R. COATES

M. H. WOLFE   GLENN BIRMINGHAM

Edited by
K. VALE NAGLE

Edited by
JOHN BAILEY

MYTHIC HOUSE

Cover Art by Fleeks Sputtelspecht (www.fleeks.art).

Interior graphics by Crystal Gafford of Crafty as a Coyote.

Dire Rada interior art by Maria Puenchir.

"An Invisible Enemy" ©2020 J. F. R. Coates

"Wolf Eyes" © 2020 Saylor Ferguson

"Kitcarer" © 2020 Saylor Ferguson

"Relwen" ©2021 Saylor Ferguson

"Embers" ©2020 M. H. Wolfe

"Dire Story" ©2020 Alexander Bizzell

"Your Dire Adventure" ©2021 Glenn Birmingham

Coldbright ©2021 K. Vale Nagle

Published by Mythic House.

Trade Paperback Edition
ISBN-13: 978-0-6486990-5-7
ISBN-10: 0-6486990-5-6

CONTENTS

Dire Rada

FOREWORD

The hardest part of any author's career is the moment right after their first book release. They're brand new on the author scene, and they're worried about what readers will think. Not only that, but as readers finish their first book, they want to know when the second will be out! The stress of completion and expectation can be daunting.

That's how it is for normal years. 2020 was something special, and I'm using 'special' here to mean 'terrible.' In April of 2020, I was expecting to house John Bailey here in Colorado. He'd spend a few days with me and some fellow fantasy authors and artists before moving on to his next convention. Alexander Bizzell was going to meet him in Canada, where a box of copies of *Dire* were waiting for him to sign and sell at conventions up there, then he'd come south to the United States to continue his tour.

Then COVID-19 hit. His trip was cancelled without a refund. Those books were stranded in Canada. And his debut was cut short.

Nobody had an easy time writing in 2020. There were too many things to worry about, too many terrible things happening. But many of the authors, artists, and fans that John would have met here in North America wanted a way to show their support—both emotionally and financially—and let him know the rest of the gryphon and dragon communities are looking forward to reading his next book.

I became the focal point for this effort almost by accident. More and more people asked if they could do anything for John. Fellow authors, fans, writers, editors, and artists donated their time and their hearts to create this anthology. All of the stories are donated, all of the proceeds from sales of this book go to John. Everyone was happy to contribute a short novel, a short story, artwork, editing, covers, proofreading, or formatting skills to make it happen.

The stories and artwork contained within take place in the world of *Dire*. None of them are necessarily canon, though John was given a copy prior to publication for his feedback and editorial notes, to make sure no one broke his world. In a sense, an anthology of this type is like fanfiction: it's an opportunity to play in someone else's sandbox. I still maintain that fanfiction is one of the greatest forms of flattery.

Most of the stories here can be read in any order, so feel free to skip around. Saylor Ferguson's stories have a progression to them, so you may want to read them in order the first time. And Glenn Birmingham's "Your Dire Adventure" offers the reader choices that play upon the first few chapters of *Dire* and have a nod to each of the other stories in the collection, so it may be best to read his last. (At the very least, read M. H. Wolfe's story ahead of time.)

If you enjoy *Dire* and this anthology celebrating it,

may I make a recommendation? Leave a review for *Dire* or recommend it to a friend. And if you've done those and there's a story you really enjoyed from here, check the contributor biographies in the back of the book to learn more about the writers.

And lastly, if you're John reading this for the first time: keep writing. Every person here, contributor or reader, loves your book and is here to support you. As much as writing can feel like a lonely, costly pursuit, I hope this serves as a reminder that your place among your peers in the gryphon and dragon author communities is secure. (And in the much smaller, but no less stylish, opinicus community.)

Your launch celebration was torn from you and left you in financial distress, the world was consumed by a horrific plague that still overshadows our lives, social and political injustices long simmering started boiling over. There is always uncertainty in life, tomorrow is never assured, but starting in 2020 our global sense of safety has been stripped away violently. That will take time to heal. The events of this budding decade have been traumatic and terrifying and they will change us.

These are the times we need stories more than ever. Stories help us process the darkness in the world by escaping to other places, other people, with simpler lives where we can expect idealism to triumph and conflict to be resolved meaningfully, where people can grow and be recognized and rewarded for it. Stories give us hope and soothe our aches so we may face the next day, and the next. And as much as we need stories, we need storytellers to bring those worlds and ideals to life, to draw us into a different place, to make people and their problems real, to give us a mirror of our own world that is more palatable to look into, to show us how it *ought to be.*

May these stories and artwork, as you see the world of *Dire* through our eyes and the love we have for it, rekindle your passion. We are excited to read the rest of the series, to see the world and characters you've brought to life continue.

-Vale Nagle

AN INVISIBLE ENEMY

J. F. R. COATES

A lone gryphon soared through the clear blue sky. Conditions were perfect for flight and hunting, but she flew alone. No one else tested their wings on the thermals, cutting into the gentle wind that blew down from the mountains at her back. Open meadows that should have been flush with hunting gryphs and herds of grazing prey remained empty. Nothing larger than a rabbit moved through the sparse grassland.

The meadows took up a wide swathe of land between the foothills and the forest that ran almost parallel to the great ranges. At its widest, the flight between the mountains and the trees was over a mark at a comfortable pace. Taera flew much faster than that. Urgent summons had forced her to leave her pride in the mountains after a flustered opinicus messenger had requested her services. Details had been vague, for the opinicus had only heard of the summons second hand, but enough had been said to push Taera to action.

Taera had brought what she could, strapping her sides with small bags of medicinal herbs, as well as food to feed herself for several days should there be no hunters at her destination. She did not know if the crisis was a series of injuries or an unknown sickness that had taken hold. To a carer such as herself, she needed to be alert and ready for whatever waited for her in the forest.

The gryphon scanned across the horizon, searching for the landmarks she had been directed towards to guide her flight. A curve in the river that looked like a claw. A rock shaped like a deer. A tall tree that towered over the rest of the canopy. Taera was not familiar with this side of the mountains, as there was little out here that interested her pride. Her wings had not taken her this direction before, but the directions had been clear enough to follow. She knew she was getting close. Her wings would be grateful for the rest.

A voice screeched out from below. Wings fluttered as a dark shape burst out from the canopy. A lone gryphon rose in a frantic flapping of wings.

"No further, please," the gryphon called out.

Taera flared her wings, arresting her speed and pulling up into a clumsy hover above the trees. "I am Taera. I was informed there were gryphs here who needed a carer?"

The other gryphon hovered on the spot, just above the canopy. His hindpaws hung low, almost brushing against the topmost leaves. His beak clacked warily, before he nodded his head once. "That is true, yes. I am Aryc. It was me who sent a messenger to your pride."

"Then could you take me through to your dire," Taera said, with a bow of her head. She struggled to maintain a steady hover, with her body rising and falling with each beat of her wings. "I would like to learn what ails your pride from them."

"Dire?" The other gryphon squawked and tilted his head.

"Yes," Taera snapped. Perhaps the affliction was a disease of the mind, one that limited the pride's ability to think clearly. "The dire who rules these lands. I desire to speak with them."

"Oh," the other gryphon said. He angled his wings to turn around in a tight spin. "I think you should come with me. I'll take you to where you need to be."

Taera gratefully followed Aryc as he began to fly away, keeping above the canopy. Grasping leaves and branches seemed to reach up for her paws as she flew low to the trees, staying in the slipstream of the other gryphon to give her wings a little rest after her long, hard flight.

Sounds of a river reached Taera's ears, getting louder with every wingbeat. Where she expected to hear other gryphs moving around, she heard only silence. But for the lone gryphon who had come to collect her, there seemed little evidence of a functioning pride out here in the forest. There were no hunters swooping after their prey. No kits playing. Taera's claws flexed. Her senses were all on alert, just in case there was some deception happening.

Taera couldn't think of any reason why she would be drawn out so far from her pride only to be ambushed by a pack of gryphs with questionable scruples. She was only a carer, and she hadn't been named by the messenger. The opinicus had only been seeking a carer – any carer, and not her specifically. The prickling at her neck feathers didn't quite go away.

There appeared nothing wrong with the other gryphon. Aryc appeared perfectly healthy to her trained eyes. His wings were strong and his flight steady. But for his apparent confusion when she questioned him about the local dire, he was not in need of a carer. Perhaps the pride had sent one of their healthy members to greet her.

The gryphon slowly descended, sinking below the canopy into a small clearing that had been cut through the trees like a giant claw swipe. A red-tinged river flowed through the clearing, travelling from north to south, perpendicular to the mountains behind Taera.

Wooden structures clung to the sides of the trees, leaning out from the thick trunks. Cabins and walkways had been constructed, wide enough even for a dire to walk across without discomfort. Dozens of trees on either side of the river had been surrounded with these elaborate buildings, lashed together with rope and cut beams of wood, as well as other techniques Taera could not immediately identify.

Nets hung from the walkways crossing the river, dangling down into the water. The nets fluttered in the current. Several fish were entangled in the ropes, though there was no one there to retrieve the catches.

Her guide fluttered down onto a wide, flat platform of wood, the surface of which had been scratched and gouged by hundreds of talons. Taera followed him, landing close to the edge and peering down at the river below. From her new vantage she could see dozens of fish caught in the nets. A dozen more lay motionless on the banks upstream.

Taera turned her focus to the trees around her. Curious eyes peered out from some of the nearest cabins, though no gryphs wandered the tree-top homes and walkways.

"What is this place?" Taera asked her guide.

"Our home," Aryc replied. He did not look back at Taera. His eyes were focused entirely on the river. "For fractures we have lived here, growing our home with care and hard work. We have been happy and healthy for so long, but that all changed two weeks ago."

"If you take me to your dire, then I can start to work things out," Taera said. She glanced around. All the gryph-made homes clinging to the side of the trees looked the same size. Apart from the landing platform, there appeared to be nowhere that might be considered a central location for the weave of homes, nowhere she would expect to see a dire's throne.

Aryc squawked in laughter. "There is no dire here. We have never had one. We have no need of one."

Taera blinked. "Oh. You're wilders. Not a pride."

"Is that going to be a problem?"

Taera took a step back from her guide. Her wings fluttered, before settling against her back. "No. I have a duty to care for any gryph who needs my help. Prided or otherwise."

"Then we are indebted to you, Taera," the gryphon said, bending his forelegs to bow before her. "I am the only healthy one left, though we have been at a loss to explain why that might be."

"What are the symptoms that have been developing?" Taera asked. She swung her head around, peering across to the eyes that gazed out from the wooden homes. No one had come to meet her, with all keeping their distance.

"It started with nausea and dizziness," Aryc explained. He flicked a wing at Taera to encourage her to follow him as he walked from the landing platform. A narrow walkway stretched out towards the closest trees, bowing and swaying with each of the larger gryphon's steps. "We grounded the gryphs who suffered symptoms, but they spread so quickly. Soon almost everyone couldn't fly."

"And why have you not developed the same symptoms?" Taera asked. She cautiously placed her weight on the walkway, feeling the wood flex beneath her paw. She clicked her beak and looked down at the riverbanks below. A fall of that distance was uncomfortable, even for a gryphon with wings. Too far to safely drop and not hurt herself, but too short to properly flare her wings and slow her fall.

Aryc hung his head low. "I wish I knew that. My store of food and water came from the same place as everyone else's. I have lived and mingled with everyone as usual, but they have grown steadily sicker while I have remained healthy."

"I would like to inspect the sick. If there are gryphs at various stages of illness, that might allow me to track how this illness progresses," Taera said, ignoring the flinch from Aryc. She knew she could be blunt with how she discussed the sick and wounded sometimes, but she needed to do that. She needed to think with reason, not emotion, when it came to curing those who needed her help.

"I will see to that," Aryc said. He glanced back at her. "I do not know how long you will be required to stay here, but we have plenty of spare shelters for you. Until we are sure what this sickness is, I do not think you should hunt. Do you have food with you?"

"I have enough to last a couple of days," Taera replied. She shuffled her wings, brushing against the packs she had strapped to her sides and belly. She looked forward to removing them, and the thought of a shelter, no matter how temporary, sounded tempting.

"Then let me get you settled in, and then I can take you to those who need your care."

Taera mantled her appreciation to the other gryphon. The prickling on her neck feathers had not fully settled down, but she could see now that there was a genuine need for her services. A mysterious illness that left just one gryphon alone. This was something that would test her skills. For the lives of every gryph in this tree-top perch, she had to succeed.

TAERA CAUTIOUSLY MADE HER WAY THROUGH THE TREES. She did not fully trust the wooden walkways beneath her paws, half expecting them to shatter from her weight, but they remained strong. The trees were close enough to each other that flying between them would be dangerous. The last thing she wanted was to clip her wing against stray branches and damage the fragile bones.

The carer tried to visit every sick gryph in the treetop shelters. Many marks passed her by until darkness began to swallow the forest, and all Taera could determine was that every gryph displayed the same symptoms. Dizziness prevented flight, and nausea prevented eating. A couple of the older gryphs had already died, before Taera's arrival. A few more looked like they could only last another day or two. Few were capable of coherently responding to Taera's questions.

One of the fittest gryphs was a hippogryph female called Seli. Her feathers were dark and matted, ungroomed for several days, but her eyes had not yet dimmed with fatigue. She was still capable of standing upright, though she needed to lean against the walls of her shelter after a few minutes.

"Most of us all got the first symptoms at the same

time," Seli explained. She wearily gestured to the mostly full store of dried fish and ceramic pot of water she had tucked away in the corner of her small shelter. They had been untouched for days. "We think it was in the fish, but Aryc has eaten from the same river as us."

"My first thought was to the fish," Taera said slowly. She caught herself from scratching her claws across the wooden floor, not wanting to damage Seli's shelter as she struggled to compose her thoughts. If Aryc had gotten sick, then that would make things simple. "I have seen such sicknesses before, but they have never killed anyone. A day of rest with water is usually enough to recover."

"The water made everyone worse," Seli said, her ears drooping.

Taera's ears perked, opposing Seli's reaction. This time, the carer's claws did tense and scrape at the wood. "Worse? How so?"

Seli's wings fluttered as she struggled to lift her head. "The water made us weaker and brought up our stomachs. None of us have been able to keep even a drop of water down. Those who drank too much could no longer stand at all."

"That's interesting," Taera said quietly. She glanced back, towards the sunset streaming through the trees. "Do you take your water from the same place you hunt for fish?"

"I can show you if you like," Seli said. She lurched forward half a pace, almost falling over until Taera managed to get her body between the hippogryph and the floor.

"You are not in any condition for that," Taera squawked. She grunted and gripped her claws into the floor as she tried to push the hippogryph upright. The weight of the sick gryph pinned down on her shoulders, straining her muscles until Seli was able to regain her balance.

"I can do this," Seli replied, weakly stomping a forepaw in irritation. She pushed at Taera until the carer gave her a little space.

Taera sighed and stepped back, giving the hippogryph the space to move. Seli swayed from side to side as she shook her head, readjusting her forepaws several times before she was able to maintain her balance. "Are you sure about this?"

"If you're to help us, then you need to know," Seli snapped, anger coming to her voice. She clacked her beak and took in a deep breath. Her steps were small and shuffling, but she was able to stop herself from falling over again, keeping her neck stiff and upright. She looked directly into the low sunlight. Her eyes remained open, not squinting her eyes at all as dappled shadows fell across her face.

"I can get Aryc to show me," Taera said, but her protests were pushed aside by the sick hippogryph.

"You said he was giving out your medicine," Seli replied. She bumped her beak against Taera's, wordlessly asking the carer to retreat from the doorway.

Taera hissed to herself. She backed out of the small shelter, carefully placing her hindpaws close to the edge of the walkway. The sunlight blazed orange and bright as it shone through the trees, casting dappled shadows through the wilders' tree-top home. Throughout the canopy, Taera could hear the pitiful and weak sounds of gryphs struggling to move. Some coughed and wheezed, while others tried to chirp and sing. Murmured voices reached her ears as Aryc moved from shelter to shelter.

She had given him simple instructions on how to distribute some of the herbal medicine she had brought with her. The carer did not have much hope for the effectiveness of the medicine until she was able to identify what had caused the illness to spread so quickly. She was buying time, that was all.

Seli permitted Taera to walk beside her. The carer's wing draped protectively over the slow-moving hippogryph. They walked painfully slowly, but Taera did not dare rush Seli any faster than she could walk. Together, they shuffled towards the landing platform in the center of the small settlement.

The ground beneath the walkways was swallowed up by the growing darkness, disappearing into shadow. Only the river remained visible, sparkling and twinkling in the dying light. Twilight had fallen by the time Seli had managed to shuffle the short distance to the platform. The hippogryph stumbled forward to lean against the raised fencing around the side, before settling down onto her haunches. Her wings both hung limply against her sides.

"You hunt from here?" Taera asked, with a tilt of her head.

The hippogryph extended a taloned forepaw. She tugged weakly at a woven strand of twine that was connected to the net extending below the platform. "We can drop and raise the net without getting wet. Fish are caught in the net, which we dry and store to eat later. We fill pitchers of water from the banks."

Taera chirruped. "That is hardly a way to hunt."

"It is our way," Seli replied. Her weakness did little to disguise the aggression or defensiveness in her tone. "We do not waste time hunting when there are more interesting things to do."

"Gryphs should take pride in how they hunt," Taera protested.

"And we take pride in how little effort we need to expend in order to feed everyone," Seli snapped back. Despite her weakness, she stamped down with her taloned paw, lifting her head up and partially unfurling her wings.

Taera closed her beak, biting down on the retort that had started to well up. She did not want to goad Seli into a challenge.

The carer turned her head aside. She allowed herself a moment to reason through Seli's explanation. She had not thought about it that way. A hunter should be praised for how quickly and efficiently they caught their prey. Did that mean a net to catch dozens of fish at once should be treated with the same respect? Taera didn't like the thought. It went against every teaching she had known in her pride. It was little more than a cheap trick that needed no skill, but it did feed the gryphs who relied on the net. Someone had used skill to weave the ropes and the net itself. Was that as valuable as the skill of a hunter who used wings and claw to bring down their prey?

"You are right, I apologize," Taera said, conceding the point vocally, even if she had not yet resolved her concerns internally. She did not want to antagonise the hippogryph, especially if she could help work out the cause of this illness. The carer approached the edge of the platform and peered down to the dark water below. "You only fish from here? You have no other food supply?"

"We hunt for game on the plains sometimes," Seli said breathlessly. She had to pause to suck in several deep gulps of air. Her eyes were squeezed closed, even as she sat with her head bowed low. "But we have only hunted for fish recently."

"You had lots stored in your shelter," Taera commented. She had seen several woven baskets of dried fish, as well as the large clay jar filled with water.

Seli nodded. "Most of us restocked with a large catch the other day." She paused a moment. Her beak remained partially open. "It was the day after that we began to get sick."

Taera had ideas on what was causing the sickness, but first she needed to be sure. She would not get those answers while the sky was ablaze with stars. She needed the light of the sun to see by, lest she risk missing some crucial clue or detail in the shadows. She bowed her head towards the panting hippogryph. "You should get some sleep."

Seli said nothing for a moment, nor did she move. She stared down at the landing platform. Her head slowly moved to look up at the carer. "You do know how to heal us, don't you?"

"It's hard to say for certain..." Taera hesitated. She saw the light fading in Seli's eyes as the hippogryph's hope began to wane. The carer tensed her claws. "I will do everything I can for you. For all of you. Wilder or prided, it does not matter. You are all gryphs, and I will cure you."

Taera extended her wing to offer assistance to the ailing hippogryph. Together, one step at a time, they slowly made their way back to Seli's home. So many thoughts swirled through Taera's head. It would take all night to sort through them all.

Taera slept restlessly that night. She often struggled to sleep in new surroundings, and the occasional sounds of discomfort were not muffled by the open spaces between the trees. There was nothing she could do to ease the gryphs overnight. Her medicine might lift some of the symptoms, but what they really needed was water to flush away the sickness. But it appeared to be the water that was making them sick, not just the food.

By the time dawn touched the trees, Taera felt like she had barely slept for a single mark. A growing chorus of song would usually greet the rising sun, but the forest was quiet. Even Taera did not feel up to adding her voice to the silence and greet the sun, and she did not have a debilitating sickness that sapped her strength. She quickly ate a simple breakfast of dried deer meat, swallowing down a mouthful of her own diminishing water supply after.

Aryc was already awake when Taera made her careful way through the treetops to his shelter. He looked to have slept as little as Taera. His feathers were unkempt and wild, and his furred hindquarters were just as untidy. He chirped in greeting to the carer.

"I'd like to see the river today," Taera said. Her eyes slowly scanned around the small shelter. All the wooden structures looked to be built the same, with dozens of cut planks being bound together with woven twine. The carer was fascinated to know what else had gone into the construction, but she had more important things to worry about.

Aryc bowed his head in acceptance. He plucked a dried fish from a storage container and tore into the meat with the tip of his beak. He showed no fear or concern for the sickness that had been present in his wilder companions.

Taera sat back on her haunches as she waited for Aryc to finish his breakfast. Her eyes were drawn to the storage baskets, which were almost empty. A thought came to her mind. "Seli told me most of the pride fished the day before the sickness spread. You didn't, did you?"

"Why do you ask?" Aryc replied, his head angled to one side.

"You don't have much left. Seli's baskets were almost full," Taera said, waving her forepaw in the direction of the empty baskets.

"Oh," Aryc said. He flicked his ears. "Yeah, I'd already stocked up a few days earlier. Do you think that's important?"

Taera could have hit the gryphon, but she held herself back. "Yes," she squawked. She contented herself with tapping her claws against the floor. "It's why you haven't gotten sick. Whatever infected the food did so after you last hunted."

The other gryphon's eyes widened. "Oh," he repeated. His wings fluttered as he rose to his paws. "So, we know something changed in the river recently. If we find out what caused the infection..."

"We might be able to stop it spreading further," Taera finished, after Aryc had trailed off.

"We need to search the river," Aryc said. He jerked into activity, almost pushing past Taera as he hastened to get outside. He flared his wings and leaped over the side of the walkway, soaring down to the leafy ground below.

Taera followed him a little further behind. With her wings outstretched, she was able to glide to the ground without a single beat, swooping around to land a few paces from the riverbank. An unpleasant smell filled her nares. Rotting flesh littered the bank, upstream of the dangling nets. Dozens of dead fish had washed up to the bank and were slowly decomposing in the mud. She grabbed one in her clawtips and tossed it away from the water.

"Are these causing the sickness?" Aryc asked, peering over Taera's shoulder.

Taera shook her head. "No. These fish are suffering from the same sickness as the gryphs. This is another symptom. Not a cause."

"We should throw away the fish, just in case," Aryc said, stepping forward to drag another dead fish from the water. He threw it away into the undergrowth.

Taera gestured with her beak to the far side of the river. "You sweep up that side. We walk upstream until we find the source."

Aryc glanced up to the shelters in the trees. "Will they be alright without us?"

"They'll be better if we work out what is causing their illness," Taera replied. She began to walk, stopping only to throw away any dead fish that had snagged in the reeds that lined the banks. She didn't worry about those that floated on the surface. They would wash away naturally. The nets would have to get cleaned on their return.

The river wound through the forest, with the trees looming close to the banks. The water was mostly clean, though it was stained slightly brown close to the edges. Taera had seen such discolouration before and knew that was nothing to do with the illness that plagued the gryphs in the treetop shelters. This was something different, an infection that had spread through the water and was targeting both fish and the gryphs who then consumed those diseased creatures. With so many gryphs infected, there were not enough healthy hunters to search for alternate sources of food, nor to supply enough water to flush away the disease. Aryc could not do it alone. Taera needed to cleanse this river to save their lives.

Taera made sure not to miss a single trapped fish. She occasionally glanced across to Aryc, keeping pace with the over gryphon as he splashed through the shallows. His focus was entirely on the river. He was more determined than Taera to scoop out the fish still caught in the current, and his legs and chest were soaked with the icy cool water. He showed no discomfort at all. Determination was etched in his eyes and the set of his beak.

The further from the wilder camp they walked, the fewer fish Taera found on the bank. She could only hope that meant they were getting closer to the source, giving the fish less chance to sicken and die.

Little moved through the forest. No prey scampered amongst the undergrowth. But for the river providing its fish, Taera doubted a pride could sustain itself out here. Or perhaps the presence of the wilders had chased away the prey, forcing them to reply on the fish. She couldn't be sure. All the mattered was the fact that the river was the lifeblood for the wilders.

The trees began to thin. Light glared through the canopy as the two gryphons reached the edge of the forest. Open grasslands stretched out before them, with the river winding like a glittering ribbon towards the distant mountains. A branching offshoot curved away to the right, sweeping around the edge of the forest. That was the river Taera had flown over on the way to the wilders' camp. If they had not yet reached the source of the infection, then that river was likely tainted too.

Taera called a brief pause to their march. The ground underpaw was soft and damp, with fragments of mud clinging to her claws. She prowled forward, moving up a small isthmus that protruded into the river, with water flowing to her left and right. The two branches of the river angled away from each other, with one skirting the edge of the forest, and the other plunging directly into the trees.

The carer could see nothing ahead that might have caused the infection. Her eyes tracked the river as far as she could see, towards the distant mountains. Nothing appeared unusual. The sky was mostly empty of life, but this was an isolated region without much prey to hunt. There were few prides here, and the dires did not feel the need to fight each other over who got to control this barren area.

"Anything over there?" Taera called out. Aryc had continued without stopping. Nothing got in his way, as the river on his bank remained unbroken.

"Just a lot of dead fish," the gryphon called back. He didn't stop moving, nor did he turn his head.

Taera flicked her ears back, pinning them to her head. There had to be something creating the illness. The whole river couldn't have soured with infection. She pawed at the soft mud, before spreading her wings and launching across the forking river. The sunlight warmed her feathers as she kept her wings extended, but there was no pleasure like usual. She could not enjoy the warm light, not yet.

The carer lost track of how far they walked. Behind the pair, the forest slowly receded until it could barely be seen anymore. Ahead, the mountains appeared to remain at the same, constant distance. The undulating lands either side of the river were mostly barren, with just thin grass covering the muddy terrain. Few animals grazed, and they ignored the two gryphs as they moved further upriver. The number of fish plucked from the water diminished further.

"I think I see something," Aryc said. He remained a few paces ahead of Taera, but that distance was quickly closed as the carer jumped into a run. A moment later, she could see what attracted Aryc's attention.

The riverbank on Taera's side had been churned up in a struggle, with mud and reed battered and crushed. Sticking up from below the surface of the water was a single hoofed foot. At least one of the prey deer had come into the river and drowned.

A grim scene emerged as Taera approached. There was not just one deer in the water, but four. All had partially rotted in the water, but Taera could still see evidence of injuries on their flanks. The flesh looked diseased, and the smell of the rot made the gryphon gag as it filled her nares. Upstream, Taera could not see any fish floating on the surface, nor caught in the reeds on the banks.

"Is this it?" Aryc asked. He turned his head away and covered his beak with a muddy paw.

"I think so," Taera replied. Though she wanted to get away from the stink of rotting flesh, she knew in her heart that she had found the source of the illness. Rotting flesh was the cause of illnesses if eaten, and these carcasses were spreading their disease downstream. Until the source was cleared, then the hidden dangers would continue to infect the water and the fish that dwelt within the river.

Aryc splashed into the river and started to tug at one of the carcasses, clamping his beak around an exposed foot. Taera quickly jumped in and swatted the gryphon away.

"You can't get any of the meat or water into your beak," she hissed, pushing the gryphon with her shoulder. "Wash your mouth out upstream, then come back and help me. Do not swallow anything."

Chastised, Aryc trudged through the deep water to dip his head beneath the surface. While he cleaned out his beak of any possible infection, Taera began to push at the carcasses with her paws. She kept her beak out of the water at all times, making sure not to splash too much. The meat was soft and tender beneath her claws, with small strips being torn away from the bone. There was little she could do to stop the infected flesh from washing away, but so long as it didn't get caught downstream, it would wash all the way through to the ocean.

Once Aryc returned to her, the two gryphons worked together to drag the carcasses from the river. All four deer had fallen into the river on top of each other in a tangle of legs and heads. They were difficult to move, especially with the cold river current tugging at the gryphons.

The work took the best part of a mark to complete, with the sun slowly moving across the sky, heating the air and creating a deep thirst in Taera's throat. She did not dare drink to quench that thirst, not until she was sure the infection had been cleansed from the river. The deer were piled up together several paces from the river, where they could not fall into the water again. Only once all four were out, did Taera allow herself to stop and rest.

The carer dropped to her haunches and leaned into Aryc, who also panted from the exertion. She could see his forepaws tremble.

"Is it done?" Aryc asked, looking down at the

disturbed riverbed. Stones and sticks had been dislodged in their attempt to remove any last scrap of diseased flesh that may have become lodged on the river, but Taera had not found anything more.

"Once the diseased water has flowed through the forest, yes. Then we must dispose of all the stored fish and water. The nets and baskets must be cleaned in the purified water, and the deer carcasses must be burned," Taera said, feeling weary just thinking about all the tasks that needed to be carried out. Her shoulders slumped. "And then we must continue giving your wilders their medicine. The source of their illness should go away, but they are not cured yet."

Aryc slumped into Taera. "Sometimes I feel more exhausted than if I had been infected this illness," he said, his eyes bright. He bumped his beak against Taera's as the two gryphons leaned together for a moment longer. "Thank you for your help. I would not have thought to look up here. My friends and family would have died were it not for you."

Taera mantled and spread her wings. "It is my responsibility and my pleasure to bring health back to the sick. I could not have done any different." The sunlight on her wings felt better now, especially as the heat began to dry the wetness that clung to her feathers and fur. She glanced towards the forest, which was little more than a dark smudge on the horizon.

"We should go back," Aryc said. He rose to his paws and stood on the riverbank, giving one last look down into the water. "I'm sure they'll be happy to know the invisible enemy has been defeated."

"The end of their discomfort is nearly here," Taera

said. She approached the gryphon and rested her wing against his back. "They'll all be healed."

Aryc extended his wing to brush against Taera's. They chirruped softly, pleased in their success. With their wings touching, the two gryphons started on the long walk back to the forest. Their eyes remained on the river, making sure there were no diseased fish they had missed, but their thoughts and words drifted far from the worries that had silenced them before.

There was still work left to do, but the hardest part had been overcome. From here, Taera knew that not a single gryph would need to die under her care. Within a few days, they would all be able to take to wing once more. Fresh water, medicine, and rest was all they needed now. Taera could provide them all.

Pride swelled her chest as she walked by Aryc's side. There were so many interesting stories she could tell when she returned home. Tales of gryphs that lived in trees like birds and hunted for their fish without having to lift a single claw. Wilders were truly strange creatures sometimes. Taera felt a new appreciation for their ways.

They did what they had to do in order to survive. Perhaps they weren't too different from prided gryphs after all.

WOLF EYES

SAYLOR FERGUSON

S tell had never been the luckiest of gryphs, but she
always reminded herself that there were some
unluckier than she. It was one of the ways she managed
day-to-day life, ranking the world around her by luck.

Exiles and the wilders ranked at the top of the list of
the unluckiest gryphs. Forbidden to live in civilized
prides, they struggled to eke a living off of the harshest
unclaimed land. Stell was thankful that she wasn't among
their numbers, though it had been a close thing when she
was young.

Also ranking high on her list were the returning
hunters who'd just had a run-in with a pack of wolves in
the mountains outside of her pride's pridegrounds. Lying
in the shade outside of the large, four-walled nursery,
Stell watched as the bedraggled hunters returned. Five
gryphs, all full-blooded gryphons, made up the hunting
party.

The largest, Hunter Kasper, eldest child of Direlord
Maylar, wore a stormy expression on his silver-feathered
face. Stell watched as he slipped into the large stone-and-

wood structure at the edge of the pridegrounds: Direlord Maylar's den.

Wolves were a common problem among Maylar's pride. Tucked between old forested mountains in a lush, green valley, Maylar's pride was small and remote. But there was a reason Stell hadn't requested to be an exchange with other prides—to get out of the remote valley—and that was Maylar herself. The direlord was the most forgiving and understanding of all direlords that Stell had ever heard of, a fact of which Stell took advantage.

"Hey!" a voice shouted from within the nursery, jolting Stell from her thoughts. As she rose to her paws, Stell twitched an ear back.

"Get your tail back in here; break's over," the rough voice continued, and Stell obeyed. Rask, head kitcarer, was her boss, and Stell did her best never to upset him.

"Coming, Rask," she said, forcing lightness into her tone as thoughts of wolves and direlords drifted out of her mind. On soft paws, she padded into the relative darkness of the nursery. The second-largest structure of the entire pridegrounds, it was the most heavily fortified to protect its precious inhabitants. The bottom half was made of stacked stone, then woven branches took over the design all the way up to the domed roof where there was a small sunlight. Despite the sunlight, the nursery was always fairly dark, and Stell's friend Relwen said Stell nearly disappeared into the shadows.

Relwen was right, Stell thought with a small smile. With her black fur and black plumage, the only thing that gave Stell away was the iridescent blue shimmer of her feathers, a reminder of her half-blooded heritage. While she was an opinicus—smaller than any full-blooded gryphon, duller of color, and having front paws instead of talons—one of Stell's parents had been a gryphon, thus giving Stell her shimmery feathers and slightly taller, slimmer stature.

"That's Kitcarer Rask to you," Rask snapped, irritable after spending the last twenty minutes alone with the kits. He shook several naughty kits from his back, where they collapsed to the soft floor in a laughing heap.

Stell dipped her head to the much larger, more heavily muscled orange gryphon. "Of course, Kitcarer Rask," she clarified. "What do you need me to do?"

Rask rattled off a list of tasks for Stell, from cleaning out the old bedding to arranging the new nests, always ending with *and don't let them kill each other* as he strode out of the nursery to report to the higher-ups.

The kits were rambunctious, sure, but things never got that bad. Stell and Rask had to break up the occasional scuffle, and shut down the occasional food fight, but never anything nearing a real threat. The kits had a good life under the watchful eyes of Stell and Rask, safe from all outside threats, and Stell would fight to keep it that way.

That hadn't always been the case, though. Several fractures ago, when Stell had been a kit in the nursery herself, a stray wyvern had attacked the pridegrounds, razing half the buildings to the ground and killing a quarter of the pride's gryphs. The nursery, at the time made completely of wood, had gone up in flames almost immediately, and the kits inside would have burned if it hadn't been for the quick thinking of Kitcarer Mar, who'd evacuated them from the burning building while the other kitcarer succumbed to the smoke, taking each kit to the stream that ran past the edge of the pridegrounds.

Safely drenched in water, the kits had all survived the attack, even when the nursery didn't.

Mar, the heroic kitcarer, had lived a few more fractures after that before dying of a smoke illness that had bothered him since the fire. Stell had been devastated to see him go, especially since unsympathetic Rask was the next kitcarer in line, but by that point she was nearly grown and vowed to herself to follow in Mar's pawsteps as a kitcarer.

"I see your head is in the clouds again," a gryph said, striding into the nursery with a flaunt to their step.

Stell once again shook herself from thoughts of Mar and the wyvern attack, which she only recalled in glimpses: the smell of smoke, the burnt orange of flames against the night sky, the scents of a hundred terrified gryphs. Her friend's arrival, as usual, was a lucky occurrence.

"Relwen," Stell said with a smile that her friend returned. Then Relwen flattened her ears to her brown-feathered head.

"The kits stink," she said, waving a paw in front of her face.

Stell just laughed. "Yeah, they're due for a rinse in the stream tomorrow." She watched as one of the smaller kits stalked across the ground towards a larger kit, tiny downy wings tight to her sides as though she were truly hunting. With a mewl, the smaller kit leapt on the back of the larger kit, tackling her opponent to the ground.

"That one'll be a hunter someday," Stell remarked, recognizing the small hunter as Merk and the much larger prey as Lendon, both spirited kits.

"You and me both, kit," Relwen said dramatically

before flopping onto Stell's nest. "Though the kit's got a better chance than me."

Old anger stirred in Stell's gut, but she shoved it down. Being angry didn't do any gryph any good, especially not a kitcarer. Well, *unofficial* kitcarer, as Stell didn't truly have her own initiated title. As a half-breed, she was lucky to be alive at all; some prides exiled half-breed kits at birth. Direlord Maylar's more accepting nature and fondness for kits was the only thing that kept Stell and others like her, such as Relwen, in the pride. But as they were neither fully gryphon nor fully opinicus, they didn't have the opportunity to become initiated.

At least you're lucky enough to work with the kits anyways, Stell told herself. "Did you talk to the group of hunters who met the wolves this morning?" she asked Relwen, to distract her friend from her woes.

Relwen perked up, brown feathers fluffing and amber eyes bright. The brown opinicus was always looking for opportunities to help the hunters and typically accompanied at least one hunting group out per day. "I just finished talking to Hunter Naylim; she got away with only a sprain on one of her hind legs. Apparently, they were up by the quartz falls after deer, they got surrounded by seven wolves. The tree cover was too dense to fly away so they had to fight their way out."

Stell shuddered. She'd just been up by the quartz falls the week prior, gathering moss for the kits' bedding. It was an excellent place for bedding—and for hunting deer, evidently—in a deep mountain cove, where one of the countless mountain streams tumbled over a large quartz outcropping, creating a pretty waterfall and giving it the name "quartz falls."

She was lucky she hadn't run into the wolves up there

last week. The pack must have their den somewhere nearby. Though they were a common sight in the mountains outside the pridegrounds, Stell had never encountered any wolves herself, as she didn't often venture far from the nursery, but Relwen had spotted wolves while accompanying hunters and even had to run from them a couple of times. She always told Stell that her black-feathered friend had wolf eyes, as several wolves of the local pack had a rare blue tint to their eyes. Stell had no wolves for comparison, but she'd seen her own reflection enough to know that her eyes were a pale, icy blue. She'd have compared them to the eyes of a goshawk fledgling, but Relwen disagreed.

"Anyway, Hunter Naylim said Kasper was going to go speak to the direlord and see if they couldn't get a group of hunters and guards out there to run the wolves further into the mountains. They're a nuisance," Relwen said, beginning to preen her feathers while still lying in Stell's nest.

Stell rolled her eyes at her dramatic, flamboyant companion, but Relwen was the closest—really the only —friend she had. Since both of them were half-breeds, they were somewhat shunned by the other gryphs, especially the gryphons, who felt insulted by their very existence. What self-respecting gryphon would dare mate with an opinicus, after all?

But at least they had each other. Uninitiated as they might be, at least they weren't wilders or exiles, and at least they didn't live in a pride with a less forgiving direlord. Yes, they were pretty lucky, as far as Stell was concerned. Though she knew she could never give up the nagging desire to be a true kitcarer.

As Relwen continued her talk of wolves and hunters,

Stell returned to clearing out the old bedding, removing the moss she'd gathered at the quartz falls from storage to prepare clean nests. It was second nature to keep an eye on the kits as she worked, one ear ticked towards the center of the nursery, the other angled to hear Relwen. Stell looked up from her work when she heard the two loudest kits go quiet; Merk and Lendon had stopped their tussling and were sitting by Relwen, tiny ears pricked forwards and faces eager as they devoured Relwen's fantastical tales of wolves as large as direlords. A warning instinct stirred in Stell's chest, and she walked over to sweep the kits away from her friend.

"That's enough stories, I think," she said, shooting a glance at Relwen.

The brown gryph fluttered a wing dismissively. "I won't scare them anymore, Wolf Eyes."

Upon hearing Stell's nickname, the two kits squealed and ran off to join the rest of their brethren. She sighed. "Great. Now they'll wake up with nightmares."

Relwen's generally jovial expression darkened. "At least their nightmares are only that," she said, and in her friend's brown eyes Stell could see the flicker of flames from the night of the wyvern attack, all those fractures ago.

Stell would've been glad to delve into their shared horrors, but she was working until Rask returned from reporting to his higher-ups. And when he got back, he'd probably kick Relwen out, as he said she was a distraction.

"Let's find something happier to talk about," Stell said, "for the kits' sakes." She and Relwen dissolved into telling jokes and helping some of the older kits practice their wing exercises until they heard a powerful voice echo across the pridegrounds.

"I call a meeting of my pride! Every gryph that is able, join me at the stream's edge." It was a voice that Stell didn't hear often, but one whose strength she recognized immediately: Direlord Malyar.

Relwen leapt to her feet from Stell's nest, her cheek feathers fluffing in excitement. "I bet this is about the wolves," she predicted, pushing aside the (ironically, wolf) pelt that made up the nursery door. Stell did a headcount of the kits, making sure that all were accounted for before positioning herself outside of the nursery's only exit. She sat down, keeping an ear angled towards the kits.

The stream's edge referred to the cleared grassy area outside Direlord Maylar's den, where the direlord herself could address her pride from atop a boulder perched next to the stream. She sat there now, adornments covering her body that accented her spiky amber feathers. She had jeweled earrings in each ear, bracelets on both forelegs, and an opal necklace that had been given to her by some visiting direlord. Surrounding her on both sides were her three children: silver-feathered Hunter Kasper, amber-feathered Guardian Reddon—the only of Maylar's children to be blessed with dirism—and golden-feathered Lila, the youngest of the direlord's children at a couple of fractures younger than Stell and still uninitiated, though likely not for long. Each of the gryphs sitting so prettily at the stream's edge was far, far luckier than Stell would ever be. She did her best not to let it bother her.

Though they were all stunning, none of Maylar's children possessed her elegance and grace; the direlord sat almost perfectly still save for the gentle rippling of her spiked feathers in the mountain breeze which smelled of damp grass and sun-warmed granite. Her orange eyes watched every gryph gather, and she even nodded to Stell, seated back from the crowd to keep an eye on the kits. Stell's heart raced at the direlord's attentions, but she nodded back, dipping her head in a respectful bow. As Relwen rushed off to join the crowd, an orange-feathered gryph returned to Stell's side.

"I hope that ruffian wasn't in the nursery for too long," Rask huffed, glaring after Relwen.

"The kits like her company," Stell said peaceably, not wanting to give a full answer but not wanting to lie to her superior either. If she were to truly anger Rask, he might kick her out of the nursery, and then where would she be? The very last thing Stell wanted to do was dishonor Mar's memory by failing as an unofficial kitcarer.

Maylar, luckily, distracted Stell from her self-doubt over the fact that she would never be a true kitcarer. The direlord opened her wings, and the sunlight through her amber feathers shaded the crowd in front of her in pale gold. "My son, Hunter Kasper, informed me of a wolf attack on a group of hunters this morning at the quartz falls. This cannot go unpunished, no more so than a group of wilders pressing at our borders. The wolves seem to have forgotten how many of their brethren lie in our nests, on our buildings, as pelts. They will be taken care of, for the safety of our pride and the honor of our gryphs."

Several gryphs in the crowd cheered and Maylar grinned, whisking her tail once. "Today, I will select our best hunters and guardians to lead an elite group to engage and defeat the wolves. For the rest of today, I place the pridegrounds under curfew, so no gryph has to face the wolf threat before we're fully prepared. But by this time tomorrow, we will have new wolf pelts to display and new stories to share!"

Stell joined in the shout that ricocheted around the valley at the direlord's words. The excitement and chaos of the pride was contagious, and even long after Rask sent Stell on her next break, her feathers still prickled with anticipation.

"I know I won't get picked," Relwen said as she and Stell sat together by the stream, eating their afternoon meal. "But I can't help but get my hopes up anyways."

Stell stared thoughtfully up at the mountains that rose past the stream, blanketed in trees, ferns, and ancient rocks. It was a beautiful place, certainly, but there was no telling what horrors its depths might hold. Stell couldn't understand her friend's fascination with the untamed places of the mountains, but she did feel for Relwen. She knew full well what it was to live in a pride but never as a true pride member. In that way, she and Relwen were deeply unlucky.

"You don't want to get mauled alive by wolves," Stell offered. Relwen nearly choked on her portion of deer haunch as she laughed.

"There won't be any gryphs getting mauled tomorrow. Those wolves are in for it!" Relwen draped a wing over Stell's back, covering the black-feathered opinicus's wings with warm brown feathers. "You, my friend, are too much of a kitcarer. Too worried about what could go wrong that you miss out on all the action!"

"I'm not a kitcarer," Stell said sourly. "But anyways, I don't think that's a bad thing. I've heard of prides further away, on the coastlines, where kitcarers are the most ferocious gryphs in the entire pride. We could be like that, too, if Rask were anything like Mar." Grief for the gryph who'd raised her stirred in Stell's chest as it did from time to time.

"Mar was a great gryph," Relwen agreed, staring down at the stream where the two friends, along with all the other kits of their age group, had sheltered during the wyvern attack of seasons ago. Then she hooked her deer haunch between her claws and the opposable digit of her paw, lifting it into the air. "A toast for Mar, the last great kitcarer."

That brought a grin to Stell's beak, and she lifted her food to do the same.

"How long do you have before Rask wants you back at the nursery?" Relwen asked once they'd toasted to the gryph who'd raised them and saved their lives.

Stell studied the sun's position in the sky. It was dipping towards the west, sunset only a couple of marks away. "Half a mark? Probably a little less," she estimated, knowing that Rask would need her to help give the kits dinner and prepare them for sleep, which was a two-gryph task.

Relwen stood and stretched, flaring her wings and arching her back. "Well, that gives us enough time for a flight around the valley. What do you say?"

STELL AND RELWEN SOARED ABOVE THE VALLEY, ONLY outmatched by the guardians who circled constantly, on alert for approaching wilders or wyverns. The crisp mountain air was fresh in Stell's nares, scented with fern and moss and hints of other animals that called the mountains home. As the sun dipped closer and closer to the western horizon, the sky exploded into color, flaming reds bleeding into inky blues as dark and deep as the most remote mountain lake. The light from the setting sun reflected on the two gryphs' feathers, making Stell's black feathers shimmer with their iridescent blue and making Relwen's brown feathers look a burnished orange.

This was Stell's favorite time of day, when the air cooled off and the woods around the pridegrounds filled with the sounds of nighttime birds and insects. She breathed deep with her beak open, letting her muscles relax.

Relwen chirped happily and brushed Stell's outstretched wing with her primary feathers. "Just think; tomorrow, we'll have a feast to celebrate the wolf capture, Maylar will display the pelts, and there might even be new initiations."

Stell knew her chances of attending such a party were slim, as Rask would definitely want to be involved and would therefore leave Stell alone with the kits, but she was glad Relwen had shaken off her mood from earlier. "It'll be a great day for our pride," she agreed. "The last feast I remember was for the guardian initiations last fracture."

Relwen sighed happily at the memory. "I can't remember ever eating anything better than the wild boar they prepared for that feast. I wonder what wolf tastes like?"

Stell chuckled but didn't know how she felt about eating another forest predator. "I don't think I'd want to eat a wolf after all these seasons of you calling me 'Wolf Eyes.'"

"Sometimes you're very boring, do you know that?" Relwen asked, nudging her friend. "Every other gryph would molt at the opportunity to taste test a wolf."

That made Stell laugh out loud. "Me? Boring? I think you've got the wrong gryph!"

Their lighthearted conversation continued as the two opinici drifted lazily above the valley but cut off abruptly when several long, low howls rose from the mountains. Stell stiffened, her ears flattening to her head, and she saw the guards circling above tighten their talons against their chests, ears flicking towards the noise.

As wolf cries continued to pierce the sky, a more familiar call echoed up from the direction of the nursery: Rask's voice. Stell checked the sky, which now had a bit more indigo around the edges.

"I've got to go get the kits ready for sleep," Stell said, angling her wings to descend.

Relwen followed. "I'm going to see if I can get an idea of who's going on the wolf hunt tomorrow," she said, dipping her right wing to circle over to the direlord's den.

Stell landed on the ground with a thump, rousing all her feathers before meeting Rask inside the nursery. He was carrying a squirming kit by the scruff to its newly cleaned nest, where he deposited it.

"Good. You're here," he said by way of introduction, smoothing his ruffled orange feathers. "Get the rest of the kits to sleep; I'm going to listen in on Maylar's meeting with the guards and hunters. As head kitcarer, I have a place in the audience."

Stell nodded, worrying that Relwen's chances of getting an audience with the direlord, her hunters, and her guards were slim. No doubt Relwen would be back at the nursery in a matter of minutes to complain.

As soon as Rask left, sure enough, Relwen showed up. "They kicked me out of the meeting," she said sourly, flopping onto Stell's nest for the second time that day.

Stell flicked her tail sympathetically but didn't look up from her current task. With a single wing, she pressed one kit into its nest, while with her paws she gathered up two more kits and placed them in their appropriate places. That was when she noticed the two empty nests. A frown crossed her face and she stalked over, dipping her head to scent who'd slept there last. *Merk and Lendon's nests,* she observed. Her heart beginning to thud fearfully, Stell gazed around the nursery, studying every possible hiding place for two bold, wayward kits.

But they weren't there.

Relwen seemed to sense that not all was well in Stell's world. She rolled to her stomach, ears pricking. "What's up?" she asked, roused from her former bad mood.

Stell's throat was dry when she answered. "Merk and Lendon aren't here."

Scenting their nests as deeply as she could, despite the fact that Stell had just changed their bedding that day, Stell tracked their movements through the nursery. She followed their scents to the stone wall of the nursery, then traced their scents upwards. Confusion flickered across Stell's mind, but she flew up regardless, where she realized what had happened. The two kits, both gryphons with dexterous, grasping talons, had climbed up and out of the nursery. It should have been impossible, but Stell knew that if any kits were determined enough to accomplish such a feat, it was Merk and Lendon. She imagined that they'd made their escape as Rask began grooming the others and tucking them into their nests, too distracted to look up.

Relwen seemed to be connecting the dots in her friend's mind. "Did they climb out?" she asked, rising to her paws with a concerned expression crossing her pleasant face.

"It looks like it," Stell said, "though I can't imagine why..."

Suddenly, Stell understood. The kits' fascination with Relwen's tales of wolves, their delight at Stell's "Wolf Eyes" nickname, accompanied with Maylar's announcement and the howls of the wolves that evening. Stell's heart sank, her feathers flattening to her body in fear. "Oh, spirits, no. They've gone wolf hunting."

Relwen made a nervous sound. "Surely they haven't..."

But Stell was already moving. "Stay here," she ordered. "I have to go tell Rask."

Her friend's questions followed Stell out of the nursery, but she ignored them. Adrenaline filled her body, making her wings feel as though lightning were running through them, flames of determination burning in her chest. She knew she was about to get in trouble for interrupting the direlord's private meeting, but as they spoke, there were kits on the loose, possibly in danger. So Stell didn't hesitate to take flight, angling towards Maylar's den. As she flew, she scanned the ground for the lost kits, but saw no sign of them.

Stell landed right in front of two disgruntled guards, and without a second's hesitation, shoved her way into the direlord's den. "Rask," she said, making every gryph inside the den stare at her, all guards and hunters and gryphs much bigger and more important than her. Maylar herself sized up the new arrival, amber eyes narrowing.

Rask's feathers were immediately on end. "What are you doing here!? You left the kits..."

"Relwen's with the kits," Stell blurted. "Merk and Lendon escaped out the sunlight to go wolf hunting; I have to find them before they get hurt."

Chaos erupted in the direlord's den. Maylar rose to

her feet, towering over everyone as she began commanding the gryphs around her. It was lucky that the direlord had a fondness for kits, Stell thought, as Maylar called for a group of hunters to scour the pridegrounds, while Rask and Lila, Maylar's golden-feathered uninitiated daughter, were to return to the nursery immediately and make sure no more kits followed their wayward brethren. It was a good plan, Stell thought, but she scooted around the guards for a second time and escaped the den before Maylar could give her an order. She was the only one who'd heard the stories that Relwen had told the kits earlier and guessed where Merk and Lendon might be headed.

Stell completely disregarded Maylar's curfew orders and leapt into the sky as soon as she was clear of the den, beating her wings to cross over the stream that made up the border between the pridegrounds and the mountains. In the deepening twilight, Stell counted on her sense of smell rather than sight and caught traces of the kits traveling towards a too-familiar deep mountain cove.

Stell tucked her wings to her sides and dove underneath the thick tree canopy after a desperate flight, landing on the damp, leaf-strewn ground beside the quartz falls. Under the trees, it was even darker, the shadows longer and more eerie. She nearly jumped out of her feathers when two delighted voices reached her ears.

"Stell!" Merk and Lendon called, racing over to meet her. These kits travelled *fast!* "Are you coming to hunt wolves with us?"

"No!" Stell hissed, relief at finding the kits nearly knocking her over. "We are going to do *no such thing.* You're going to let me carry you back to the nursery, where you'll be in big trouble!"

As Stell spoke, the kits shifted from excited to defiant to afraid. *Good,* Stell thought. *I'm getting to them.* "Do you understand?" she asked, standing tall to show dominance as the kits began to press themselves to the forest floor.

"Stell," Merk whimpered, staring behind Stell.

A low growl sounded from behind Stell. *Oh, spirits help me.* Carefully, Stell turned around, keeping the kits firmly behind her, and found herself face-to-face with a wolf.

Relwen had been right all along, it seemed. For as Stell stared at the wolf before her—it must have crept up unnoticed over the sound of the waterfall—she recognized the wolf's pale blue eyes as her own. *Wolf eyes.* She swallowed hard and stood as tall as she could, even though her head only came to the wolf's shoulder.

The wolf's tongue lolled, showing fangs as long as a gryphon's talons, and its light gray-furred ears pinned back to its head.

Stell shoved her ears forward. "Kits, stay behind me," she said softly. Then she addressed the wolf. "We'll just be leaving..."

The wolf leapt. Teeth met in Stell's wing, and she was forced backwards, screeching. The wolf used its weight to pin Stell to the ground, snapping its jaws closer and closer to Stell's throat. Ice blue eyes stared at her in the dark woods, and Stell knew they were the last thing she'd ever see. Just her luck.

No. Stell remembered the kits whimpering behind her, the kits who would certainly die should she fail to protect them. She'd be a lousy kitcarer indeed if she didn't even try.

With a screech, Stell kicked her muscles into motion, biting down on the wolf's foreleg with her hooked beak. The wolf reeled back with a yelp, giving Stell just enough time to get to her feet and launch her own attack, digging into the beast's coarse fur with her claws and beak.

The wolf retaliated, flinging Stell from its back. She landed on her already-bitten wing, wincing, but got back up again and threw herself at her enemy. Pure instinct took over Stell's body, directing her every movement, fueled by the need to protect the kits. Flames roared in her memory, and Stell knew that the spirit of Mar was there, giving her strength, one kitcarer to another.

How long the battle had been raging, Stell didn't know, but she began hearing gryph shouts as they tracked her and the kits. Surely, between her screeches and the wolf's earth-shaking growls, they could find her. Wing-beats sounded overhead just as Stell's beak got a lucky grip on the wolf's neck, and she twisted her head, snapping the wolf's spine. As her opponent collapsed to the ground, dead, Stell forced herself to stand on unsteady legs and check on the kits. Though shaken, they were alive.

Stell felt a touch on her shoulder and whirled around to see that Hunter Kasper and four other gryphs had landed, all staring at her in awe.

"Wolfslayer," one gryph said.

Kasper just said, "Can you fly?"

A DAY PASSED BEFORE THE HEALER DECLARED STELL FREE from infection and broken bones and able to return to her duties. Her bitten wing hurt worse than any of her other injuries, and Stell still didn't fully understand how she'd managed the flight back to the pridegrounds the night before. Especially after she insisted on carrying one of the kits. Relwen had been the first gryph to welcome her back, as soon as Stell knew the kits were safely in the care of Rask and the direlord's daughter Lila.

"Are you okay?" Relwen's eyes had been wide with fear for her friend in the rising moonlight. Stell had managed to nod, leaning more and more heavily on her friend as Relwen guided her towards the healer's den. As soon as she entered the herb-scented darkness of the den, Stell collapsed with exhaustion, and the rest of the night was lost to her memory.

"A bad bite on your wing," the head healer, a gray-feathered opinicus, told Stell the following morning. "But luckily I was able to treat it before infection set in." Nonetheless, Stell looked down at her wing and saw that it was tucked to her side, encased in healing leaves and tied in place with honeysuckle vines. "Bad bruising all over the rest of your body," the healer continued. "And a sprain in your right shoulder. Don't hesitate to come by if you need anything for the pain."

"I will," Stell promised, already gritting her beak against the aches that ran up and down the length of her body, nothing that wouldn't be fixed given a bit of time. "Thank you, Healer."

The healer dipped her head dismissively, waving Stell away with a flick of her wing. "Then I don't see any reason to keep you here any longer. Besides, I think there are gryphs who want to speak to you."

With a sinking feeling, Stell imagined who those gryphs might be. Rask, ready to punish her for leaving the kits in Relwen's care. Direlord Maylar, for interrupting her private meeting and breaking her curfew orders. Or even the kits' parents, for not realizing their children had escaped until they were nearly brushing feathers with death.

But none of that happened when Stell left the healer's den. Instead, a familiar face greeted her, throwing a wing over Stell's back. Stell winced but leaned over to preen at her friend's brown feathers.

"I thought you were dead for sure after you passed out last night!" Relwen exclaimed. "You're never, ever allowed to do that again."

"Believe me, I don't have any plans," Stell assured. Then she remembered her worries, and her ears pressed back against her head nervously. "Have you overheard anything from the other gryphs? Do you know if Rask is going to kick me out from working in the nursery? Or if Maylar's going to exile me for disobeying her curfew orders? Or..."

"Go over to the stream's edge and maybe you'll find out," Relwen said conspiratorially, making Stell feel in no way better.

"A meeting?" she asked, nerves making her beak dry. So Maylar wanted to make her exile a public event, then.

She rounded the corner of the healer's den, nearly halting when she saw all the gryphs gathered at Maylar's meeting grounds. There was the direlord herself, perched atop her announcement boulder and dwarfing all the other gryphs save for her dired son Reddon. As before, her three children stood on either side of her. Golden-feathered Lila, who Stell remembered had been tasked with caring for the kits last night, dipped her head encouragingly to Stell, a small grin on her beak.

Encouragement from the pretty gryphon made Stell's insides turn, not knowing how she was supposed to feel about this situation. Stell caught a glimpse of Rask some ways back, blocking the doorway of the nursery but watching the meeting, nonetheless. When he made eye contact with Stell, he lifted his chin. *Head held high.* Stell followed his lead, not wanting her boss to see her exiled in complete shame.

Relwen nudged Stell forward once they'd reached the stream's edge, and Stell found herself in front of Direlord Maylar. Ignoring the protestations of her muscles, Stell leaned into a bow, mantling her one good wing.

"Rise, Stell, opinicus of the Maylar pride," the direlord's voice boomed, and Stell hastened to straighten her back. "Last night, you disobeyed my curfew orders, left the nursery in the claws of a gryph untrained to watch kits, and foolishly engaged in single combat with a wolf." Stell's heart sank and she felt tears prickle in her eyes but remained standing tall. None of these gryphs would see her cry, especially not Rask or Relwen.

"And yet..." the direlord said, tilting her head like an inquisitive raven. "You did all of these things to save two kits, who most certainly would have met their end had you not been there." Maylar nodded to her son Kasper, who'd found Stell and the kits last night, and he presented his mother with a very familiar wolf pelt.

Stell couldn't hide her gasp. The pelt was beautiful where the wolf had been harsh, its former violence reduced to soft fur that would keep a gryph warm in the winter months. "This is the pelt of the wolf you killed, Wolfslayer," Maylar continued. "And I gift it to you, to keep your nest warm..." she passed the pelt to Stell, who took it thankfully, realizing that this meeting wasn't at all what she had expected. "... Kitcarer Stell of the Maylar pride," the direlord finished.

Stell's good wing fell to her side in shock, flashing its

blue iridescence. "Kitcarer?" she asked, her eyes wide. The direlord chuckled and several other gryphs followed.

"Yes," Maylar assured her. "Your heroics were on a level with those of our former Kitcarer Mar, and your battle with the wolf served as an excellent initiation, proving how far you're willing to go to protect our most vulnerable members." Maylar dipped her head to brush Stell's crest feathers with her enormous beak. "Kitcarer Stell."

As cheers erupted around the stream's edge, Stell reflected on how lucky she was. Lucky to be in Maylar's pride, where the direlord was so fond of kits that a half-breed kit could rise from being nobody to being a kitcarer, all because of her willingness to track and save missing kits. Lucky that her injuries last night hadn't been fatal, and lucky to have earned a wolf pelt to warm her den in the winter. Stell glanced around the gathered gryphs, all shouting "Kitcarer Stell" and "Wolfslayer," and heard one gryph shouting "Wolf Eyes!" Stell's gaze searched until she saw her friend, grinning at Stell like a fool, even though it had been Stell and not Relwen to have been initiated. Seeing her friend, Stell flared her good wing and held the wolf pelt high in the air, to the heightened cheers of the gathered gryphs.

Perhaps Stell wasn't so unlucky, after all.

EMBERS

M. H. WOLFE

"Flames be smothered!" Kinira snarled as she caught her breath. "At this rate, our attack will fail before it begins!" She whipped her slender, scaled tail back and forth, bracing her lean frame upon her powerful, winged forelimbs.

The three wyverns before her rumbled their understanding of the situation, each bowing their heads and letting their massive wings droop. They panted as hard as she did. The scramble to catch the interloper had been fruitless, save for a newfound wave of exhaustion.

"Tarak," she said. The smallest of their four-member wing dropped his head lower, the basalt-colored scales on his chin nearly touching the dirt of the forest's floor. "It was your fault the reconnaissance was a disaster...again. Last time, the hippogryphs spotted you at a distance and bolted. This time, you were within maw's reach of the stinking gryph. Yet, you let it get away."

Kinira jabbed her wing talon at the runt. "You are supposed to be the stealthiest drake in the clan. Yet, you have only shown an ability for being discovered. If I didn't need your flame, I would crush your spine now and leave you for the forest animals to devour."

She snapped her jaws at him to accentuate her point.

"And, you two. What part of 'two-wyvern reconnaissance' do you not understand? Running out here at the smallest commotion. By the Direlord! You revealed our numbers to them!"

Kinira felt a rising heat in her core. It licked at her throat, urging her to lash out, teach them a real lesson. Her body tensed. The muscles of her jaws ached with her efforts to keep them closed for a moment longer. She took a deep breath and closed her eyes.

Anger fogs the mind. Her wit was the greatest weapon they had. *Focus.*

Xhorin, a hulking male with rich amber scales and eyes to match, raised his head and locked his gaze upon her. "With the respect that is due, wingleader, we heard the growls and clamor. It was quite loud. We felt you may need reinforcement, whatever the trouble might be."

His voice was deep and he was well spoken, his words a measured, rhythmic staccato. His glare was steady, his enunciation annoyingly precise. All that one would be expected from the condescending son of a dire.

Reinforcement, indeed. Because you are weak to me, more like. He and his kin were blessed with superior physique – massive bodies with powerful muscle encased by thick scale plates that served as natural armor. Still, *she* was the commander.

Kinira narrowed her eyes. "Do not speak down to me within my own wing."

Though she felt the flame within her cooling, she knew the wyvern ways, and she could not let his challenge go without response. She stared him down, her eyes unblinking, gaze unwavering...for a time. She glanced away with a snarl. Xhorin let out a satisfied huff. She despised this dominance play.

"I am certain you all will agree," she said, her tone even, her back to them. "We should not have been spotted and we should not have been seen in our entirety. Now, we run the risk of the entire forest being alerted to our presence. The first sighting could have been dismissed as an unwanted wyvern passing through. But now, days later, with the sighting of four wyverns? They will have reason to be on guard. Our chances of success evaporate if they are prepared."

She looked deeper into the forest, in the direction where the hippogryph had escaped. The trees grew thicker and denser further into the heart of the wood. Perfect terrain for a hidden camp. They needed to act fast and she needed a plan to correct the course of things. Her thoughts raced, straying briefly to the words that Direlord Xhililm had spoken to her before their departure to the heart of gryphon territory.

I have watched you. You lack muscle and intensity of flame. Yet, your cunning has set you apart from the others. Proceed with the surprise attack you proposed. Prove to me that your way, the strength of cold wit, can be more powerful than pure flame alone.

Kinira knew that more than her life was at stake with this mission. Her success would ensure that the intellectually superior wyverns of her clan could have the ear of the Direlord. It meant that those seen as physically inferior could have political power. She would not fail. She *must* not fail.

She glanced back to her subordinates. Their heads were bowed, and they spoke in low grunts and growls. She took a step toward them, getting their attention. "We need intelligence on the hippogryphs and their relationship to Rada. If they are somehow allied with the gryphon direlord, we may have to change our plan of attack. Return to the cave. I will find the hippogryph camp and determine the risk myself."

"Wingleader," Tarak said, "allow me to redeem myself."

She weighed his offer for a brief moment. Tarak was even smaller than she was and should be stealthier than the rest of them. But, his repeated lapses of judgement overcame any natural clandestine skills he might possess.

"No. We have no room for failure," she said. "Get back to the cave. All of you."

Her order caused a general grumble to arise from her subordinates. Gral, the quietest of the bunch, spoke a single syllable. "Aye."

She watched as the three plodded back toward the clearing they had established as their base. The cavern there was large enough to accommodate all four of them with room to spare. In addition, the clearing was dry and desolate – unfit hunting ground and undesirable land for any gryph. There was little chance that they would be disturbed there.

Once the others had cleared out of sight, Kinira turned to the task before her. She sniffed the air, taking in the rich textures of the forest around her. The smell of greenery was ample, as was the presence of life. Delicious fragrances. Prey, all of it. Her mouth watered at just the thought.

She stepped slowly in the direction that the hippogryph had run as it had eluded them. A musty odor with a pungent edge arose above the landscape of scents. She could almost taste its stink.

Hippogryph.

A single tattered leather cloth with red markings lay on the ground before her. She sniffed it and recoiled. The stench of hippogryph was strongly embedded in the fabric. She snorted, clearing her nostrils. With that unpleasantness now firmly etched into her mind, she would find the interloper's camp for sure.

IT WAS NIGHTFALL BY THE TIME KINIRA NOTICED THE wafting odor of hippogryph growing stronger. She slowed her pace, crawling into the thickening forest undergrowth. She grimaced as her scaled hide scraped against branches. Thankfully, she was still a distance from the source of the scent. It was unlikely any of them heard her approach.

Her sharp vision caught the distant flicker of fire, then as the wind gusted toward her, she caught the whiff of burning wood. Several intermingled smells came with the breeze – the heavy tang of hippogryphs and the lighter musk of gryphons, perhaps opinici as well. The camp was mixed, and it was full of creatures that would easily sense her should she attempt to move closer. She would have to forgo looking directly at the camp and its inhabitants.

Fine. A wyvern's prowess came from their entire being, not just their keen vision. She would sweep the area with her other senses to get the information she needed. She closed her eyes and let her breathing deepen. Her rising irritation settled. Then, she let her hearing, smell, and touch map the area, looking for anything that could serve as evidence of a connection between the outcasts and Rada.

She heard the din of conversation in the camp – chattered and warbled words that she couldn't understand. Then, outside the camp of gryphs, much closer to her, she felt the light trembling of the ground through her claws. The minute vibrations, mixed with the odors carried by the breeze, gave her a clear image. A gryphon, male and alone, was leaving the camp. His trajectory took him past Kinira's hiding spot at a safe distance.

She ducked her head, pulled her wings and tail tighter about her. With the wind shifting and the shadows darkening, she would be difficult to spot. After several slow breaths had passed, she saw the gryphon through the trees. Her wyvern's eyes saw him clearly through the gloom of the forest. The gryphon was red in hue and large – but not dired. He had a somber but hurried air about him. His wings drooped despite the regal upward tilt he maintained in his beak. He trotted up a lightly-worn path that ran between the thicker reaches of the forest.

Kinira watched him pass by. He was, without a doubt, heading deeper into Rada's territory. Judging from the simple leather cloth he wore around his neck, just like the hippogryph cloth she had found earlier, he was a wilder. Outcast, vagabond, and unwanted.

But, a wilder interacting with Rada's court confirmed her fears. She breathed deeply while an icy ball of fear filled her chest, feeling like it would overwhelm her. If the wilder told Rada about the wyverns' presence, the gryphons would prepare their forces. Kinira's mission would fail. Four wyverns would not be enough to stop an alert force of guards. She could already feel Direlord Xhililm's glare of disappointment and rage, all of her kin thrown out into the desolate wastes.

No, there was still a way. Once the gryphon had moved out of earshot and she had ensured no one else was nearby, Kinira retraced her steps. As she approached the discarded wilder's leather, a plan coalesced. She snatched up the cloth with her wing talon and made her way back to their cave.

"LISTEN CAREFULLY," KINIRA RUMBLED AT HER subordinates. Gral and Tarak glanced at her, yet they continued to bicker, nipping and growling at each other. Xhorin lifted his eyes but remained curled in an alcove along one wall of the cave.

They listen, but with disinterest and disrespect. The heat of her irritation grew. Oh, how she wanted to grab the nearest one with her jaws and shake them into submission. She bit her tongue so as not to lash out.

Calm. Calm winds secure victory.

"Your part is simple," she said. "Just stay here in this cave until I return. No additional raucous. Especially fighting."

Xhorin grunted. "If silence is what you want, you may as well gut us now and leave us to rot." He glanced at the other two, who were already sending silent signs of aggression. A bared fang here, a slow adjustment of height there. A glance, then a glare.

"Behave!" she snapped. "Or know that the Direlord's wrath will be upon us. His vision of the future hinges upon our success. When I return, we will prepare for our assault."

The mention of attack silenced Tarak and Gral for a few moments. As she left, she heard a few tentative rumbles and the snap of jaws. She rolled her eyes and muttered a curse to the winds. She hoped that she could be back quick enough so these fools wouldn't reveal their presence yet again.

Kinira reviewed her plans, creating several contingencies just in case. She stepped swiftly through the thicker parts of the forest, using the deeper shaded areas there as cover. She needed to be fast, quiet, and precise. But, more important would be the location – a perfect place for a trap.

She searched until she found a long, narrow clearing just within Rada's hunting grounds. It was ideal, surrounded on all sides by large trees that would provide deep enough shadow to obscure her. She used the scents of the forest to pick a spot where animals were likely to congregate – and where hunters were likely to land. This particular locale had a small stream running through it and a stony outcropping that harbored a small pond.

Perfect.

She nestled into the shadows again, careful to stay downwind from the clearing. As she watched, a deer cautiously stepped out of the forest. Its ears swiveled back and forth, its eyes alert, gleaming. Then, once it was satisfied that no predators were around, it bowed its head to sip from the clear water of the pond.

Given the time of morning, Kinira was certain hunters would find this spot. And, with their arrival, she would launch her ambush. She settled in to wait, stalking her prey.

Kinira waited. And waited.

The sun passed by overhead with no visitors. She was

disappointed, hot, and ready to leave when three gryphons landed. They scanned the edges of the treeline opposite of her hiding spot, then exchanged words. A sparkle adorned the gryphons' necks, beaks, and talons. Gold and jewels.

These were not members of Rada's pride. Kristel, she recalled, was the gryphon lord that encouraged such extravagance. If they were envoys of some sort, they were likely waiting for a similar presence from Rada's pride. This was even better.

Kinira had planned to use Rada's own clan members as the catalyst for her plan. But, foreign envoys would serve even better. She could use the political implications – envoys murdered in Rada's territory – to her advantage.

She held herself still and watched as the gryphons explored the clearing. One dipped its head for a sip of water. Another began to whistle a tune. Oblivious and bored prey was easy prey. She mapped her attack, envisioning each maneuver and strike, then crouched ready.

The first target approached her part of the clearing, as she had anticipated. She tensed her legs, then vaulted out of the foliage and slammed into the gryphon. It squawked pitifully as she collided with it. The claws on her wings struck their marks, raking gashes across the gryph's chest. One last thrust through its eye, mimicking the peck of a gryph's beak, and it collapsed in a bloody heap. The second gryphon was further away than she had calculated, having reeled backward upon seeing her.

No matter.

Kinira closed the distance with a gliding bound. She opened her mouth briefly, but resisted the urge to crush it with her jaws. She would use no methods that would give clear signs of a wyvern attack. Instead, she swept the gryphon off its feet with a well-placed tail lash. Then, she pivoted swiftly with the momentum of the blow, her talons slicing through the delicate flesh of its underbelly.

The last gryphon froze. It stared at her, wide-eyed and gibbering a rapid succession of sounds. She rewarded its terror with a similarly quick and precise death.

The dirty work done, Kinira eyed the corpses. They were as good as she had planned. The wounds were savage but not beyond what a hippogryph or rogue gryphon could muster. All she needed now was a piece of evidence and a skillful escape.

She returned to her hiding spot and retrieved the smelly hippogryph cloth. She moved to the carcass furthest from her refuge and dropped the fabric nearby. Then, she stepped deftly back to her hiding spot, sweeping her tail from side to side across the loose dirt and rock as she left. Tracks obliterated and false evidence planted, she retreated into hiding. She would only leave once she had witnessed Rada's gryphons' discovery of the carnage.

By the time two gryphons landed in the clearing, the sun was setting, casting streaks of pastel pinks and blues across the lightly cloudy sky. The gryphons glanced quickly about. They squawked and fluffed their feathers in distress upon seeing the slain, gem-encrusted gryphons. One of the two immediately spotted the wilder cloth that Kinira had planted. Upon seeing it, both gryphs fell into rapid chittering. Kinira couldn't understand the meaning of their warbling, but the tone and tempo was enough. They were clearly disturbed to see Krystel's fallen gryphs and even more unsettled to find the wilder's cloth with the bodies.

The two gryphs moved slowly, hauling their fallen allies back toward the heart of Rada's territory.

So it was. Another scheme completed flawlessly.

The wilders were implicated in the gryphons' deaths. They would be discredited once Rada was presented with the undeniable "evidence" of their treachery. She stifled a chuckle, then waited until the gryphons were gone before making her way back to camp.

DESPITE WHAT SHE KNEW WOULD BE A BLOW TO MORALE and her subordinates' patience, Kinira ordered them to lie low for several days. Even with the wilders out of the way, she needed to be sure that no gryphs had a recent wyvern sighting. With the exception of a few nearby hunts at night, the four wyverns stayed within the confines of the cavern. The three males were surprisingly well behaved, perhaps because they knew that their attack drew nearer with each passing hour.

The peace between the wyverns lasted only a few days. Clouds suddenly rolled in, bringing light showers into the area. Then, the bickering resumed in force. Kinira postponed their assault for a few more days, which sparked a new round of fighting. Soggy ground and leaves made for poor fuel for fire, she explained. But, they were beyond logic.

At least they listened and stayed within the cave, she thought.

Just as she was afraid she would go mad from Gral and Tarak's constant nipping and growling, the skies cleared. The ground and air lost their excess moisture. With the shifting atmosphere, she could feel it. The time to act was upon them.

The others had already left the cave, with her leave, likely sensing that today would be ideal for attack. She appreciated the short respite alone, and she took a brief moment to gnaw on a few bones that littered the cavern floor.

A sudden roar from outside the cave drew her to her feet. Kinira lunged out of the cavern, wings carrying her fast. Tarak stood a short distance from their cave. His maw was smeared red with blood. At his feet were the mangled remains of a gryph – she could not tell what type as it had been completely annihilated by Tarak's attack.

"We were spotted," he growled. He punted the pile of flesh and feathers. It rolled toward Kinira. "But this time, I caught the scout."

Was it really a scout? Or a careless hunter? Were there others, notifying Rada's guard as they stood idly by?

A groan shook her from her thoughts.

"Dull-spined worm," Xhorin rumbled at Tarak, "Kinira would have had better use of it alive." He was right. Even without the benefit of understanding gryphon language, she could have learned something.

Tarak rose up, taking offense at Xhorin's remark. He snapped his jaws at the larger wyvern. Xhorin let out a hiss and swiped Tarak in the face with a long wing talon.

Gral watched as the two circled each other, his tail slamming into the ground in excitement, cracking the dried earth beneath him.

Kinira gaped at the three, dumbfounded. All her planning, the efforts to keep them on track for the attack, and it was plain wyvern brutishness that would be their undoing. With each growl and snap of jaws, her flames grew hotter.

No!

Calm. Reason.

The words evaporated before the rising blaze within her. She could only see her cousins cast out to the desert plains. The wind-blasted wastes would leech the life from them, then leave nothing but bone. Their collective wisdom and intellect would fall prey to stubborn instinct until there was nothing left but fools. Like these three before her.

A growl grew in her throat. *No, it would not be so.*

Her flames flared. At first, she shied away from it, but she quickly realized that the cool edge of her cunning was still there, empowered by her fury. She bared her teeth in a wicked grin.

Kinira released a deafening roar that filled the clearing and echoed within the nearby cavern. The other three froze in place and immediately assumed bowed stances.

"Fall in line," she snarled. "I've had enough. It's time."

She gestured toward the forest and spoke with a deep, growling authority. "Simple plan for simple minds. We move fast. Gral and Xhorin, to the skies. Once you see smoke, burn everything."

The two exchanged glances and let out excited rumbles.

"Tarak, sweep north on foot, I will sweep south. We converge on Rada and light the first flames. Now, *together!* Burn them to ashes!"

The four wyverns roared in unison, then separated.

Tarak wiped the gore from his face as he loped

through the tree line. The other two had already lifted into the air, clearing the forest's canopy.

Kinira felt her pride swell as she rushed into the forest. This plan would now come to fruition. Success. Vindication. Honor.

As she cleared past the first trees, instinct made her pause. She smelled deer blood mixed with the undeniable stench of terror – gryph terror. She slowed and sniffed the air, tracing the scent to a copse of thick bushes. She let out an amused grunt.

Another witness. How unfortunate.

She took a step closer, but was interrupted by a call from above.

"Waiting on you," Xhorin growled.

She shot him a look. "Patience," she grunted. She was annoyed, but he was right. Stragglers could be dealt with later. She turned and continued her charge forward.

As she raced through the woods, her thoughts returned to the terrified gryph, left hiding in the bushes. She let out an amused huff. It had been right to hide. *After all, what could one gryph do against a wyvern?* She doubled her pace – head down, wings pushing against the ground – and hurtled forward to her target.

Ahead, she could see the gryphon dwellings. They would be kindling for their four embers, just right to light the coming conflagration. Soon, very soon, the entire world would be ablaze.

DIRE STORY
ALEXANDER BIZZELL

Florence sat at the beach's shoreline, staring out at the horizon as the sun broke over the waves. She took in a deep breath through her nares and let the cool, salty breeze brush through her white-crested feathers. She closed yellow eyes, surrounded by deep brown accents, and let out a sigh. The sound of rolling waves breaking along the sandbar calmed her thoughts. Rhythmic rushing water mixing with the loud seagulls in the distance put her mind at ease.

She glanced to the crude fishing rod lodged in the sand next to her. Now, the fishing pole was straight with the line cast into the crystal-clear blue water. She hadn't seen a single fish that morning and cursed her luck. Sure, she could easily take to the skies and patiently wait for a fish to show itself towards the surface, but she had already met the week's quota for rations days ago. This day, she wanted to try out a new gryphon clan invention, the fishing pole. It seemed simple enough, cast a line out with bait and let the fish come to them. It was far more relaxing and easier than hunting with talon.

The osprey gryphon closed her eyes once again and concentrated on the rhythmic sounds of the ocean. The early mornings were her time of peace before the rest of her clan awoke. After first sunmark, the area was full of life and vigor. All thoughts of peace were out of the question during those times. She was an early riser for that reason alone.

"Trying out Uri's new invention, are we?" came a deep voice from behind her.

Florence sighed and lazily opened one eye to glance at the opincus walking towards her on the beach. His dull, sandy-white feathers almost made him blend completely into the surrounding beach. The opincus chuckled as he saw the intrusion upon her expression.

"Oh, excuse me, my great gryphoness," he said with a mocking bow, forepaws digging into the sand.

Florence waved a foretalon dismissively and huffed. "Save your grubbing for later, Kernith." She spoke in a low, stern tone, but her yellow eyes gleamed in the early sunrise. "What do you want?"

"What? I can't visit an old friend now and again without there being some sort of business attached to it?" Kernith sat down in the sand next to her. He was a full head shorter and had dull, grey eyes like a stormy sea day.

A seagull circled around them, calling out its taunts and remarks in the feral language of birds. Florence ground her sharp curved black beak and glanced over to her visitor.

"Every time you visit me, it's about business," the osprey said sharply, wings readjusting. Kernith picked up a nearby stick and started to sketch in the wet sand between them. As he drew, he spoke.

"It's not about business this time," he stated, drawing

an avian face in the sand. "It's about a rumor, one that may very well be more than a rumor."

His firm tone drew in Florence's attention. The opinicus was known as a gossiper, but for good reasons. He was a courier for Dire Rayne, carrying both verbal and written messages to the other dire clans within close vicinity of their own. There was no reason to discount what he had to say.

"Well? You going to leave me hanging or what?" Florence flicked her white-furred tail across the sand in agitation.

Kernith grinned and threw his stick to the side. "Why would I do that? After all, I am the one that came down here, but," he pointed at the rod with a furred foreclaw, "the next tuna you catch is mine, deal?"

Florence sighed and nodded her head. "I knew you weren't down here to just visit an old friend, you manipulative snake."

The opincus held both forepaws up in defense, shaking his head. "Oh no, no! You clearly misunderstand! I simply..."

"Shut your beak before I bury it in the sand," Florence replied sternly.

A sly smile crept along the male's beak, and he chuckled deeply. His forepaws returned to the ground as the silence between them grew. She was already ahead of her ration quota for the week, and an extra tuna would not be difficult to obtain.

She knew it was his favorite, after all. "Fine, tell me what you know."

Kernith laughed and clapped his paws together. "Splendid! Ok, well to begin all of this, you know of Dire Rada?"

Florence nodded. "The insane traditionalist dire that makes his subjects swear complete oath to him? The same one that raises gryphons and opinici to hate one another?" Florence stated.

"The very same! Well, he and his clan are no more," Kernith began.

This news made the dark eye ridges on Florence's face rise with attention. "No more? As in the dire is dead?"

"Burned to the ground, by wyverns none-the-less," Kernith responded.

The very mention of wyverns caused the osprey's feathers to flatten firmly against her body. She felt a disgusting cold shiver run up her spine. Memories of mountain-sized, scaled beasts came rushing back. Her ears rang with the overpowering screeching they produced. Her heart began to race, and her vision blurred.

"Florence?" the opinicus repeated for the third time.

She took a deep breath and stared out at the sea once again. "I'm fine. A pity to hear about the clan. Not so much for dire Rada. I hope his spirit is being obliterated right now," she said sternly.

"My, my! Someone certainly has some history with the dire," Kernith pressed.

Before the gryphoness had time to respond, the fishing rod in the sand sprang to life. The line tightened and threatened to pull out the stick from the earth. Both gryphon and opincus ears perked to attention, and Florence acted quickly. She grabbed the rod with both foretalons and yanked.

"You must have caught something!" Kernith yelled excitedly.

Florence ground her beak and yanked again, watching as a large tuna jumped out of the water.

"Obviously, genius!" the gryphoness yelled and walked away from the ocean, pulling the line with her. Kernith cheered her on as the tuna came closer and closer to shore until it was flopping on the beach line. He ran to the fish and dispatched it with his paws, slicing it across the throat.

Florence placed the fishing pole down on the ground and approached the opinicus with a half-smile.

"Looks like the fishing pole works after all." He pointed out and drug the fish farther from the water.

"I'll have to thank Uri later, but there has to be some sort of way to bring the line in without me having to walk backwards," Florence thought out loud. "Anyways, as promised, that tuna is yours."

"Thanks, but I'm not done yet," Kernith mentioned, working along the fish's stomach with a sharp claw. He bled the fish and started to clean it. "As you know, Dire Rada's land was not impressive, but it's still land none-the-less. Unclaimed land."

"And now all the direlords are fighting for that land?" Florence finished for him.

He cut out a sizable piece from the tuna and held it in his dirty paws. A slight grin appeared on his beak, and he motioned to her with it.

"Precisely!" Kernith explained and tossed the piece in his beak. He savored the flavor for a minute and let out a pleasant trill. "Nothing like a fresh piece of tuna in the morning."

"Don't tell me our Dire plans on trying to claim that land also," Florence pleaded, already knowing the answer to her question. Their Dire was one of the more relaxed and intelligent leaders known, but still, a direlord was a direlord for a reason. All dires were greedy by nature, and if there was something worth taking, they would try their hardest to get it.

"I believe you already know the answer to that one," The opinicus confirmed her fears. He cut another piece from the fish and offered it to Florence, who happily took it. He let the osprey gryphoness enjoy her piece before adding in, "And your name was mentioned to lead the hunting party that will accompany the strikers."

Florence was grateful that he paused to break the news to her, or she would have chocked on the tuna. Her blood began to boil almost instantly, and her hackle feathers stood on end.

"She what?!" Florence yelled.

Again, the opinicus held his forepaws up in defense, trying not to laugh. He clearly enjoyed being the bearer of bad news. "Hey, hey don't kill the messenger! Literally or figuratively. I'm just giving you a heads up before you receive your official summons."

As if on command, the sound of beating wings drew their attention to the sky. A brightly-colored gryphon landed beside them, kicking up sand with the backstrokes of his blue and yellow wings. His beak was short and curved, with bright blue feathers adorning his head. Florence recognized him instantly, being the only macaw gryphon in their colony. He was a personal advisor to Dire Rayne. It was rare he sought out others individually. Usually, they were summoned to meet with him.

"Good morning, Florence," he said calmly and approached the two of them. "And to you, Kernith. Wait, what are you doing here?" The brightly-colored gryphon questioned.

"None of your business, Poulsen," Kernith sharply replied. Poulsen did not seem to be bothered by the fiery retort. He sat down to reach into his leather bag hanging around his neck and pulled out a sealed piece of parchment.

"I believe you know what this is, now that I see Kernith with you," the macaw said, glancing over at the opincus.

Kernith huffed through his nares and looked away. Poulsen handed the letter over to Florence. She sighed and took it from him.

"Unfortunately, yes. And here I was trying to have a quiet morning." Florence broke the red wax seal with a foretalon and unrolled the piece of parchment. She scanned over it for a minute, ears falling flat. Once she was finished, she rolled the piece back up and handed it over to Poulsen. "Tell Dire Rayne that I will be there by midmark."

Poulsen put the piece away and bowed politely before her. Florence returned the gesture as he began to speak.

"Splendid. As always, a pleasure to see you again." He turned to leave. The fishing pole caught his eye, and he paused to point at it. "Is that Uri's new invention?"

The osprey gryphoness nodded in response. "Yes. I was trying to test it out for the next couple days and give her some recommendations, but it looks like that will have to wait."

"A shame. I'm sure Uri will have a dozen new versions by the time you come back," Poulsen said and quickly took to the sky.

"That macaw thinks he's just all that. I can't stand him!" Kernith slammed his paw down on the fish. The force splashed some of the leftover salt water onto Florence's face. Kernith's angry expression quickly changed as he cowered before the gryphoness. "I'm so sorry! I...!"

"Beat it, Kernith!" Florence yelled at the top of her lungs. The opinicus squawked and picked up the fish, quickly taking to the sky as well.

She took in a deep breath and wiped her face with a wing tip. Once again, she was left in silence. The sounds of the waves broke along the shoreline as the sun continued to rise higher by the minute.

"Well, here we go again."

KITCARER

SAYLOR FERGUSON

It was a chill autumn day, and Stell had wolves on the brain.

Then again, Stell often was reminded of the wolf she'd battled and killed a fracture ago, especially on colder days, as her former wing injury had a tendency to ache in the cold air. She could fly fine, but the scar on her wing—right where her wing bent at the wrist, and only visible if the feathers were parted—was prone to aching if overused or exposed to cold air.

Stell's mind jumped from thoughts of wolves to the present, as it always did when her lifelong friend Relwen strode into the nursery.

"How're things, Kitcarer?" Relwen asked, a laugh puffing the brown feathers of her face.

"Same as last time you checked in, which, I think, was maybe one mark ago...?" Stell returned with her own chuckle. "What can I do for you?"

"Oh, nothing," Relwen said, draping herself across Stell's nest as she always did. "I just finished talking with some of the hunters, and now I'm bored."

Relwen was often bored and was always over at the nursery with the sole purpose of bothering Stell. Before Stell had become a true kitcarer—rare, given her half-breed status, but earned when she fought a wolf to save two kits—Rask, the other kitcarer, would've kicked Relwen out of the nursery in a matter of seconds. Now that Stell was of an equal rank with Rask, and as the older gryph began to move toward retirement, nobody could make Relwen leave. Well, nobody but...

"Relwen," a new voice said as a lovely golden gryphon ducked under the wolf pelt that made up the nursery door. "A pleasure as always."

Relwen chirped a greeting. "The pleasure is all mine, Lila."

Stell flushed under her feathers when the newest kitcarer entered into the nursery but continued her current task of portioning out meals for the kits. Kitcarer Lila was Direlord Maylar's youngest child, just a fracture or two younger than Stell. She'd recently been initiated as a kitcarer, set to replace Rask as he began pursuing other tasks that were less intense.

As Lila began play-wrestling with the kits, distracting them so that Stell could continue her meal planning uninterrupted, Relwen rose from Stell's nest and stretched her wings. "Well, I won't bother you two," she said with a laughing glance at Stell that had the black-feathered opinicus's cere flushing. With a flick of her wing, Relwen was out of the nursery, off to find some hunters to accompany.

Life hadn't been particularly fair to Relwen, Stell thought, but the brown-feathered opinicus was never one to stay bitter for long. Half-breed like Stell, Relwen had never had the opportunity to advance to initiation, and it wasn't very likely she ever would. As far as Stell knew, she herself was the only half-breed to have ever risen to a title.

"I swear, that gryph can never sit still," Lila said with a laugh as kits climbed all over her. Merk, the smaller kit Stell had saved from the wolf, was now a much larger kit, though still in the nursery; Lendon, however, had moved out recently to begin training. He still stopped by on occasion to visit Stell, as she shared a close bond with the two kits she'd rescued.

"She'll be back before too long," Stell warned, avoiding eye contact with her fellow kitcarer. "If the hunters let her tag along, it'll be a couple of marks. If they don't, it'll be even sooner."

"I'd come by all the time, too, if I were her," Lila said furtively.

And there it was, the reason that Relwen made such fun of Stell, the reason that Stell could barely make herself look at Lila. The direlord's golden daughter was a shameless flirt, and Stell found herself more and more unable to ignore Lila's words. The two kitcarers worked well together, and Stell *knew* that it would be worth it to test the waters with the pretty gryph, but she also knew she couldn't.

Get your head out of the clouds, Stell warned herself. *A half-breed has no place courting a direlord's daughter.*

Lila seemed to sense Stell drawing further into herself. "Because of your excellent stories, of course," she said, smoothing things over. "Relwen loves a good story, and every gryph here knows you've got one of the best stories this pride has ever heard."

Stell accepted Lila's peace offering. "I was just doing my job," she said, turning from her meal planning to face the eager kits. "Now, who wants a story?"

Excited cheers met her ears, none more so than from Merk, a central figure of Stell's wolf tale. Lila lay down on the soft nursery floor, allowing the kits to snuggle up against her, and Stell sat in front of the gathered gryphs. "It all started when a group of hunters was attacked up by the quartz falls..."

As Stell's words bled into her well-memorized story, she spent a few moments studying Lila. Her fellow kitcarer was larger than Stell, as all gryphons were, but Lila was larger still, being the daughter of a direlord. Stell reached the golden gryph's shoulder, always having to tilt back her head to meet Lila's eyes. Eyes that were a mesmerizing moss green flecked with amber.

"You're a hero to them, you know," Lila said later, once the kits had been tucked into their nests and the two kitcarers were in their own nests, between the kits and the exit. Rask had returned some marks ago and almost immediately retreated into his own bed, and Stell could hear the orange gryphon's soft snoring.

"Just Merk, I think," Stell murmured back, nuzzling herself deeper into her wolf-lined nest, hoping the warm pelt would chase away the autumn chill and the ache in her wing. "The rest of them just enjoy a good story, no matter who it's about."

"Don't downplay yourself," Lila said, an exasperated note in her voice as she rolled over in her nest to face Stell.

Lila's eyes shone like flames in the darkness, but for once Stell wasn't reminded of the traumas of her kithood, when a wyvern attack had destroyed the pridegrounds and very nearly killed the kits, save for the quick thinking of Kitcarer Mar, Stell's personal hero.

"I hear the things they say about you, Wolfslayer," Lila

continued in a tone that made Stell's heart beat faster. "You *are* a hero, whether you like it or not." The golden gryphon was silent for a moment more before adding, "I, for one, like it quite a bit."

Stell looked away, heat flashing through her pelt. She knew in that moment she could give into instinct, let Lila into her life, but instead she simply rolled over, tucking her wings close to her sides. "Goodnight, Lila," she said, and closed her eyes.

She could feel Lila's burning stare on her back until sleep claimed her.

LILA AWOKE JUST BEFORE DAWN. FIRST, SHE GLANCED OVER at the kits, most of whom slept in a feathery bundle that spanned several nests. She did a brief headcount, confirmed that all the kits were there, and sighed softly with relief. Still being new to kitcaring, Lila often worried she'd make a mistake and lose a kit, but so far things had been easy.

Except with Stell, of course. Lila tilted her head to regard her fellow kitcarer, who was fast asleep with her iridescent black feathers fluffed to keep out the chill. Lila found herself vaguely jealous of the way Stell's paws were wrapped around the wolf pelt she slept with.

This is ridiculous, Lila thought. *I've been subtle for long enough.* Rising softly to her feet, Lila padded around Stell, Rask, and the kits, and made her way into the predawn dark.

She stretched her back and wings once outside, reveling in the way her breath fogged before her in the chilly air. The sky was clear, the stars fading back into the night as pale light touched the edges of the horizon. The outline of a lone gryph circled far above the pride-grounds: that night's guard. Few other gryphs were awake at this early hour, particularly with the cold keeping them bundled in their nests. But Lila knew at least one other gryph who would be up; she'd inherited her enjoyment of the earliest time of day from her mother. A short flight led Lila to the direlord's den, the only structure in the pride that was larger than the nursery. Standing outside the bear pelt door, Lila cleared her throat.

"Mother?" she called softly.

There was movement inside the den. Around the edges of the door, Lila saw light flicker into existence as her mother lit the brazier inside her home.

"Enter," Maylar replied.

Pushing aside the bear pelt, Lila made her way into the direlord's den. Maylar was lounging on a cushion beside the fire, her spiky amber feathers looking almost as golden as Lila's in the wavering light. Nearly twice the size of Lila, Maylar regarded her daughter in a way that required her to stare down her beak at the smaller gryphon, even though Lila was standing and her mother was reclining.

"What brings you here, Lila?" Maylar asked in her deep, rich voice.

Lila sat down across the brazier from her mother. "I need relationship advice."

Maylar laughed, a sound that reverberated in Lila's chest. "I may be the wrong person to ask," she chuckled. "Considering that I've never stayed with one gryph longer than the time it took to have a kit."

Lila smiled weakly.

"But that's beside the point," Maylar said. "Who've you got your eye on?"

"Stell," Lila replied, feeling herself blush under her facial feathers at the mention of the gryph who so frequently occupied her thoughts.

Maylar tensed, her feathers smoothing to her body in displeasure. "Stell," she repeated, the laughter gone from her voice. "The mix-breed kitcarer?"

Her mother's tone rubbed Lila the wrong way and she fought to keep her feathers from hackling. "Yes," she said with restrained temper. "Is that a problem?"

Maylar thought for a moment, her eyes flickering in the firelight. She was so still she might have been a gryph carved from stone. "You are a gryphon. She is an opinicus," the direlord said finally. "It is not proper, nor is it permitted in my pride."

This was news to Lila, though she'd never really considered it before. Still, it sounded ridiculous. "But Stell is titled, initiated," Lila argued. "Besides, she's half gryphon. Her parents got together and..."

"And where are they now?" Maylar interrupted.

Lila's ears pinned back.

"They're exiles, or wilders, or dead," Maylar continued. "They broke a law more ancient than even this pride —gryphons and opinici do not mate, no matter where they come from. I spare the kits because it is not their fault they were born. But they will not take mates, and they will especially have nothing to do with the child of a direlord."

At this, Lila's fine hold on her temper snapped. She stood, flaring her wings. "Who I care for is my business, not yours," she growled. "I came here for a lighthearted conversation about how I could properly court a gryph who I intend to take as my mate. I didn't come here to listen to your stupid rules, and I certainly didn't come here to hear that my feelings should be ignored."

Maylar looked troubled, her tail tapping on the ground. "Sit down," she commanded, and despite Lila's anger, her mother's tone forced her rump to the ground, though her wings remained open.

"I would never tell a gryph their feelings aren't valid," Maylar explained, and Lila huffed a sarcastic laugh through her nares.

"You're sure that isn't what you told Stell's parents when you exiled them for being mates?" Lila asked. "Because what you're saying and what I'm hearing are very different things."

Maylar growled, and although she knew her mother would never raise a talon against her, Lila flinched.

"You misinterpret my words," the direlord said.

"You misinterpret yourself," Lila countered. "You say that I should act on my wishes yet tell me I can't because of some law that originated spirits-know-when." When Maylar remained silent, brooding, Lila continued. "I'm going to court Stell," she said. "And you'll just have to see if you're the kind of direlord who would exile her own daughter for doing so."

Lila didn't miss the contemplative look in her mother's eyes as she turned and stalked from the tent.

WHEN STELL AWOKE AT DAWN, LILA WAS GONE. RASK, ON his way out of the nursery, told Stell she'd gone to visit her mother for a few marks. Stell very nearly sighed with relief, though a part of her missed seeing her lovely, energetic fellow kitcarer.

Relwen burst into the nursery with enough energy to make Stell jump. "A storm's coming," the brown gryph announced before making her way to her designated lounging place in Stell's nest.

Stell glanced up at the skylight, but as far as she could see the sky was blue. "What makes you say that?"

Relwen joined Stell in staring outside, her pupils dilating and contracting as she focused on fast-moving white clouds. "That's what all the hunters are saying. The sky's got a sort of electricity to it, the clouds are moving fast, and the air is damp."

"I'll believe you, then," Stell said, "if that's what the hunters are saying. But I've got kits that need a wash in the stream today, so I hope the storm holds off until later."

Relwen shrugged. "I can help you get the kits together if you want, since I see pretty feathers isn't here."

"If you think she's so pretty, why don't you court her yourself?" Stell asked, her face feathers fluffing.

"Oh, Wolf Eyes," Relwen said, tapping Stell's beak with a paw and making her blink. "Anyone who's paying attention can see that the direlord's daughter has eyes only for you."

"That's really too bad, then," Stell said dismissively.

"I don't see why..." Relwen began, but Stell turned on her with a low hiss, making several kits jump.

"It just can't happen! Okay? Please stop asking me about it."

Relwen raised her front paws in surrender. "Okay, I'll stop bothering you about it. For now, at least. Now, let's go wash off some stinky kits."

Herding kits was one of the most demanding tasks of

being a kitcarer. Once free from the confines of the nursery, the kits were prone to wandering all around the pridegrounds, and those who were developing flight feathers
would try and flap off to spirits knew where. It was definitely a task for multiple gryphs, and as Relwen was
largely untrained in kitcaring, Stell was relieved when Lila
flew over from the direlord's den.

"Have you seen Rask at all?" Stell said by way of introduction, blocking a smaller kit from escaping the group
with her wing.

Lila looked tense but answered Stell's question nonetheless. "He's made it pretty clear to Maylar that his
kitcaring days are just about over. He says he wants to be a
coordinator; he thinks it might be easier for him."

"Well," was all Stell said, but in truth, she'd miss the
grumpy old kitcarer. He'd half raised her, after Mar died,
and had taught her all she knew about kitcaring. But Stell
didn't have time to worry about that right now; they'd
reached the stream and had to line the kits up in order to
be washed.

Relwen left Stell and Lila to scout around the pridegrounds, to "make sure there weren't any kits wandering
off to fight wolves," as she put it. Stell sat in the chilly
water of the stream, receiving one kit after the other and
giving them a thorough wash. She checked the sky from
time to time, noting the gathering clouds and rising
breeze. It seemed that the hunters were right, though she
didn't think the storm would break for a while longer.

As the kits dried out at the stream's edge—the grassy
field where the direlord made announcements—Rask
ambled over and agreed to watch over them so that the
other kitcarers could get clean, too. Stell preened water
from her iridescent black feathers, watching as Lila did

the same in the yellowing light that always came before a storm.

Stell was startled when Lila looked up to notice her staring.

"I want to talk, gryph to gryph, if that's alright with you," Lila said firmly.

Stell knew what this was about. "Okay," she said cautiously.

"Are you deaf to my flirting or am I just that bad?" Lila asked, her eye ridges furrowed seriously. Stell nearly inhaled a feather and choked a few times. Lila cocked her head to the side, beginning to look embarrassed. "What?"

Stell didn't want the beautiful golden gryphon to think that Stell disliked her. "Your flirting is quite good, actually," she finally confessed. "I just... can't."

"Can't what?" Lila stopped preening altogether, staring hard at Stell with those mesmerizing green eyes.

"I can't... we can't...," Stell stammered.

At this, Lila smiled. "Why not? If we like each other, I don't see any reason we shouldn't court."

Stell roused her feathers, trying to get them to lay flat, but they remained ruffled. "Don't you know what the direlord does to gryphon-opinicus pairs?" Stell snapped. "She's your own mother, you ought to know how she treats those sorts of gryphs."

Understanding dawned in Lila's eyes. "I know, but..." she started, but Stell wasn't done.

"I was born because a gryphon and an opinicus became mates. I never knew my parents; Maylar exiled them as soon as I was born. She did the same thing with Relwen's parents, with the parents of every other half-breed gryph ever born in the pride. She only spares the kits because she has a soft spot for children; everyone knows it. But if you and I were to court... I don't know that she'd exile you, but I could kiss my title as Kitcarer goodbye!"

Stell realized she'd maybe gone too far, based off the look on Lila's face. "Look, Lila, I didn't mean to say all that."

"Oh, Kitcarer Stell," Lila said coldly, "I think you did."

Stell didn't have any time to feel sorry for herself before a clap of thunder resonated around the valley, and the rain began in a downpour. Squawking indecently, Rask started herding the kits together. Stell's heart raced and she, too, screeched when lightning split the sky, causing thunder to roar all around her. This was a true autumn storm, sudden and fierce. As the cold rain soaked her through, Stell's old injury twanged at every movement. Rushing forwards, Stell helped Rask herd the now-soaking, terrified kits.

But one of the older kits who had just enough of their flight feathers to be problematic startled at the next clap of thunder, leaping into the sky and smacking Stell in the face with their wings before careening off toward the stream. Kitcarer instinct took over and Stell whirled around to follow the wayward kit. She searched frantically through the driving rain, blinking to rid the water from her eyes, and finally caught sight of the kit. And *of course* it was Merk, the kit closest to Stell's heart.

Stell felt her chest seize as she realized that Merk hadn't been able to sustain her flight for very long in the pouring rain and had fallen into the stream, which in the past few minutes had transformed into muddy, roaring rapids. Stell was about to dive into the stream when a golden-feathered gryph beat her to it, plunging into the water like an osprey and grasping Merk in her talons.

Stell gasped, watching as Lila almost pulled herself and Merk from the water, until a large branch crashed into her, causing her to collapse into the flooded stream and drop Merk.

Shoving caution aside, Stell flared her wings to follow the other kitcarer, the gryph she had come to care about in a way she'd never cared for anyone else before.

But... "No!" Lila spluttered, lifting her head above water. "The other kits," she managed to say before she began swimming downstream, desperate to catch up to Merk.

Stell knew what she meant. But it took nearly all of her resolve to let the golden gryphon go, to let her disappear downstream into the pouring rain, and to turn around and sprint back to the other kits, still being watched by Rask.

"Back to the nursery!" Stell shouted. "Now!" And within minutes, they'd reached the safety of the nursery, where Stell ushered the exhausted kits inside and held them in her soggy embrace, crying herself to sleep as the storm raged outside.

DESPITE BEING FILLED WITH WATER, LILA'S LUNGS FELT ON fire. She hacked and gasped, vomiting up muddy water as she simultaneously tried to stay afloat and look for Merk. *I should've paid more attention when Rask taught me to swim as a kit,* she thought, but gryphon talons were ill-suited for swimming no matter how skilled one was. She was distracted, trying to paddle with her hind paws, when a rogue tree limb struck her in the side. With a yelp, she was pulled under again, spinning out of control in the flood.

Unable to see anything through the gritty water, Lila closed her eyes, pain jolting through her as her back bounced off of a submerged boulder and a cluster of uprooted thorns scraped along her flank. But then Lila felt something soft brush past her wing, something kit-sized. A shocked exhalation leaving her beak as a stream of bubbles, Lila grabbed the limp kit and found the strength to push up from the bottom of the river.

She broke the surface of the water with a gasp of exertion. Wiping water from her eyes with flicks of her nictitating membranes, Lila tried to get a bearing on her situation. The sky above her was roiling gray clouds—or was that the surging water beneath her? Somewhat dazedly, Lila remembered the kit grasped in her talons, and she pushed Merk's head above the water. The kit was alarmingly limp.

"No," Lila managed to rasp, her chest still heaving as she fought for breath. "No!" But before she could cry her sorrow to the world, an unusual current tugged against Lila's submerged wing, pulling her to the left. Her burning muscles were too weak to fight the water anymore, so Lila cradled Merk's limp form to her chest as the river swept her away. In her delusional state, Lila thought she could make out the dark outline of a great beast's maw, ready to swallow her whole. But she couldn't fight any more, and as dark spots flashed across her vision, she was sucked into a blackness as final as death.

After a few moments of darkness, Lila realized she was still breathing. That, and the water was growing shallower, her hind paws brushing up against a creek bed that was made up of soft sand. The creek itself was much colder than the river, but the current had slowed, and before too long Lila felt herself halfway deposited on a pebbly beach.

A dark pebbly beach, Lila thought, her eyes adjusting to the dim light inside of what she was now realizing was a cave. Pale blue luminescent moss coated the walls around her, and the ceiling was made up of dripping limestone stalactites. She wondered if she'd ever find the strength to drag herself fully from the cold water when she remembered the small feathered form pressed against her chest. *Merk.*

Harnessing a strength she didn't know she still possessed, Lila placed Merk gently on the pebbled beach and stood shakily over her motionless form. The kit wasn't moving. Alarm sparked in Lila's veins, filling her with adrenaline as electric as the storm's lightning. Breathing hard, she lowered her head to press her ear against Merk's beak. She didn't hear anything, didn't register any breath brushing her ear feathers.

Merk was dead.

You failed, a nasty voice in Lila's mind whispered. *You knew you'd be a failure of a kitcarer.* But then Lila remembered something Rask had taught her in her first days of kitcaring.

"It won't always work," he'd warned. "But if a kit isn't breathing you can try this."

Forcing steadiness into her talons, Lila began gentle compressions on Merk's chest. Not too hard, because she didn't want to break the kit's small ribs, but with just enough force to pump the heart that refused to beat for itself.

"Come on," Lila muttered. "Come on, Merk! You survived a midnight adventure into the woods. You survived a wolf, for spirits' sake! Now wake up!"

Lila was moments away from giving up hope when Merk gasped to life, convulsing as she threw up muddy river water. Lila immediately pulled the kit's shivering form to her chest, settling herself on the pebbles and fluffing her feathers in an effort to warm Merk.

"You're okay," she said, stroking Merk's back as tears ran down her face. The trembling kit, shocked and scared, began to cry, pressing her face into Lila's feathers. Lila simply held her until both of them had overcome their emotions. *You didn't fail,* Lila told herself. *You saved Merk, just like Stell saved her before.*

Stell. She needed to get back to Stell.

It dawned on Lila that she was beginning to shiver, the cold water and chill air of the cave threatening hypothermia. Merk was likewise shaking.

"We can't stay here," Lila muttered to herself. No search party would ever find them here. Spirits above, did anyone even know this cave existed? Lila had certainly never heard anything of a limestone cave that branched off from the river. They were on their own, and with the afternoon beginning to fade, making the water flowing into the cave even colder, Lila began to fear that they were much farther from home than she'd previously thought.

"Merk," she said gently, nudging the traumatized kit. "Merk, honey, we have to get up." She stood, and Merk rose on shaky legs. She looked so small with her feathers plastered to her body, and Lila worried that the kit was still in just as much danger of not surviving the ordeal as before.

Exhaustion weighed heavily on Lila's shoulders, but she told herself she'd just have to overcome it. She hadn't brought Merk back to life just to have the both of them die. She hadn't left things with her mother like that. She hadn't left Stell with their final conversation being an argument...

"Here, climb onto my shoulders," Lila said, stooping down to let Merk settle herself between Lila's wings. "I'm going to get us out of this cave."

Lila turned and stepped back into the shallow creek, carefully wading upstream. Here, the water was no deeper than her stomach, the sandy creek bed soft beneath her feet. If they survived long enough to get back to the pride, Lila would consider herself and Merk lucky for being swept into the cave and not further downriver.

Lila was beginning to wonder how far into the cave she and Merk had been carried, beginning to think they'd certainly become lost amid the soft, musical dripping sound of moisture off the stalactites, the swish of Lila's legs against the current, and the echoes of the two gryphs' breathing. Just when it seemed like the world would never again contain anything other than stone, water, and glowing moss, Lila spotted a faint yellow light up ahead.

Sunlight.

Her confidence restored at this sign of the outside world, she waded faster through the water, even as the creek gradually deepened and she found herself halfway swimming. The weight of Merk on her back didn't drag her down whatsoever, so encouraged was she by the glimpse of sunlight. When she finally made it to the cave exit, standing clumsily on her hind paws to stay upright in the deeper water, Lila turned back and realized that the cave mouth was not the terrifying maw she'd previously thought. It was a nondescript crack in the stone that lined the banks of the larger river. It had also been the only thing which saved her from being swept further downriver, and for that she was thankful.

The late afternoon light was golden in the way it often was after a storm, the air thick with steam rising from the river and plants. The flood had subsided, leaving behind water that was still muddy but not powerful enough to drag Lila away; she managed to climb up the rocks surrounding the cave entrance, finally emerging on dry ground.

Thank the spirits.

But their ordeal wasn't over yet. Turning in a complete circle, Lila surveyed the land around her, finding it completely unfamiliar. She stood in a large field that bordered on a thick forest several leaps away; staring upriver, she could see the mountains of her home pride, but out here the rolling mountains had worn down into even more gently sloping hills.

You're not in your pridegrounds, then, she told herself. The lands surrounding Maylar's pride weren't inhabited by other prides for nearly a hundred miles, although there were certainly camps of exiles and wilders who called this place home. Lila shivered as the air began to cool, bringing with it the sounds of evening crickets and the faint hoots of waking owls.

"Lila?" a small voice asked from Lila's back, reminding her that she wasn't alone. "Where are we?"

Far from anyone who cares about us, Lila wanted to say. But instead she set her jaw, turning to look Merk in the eye. "I don't know," she admitted, "but we're going home."

STELL WAS ABRUPTLY WOKEN FROM TURBULENT DREAMS BY A gryph shaking her shoulder and proclaiming, "You look like a wreck!" Stell cracked her eyes open, noting the persistent ache in her formerly injured wing, the dampness of her feathers, and the smell of dirty water.

"Lila?" she asked, even though she knew it wasn't. Rather, Relwen clicked her beak once before leaning over to preen at Stell's messy feathers.

"Oh, Stell..." she murmured. And Stell *knew*. Knew that Lila, the gryph she refused to let herself love, and Merk, the kit who had held such a large place in her heart, hadn't returned. The search parties had come home empty-pawed.

Stell had failed. As a kitcarer, as a gryph, she'd failed miserably.

"I need to speak to the direlord," Stell said, her voice raw.

Relwen drew back to stare Stell in the eyes. "Not looking like that, you won't. Let me help you." So Relwen helped her friend preen, grooming some of the rainwater smell from her feathers and fur. Within a half mark, Stell stood outside the direlord's den, satisfied at least that Rask and Relwen were watching the kits. The guards, surprisingly, allowed her to enter.

Direlord Maylar was putting on her ceremonial jewelry, complete with earrings, bangles, and her lovely opal necklace. "Kitcarer Stell," she said shortly, not looking in Stell's direction. "I assume this is about the disaster of yesterday afternoon."

Stell nodded, but when she realized that Maylar didn't see her, she instead swallowed hard and said, "Direlord, I am so sorry. Everything that happened is my fault. As senior kitcarer, I should have been monitoring the storm more closely, I shouldn't have let Lila go after the lost kit."

"I seem to remember you going after several lost kits and becoming a hero," Maylar said, finally turning to meet Stell's eyes. Matching grief shone from both gazes.

"My daughter did as her role demanded, and she has died a hero. Nothing can take that away from her."

Stell's throat grew tight, and she scuffed at the direlord's rug with her forepaws. "She was a wonderful gryph," Stell agreed.

"... who seemed to think highly of you," Direlord Maylar finished, tilting her massive head at Stell in a way that reminded Stell of Lila. "Just yesterday, she was seeking my approval to court you with the motive of making you her mate." Stell's heart sank to her stomach. "I was prepared to say yes," the direlord continued. "As I'm sure you know, we have ancient rules that forbid such a thing between gryphons and opinci, but I trust my daughter, and I was open to change, for the sake of her happiness."

"I'm so sorry," was all Stell could bring herself to say, before she stumbled out into the too-bright light of the morning to return to her job. After all, a kitcarer's duties were never over—heartbreak or no—and she was the only true kitcarer left in Maylar's pride.

STELL SPENT THE NEXT THREE DAYS IN A DAZE. FROM THE doorway of the nursery, she listened to the meeting in which the direlord announced Lila's and Merk's deaths. She forced herself to continue her duties, to find joy in the kits that *had* survived the storm.

Sleep brought little relief. She dreamed of the her argument with Lila before the storm; she dreamed of the night, fractures ago, when she'd battled a wolf to save two kits; she dreamed of wyvern flames and the thick stench of fear; she dreamed of a faceless gryphon and opinicus—

her parents—and of Maylar's voice: *"I was open to change, for the sake of her happiness."*

They're dead! Stell screamed in her dreams. *Merk, Lila, Mar, my parents, they're all dead!*

On the fourth night after the flood, just as the sun was setting, a commotion rose up on the edge of the pridegrounds, near the river. Stell had been getting the kits ready for bed with help from Rask—and Relwen, who had rarely left Stell's side since the storm—when words floated into the nursery, carried by the wind: "They're alive!"

Stell's heart leapt into her throat, her eyes widening as she turned to face Relwen. The brown-feathered gryph waved her friend forward with a paw.

Stell burst from the nursery, her paws pounding on the grassy ground until she got enough lift under her wings and leapt into the air. Rapid wingbeats carried her to the edge of the pridegrounds, where a small crowd was gathering around two gryphs: a golden-feathered gryphon and a half-fledged kit.

Stell tucked her wings and fell, stooping like a falcon until she pulled up on the grass directly in front of the two gryphs she'd lost, who had returned to her. Merk chirped an excited greeting. Stell stared at Lila—wolf eyes gazing into mossy green eyes.

"Lila," she breathed, and the golden gryphon leapt forward, wrapping her front legs around Stell's neck in a tight hug. Shocked, Stell stiffened for a moment, but then threw her wings around Lila, holding her tight.

"I thought you were dead!" Stell said, her voice somewhere in between laughing and crying as the two kitcarers drew apart and Merk took the opportunity to leap at

Stell's chest, purring as she embraced Stell and was in turn held close by Stell's paw.

Now that she was having a good look at her fellow kitcarer, Stell could see exhaustion dulling her eyes, mud plastered to her feathers, and scrapes along her body. But Lila found it within herself to smile at Stell as though they weren't being stared at by a growing crowd of gryphs.

"It takes more than a little water to kill Merk and me," Lila said, gazing fondly at the kit who was still plastered to Stell, nuzzling her shimmery blue-black feathers.

Stell surprised herself with her next words. "I'm sorry," she blurted, drawing Lila's eyes back to her own.

"I was cruel to you when I shouldn't have been," Stell continued. "And it shouldn't have taken a flood for me to tell you... I like you. And I'd want to give us a chance, if you're still willing."

Lila was contemplative. "Even though I'm a gryphon?"

"And even though I'm an opinicus," Stell confirmed. "We'll find a way to make the laws work for us."

A slow smile spread across Lila's lovely face as she realized her mother was going to allow her and Stell to court. "Am I willing to give us a chance?" she asked, rephrasing Stell's words. "I'd love to, Wolfslayer."

"But first," Lila continued, "Merk and I need a proper preening. And a proper meal." The gryphs gathered around them began departing to find something for Lila and Merk to eat, and undoubtedly to find the direlord to tell her that her daughter was alive.

Finding herself relatively alone with Lila, Stell—still holding Merk—tilted her head to the side inquisitively. "How did you survive?" Lila paced up to Stell's side, draping a golden wing across Stell's back.

"All in good time," Lila replied. "But first, let's go home."

As the two lovers meandered back to the nursery, Merk darting around them and fluttering in the air for a few moments at a time, Stell saw a brown-feathered figure dart from the nursery door and jog toward her. As Relwen arrived in front of them, she dipped her head at Lila.

"Good to see you alive, pretty feathers," she said.

"And you, Relwen," Lila replied.

Relwen seemed to notice the way Lila and Stell were leaning into each other, the golden wing resting across Stell's back. A wide smile broke across her face. "Oh, good," Relwen said, relieved. "Thank the spirits I don't have to tiptoe around you two lovebirds anymore."

Stell felt herself blushing under her feathers when a clamor arose from the nursery. She pricked her ears at the noise as Merk squealed and ran into the building to reunite with her friends.

"Yeah, about that," Relwen said guiltily. "The kits heard all the commotion about Lila and Merk coming back. They're wide awake now."

"Great," Stell said, staring at the sky, which was dark enough for Stell to know it was beyond time for the kits to start winding down for the night.

Lila leaned her head down to nudge the top of Stell's head. "Well, come on, Kitcarer," she said. "Sounds like you've got a job to do."

"*I've* got a job to do?" Stell exclaimed. "Last time I checked, you were a kitcarer too."

Lila shook her head, clicking her tongue. "The only thing I've got to do is eat something and go to bed. I'm beat."

"Well," Stell said, watching Relwen pace off to the

nursery—shouting for the kits to *shut up and settle down before the real kitcarers get here*—"My nest is available."

At this, Lila flushed, staring down at the ground as a small smile touched the edges of her beak. "Let's go get those kits settled down so you can make good on that offer," she said.

Stell walked toward the cacophony of the nursery with Lila by her side. And Stell had to wonder why she'd ever thought she was unlucky.

COLDBRIGHT

K. VALE NAGLE

1

SNOW FIELDS
COLDBRIGHT

S now swirled through the misty mountains, coating trees and gryphs alike. Thick flakes clung to feathers and fur, grounding the small expedition.

If the storm hadn't hit, they'd have arrived at the first outpost marks ago. Instead, they were crawling through the rime-coated forest, pushing towards a safety they could no longer see.

"We should turn back," Trisk shouted. The small opinicus's grey plumage was lost to the snow, giving his dark beak and black markings a disembodied look. "I've lost feeling in my paws, and we aren't going to make it by nightfall."

Njorn, their gryphon leader, shot a look of warning in return. Where Trisk was small for a gryph, Njorn was one of Dire Haynil's children, and he stood twice as tall as his escort.

A supply run shouldn't require a dire, and normally it wouldn't—but reserves at the pridelands were danger-ously low, and the Blackwald was one of the few places where game had always been plentiful.

Missing one shipment was normal. The white skies and soaked expedition testified to the temperamental nature of the weather on the foothills approaching the mountains surrounding the wald. Three shipments put the pride in a predicament.

Njorn, with his massive size, golden plumage, and voluminous mane, was here to take control of the local aerie and make sure there were no further delays. He'd been sent instead of his siblings because Dire Haynil needed a charismatic dire to keep the aerie gryphs in line.

Most of the hunting in these fringe aeries was done by opinici, the sort who didn't take kindly to threats, and that's what a dire gryphon was to them: the threat of violence. Njorn had a reputation for being kind to opinici, insomuch as any dire could have that reputation. There were rumors of more than that, of course, but those were mostly just rumors.

Mostly.

Trisk looked at Njorn's warm mane and wished he could curl up and sleep through the storm in it. The dire ran warm and even now showed no signs that the storm was affecting him. Curling up against that mane was like reaching up and grabbing the sun for a quick nap.

Trisk's eyes were on his former lover and not the snow, and he placed his paw into one of the talon-holes left by the dire and fell beak-first into the snowdrift.

He struggled to right himself with a cough, swearing a little louder than was polite in the company of dires.

Our big ears are sensitive! Njorn had once joked when pretending to escort Trisk to pick up rocks as punishment for 'profaning the pridelands with language not fit for civilized creatures.'

Njorn turned to pull Trisk out of the snow with his

massive talons, taking stock of the situation for the first time since they'd landed. To Trisk's relief, the dire's features softened.

Njorn led them to a cluster of evergreens. With a few slashes of his talons, he carved through the branches to create a small hideaway for the eight opinici under his care. Once they were inside, he stood at the entrance and spread his wings, blocking the wind.

"Are we staying the night out here?" Jenell asked. Her soft greys and blues meant if she fell in the storm, they'd never be able to locate her. She didn't have the benefit of Trisk's black markings, though she wore a bright turquoise bracelet she hadn't taken off in days.

"Just long enough to get warm," Njorn replied. "Trisk's right, we can't be out here past nightfall. I have some feather oil in my packs. It's supposed to help against the Blackwald mist. Hopefully, it'll also keep the snow from soaking in."

The dire's packs were strapped to his body. They were only half full as the mission was to bring *back* supplies from the wald, not the other way around.

The other opinici were too frightened to rifle through the packs of a dire, leaving Trisk to the task. He climbed a half-broken branch and stood on his back legs to reach the bag in question, resting one paw on Njorn's hip for balance.

Trisk tensed, realizing his mistake. No opinicus would dare put a paw on a dire in such a familiar way. He only relaxed when he saw that the others were too busy preening themselves to care what he was up to.

Njorn doesn't show it, but he's freezing, too. I can feel him shivering. It's like a small quake.

Except it wasn't a shiver. Trisk could have laughed

when he realized he was feeling a purr. Thankfully, his chattering beak hid the sound.

Good to see you've missed me, too. He beaked through the pack, finding the oil. He gave them to Njorn to open with a whispered thank you, then distributed the open vials to the opinici.

Their break was far too short, but when they stepped back into the storm, it was with renewed vigor.

ACCORDING TO THE MAP HANGING IN DIRE HAYNIL'S GREAT hall, the Blackwald was nestled in the mountains, a frozen lake at its northern tip, an aerie looking down on it from the mountains making up the eastern border, a large lodge in the middle of the valley, and a pawpath in the southeast through the mountains led to a smaller lodge where food was stored before being flown to the pride-lands. Trisk, Njorn, and the others would check the second, smaller lodge first. If nothing else, it would tell them if the supplies were there at all.

The snow near their destination was old, having melted and refrozen several times, and the opinici were light enough to walk on top of it with their soft, wide paws.

The storm here, too, lightened as they moved away from the plains. It was still too windy for Trisk to fly, but if worse came to worst, he thought Njorn could go for help and lead them back to the opinici.

Assuming there's anyone else out here to help us.

The mountain gryphs weren't punctual, but they had always been reliable; a month without messengers was unheard of. That's why Trisk had initially pushed back when he was ordered to come out here. If there was a problem, it was a *big* problem. Wilders gone feral, another dire encroaching on Haynil's lands, maybe some wyverns setting up a new warren. Not something an opinicus could take care of on his own.

Hence Njorn's inclusion.

Poor Njorn. The dire's talons sunk deep into the snow. He wasn't leaving paw prints so much as pushing through the snow as he went, stopping to pant every so often.

Trisk didn't know if Njorn had volunteered or been ordered to come along. The golden dire had a reputation for being able to keep Trisk in line, and Trisk had a reputation for being popular among the opinici, so it was natural to think that was why Trisk was responsible for his old paramour's inclusion.

Then again, judging by the purr, Njorn may have just been worried about Trisk's safety and volunteered.

I flatter myself.

Trisk knew there was little future for the two of them. Direlords, even those as relatively kind as Dire Haynil, managed their children's relationships and partners to try to make sure the offspring ended up dired. A pride with dires was strong. A pride without them was prey.

While the storm had slowed, snow fell in large flakes now. The clouds ahead were darker than those behind. Between the shower of white, Trisk could just make out the start of the mountain pass leading to the Blackwald, and nestled against the mountains, a small outpost.

"Njorn," he called back. "I can see the lodge. Do you want to fly ahead and tell them we're coming?"

The golden dire stopped to catch his breath. "I'm too wet to fly. I must have a lake in my mane. Take everyone else ahead. I'll catch up."

Trisk checked his surroundings. If the storm picked up and visibility disappeared, he wanted to know the general direction Njorn was at.

With a few chirps and an encouraging swat or two, Trisk gathered the opinici around him, and they pushed towards the building, dancing atop the snow.

During such a heavy storm, it would be natural to have a fire going. That was the only reason Trisk could think of that he missed the danger ahead of them.

Jenell stopped to lick one of the snowflakes, then coughed and spit it out. The pack of opinici stopped to console her, and Trisk caught a snowflake between his paw pads.

It smeared from white to black.

Ash?

The dark clouds ahead weren't clouds, they were smoke, and they were coming off of the lodge. He left his companions behind so he could check for threats. Jenell's plumage might keep her hidden in the bad weather, but she wasn't as experienced at sneaking as he was. He'd have to trust his greys and blacks to do the job of reconnaissance.

From the front, the squat building with the triangular roof looked fine. It was only once he went around the side that he discovered the charred remains of the back half. The snow and winds had put out most of the fire, but bedding and nesting material in the basement still burned, sending flames up through the floorboards.

He started to call out for survivors, then caught himself. What if whoever did this were still around, waiting? Surely, the snowstorm would have dissuaded them. Wyverns were cold-blooded, and when their flame ran out, they'd freeze to death. Wilders, though, could be hiding in the mountains—could be hunting down the outpost survivors in the mountains.

Trisk waited for a break in the winds, then tried to flutter back to warn the others. He'd gone twenty feet before a gust caught him, flinging him into the air with a frightening speed.

Jenell shouted in alarm as he flew past. Trisk didn't know what to do. The winds were so violent, they could tear his feathers out if he kept his wings spread. But with his wings folded out of fear, he had no way to slow down.

He kept them closed. A grounded opinicus was like an undired pride: prey. He'd just have to hope for the best.

He tumbled tail-over-beak through the air, trying to take into his surroundings, when he crashed into a giant, golden cloud and clung on for dear life.

With Njorn's wings spread, he was a wall of sunshine in defiance of the gloom. He flapped against the air currents, catching some lift, and flew towards the lodge. Each beat of his wings splashed water in all directions, and he panted with exertion at the effort.

"You're an idiot, you know that?" Njorn scolded Trisk. "What was so important that you thought you could fly in a snowstorm?"

"Just, y'know, wanted a hug." Trisk clung to the dire's mane, a mane so impressive that when Njorn had asserted his gender at a young age, none of the pride had dared challenge him. "I love you, too."

He couldn't see Njorn rolling his eyes, but Trisk could feel it—along with a slight purr that only stopped when they alighted by the lodge and Njorn shook Trisk off.

The opinicus landed on the hard snow with an *oomph* and some bruises, but it was better than if the storm had been allowed to have its way with him.

Jenell and the other opinici came out from their hiding places now that Njorn was here to protect them.

"What did you find that set you off like that?" She was yelling, but with the wind, it came across more like a whisper.

Trisk led everyone around to the back, showing them the burnt-out husk of the rear half of the building. A mottled green opinicus whose name evaded Trisk leapt back when some of the flames in the basement licked up against the exposed floor.

"Well, we can't stay here now." Njorn sniffed the smoke, a plan that caused a coughing fit in the opinici who tried to replicate it. "I smell wild mint, dried mushrooms, and truffles. If they're storing northistle down there, and the fires reach it..."

The dire mimed an explosion, and several of the opinici stepped back from the lodge. It was important to be careful with flames and dried herbs. Most were safe enough, but some were inflammable, and others, like northistle, explosive.

Tasty, but volatile. Just like me.

The wind howled, drawing attention to the mountains separating them from the Blackwald. The small foot path heading into the mountains, more an afterthought for dragging large game since all of the locals could fly, disappeared into a wall of collapsed snow and ice.

Jenell sighed. She was the only one of them who had been to the Blackwald before. "I think we *have* to stay here. We can't reach the mountain aerie tonight, and we'll never get through the pass on foot to find the lodge inside the wald."

Njorn frowned but didn't disagree. "I'll pull up the floorboards, and you all shovel snow down to put out the fire. Once it dies down, we'll find the warmest place in the cabin to shelter the storm."

The dire reached for a plank that had broken off on one side, pausing when a bit of snow tossed down by an over-excited opinicus sizzled against it.

Njorn turned and stuffed his talons deep into the snow, holding them there until he began to shiver, then reached and pulled up the smoldering wood with a yelp.

A cry that was soon joined by several smaller shouts when air rushed in, sending a plume of flame high into the sky and singeing a bit of fur, quickly doused by the snow.

Trisk hopped into the thick snow, balanced on his back paws, and used his forepaws to shove the snow back between his legs and into the lodge like he was digging a hole.

Dignity has never gotten me anything, he thought as Jenell stifled a laugh.

"Well, what're you waiting for?" Njorn shouted. "Get to it!"

She hurriedly joined Trisk, digging as fast as she could. Once two opinici abandoned their self-consciousness, the others joined in. It was obvious they'd never dug a hole in a hurry before, because their aim was terrible. Trisk was the only one regularly getting white stuff down into the fire. But their lack of accuracy ended up helping cool off the surrounding planks, allowing Njorn to pull up several more.

Once there was a sizable hole in the floor, the dire used his bulk to push a small glacier's worth in, killing the last of the flames and bathing them in white, icy darkness.

"Jenell, take four opinici and grab whatever food you can find down there," Njorn ordered. "If you find any northistle—you know what it looks and smells like, yes? —evacuate and bring it out one bushel at a time."

Jenell shivered but bowed her head. She feared fire, of course. All opinici had burned their paws at some point. But Trisk knew she'd also had some nasty run-ins with fresh northistle. It smelled good, it tasted good, but there was no way to get to the tasty bits without talons to pick off the prickles.

Njorn turned his attention to Trisk. "I want *you* to go inside and find the warmest, driest space that will fit everyone. Ideally, I want us all in one room."

"Lord Njorn, you shouldn't be forced to sleep among the opinici," Trisk protested.

There was a spark of amusement in Njorn's eyes. "I will not have you all freeze to death to protect my dignity. This isn't the pridelands. I imagine those who stand on propriety in the Blackwald become victim to its... peculiarities."

2

LODGE
COLDBRIGHT

The interior of the lodge—the half that hadn't burned down, courtesy of a stone center wall that housed the fireplace—was eerily vacant. Trisk hadn't expected to find a living soul there, but if the fire had been an act of arson, he'd have expected to find several dead ones. Instead, it was just... empty.

'Abandoned' might be a better word.

Heavy leather hung as a divider between entryways. He reached up a paw. Elk? Moose? Reindeer? The hide was thick, and he didn't recognize the pattern. He'd hunted bear and white-tailed deer, but this was something different. The antlers had been removed, further foiling identification.

"What's a moose?" Trisk had once asked Njorn, the first time he'd been sent to escort the dire as 'punishment.'

Njorn, always much more candid when they were alone, replied, "It's like a white-tailed deer, but much larger and more foul-tempered."

"So a dire deer." Trisk waited for Njorn's response.

"Right, like a—" Njorn began before his brain remembered the foul-tempered part of the statement. *"Hey!"*

Trisk grinned. *"Come on, you foul-tempered moose, we have work to do!"*

Trisk reached up a paw to the top of one hide. Room had been left above the head, presumably for antlers, but they'd been snapped off and taken.

By wilders? By poachers? What's the point?

He had a few ideas. Some of the mountain aeries had craftsgryphs who specialized in... 'creative leather-working.' They put antlers or wings on rabbits. Those sorts of things. According to the rumors, someone had once sold a particularly magnificent forgery to Dire Rada, one of the less intelligent direlords, claiming it was a kirin hide.

Trisk laughed at the thought, puffs of white vapor leaving his beak. *A kirin hide, perfectly intact, and for sale! And if you believe that, I have a dragon skeleton to sell you. Pristine, except for the front two legs.*

He finished checking the large, main area next to the fireplace and climbed up to the openings to the attic. There were a few ways up, each with a small platform hanging next to it, but he picked the closest to the lodge entrance, poking his head through the open door.

The attic was full of nests. With the heat from the fire rising and so many bodies packed in together, it would get quite warm in here. He tallied the beds. About twenty in total, five of which had been stretched big enough to fit two gryphs.

Thirty missing gryphs. Where did they go?

Njorn wouldn't worry about that until he'd contacted the aerie, but Trisk wanted to make sure they weren't walking into a trap. Nobody who lived out here would abandon safety during a snowstorm, not unless they had no other choice, and this half of the lodge was unscathed.

From down below, he heard Jenell dragging in supplies. The snowstorm screamed outside when she opened the weather barrier.

It's a good thing we didn't try to make for the aerie. That's even worse than what we walked through.

He finished checking the ceiling, but it seemed solid enough. The kind of roof that could keep out a snowstorm would be too strong for Njorn to break through if they all slept up there and someone lit the door on fire.

"Hey Jenell," Trisk called from above. "When you're done, can you help me drag some of these nests down? We're sleeping in the main hall tonight."

She chirped her affirmative reply. While she was the senior opinicus, they had an understanding that when things were going wrong, he was in charge. She was good at keeping things going right, but when all hell broke loose, he was the opinicus who could get things back on track.

AFTER DETERMINING THAT THE FIREPLACE HADN'T STARTED the flames that had burned down the back half of the lodge and charred the basement, Trisk braved the storm one last time to bring up some firewood from storage. If there were a way down to the basement on their half of the lodge, nobody had been able to find it.

It took Njorn a few tries with his large, cold talons, but he managed to get the fire going again. When Trisk had considered what room they'd sleep in, he hadn't taken into account how much space a sleeping dire took up. In the end, with the fire going, Njorn slept in the main room and the opinici slept up in the attic.

Once they were settled, Trisk announced very loudly that he was tired, so Jenell would take first watch at the weather barrier while he slept.

"Can't Njorn do that?" Jenell asked.

Trisk made a *tsk* sound. "If some wilders or a baby wyvern comes crashing through the front door, do you want Njorn to be exhausted or well-rested? Because I'll tell you which I want."

With that matter settled, Trisk pulled himself through the opening to the attic and curled up in one of the nests, drifting off to sleep. The other opinici were happy to sleep in warm nests. The bedding material held a pine scent that was pleasant but which Trisk suspected they'd all be sick of before they returned home.

He was in the middle of his own nightmare about a patch of conflagrated-yet-tasty northistles when Jenell woke him.

"I'm sorry, I can't stay awake any longer." She collapsed into the bed next to his, not waiting to see if he'd get out to take over.

Trisk groaned. If Njorn weren't waiting for him downstairs, he'd have gone back to sleep. Instead, he carefully checked on each opinicus. They slept like the dead, even the mottled green opinicus who was using the now-drool-drenched haunch of the orange opinicus next to her as a pillow.

With everything in order, Trisk made his way downstairs, curling up by his dire friend's beak, which was pointed at the door. It didn't take long before Njorn's snoring turned into sniffing.

"I wondered how long it'd be before you came down."

Njorn's eyes may be closed, but the glint of the firelight showed that he was peering through his lashes at the newcomer.

"Quiet, you dire moose," Trisk said as he nudged the gryphon's shoulder with his hip. "I'm here to protect you while you sleep."

Njorn snorted. "Just don't get too cozy."

"Oh? Like don't knead your wing joints?" Trisk hopped up and began working on the sore spot where the wing met the shoulder blade.

The dire purred, nearly dislodging his opinicus masseuse. "No, no. That's fine. A little lower."

"My sacred charge is to protect you while you sleep," Trisk explained. "I can't do that if you keep harrumphing and shrugging your sore shoulders instead of actually sleeping."

It was hard to tell time in the cabin, but it felt like it took Trisk the better part of a mark to get Njorn back to sleep. Once his dire friend was snoring soundly—a sound that shook Trisk's poor contour feathers—he curled up in front of the door to keep watch.

If some wilders tried to break in, his job was to scream his head off, startling the offending hippogryphs and alerting Njorn. Wilders could include gryphons, opinici, and hippogryphs, but they never had dires with them. One look at the gold mane filling the common room and they'd flee for their lives.

Trisk shivered, and this time it wasn't from the cold seeping through the door. The last time he and Njorn had been together—like *together* together—he'd been escorting the dire to an outpost not too dissimilar from the one they were visiting today.

It was routine; the local aerie just wanted Njorn's help

moving an exceptional amount of food to the pridelands. When the couple arrived, however, they found the outpost razed and wilders scavenging the food in small groups of twos and threes, retreating into the woods with it.

The gryphons at that aerie had been armored, trained, and prepared for anything. The wilders—all hippogryphs, one of the few species that never produced dires of their own—could not have taken the aerie. It was impossible, unthinkable.

What wasn't unthinkable was that they were starving and all that stood between them dying or living another fortnight were a couple of already-dead bodies. When Njorn and Trisk—Njorn had insisted he was fine alone, but pretended to bring Trisk along as punishment so they could spend the time flying together—found the wilder camp, there wasn't much food stashed away. It was more likely another direlord, Caslir or Caranel, had seen the remote aerie as an opportunity and these hippogryphs were just cleaning up the scraps left behind.

But Njorn had lost it. His fiery orange eyes, reminiscent of his father's, had lost all sense of proportion. He landed upon the hippogryphs like a tornado, cutting through them even as they screamed.

Trisk considered himself fortunate to be friends with a dire—and a gryphon, at that. But somewhere in the flirting and long flights together, waking up enveloped in that soft, flowing mane, he'd forgotten that when a dire looked at the undired, they didn't see equals. They didn't even see a gryph, really. They saw... something disposable.

There were places in the world where an opinicus wasn't thought of as much better than a hippogryph. Since visiting those places, Trisk had judged every gryphon, every dire he met based on how they treated hippogryphs. In his eyes, they all came up wanting.

So he resisted the urge to reach back and stroke Njorn's mane. To curl up against his paws, to touch their beaks together, to pet the dire's head as he had a nightmare.

If the day came when Trisk was cast out of the pride, only the hippogryphs would take him in. Njorn would not stand up to his father, would be struck down if he tried. Not killed—oh no, dires were too important for that. Trisk had long suspected that if hippogryphs were capable of producing dires, they'd be allowed in the prides. But Njorn would regret the day.

Trisk sighed. Why couldn't Njorn have been born an undired opinicus? Life would be so much simpler.

Njorn probably wishes I had been born a dire gryphon. But if wishes were kits, the mewing would never cease.

Having used up his physical strength on the trip here, having bankrupted his emotional strength with thoughts of what could have been, the only guard watching the door closed his eyes and dozed off.

THE WIND SCREAMED OUTSIDE, SCRAPING LONG BRANCHES like claws across the wall of the lodge, and Trisk flung himself out of a dream of burning northistle, hackle feathers raised, to protect Njorn with a loud hiss.

The dire very carefully put his talons over Trisk's beak. "Enough of that. You're like an offended hedgehog when you get angry, little deer."

The howl and clawing picked up again, and Trisk pushed himself closer to Njorn. "That can't be the storm can it? It sounds like the screams of the souls escaping from a Fracture."

Blackwald: a place so dark, none within it can see the light of a Fracture. The souls who die there never see release, being pulled deep within the earth. I should never have listened to Jenell tell her stories with her spooky voice.

Trisk wasn't superstitious, but there was a reason no sane gryph wanted to be assigned out here. The food was plentiful, but it took a mental toll. Dire Haynil had been forced to rotate out his gryphs here every few fractures. And he'd had to move the aerie up into the mountains above the Blackwald. Only the bravest were willing to stay here all year long, and they had a reputation for being... eccentric.

"What else could it be except the wind?" Njorn's tone was casual, but he shifted to tend to the fire, playfully knocking Trisk against some of the horn-stripped moose and deer hides with his tail.

Above the fireplace, there were several spots for more antlers, all removed. The chimney was thick, sturdy. When the wind pushed some loose branches against the side of the lodge, Trisk weighed the odds that he could hide in there safely.

The smoke would kill me. Besides, there's no way to know if there's a grate at the top of it or not.

"Shouldn't it be daylight?" he wondered. None of the other opinici were awake, but he was careful to keep distance between himself and Njorn in case any looked down.

Not an easy task, considering how large the dire was. Even in the spaces where Njorn wasn't physically present, his pleasant, spicy scent and heat filled the room.

"Go and check. If it is daylight, we should head for the

aerie." Njorn didn't say why it was important—if the aerie had fallen, they'd need to check the camp inside the Blackwald itself, and they wouldn't want to stay overnight there.

Trisk pushed the door, but it didn't budge. "Could I get a little help here? Maybe your moose hips can get it open."

Njorn idly pushed the door with his back, leonine paws while tending to the fire with his talons, but he didn't have any better luck than Trisk did.

The dire adjusted himself, facing the door. He braced his back legs against two of the side walls, digging his claws in, and pushed until the snow sealing the door shut finally gave way the smallest amount.

"See?" he panted. "Nothing to it. Just takes some paw grease."

The door had opened just enough to let Trisk squeeze through, revealing a wall of snow piled above its top. He'd need to bring some opinici out here to dig it out if they didn't want Njorn trapped inside.

It was a silly, idle thought, but it turned into something more when he burrowed up through the snow to the surface and climbed high enough to see the lodge. Whatever the screams and scratching had been, the storm was no longer raging. But the lodge had been buried with snow.

It was set far enough from the pass that it stood out in the open—probably to avoid the avalanche that blocked the path. But something was wrong. There was a lot of snow around, sure, maybe four feet on the ground. The lodge, however, was entombed in snow and ice. There was no sign of the wood that made up its walls from the outside.

If someone from the pridelands or aerie had come looking for them, they'd have been invisible from the sky. The building must be twenty feet high, but it looked like a mound of snow from the outside.

Trisk licked a paw and held it up. No wind tickled his fur. Behind a film of white, the sun shone, unseen and forgotten. Flakes of crystallized water hung in stasis in the air, dislodging as he walked through them.

Cautious of what had happened yesterday, he opened his aching wings and beat them a few times, tempting the predatory storm to come out of hiding and pounce.

The weather didn't take the bait.

He landed on the roof first, digging with his paws. He dug a hole as tall as he was, but he didn't hit the roof, so he gave up and flew to the burned down section of the lodge and found another wall of snow.

How is that possible? We tore up the floorboards here to get to the spices. The snow would have had to fill the basement and then pile up this high.

Round holes surrounded the building. Hopping mice, some quirk of the weather—Trisk had no idea what had caused them. Had they made the sounds he'd assumed were branches thrown by the storm against the side of the cabin? For anything to touch the cabin walls, it must not have been entombed yet. Surely the snow against the unburned lodge walls couldn't be as thick as it was here.

He burrowed against the closest wall where he was certain he'd heard the scratching come from. The wall of snow was longer than he was, and he had visions of it all collapsing down around him, but he finally prevailed and felt his paw hit the wood of the cabin.

To his reassurance, there were long scratches against it. But they didn't feel like they'd been caused by branches. Instead, they were three long gashes, as though a massive gryphon had clawed against the wall to try to break in.

He slowly backed out of his snow burrow. He'd been the first gryph at the cabin last night, and there hadn't been any talon marks... right?

I'm certain there weren't, but I was so tired. Perhaps it was just branches from the storm. Or perhaps Njorn scratched the wall in frustration while I was exploring the inside.

From the direction of the evergreens marking the entrance to the Blackwald, a branch snapped and a pile of snow collapsed down the tree to the ground.

Trisk watched the trees. The weight of snow broke tree branches all the time. But he couldn't shake the feeling that within the dark pine needles, something was staring out at him. Some of the shadows between the branches looked almost purple in the light.

"Trisk?" Njorn's voice came from the direction of the door. His large beak poked out of it. "Trisk, get the other opinici and get this door all the way open. I have to pee."

Trisk laughed. He laughed so loud, it shook the branches, and more snow collapsed off the evergreens. The shadows no longer looked purple.

"I'm coming, I'm coming," he shouted back. "You'd better cross your legs, though. It's going to take some time to dig this out."

WITH ALL OF THE OPINICI DIGGING, THEY GOT THE DOOR open just in time. Trisk had never heard a dire whimper like a kit who'd had too much to drink and was being rushed outside by its kitcarer before now, but he'd had to bury his head in the snow to stop from laughing.

"Are you okay?" Jenell asked him.

Trisk just laughed more and waved her away.

"He's a *dire*," she scolded. "He's the son of Direlord Haynil, and we should respect his dignity!"

Trisk caught his breath. "Nell, he got trapped inside by snow and needed the help of eight opinici to pee. Of *course* we won't mention this to anyone at the pridelands. Haynil would make wilders of us all. But right here, right now? With just us here where he can't hear us? It is *hilarious*."

She started to protest, but one of the opinici behind her with mottled green plumage had just lost her own battle against mirth, and once she started, the others began to giggle.

Trisk hopped on top of the overhang above the door, careful not to sink into the snow. "I may not be a dire. I may not even be a gryphon. But I can pee where I want to."

By that point, the last of the opinici gave in and there was no hope of stopping the laughter. Thankfully, Jenell caught sight of gold in the sky and let out a warning chirp so they could compose themselves before Njorn landed.

"You said there was something you wanted to show me?" the dire asked.

Trisk brought everyone around to the side of the cabin, then led them to where he'd excavated more of the wall and claw marks. "I don't think we were hearing branches last night. I think something was trying to get inside."

Jenell pushed past Trisk and Njorn and ran her paw along the gash. When she wasn't cold and wet, she was surprisingly good at taking charge. "This is too big to be wilders. Do you think it was Caslir?"

"*Dire* Caslir," Njorn automatically corrected. There were only so many direlords out there, and the ones with many dire gryphons under them like Naralin and Kristel didn't need to stoop to tactics like this. Caranel, as one of the only dire opinici, would have left paw marks and not talon marks. And then there was Rada, leader of the lone small pride, sometimes called a clan. Rada wouldn't have traveled this far from the safety of his clangrounds.

Trisk's tail twitched back and forth. It wasn't that he didn't trust Njorn in a fight. No undired had killed a dire since the days of the Blackbeak Rebellion. But if there were a dire out there, that didn't bode well for the opinici.

"A dire could have covered us in snow, knowing it'd seal shut in the sun, leaving us frozen inside," Trisk added. "I couldn't have opened that door without your help. We'd have starved."

Njorn's mind had gone elsewhere, however. "Nothing we've seen here *had* to have been caused by a dire. It could easily be tricks to scare us away. Enough hippogryphs could have carried the snow here. And it really did sound like branches scratching against the sides of the walls. This is just some wilders trying to scare us away. Once they see I'm here, they'll relocate."

"Did the wilders kill the previous occupants?" Jenell inspected the strange holes around the outside of the cabin. "Did wilders stop shipments for weeks?"

Trisk stepped in before Njorn corrected Jenell. "We don't actually know that anyone is dead. The fire was recent, and there's no blood inside. *If* the occupants were killed, they weren't killed here."

Njorn stalked around the lodge. "We don't actually

know that it was our pride staying here. It could have been squatters, and they caught sight of us before the snowstorm grounded us and tried to burn down the cabin."

He didn't say if the squatters—really, wilders—had killed the original occupants, but just the suggestion that they came in later was an improvement. Trisk's heart softened a little, but as much as he didn't want to see Njorn scourge every wilder from this section of Dire Haynil's lands, he also didn't know what had happened to the lodge.

The wall had been clear when they heard the scratches. It had been buried two opinicus-lengths thick by the time morning came. How many hippogryphs packing snow against the cabin would it take to pull that off? At night? In the cold?

"Lord Njorn, you said you wanted to reach the aerie before midday?" Trisk asked. Overhead, the chimney let clouds of dark smoke into the skies.

The dire nodded. "Jenell, put out the fireplace. Then we'll close the door in case we need to use the lodge as shelter on our way home. Toss the snow back down against it, maybe that'll keep bandits from stealing the few spices we managed to scavenge."

Trisk did *not* want to spend another night inside the ice tomb.

"Um, dire?" Jenell squeaked. "I covered myself in the waterproof oil in case it was storming at the peak. I'm rather... flammable, as it were, right now."

Trisk sniffed her. The cold dulled his sense of smell, but now that he knew what he was smelling, he realized she was marinated in the oil. "You must really hate the snow. Are you going to be able to fly?"

"I had a little trouble getting the bottle open and didn't want what spilled to go to waste," she admitted. "And I've been to the Blackwald once before. Once you get down from the aerie, there's a mist that covers the forest. Tell me if you think I used too much once you're soaking in *that*."

Njorn shook his head. "It's not cooking oil, Jenell. It doesn't repel fire quite as well as it does water, but you're now the least likely of any of us to combust."

Trisk and Njorn moved away from the group, staring at the mountains dividing them from the Blackwald. The sky was still white, a bright spot marking the sun directly overhead, as the weather decided if more snow was coming.

"We should send someone back," Trisk whispered. "I have a bad feeling about this."

Njorn pretended to stretch his wings and spine, bringing his beak down close enough to whisper back to Trisk. "Let's see what the aerie holds for us first. If there is a problem, that's where gryphs would gather to wait for help. If no one's there, we'll send the rest home while you and I check the Blackwald."

There definitely is *a problem*, Trisk thought, but he left it. He couldn't force Njorn to do anything the dire didn't want to, and Trisk felt pretty certain the aerie would be abandoned, making it a moot point.

Jenell shouted from the cabin. The fire was out. Njorn helped wedge the door closed and seal it with snow, then they took off into the mountains to find the aerie, a thick mist spilling out of the forest to their right.

3

AERIE
COLDBRIGHT

The aerie was a system of caves nestled in the side of the mountain, well above the Blackwald mists. Trisk had visited many aeries in his days, both Dire Haynil's and several along their border with Naralin. Never before now had he been so surprised to find an aerie *not* on fire.

It wasn't even abandoned. To Trisk's annoyance, a red gryphon and a blue gryphon flew through the skies together, laughing and chatting. Then *they* had the audacity to seem surprised to see *Trisk*.

"Mind your manners," Njorn said to his entire opinicus retinue, but his eyes were on Trisk.

The patrols chirped a greeting to the dire, ignoring Trisk, Jenell, and the rest, and guided them towards the aerie.

A gust of wind shifted the mist, revealing a stretch of black rocks along the mountains' lower levels.

"What's that?" Trisk asked Jenell.

"You didn't think they called it the Blackwald because of the white mist or dark green trees, did you?" Jenell laughed. Her mood had brightened with the arrival of the gryphons. "Below the mist, there's a lot of dark stone. It certainly adds to the atmosphere when you're down there hunting. I'm sure you'll see tomorrow."

There must have been some trepidation on Trisk's face, because Jenell continued on. "It's just stories, Trisk. The Blackwald is all scary stories told over a fire. When you're in the mist, the rest of the world seems to disappear, but when you fly back up before sundown, the aerie is still here."

"The burnt lodge wasn't a story. The fact they're four shipments late isn't an amusing fable," he said, but Jenell had already begun her descent. The other opinici followed her lead, likely eager to sleep somewhere safe and warm tonight.

Trisk looked up at Njorn. The aerie's patrol was leading him to a higher cave. Despite the protests of his wings and stomach, Trisk changed course and flapped his wings harder to follow the gryphons.

Something is going on here, and I'm going to figure out what it is.

The aerie had been built in three levels. Tanned hides and treated wood filled the bottom terrace, leaving him to wonder if the snowstorm hadn't made it over the mountains. The next level up had a fire pit with food roasting over top, and Trisk's friends headed straight for it. The charms and bangles hanging from the different caves suggested this was also where the majority of gryphs slept, too. There were grooves in the rocks to keep moisture out of the nests and hides covering the entrances instead of doors.

Like the hides at the lodge from the previous night, these were missing their horns or antlers.

Maybe that's just a thing they do here. Maybe a kit lost an eye or something after flying into them, so they took them all down.

Stranger things had happened, but when he looked to see if there were any kitcarers, he didn't see any signs of children at all. It wasn't unusual for the more dangerous aeries to send their young back to the pridelands, but something else was bothering Trisk, he just couldn't quite put a paw on it.

Njorn was headed towards the top level, a single open cavern large enough to house a dire. The entrance was surrounded by wooden branches twisted around each other. They'd been stained a red so dark it appeared black except where it faced the direct sunlight—the sun having finally decided to make an appearance now that they were at their destination. At least, Trisk assumed the wood was stained that color. The mist still covered the Blackwald below them, and he could only see the dark green leaves of the canopy poking through, not the trunks to confirm his theory.

He alighted on the ledge behind Njorn, earning him a look of disapproval from the gryphons.

Perhaps they're unaware that no gryphons were dispatched to help them. Or perhaps they just don't like opinici.

Njorn set them straight, using the rumbling voice he saved for impressing aerie folk. "The opinicus is with me. Once we ascertain what went wrong here, he'll lead the other opinici in hunting to get the food stores where they need to be, then we'll escort the next shipment home."

'The opinicus' didn't appreciate being called that, but it was enough that the undired gryphons switched from treating him like a hostile invader to treating him as invisible, which was how he liked it, just as long as no one stepped on him. Again.

Other than disliking him, the aerie gryphons were quiet. The large chamber, meant to house dires or whoever ran the aerie, was empty. 'Empty' was underselling it: the place was decrepit, abandoned. Spiderwebs large enough to capture birds spanned the upper reaches. Trisk hoped his brain was being hyperbolic, but the arrival of the aerie's leader removed that hope.

"Ah, Dire Haynil has sent one of his children to check in on us!" The gryphon was dull brown, a color usually more characteristic of opinici than gryphons, with spots and splotches of a yellow-green so vibrant it looked unnatural. "My name is Cerris. I apologize for the cobwebs. The spiders come with the black heartwood. Almost seem to hatch with it. They keep bats from taking roost here. Temperance, would you see to clearing out the dire's quarters? I assume you're staying here tonight, Lord...?"

"Njorn," the golden dire responded. "Yes, we'll be here several nights. I'll also need quarters cleared out for my escort. There are eight of them. Trisk here has been charged with hunting. They'll be moving down into the Blackwald tomorrow. Unless that lodge has also been abandoned?"

"Abandoned?" Cerris looked, or at least feigned, surprised. "Why would the lodges be abandoned?"

While Njorn filled the aerie leader in on what they'd found in the cabin, Trisk inspected the cavern. He'd hoped the nests were the work of many smaller spiders working together, especially once he noticed bat- and even bird-sized cocoons wrapped up in them. His eyes were having a hard time finding the spiders. Instead, he saw small, flickering lights around the webs, like a tiny swarm of green, red, or blue fireflies that stayed in formation.

While Cerris ignored Trisk, Temperance took an interest in him. She used a talon to hold him back.

"Not too close." She pulled out a piece of glass, perhaps a mirror, and used it to reflect some of the high mountain sunlight next to the web Trisk had been looking at. When light shone on the small sparkling lights, they revealed the shape of a very large spider—the tiny, bright design painted on its massive abdomen.

Trisk's hackles raised out of instinct. "Are they... poisonous?"

Temperance smirked. "Only if you try to eat them."

He adjusted his language. Gryphons were always pedantic when they spoke to opinici. "Are they *venomous*."

"Only if they're trying to eat you." She put away her light, and the large spider vanished into the darkness, bringing back the sparkles. "You can see them sunning themselves sometimes atop the trees when it's warm out, soaking up the light and heat like mountain cats. It seems to make their pattern glow better in the darkness of the Blackwald, where they lure moths to their nests. You have to be careful with any kind of light down there."

Trisk's beak was open in disgust. The disturbed spider had retreated, but now that he knew what to look for, there were moving constellations of arachnids on the roof. He would *definitely* advise Njorn to find some pretense, *any* pretense, to sleep outside tonight.

Temperance laughed. "They're not so bad; they're just spiders. Each has its own unique pattern. See up there, the one with the four dots and the angular crescent? I call that one Cuddles."

Trisk shivered. Aerie gryphs were unusual, there was no doubt, but this was a new level of weird. It was made worse by the fact that 'Cuddles' had stopped moving when Temperance called its name. Up among the stars —*spider* stars—there was a slight mist that shifted when they moved, as though by taking the black heartwood from the Blackwald's trees, the gryphs here had brought up a piece of the Blackwald itself.

He was so busy keeping his eyes on the ceiling, he'd forgotten to listen in on Njorn's conversation. He was caught off guard when the dire said, "Trisk will help you make up the deficit. If you would?"

Trisk shook his head free of the metaphorical cobwebs. "Yes, of course. If you could show me to your opinici?"

Cerris waved a talon at Temperance, who led Trisk out of the cavern. He watched the way she moved, and she was very careful not to brush against the black heartwood decorations. Maybe it was superstition, but he followed her example. If the spiders liked the wood for some reason, he didn't want any of its scent on him.

He took one look back at Njorn, but his friend was busy talking. Behind them, Trisk noticed that the spiders on the rear wall hadn't moved at all during the conversation. Something about that bothered him, but he put it to the back of his mind to consider later.

"THERE ARE NO OPINICI," TEMPERANCE EXPLAINED. "I'VE hunted in the Blackwald before, so I can answer your questions. You know about the spiders. If you light a fire outside the lodge, it'll attract moths, which brings in the screechers, so don't do that. You may not like Cuddles, but the spiders won't bother you unless you climb trees or try to fly."

No opinici here at the aerie, or no opinici at all?

Trisk had gone over the lists of supplies and logistics for each aerie ever since food started going missing. He may not know the name of every gryph in Dire Haynil's pride, but none of the aeries were made up of only opinici or only gryphons. Opinici were usually obligated to do the jobs gryphons hated, like hunting. And most menders were gryphons thanks to their talons. Opinici benefited from having at least one gryphon surgeon at each aerie.

"Oh!" Temperance acted like she'd just remembered a small trivia. "The lodge in the Blackwald was built to rise above the mists. That way, if you get lost, you can fly up and spot your way home."

"Won't that put you at odds with the spiders?" he asked.

She shrugged. "You just need to be very, very sure you're lost first. But the lodge's tower has an entrance up top, so you can land there, then climb down. That way you don't have to deal with the spiders, just the occasional screecher nest."

Trisk still had no idea what a screecher was. He was sure he'd find out tomorrow. Hopefully, if they were so numerous, they'd be more edible than the spiders. Her comments on the tower entrance into the Blackwald and not flying brought up two more questions.

"How will Lord Njorn reach us? Is the tower large enough to fit a dire?" Trisk asked.

"Dires don't go into the Blackwald. There's no need," she explained. "Just bring your game and wounded up the tower each day, and some gryphons will pick them up."

Trisk ran over the geography from the maps in his mind. The pass blocked by snow was along the eastern ridge, south of the aerie they were in now. The Blackwald stretched west into another direlord's territory, then more mountains. But to the north, there should be a lake.

"What about the frozen lake? Couldn't Lord Njorn come down there and walk in? Or could we fly out?" he asked.

Temperance feigned nonchalance, but there was a warning in her words. "You're welcome to try. The mists are strongest by the lake. I'd recommend you avoid hunting there."

"Fish fill a belly just as fast as deer." He'd never met a gryph who claimed they didn't like fish, and he'd met a lot of liars.

She stared at him. "The lake is frozen."

"We can break the ice, use bait to bring fish to the surface," he pushed.

"You really don't want to disturb what's under the ice." Her ominous words came with the tone of boredom.

He frowned. These topics of conversation were getting him nowhere, so he switched to asking about what types of game he should expect. The answers were fairly straightforward: deer, moose, elk, caribou, northistle hogs. No edible birds were mentioned, presumably due to the spiders, but there were bugs called dragonflies that were large enough to eat.

Temperance stressed that dragonflies were how the opinici should feed themselves. Gryphons required 'real meat.' "Don't you leave dead bugs on the platform."

"One last thing," he said when she turned to leave. "What happened to your opinici? Are they dead?"

"How should I know?" she asked, her shoulders apparently out of shrugs. "They all left to chase a grey hippogryph with pretty red tailfeathers. You know how your kind get when they're in heat."

Trisk kept his anger in check, but he was beginning to understand why an entire aerie's worth of opinici might decide life was better as wilders. He hissed something obscene once Temperance was out of hearing, then he went to check on his opinici to see if they had decent lodgings.

Decent, in this case, meant free of star spiders, evil heartwood, and whatever a *screecher* was supposed to be.

4

STAR CAVE
COLDBRIGHT

"What are you *looking* for?" Jenell scolded Trisk as he searched every nook and cranny of their quarters for colorful constellations or webbing.

He didn't find any. "You're better off not knowing. Don't go into the dire's quarters."

"What did Njorn discover?" she asked. "What happened to the lodge we stayed in last night? And why were all of the opinicus quarters cleared out? They had to fetch new nesting materials for all of us."

Trisk opened his beak, then shut it, realizing he didn't know what Njorn had found out. So he decided to lie. "We're going into the Blackwald tomorrow to hunt, but Njorn said he'd meet us in the morning and explain everything."

"I guess if our dire isn't worried, we shouldn't be, either," the mottled opinicus whose name escaped Trisk said.

Trisk disagreed. He'd seen dires talk of their conquests against wilders, small wyvern warrens, and each other.

What they described as a *bloodless victory* had often been paid for in the lives of the undired, especially opinici.

"With our luck, Njorn will sleep in and forget to tell us. I guess the best we can do is trust." Jenell shoved some soft hides and pine needles at Trisk. "Here, let's get you a nest going. We should all have been asleep two marks ago if we're waking up at dawn."

He built his bed next to hers and waited until the other opinici were asleep before poking her braceleted ankle with a paw. The nice thing about Jenell was that she was a light sleeper when she wasn't around her mate.

"I'm awake, Trisk," she grumbled. "I figured you'd have questions."

He stopped poking. "Is all of this normal? Giant dragonflies, bat-eating star spiders, *shriekers?* Just what is a shrieker, anyways?"

"Screecher, not shrieker. An ugly, leathery bird that's exceptionally loud." She shifted in her nest so her beak faced his, putting a wing over them to muffle the sound. "It's been fractures since I did a stint out here, but the Blackwald has always been a strange place. The lake stays frozen even in summer. The spiders are striking, sure, but they stay out of the sunlight. It's creepy when the mists roll in, but the sun burns them away quickly."

He thought of Temperance's comment about spiders having to crawl above the mist and wondered if they still 'burned off' when it became light out. Certainly, they'd arrived here in the afternoon and the Blackwald was still smothered with mist, but that could have been a side effect of the snowstorm raging out on the plains.

"There's something beautiful about it, though," Jenell continued. "Some days, it's quiet, and the mist hangs in the area, and nothing moves, and it feels like the forest is in a kind of stasis. Other times, the birdsong is deafening, and the deer walk up to gryphs without fear.

"It's an easy place to tell stories about because it feels like it's out of one of those old tales—before Blackbeak, before the God's Tear, back when dragons and kirin roamed the land.

"And it's an easy place to fall in love. My mate's brown feathers glistened in the mist like they were made of bronze starfire. Her eyes were the green of forest ponds."

"You've only been away from her for a couple of days. 'Great place to fall in love,' pshaw." Trisk rolled his eyes. He couldn't imagine anything like romance from the gloomy, misty forest they'd flown over.

Jenell turned away from him to sleep, whispering one last parting retort under her wing as she covered her bracelet with her other paw. "Or a great place to fall *back* in love."

I guess Njorn and I haven't been as careful as we should have. Not that Jenell would tell anyone, but if she picked it up on it, others might, too.

Trisk did his best fake snore, the sort of embarrassing, slightly-too-loud snore anyone who cared about their own dignity would never fake. Only once Jenell was asleep did he crawl out of his nest and into the open.

He found a good spot by some cured moose blankets and hid, scanning the higher levels of the aerie for signs of activity.

Nothing.

He didn't want to risk someone looking out of their cave and seeing him, so he crawled along the northern edge of the aerie, climbing instead of flying towards the dire chambers.

A couple times, his paws dislodged some scree, but no

movement came, and he resumed his climbing until he reached Njorn, who was sleeping outside the chamber.

That reduces the chance he'll end up as spider bait.

A little of the dire's golden mane was caught in his beak from grooming, and it took all of Trisk's self-control to keep from sneaking over to pull it out. The stakes were too high, however, so he kept his distance while he searched for a mirror like he'd seen Temperance use.

He finally located one just inside the cave. While the moon was full outside, the cave's interior was as dark as the inside of a dire's soul. He was careful to avoid the twisted heartwood, running in, grabbing the mirror, and dashing back out. He opened it with his paw and reflected the light inside at each arachnoid constellation.

Most crawled away, but the ones at the very back of the cave didn't. He returned to annoying the spiders on the ceiling, and only when the cave's night sky turned black did he grab a rock in his mouth and dash straight for the far side.

Staying back a ways, he faced one of the static constellations and tossed the rock at it. The stone made a dull thud, but the starry pattern didn't move.

Trisk gathered all of his courage and put his paw against the bright green constellation. There was no fuzz, no spider fangs, just wood. He scraped at the paint and it came off easily.

He waited a few moments for his eyes to adjust. Tucked away at the back of the cave, there were stacks and stacks of crates hidden just out of view. He sniffed at the one nearest him, and the smell was salt and meat, like some sort of jerky.

He could make out enough food to feed the aerie and send two full shipments back to the pridelands. He wanted to get an accurate count, but his eyes were having trouble adjusting, and when he looked back, he saw blue, red, and green constellations crawling out of their hiding spaces now that he'd stopped annoying them with moonlight.

His courage finally gave way, and he fled the cave.

TRISK DREAMT THE SKY WAS FULL OF SPIDERS AND THE MIST was a fine, wet web they wove above him. Wherever he ran, he could not find a way out from under the mist.

When Jenell tickled his paw to wake him and he accidentally kicked her in the face with a scream, however, he claimed that he'd been having flashbacks to clearing out a wyvern warren.

She rubbed her beak. "You kick like a mule deer. Scream like one, too. Remind me not to sneak up behind you again."

"Sorry about that." His nares were red with a hot blush. He liked Jenell and was grateful she didn't seem hurt or upset, just embarrassed.

She shook her head. "It's fine. Sun's up, time for us to go. The gryphons didn't leave out food, but a few of our own squirreled some away, so there'll be enough to eat."

"Any sign of Njorn?" Trisk stretched his paws and preened a few feathers back in place. There were gryphs who needed every strand of hair, every microfeather groomed within an inch of its life before they'd get out of the nest. He took a different approach. They were only gliding down to a tower, so nothing had to be perfect.

"Nothing yet," Jenell said. "Like you said, he's a deep

sleeper. Normally, both of you are, though not this morning."

The thought of Njorn covered in spiders sent a shiver down Trisk's spine. He came outside and picked over the cold meat the other opinici had hid. It was typical of the fare aerie gryphons offered opinici—it was the worst they had, which was much better than they'd normally have given opinici.

I guess the spiders ate all the dragonflies hiding in their larder.

He wiped the sleep out of his eyes. The sun was bright, giving him hope that Jenell could be right about the mist burning away. He looked west and caught sight of another sun, the golden feathers of Njorn gliding down to greet them.

"Good morning, hunters," the dire trilled. "Did everyone get enough to eat? Ready to head off and show these aerie dust-tails how real hunters handle things?"

Trisk shook his paw a few times like it was asleep, then pretended to trot around to get feeling back in it so he could check Njorn's flank and tail for spiders.

"Morning's greetings, Lord Njorn," Jenell said with a chirp. "Trisk said you'd be here to send us off. Tell the gryphons we hope to return a similar level of hospitality."

Njorn looked pleased, but considering the opinici hadn't been provided with breakfast, Trisk suspected there was an insult hiding in Jenell's words.

"Trisk, what are you doing?" Njorn asked the opinicus running circles around him.

Trisk marched in place. "I like to get out of bed extra early so I can get a little exercise and stretching done before the other gryphs get up."

The long pause before Njorn opened his beak spoke to

his knowledge that Trisk was exceptionally hard to wake up in the morning, let alone get upright, let alone get both upright *and* out of the nest.

Instead, all he said was, "I see."

Once Njorn had finished calming the opinici and encouraging them with promises they'd meet their quota in under a week, he came over to where Trisk was grilling Jenell about the things they'd be hunting.

Neither male gryph could find a way to get Jenell to go away, so finally Trisk just said what he was going to say in private in front of her.

"Lord Njorn, something's very wrong here," he began. "Every single opinicus in an aerie doesn't defect to become a wilder. Not unless they were severely mistreated, and even then, they'd have filed a complaint with your father first. What did they say happened to the burned-out lodge we found by the pass?"

"You forget yourself, Striker Trisk. I'll handle questions, and I don't owe you any information." The dire's tone was more for Jenell's sake than Trisk's. "Besides, the answer was simple. Aerie Leader Cerris assumed the food made it to the lodge just fine. They always sent it with gryphs who were done with their rotation out here. When they didn't return, he just assumed since the aerie was doing so well, Dire Haynil hadn't sent anyone to replace them. Cerris had no idea there was a problem."

Trisk picked his words carefully to avoid indicating his nocturnal adventures. "When we first showed up at the dire cave, there were a lot of boxes of supplies..."

"Being prepared isn't a vice," Njorn interrupted. "If their shipments had arrived at the pridelands just fine, no one would care how much they had stored up here. It's like Jenell said on the flight over, the Blackwald is full of things to eat. The most likely explanation is bandits were hitting the convoy on the plains. There's nothing to worry about."

Jenell nodded her head, though she seemed like she would have said more were she not in the presence of a dire. Trisk could guess what was on her mind: without any opinici hunting, just how were the gryphons staying stocked? They certainly seemed disinclined to enter the wald itself.

He hoped he wouldn't regret his decision later, but Trisk decided not to press the issue, not in front of Jenell. An angry dire was more dangerous to him than a clueless dire. The aerie wouldn't try to hurt Njorn. Even if their plan was to defect to another pride, they'd wait until he left.

"We'll send someone to report to the aerie after a week," Trisk said. "Temperance wants us to leave the cleaned kills atop the tower for the gryphons to pick up, along with any wounded, so we can send messages back that we if we need to."

Njorn's eyes showed a hint of concern. "There's no mender going with you?"

Jenell nuzzled the pack around her neck with her beak. "I've assisted gryphon menders in the past, and half of being a kitcarer is fixing small cuts, tangled fur, and bruised beaks."

That last bit included a glance at Trisk's back foot. He bowed his head in apology for earlier.

"A kitcarer?" Njorn looked surprised, and for the first time, Trisk realized that their leader had no idea the jobs of the opinici here with him. "That seems a strange choice for this mission. Were you assigned here because of your past experience in the Blackwald?"

"A little bit. I'm also very good at keeping track of bickering kits," she said coyly while covering her bracelet. This time, she looked at both Njorn and Trisk.

The golden dire laughed. "Ouch, Kitcarer Jenell. My ears are burning."

She bowed a little, then went to gather the other opinici, giving the two ex-lovers a brief moment alone.

"Watch yourself, you dire moose." Despite the moose comment, Trisk was surprised at how worried his voice sounded.

Njorn lowered his head to look Trisk in the eye. "I was about to say the same to you, little deer. Cerris claims all of the opinici rotated back to the pridelands and disappeared en route, but I found the ledger from the previous leader, and it sounds like *he* believed something was hunting them in the Blackwald. Several went missing, and he was leading an expedition to locate them when he also vanished.

"Cerris's first act was to ban gryphons from going lower than the mist. There are a few pages missing, and based on the surrounding context, it seems Cerris removed any remarks about himself from the journal."

"Hunted is a strong word." Trisk tapped the tip of his beak with a claw, lost in thought.

"Temperance found the partially-eaten remains of a gryph, but it could have just been scavengers." Njorn lifted his head. The aerie gryphons were starting to rise. "Anyways, that's what the previous aerie leader said in his ledger. Watch for wolf or boar tracks. They've both been known to develop a taste for gryph flesh."

Trisk watched his dire friend fly back up to greet the gryphons. Jenell was ready to go, and he didn't particularly want to talk to Temperance again, so he allowed himself to be led down the mountains, gliding towards the mist.

He'd have Jenell run him through a list of predators big enough to attack an opinicus once they were settled in. He had his own theories, however, that didn't include wilders, cannibals, or feral animals. If all gryphons had been banned from going below the mist, no one would expect a gryphon to be the killer.

The difference between a bigoted gryphon and a murderer is only opportunity. It was a sentiment his mother had told him before her death, one he'd ignored because he was already falling in love with Njorn.

5

TOWER
COLDBRIGHT

F rom directly above, the mist caused the Blackwald to resemble a snowfield. The sun sparkled off of the moisture in the area. Occasionally, bits of dark green foliage poked through, but otherwise, the false tundra was unbroken except for a landing spot atop the tower.

Not only had the sun failed to burn off the mist, it didn't seem to have thinned it at all. The tower was, in essence, sticking out of the miasma. None of them could see how deep it went.

Trisk shook his head. Despite Jenell's promise of deafening birdsong, the air was silent as the party landed. The platform had blood stains, presumably from game brought up by the previous opinicus occupants and not something more sinister, though Temperance's comments about potential wounded did little to reassure Trisk, especially after finding out she'd been found over a partially-consumed body.

Other than the stains, the platform was clean. If any game or wounded had been left up here, Jenell's screechers must have cleared them out.

"Cheer up." She nuzzled his shoulder as she walked past him. "You're spooking the others."

They should be a little spooked. This is weird.

He pretended to smile, which seemed to unsettle them more, then switched to putting on a grumpy face, which they all treated as normal. He didn't pause to think about what that meant about him as a gryph but instead got to work trying to figure out how to open the way into the tower.

There was no reason to have such a complicated mechanism. He'd heard of aerie woodworkers getting bored with the quiet life and creating puzzle boxes out of different types of wood. This wasn't that bad, but it still took him a quarter mark to get it open the first time. While he worked, the other opinici groomed the water-resistant oil into their fur and feathers.

At least the tower's not made of that black heartwood. This looks like pine, maybe, or aneda. Once he got it open again, he asked Jenell to shut it closed behind him to see if he could get it open from the other side.

From within the tower, there were two heavy bars he had to push on at the same time to release the catch, so it was somewhat easier. It seemed safe enough, and the other opinici were reassured by the door opening, but something about the unnecessary complexity bothered him. It would be easy to trap it shut from the other side and claim the mechanism had malfunctioned.

He didn't know what the purpose of that would be, but he also didn't want to find out the hard way if there was a reason for it.

He pushed past the opinici examining the heavy bars. Despite Temperance's comments that a dire couldn't get into the tower, the spiral ramp leading down it was wide enough to fit several opinici shoulder-to-shoulder. This was likely intentional, as the ramp gave small opinici a way to work together to pull a large carcass up the tower to their gryphon overlords.

The last opinicus inside shut the door, and Trisk had his first panic attack.

The sides of the tower lit up bright red, blue, and lime, and only the fact that he was too paralyzed with fear kept him from screaming and embarrassing himself.

He waited, but none of the marks moved. Behind him, one of the other opinici scratched idly at the floor, unaware of the existence of giant, celestial spiders. When a few minutes had passed and nothing moved, he took a few steps down.

On closer inspection, these weren't constellation patterns like the spiders had. It was just a series of glowing stripes leading deeper. Paint, like the type used on the crates.

"Er, sorry," he said at last. "I wanted to give your eyes time to adjust so no one slipped. Safety first."

"Safety first," several of the opinici echoed.

Another two added, "A safe kit is a happy kit," leaving Trisk to wonder if he'd just stumbled upon the kitcarer motto.

The thing about going down a series of spiral ramps was that it made the tower feel needlessly long. Intellectually, he knew that the Blackwald trees weren't hundreds of feet high. They were so twisted, they probably clung close to the earth. So if he had seen their leaves above the mist, the tower must be relatively short.

However, because it was so slow going, they'd been walking for half a mark with no sign of the lodge the tower was supposedly attached to. This left Trisk with the terrible feeling that they were descending deeper and deeper into the earth, into the eternal wyvern den some spiritual opinici said the unrighteous were cast upon if their spirits weren't released properly.

The only thing that kept Trisk from succumbing to his fears like he had with the non-arachnid paint earlier was that Jenell was humming a nursery rhyme from the back of the group.

"Little kirin, little kirin, don't eat me," she sang. "Little kirin, little kirin, I have no meat."

What is that song? He'd never been much for music, but all of his kit songs had been about gusty wolves or angry songbirds.

"Little kirin, little kirin, tell me of the dragons of old," she continued. "Little kirin, little kirin, such a sight to behold."

Trisk's mind wandered, and he tried to remember what kirin were supposed to look like. *Wyverns with too many legs? Wait, those are dragons.*

He took a step and stumbled as his paw hit flat ground instead of ramp. He started to shout back to warn the others, but not before the mottled green opinicus behind him hit his rump beak-first.

"Sorry," she grumbled. Her voice was a mixture of embarrassment and fear, and he wondered if Jenell was right and he was having a negative influence on the other hunters.

He reached back with a paw and rubbed the sore spot. When he brought it back, it was stained red.

"Looks like we have first blood," he shouted back to Jenell.

When she laughed, the other opinici joined in, and it helped diffuse the tension a bit. Trisk searched for another bar to push down on, and the way into the lodge opened before them.

THE TOWER'S EXIT OPENED INTO A LARGE, DARK ROOM THE size of the nearby aerie's dire quarters. The slight light from the door seemed to be enough to illuminate the paint even this far down, casting it all in a faint multicolored glow. The southern wall was made up of brick and housed a fireplace and a raised kitchen for cooking. The other walls were wood.

Crates of salt, spices, northistle, and other preservatives were stacked high, wisely away from the flames. Like the cooking fire, the spices were on raised stone platforms, leaving Trisk to wonder if the basement might have a flooding problem in the rainy season.

The western wall featured some sort of stone shrine. It looked like it had once been in the shape of a gryphon, but someone had chipped away at it until it was just a gryph-like shape with a beak. The grooves around it proved a mystery to Trisk, but when Jenell found another lever, their purpose became clear.

"Ha!" Jenell shouted as water spewed from the stone gryphon's beak, forming a small river as it flowed through the grooves and into a basin.

Trisk inspected the mechanism. A piece of wood could be pulled down and then notched in one of three areas, resembling the letter 'E'. It hadn't been in any of the grooves when it was off, and the top groove filled the basin.

He pushed it back, and the water stopped flowing

from the gryph's beak. Then he pushed it down and locked it in the second location.

The water drained out of the basin, leaving it empty. He could hear the sounds of the water moving under the stone floor, and he paced over to the large grate in the middle of the room. He pushed his ear against the slats, and he could hear the water down below.

"Hey, what's the bottom setting do?" the mottled green opinicus who had impaled his rear on the ramp down said and pushed it down.

A loud creaking erupted from behind the shrine, and for a moment, nothing happened. The poky opinicus moved in front of the fountain, trying to find where the problem was.

Then it was like a river erupted from the stone gryphon, spraying the center of the room and sending one startled green opinicus flying straight into Trisk.

Jenell calmly stepped up to the kitchen level as the lower area swirled with water. With a leap and glide, she reached the crates of salt, then stretched herself long to knock the lever out of place.

Water circled and drained, leaving the bulk of the room damp but dryer than it had been a moment ago.

Trisk pulled himself out from beneath the opinicus who was causing problems. "What was your name again?"

"Yenni," she coughed. "Sorry about that."

Jenell hopped down and stopped Yenni from shaking the water off. "We don't want to get the crates wet."

"That's an extreme way to clean a kitchen," Yenni said.

Trisk found himself surprisingly grateful for the waterproofing oil. With a light touch of the beak, he managed to persuade the water out of his feathers. "A handy thing to have in a butchery, though."

Jenell looked from the salt crates to the ramp. "Yeah, I suppose it is. This wasn't here during my tour of duty. Not the tower, not the... 'butchery,' as you put it."

"Hey, I found the door!" an orange opinicus chirped from the southwest corner of the room, in the raised cooking area.

The other gryphs lined up and waited for Trisk to go through first. While he appreciated the vote of confidence, he wondered if he'd have trouble getting them to go out and hunt on their own later.

He was also concerned by the size of the butchery. In a sense, this was what all predators did—they existed inside an ecosystem to eat other animals. And for all of their civilization and culture, gryphs were predators. Even hippogryphs ate meat.

But there were locations where wolves moved in and the local deer populations collapsed. Valleys and islands were most vulnerable, but in many places, if gryphs didn't step in to cull the wolf packs, the delicate balance between plants and animals would fall apart.

Maybe that's why the opinici left. It wasn't that the gryphons were bullying them, it's that they foresaw the impact being forced to kill so much prey had on the Blackwald.

He shook his head. There was no point thistle-gathering before he saw the game situation from the ground. With the help of Jenell and Yenni the Problem Kit, Trisk pushed open the door from the kitchen and stepped into the lodge.

TRISK EXPECTED CHAOS, BUT WHAT HE GOT ON THE OTHER side of the kitchen door was order. He took a few steps into the darkness, and when nothing tried to eat him, he ordered Jenell to get the fireplace going.

The room danced in the firelight, a mirror to the lodge on the other side of the mountains. The deer-hide dividers still had their antlers. Small, paw-made antler decorations hung from the walls. The cushions and furniture looked designed with opinici in mind instead of gryphons. And under the oppression of the mists, someone had set glass vases along the walls.

He padded over and sniffed one. It smelled... oily. He prodded it with a paw. Someone had secured it against theft, it felt like.

"It's a lantern," Yenni said, causing him to jump. "Dire Kristel sent some to Haynil two fractures ago. The opinici were probably tired of the gloom below the mists."

The mottled green gryph padded over to the fire and found some long, thick reeds. With one side in her beak, she lit the other side at the fireplace and went from lantern to lantern, transforming the cabin at the bottom of the pit from darkness to day-bright.

"Hey, this one has a leather strap so you can hold it in your beak!" Yenni's excitement attracted the others. She pranced around the room with it, causing both Trisk and Jenell to take stock of what could catch fire in here.

The wooden walls had been treated with something the previous lodge hadn't been, but the best he could expect was flame resistant, not fireproof.

Jenell caught up with Yenni and carefully took the portable lantern, then wiped Trisk's blood from Yenni's beak. "Why don't we just take that one up to the nests to get a look around?"

He trusted Jenell with the lantern a lot more than Yenni. "Also, no taking the lanterns outside unless there's an emergency. The moths down here flock to any kind of light, and where the moths go, screechers are sure to follow."

The opinici stared at him with a mixture of respect for his leadership skills and surprise that he seemed to know something useful. He decided if he got through this ordeal unscathed, he would spend some time perfecting a smile that didn't alarm others and maybe try to learn something about real leadership.

Maybe.

He pushed aside the thick hide separating one of the downstairs rooms from the main open gathering area, figuring that if he were in charge—and he supposed without Njorn here, he was, in a sense, the Direlord Under the Mists—this is where he'd want his working area to be.

Direlord Under the Mists. Undired Lord Under the Mists. Lord of the Mists?

He looked around and reconsidered that proposition. This wasn't an office or a throne room, this was the mender's room.

Despite everything he'd learned from hanging out in the mender's quarters at the pridelands every time he did something inadvisable, despite the marks he'd spent listening to menders chat while they tried to pull northistle vines out of his feathers and fur, Trisk did the inadvisable and poked some of the bloody bandages.

They didn't feel like they'd been left here for months, but they also weren't wet. As he looked around the room further, he saw things that felt out of place in an all-opinicus camp. There was a bone saw and other medical equipment that he couldn't imagine himself operating.

I need to ask Jenell about this. Cerris supposedly banned all gryphons, so either someone disobeyed orders to help the opinici, or the opinici tried to use these for themselves.

There were several glass vials of medicine, another indication this lodge had been intended for better than just opinici, but the supplies were fairly low. If he were stocking the lodge for a year's worth of hunting, he'd be worried. For a few weeks, they had enough.

Jenell pushed aside the hide and poked her beak into the room. "Hey fearless leader, we've got something you want to see upstairs."

Trisk didn't jump this time. "Sounds good. Before I head up, could you take a look down here? I'm trying to figure out if the previous opinicus occupants had a taloned helper."

"You think a gryphon disobeyed orders to aid them?" She put her satchel down and looked through the equipment and the supplies.

He watched her, trying to figure out what she was seeing. "Or it could have been another pride seeking to recruit them. They could have bargained the food they had down here for entry."

"Dire Haynil would throw a fit if he found out." Jenell turned each glass vial around to read the glyph etched into it. "There are ways to leave and join a new pride, and circumventing them would leave a smaller direlord open to attacks from the larger Dires."

"Unless it was Naralin or Kristel making the move." Trisk didn't know how likely that was. Kristel owned the mountains on the other side of the range, but all of Naralin's territory separated the Blackwald from her. "Greed is a powerful motivator."

Jenell looked down at the bloody bandages. "So's compassion. If you saw terrified opinici down here, wounded and dying, abandoned by aerie and direlord alike, would you risk war to save them?"

"If I'm a gryphon and they're an opinicus? Probably not." He hated that he honestly believed that.

"What if you thought nobody would find out?" she pushed. "And what if they came with half a medicine cabinet, a butchery full of food, and knowledge of where the cruelest gryphs were holed up far from aerie eyes with the rest of it in a particularly flammable cabin?"

"Maybe?" It still didn't sound like something a prided gryphon would do, but he shrugged his shoulders. "Wait, you said half a medicine cabinet. How do you know they hadn't just used half of the medicines?"

She gestured around the room with her forepaws. "There's no empty glass bottles. Medicine stores better in glass, it doesn't go bad as fast, but do you know what we have to trade Kristel for it? One vial is worth more than everything you own combined."

She's greatly underestimated how much I've stashed away over the years. Or I've underestimated the price of glass. One of the two.

Trisk wasn't a kleptomaniac. He didn't steal because he was compelled to. But the day he saw Njorn tear apart an entire wilder camp of hippogryphs for the crime of 'not starving,' Trisk had started taking small, precious things and hiding them away in case he ever had to flee.

Opinici who saw the dired at their worst didn't tend to last long. The cheap trinkets on his pouch were heavy because they hid more precious things beneath them. Hidden pockets, inner linings. The leather looked heavy, but that just concealed his satchel's true purpose. It was his escape plan.

"You said you had something to show me?" he

prompted. That the missing opinici had a taloned, presumably gryphonic, friend and had taken medicine with them when they left was interesting knowledge, but he couldn't do anything with that information right now.

Jenell blinked. "Oh, right. Allow me to show you the upstairs quarters."

THE ATTIC HAD SEALED CRATES OF NESTING MATERIAL, mostly the basic kind that smelled of pine, a few hides, and around twenty abandoned nests. That part, Trisk had expected.

It also had nearly a hundred paw prints all over the walls and a few on the ceiling. This part, he had not.

His first thought was of a particularly hyper opinicus running around wildly, moving so quickly they could get a few paw prints on the walls. But there were none on the floor, and when he looked closer, the paw pads were all different shapes and sizes, and almost all of them were front paws save four.

"This is weird, right?" he asked his expedition. They all nodded back. "Okay, just making sure."

Yenni brought up a long reed to light the heavily-secured lantern from a pedestal against the west wall of the attic. "It must be every opinicus who hunted here. They left their mark."

Trisk blinked. That did make sense. He looked closer at each print. He wasn't sure what ink they'd put a paw in to stamp the wall, but he did see a few places where it had dripped to the floor.

"What're these scribbles?" he asked. "They're not decorative, right?"

Some paws had a small design traced in what looked like blood in their center. Others had a different glyph. Still others had something written underneath the paw print in a flowing script.

"The blood probably means they're dead," Jenell offered. "And this other glyph here is used sometimes to mark a grave when someone has gone missing. It's a kind of prayer that wherever the gryph died, may someone find their body and release the soul so the spirit can be free."

Dead, missing, and... what's the other option? Lived happily ever after?

He pointed to one of the others. "I wish my clawscript flowed that well. Does any opinicus have such pretty writing? What's this glyph mean?"

"It's not a glyph," Yenni stuttered. Everyone stared at her. "The way it flows, with heavy parts at the top and bottom? I was a messenger for a little. When dires write secret messages to each other, that's what the words look like. I've only had a glimpse."

"You're mistaken," Trisk said, even though she was absolutely correct. "It may look like dire script, which we're all forbidden to see and so none of us will relay Yenni's incorrect comments here to another living soul, but I've seen this used by gryphon merchants before. I just forget what it means."

Jenell gave him a funny look.

"Jenell, I've heard your writing is passable—for an opinicus," he continued. "Will you find something to write that symbol on? I'll ask a friendly gryphon what it means next time I see one. I'm sure it's mundane. Something stupid like 'shipped off to the pridelands.'"

Jenell's look showed that she doubted him and knew

he was going to show it to Njorn, but she still humored him.

"Just promise me you don't say *I* was the one who copied down dire script," she whispered when she handed it over. "I'll deny it because I don't want to get killed."

While the other opinici picked out their beds, either taking existing ones that looked relatively fresh or opening a crate to make a new one, Trisk led Jenell to an attic exit so they could glide back down.

"How can it be dired script?" He pointed at the small platforms and holes the opinici used to get to and from the attic. "You think the world's tiniest dire crawled up there and wrote it?"

She opened her beak to protest, stopped, then chuckled.

"What? What is it?" he asked.

She waved a paw. "Sometimes, with your false gravitas and pigheadedness, I sort of think of *you* as the world's tiniest dire."

He blinked, thought back to his own thoughts about being 'Undired Lord Under the Mists,' then burst out laughing. "That's terrible! I wish you weren't right. If we get out of this, you and your mate can teach me to be a nice gryph."

Her beak was open in a grin. "Our own tiny dire we can bully? Isn't that every opinicus's dream?"

The others came down to see what the fuss was, and Trisk cleared his throat.

"Well, we found our quarters for the next few weeks." He looked at their eyes and was relieved that none of them believed Njorn's claim that they'd be done in a few days. Hunters were used to hard work. "You were all paw-picked because you're some of the best at what you do.

For most of you, that's hunting. For some, like Jenell, it's organization and medicine. For myself, I was chosen because I was the only one loud enough to give these speeches."

It warmed his heart that a few faces were willing to entertain the idea of him being nice and friendly. Yenni stood closest to him, which made him nervous when he remembered the feeling of her sharp beak going into his flesh. Jenell stood in the back, keeping watch.

"It's time for us to go out into the mists and get the lay of the land," he continued. "I know it's tempting to do some hunting here today, especially since prey animals may be coming closer to the lodge. But I want everyone to be safe. We're going to go out there together, as a group, and scout the area.

"Our number one priority is safety. There've been some lost, wounded, or missing gryphs down here in the past. There won't be in the future. I don't know if it's carelessness, wolves, bears, or a giant gryph-eating dire wyvern"—this earned him his first genuine chuckle, though it came from Yenni, who still felt bad about impaling him—"but I'm a lot more concerned about keeping you safe than I am about filling gryphon bellies.

"Stick with me, and we'll get through this as safely and quickly as we can. Whatever we see when we open those doors, just remember: this is not your new home. This is a job. We're here until two shipments worth of game are caught and sent up top, then we're out."

Yenni stuck a wing up like she had a question, and he nodded at her. "Do we put our paw print up on the wall like the ones who came before us?"

"Yenni," he began, "on the day we leave, you can put your paw print up on the wall, and I'll even let Jenell write

'Alive and Happy' underneath it with her prettiest writing. Sound good?"

Yenni perked up. "Sounds good!"

"Great!" he responded. "Now let's open the giant ominous door into the killer mists full of spiders and death and get this over with."

6

LAKE
COLDBRIGHT

The same way the second lodge had defied Trisk's expectations, stepping out into the Blackwald once again caught him off guard. What awaited him on the other side of this door wasn't horror, it wasn't spiders, it was...

"Beautiful," Yenni gasped. "This must be the most beautiful place in the entire world!"

Though the mist still obscured the world above the canopy, it was neither dark nor gloomy below them. It was surprisingly bright. And despite the silence as they flew down into the wald to find the tower, the late morning air hummed with the deafening call of a hundred different birds.

Trisk moved closer to Jenell so she'd be able to hear him. "You should have told me it was this light down here. I thought we were going to need Yenni's lantern."

"Everything else had changed," Jenell replied, "so I assumed this had, too.

The lodge stood tall in a clearing, but the gnarled, twisting wald trees stretched even taller. At some point, gryphs had cleared out bushes and everything except a soft, springy grass from an area ten meters wide around the cabin. A couple of vines were hidden in the grass, tripping some of the opinici running circles around the lodge. The density of the soft grass saved them from any injuries.

He tried to pick out the different species of birds to see if he could recognize any. He thought he heard some pheasant and grouse, but it was hard to tell them apart. His ears were deafened by the symphonic cacophony.

He made use of his wings and paws to get everyone's attention so they'd gather close enough for him to talk.

"This isn't nearly as dangerous as I thought it would be," Yenni chirped.

He tended to agree with her, but he didn't tell her that. "Gather into two groups of three. Jenell, you and I will form our own group together. First group, I want you to head east. Find landmarks and locate the old paths. I trust you can tell the difference between a deer path and a hunting trail. Figure out how to get to and from the lodge from each landmark.

"Yenni, take your group west and do the same. I'm not expecting you to reach the mountains today. I just want you to start memorizing the territory around the lodge so you'll recognize it in the future when you're out hunting."

The mottled green opinicus nodded. "Where are you and Jenell going?"

"North." Trisk wanted the entire group to explore the south together tomorrow. If there were wilders near the pass who attacked the snowed-in lodge, they were more likely to be hiding near where the pass entered the Black-wald. "There's supposed to be a lake, and I'd like to see if it's fishable. It would be nice to have an easy way to feed ourselves if the game has become skittish."

And I want a water source that doesn't come from a creepy stone statue.

The groups dispersed, leaving Trisk and Jenell alone at the lodge. She started walking north, but he called her back.

"I'd like to get a better look at the lodge's exterior first," he explained.

A hop and a few wingbeats put him atop the overhang protecting the only way in and out. He could smell the moisture in the air, but he wasn't in the mist yet. Oddly, the world above the mists seemed more opaque the closer he got to it. Both the main gathering area and the attic had very tall ceilings, and the roof of the cabin was in the mists proper.

"Do you see any of your screechers flying above us?" he shouted down to Jenell, but she wasn't able to hear him over the birdsong.

Well, if she sees something flying at me, I'm sure she'll warn me.

He pushed off the overhang and flapped his wings, circling the lodge and gaining height. The higher he went, the smaller his field of vision became. He nearly hit the lodge once, unable to see it, and when it disappeared, he had to glide down until the roof materialized under his feet, giving his knees a jolt.

The roof was sloped, and the mist made it slippery. He made his way towards what he thought was north, but instead found himself in the south. He went to the edge and tracked back the other way, finally locating the tower. The wood that had looked sturdy from the inside was actually starting to rot from the moisture. He was mentally preparing himself to try to climb it when something flew past him in the swirling white.

Something about the size of an opinicus. Something that made him wonder just how big these screechers grew.

He reconsidered his plan. He wanted to know how feasible it would be to fly out of the wald without climbing up the tower first. But if there were things hiding in the mist, it would be better to hope they didn't need to go out this way.

He crawled back to the southern side of the roof, then glided down.

"Looks like you had fun up there," Jenell said with a yawn. "No holes in the roof?"

He looked up. Inside the mist, visibility low, he'd felt a hundred feet in the air. Here on the ground, he thought he could see well past that.

"Could you see me the whole time?" he asked. "Did you see the thing in the mist?"

She pulled herself up from the soft grass. "Thing in the mist? No, was it a bird or a screecher? The skies are clear. It must have been on the other side of the tower."

Trisk and Jenell circled from the ground, but there was nothing above them. Trisk kept staring at the sky, trying to figure it out. He couldn't see clouds, so visibility wasn't entirely clear. The sun itself seemed a fuzzy, white blob in the sky. But the mist looked the same blue as a clear sky.

It was unlikely that was the color of the mist itself. It had seemed white and cloudy when he was inside of it. More likely, it was getting its color from the sky behind it. While the sky was probably full of clouds and things flying overhead, it looked empty from down here.

Some kind of illusion of light, he thought. *Which means the sky could be full of screechers but it would feel empty because of all the blue.*

Not a reassuring thought.

He took a step and his foot caught one of the vines, sending him sprawling. "Looks like the wald is trying to reach out and reclaim the lodge."

"Actually, you have it backwards." Jenell helped him up. "The vines are all growing out from the lodge."

She showed him where she'd traced one of the vines back to the base of the building. There were signs of digging, and the vines had been planted at regular intervals with small charms hanging on the lodge wall above each. Instead of climbing the cabin walls, however, they'd fled in the other direction, heading back to the wald.

"Damn peculiar," Trisk muttered. "A vine that doesn't want to climb?"

Jenell shrugged. "Ecosystems evolve together. Lumber is dead wood, and the type you build lodges with isn't from the trees that grow down here. Local vines need the heartwoods to survive. Live heartwoods with nutrients they can steal, not dead ones. It's not weird, it's just bad gardening."

"Okay, okay, enough with the nature class," he said with a wink. "I get it. The Blackwald is just a forest. I'll stop making it seem creepy once I know what happened to the missing hunters."

Jenell's stomach growled. "They probably starved to death. Come on, let's see if we can find some fish."

THE BLACKWALD'S TREES GREW TOGETHER AS THEY REACHED into the mist, creating a pattern of interlocking shadows on the forest floor as Trisk and Jenell trekked their way north. The greys in their plumage had made them hard to spot in the snow but stood out in the forest. Every so often, where erosion or rains had cleared away a section of the stone, obsidian-like crystals jutted out of the foliage.

"Ah, here we go." Jenell pointed to a dry creek filled with vibrant moss, turning it into a bright yellow-green river.

Trisk glided down into the creek bed, his paws sinking into the moss with a squelching sound. The path was springy, and he found himself using the extra bounce to leap and glide short distances, finally stopping on an obsidian outcropping.

He lifted a paw and shook the water off. "For a place without running water, everything here is very wet."

"Like a dry lake," she said. "That's what my mate always called it down here. The wet parts are dry and the dry parts are wet. Like you've dived so deep you came out the other side, so the more up you fly, the wetter you get."

He leapt from one obsidian chunk in the verdant river to the next, but the crystal was harsh against his paws, so he gave up and joined Jenell in the wet moss.

They walked on for another half mark in silence when Trisk got his first look at a screecher. There was no noise, at least none audible enough to rise above the birdsong, no warning. The slightest swirl in the mist above, about thirty meters ahead, heralded two creatures tumbling from the sky.

One was a plump canopy grouse, crushed by the fall against a chunk of obsidian. Atop the bird, its wings enveloping the kill, was the screecher.

In his mind, Trisk had imagined screechers to be some sort of large black eagle based on the size of the wing he felt move past him in the mist. What stood before him was not a bird, not exactly, and its skin was a mixture of white with grey stripes.

If a bird could be said to resemble a gryphon, a screecher could be said to resemble a wyvern. Its hide was leathery, and it had the right number of legs and wings. It even had the horns, the snake-like tail, and the reptilian eyes. But its face was long, almost beak-like, except with pointy teeth.

Trisk put his beak by Jenell's ear so the creature wouldn't hear them. "It looks like a tiny wyvern. Is it sentient?"

"Sentient or sapient?" she asked.

He rolled his eyes. It was like talking to Temperance. "Sorry, is it *sapient?*"

"No," Jenell replied. "Nor does it breathe fire."

"We could kill it. Eat it and its prey." This one was smaller than what he'd felt go by in the mist. He was sure he could take it, especially with help.

She looked from its spread, mantled wings up to the sky. "No, we should avoid it. See what it's doing there? There are more above us. It doesn't want them to know it's eating. But if we get in the way, it'll screech for help, and we don't know how many are out there."

Trisk retracted his claws, and they slipped into the thick forest on either side of the creek, giving the creatures a wide berth. Once they were back on the moss again, they reached the first signs the lake was nearby. Despite the temperature staying pleasant, the creek changed from moss to frozen water, and the opinici were forced to move back to the bank. Another quarter mark after that and the Blackwald gave way to an expanse of frozen lake.

Gave way wasn't quite right to Trisk's mind. Though

the mist still hovered over the lake, the light was brighter here, and he could see under the surface. The trees continued along the bank, into the water, and into the depths, frozen in time by the ice. It looked as though a sinkhole had opened up, the land had started to collapse, then it had flash frozen.

Walking along the edge, he found where the Black-wald itself stopped and the shore became rocky. He even located what appeared to be an old gryph fishing hut —*under* the ice. The surface was so clear, he could see gutted fish hanging from hooks inside the hut.

Jenell walked out past where the trees were visible under the ice, spreading her paws for traction. She leapt up and down a few times before declaring the surface too thick to break through for fishing.

While the lake edges were all solid, Trisk hadn't considered that the entire thing wasn't one block of ice until a dark shape rose up beneath Jenell and slammed the ice from the underside, knocking her off her feet.

"Nell, are you okay?!" he shouted to her, using an old nickname, as she slid towards the center.

Beneath the lake's surface, the dark, brown shape of a sturgeon with spikes along its back and fins sped towards her, hitting the ice again, causing her to slide closer to the center.

Had they been in the air, Trisk would have seen what was coming long before now. But because even the waves had been flash frozen, he only now realized that his sink-hole analogy was more accurate than he expected.

The surface of the lake was not, in fact, one contin-uous surface. Instead, it opened up into a giant, gaping abyss. Mist swirled around the blackness.

He shouted at Jenell. "Look behind you!"

Yet the birdsong was deafening even so far from the trees. It was as though the memory of every bird who had ever lived here had been trapped beneath the mist, echoing to eternity, unable to escape.

She tried to stand again, just for the dire-sized fish to slam the ice, knocking her down. The flat surface of the lake curved slightly inward here, and she slid farther, not stopping.

He ran as fast as he could without risking falling on his beak, then leapt into the air. Just as the fish prepared to knock her over the edge, Trisk caught her and pulled her up enough for her to get lift and fly on her own.

Together, they soared over the frozen waterfalls that disappeared into the mist. Along the edges of the abyss, he thought he saw a flowing script carved into the ice, but if they were the same symbols as the ones in the lodge, he couldn't tell.

They flew as low as they dared, and when he looked down at their shadows on the lake's surface, he saw the dark shape swimming behind them, only stopping when they hit the tree line again.

Jenell caught her breath. She was visibly shaken.

"I'm going to guess the monster fish wasn't there last time you visited?" he asked her.

She shook her head. "I don't know. We saw the lake was frozen and left it alone. None of us knew how to ice fish, so we didn't really go looking."

Trisk had assumed the south would be the dangerous part of the Blackwald, but he decided the north would be off limits, too. Better they risk going west and step into Dire Naralin's lands than find out where the hole in the ice led to.

"It's stupid," he said as the frozen river became the

green moss creek, "but I can't shake this strange feeling that if we'd fallen into the sinkhole, we'd have come out on top in the mist again."

Jenell laughed, but it was half-hearted at best with a touch of fear. "Did you see all of the mist in there? I kept thinking that this must be where it's coming from. Maybe they should try to build a door on top of it."

"I don't think the sturgeon would like that." He meant it as a joke, but it came out serious. The birdsong ate nuance from speech, forcing everything to be louder than intended, harder.

They continued on in silence until they had their first bit of good luck—there was a white doe licking something off of an obsidian crystal in the middle of the creek with its back to both of them.

He nodded to Jenell, and she snuck through the forest to get ahead of it. Trisk got a running start, trusting the bird noise and moss to hide his footfalls, and leapt on the animal.

While he clawed his way up its back towards its neck, it fled south, along the creek. Just as it was about to slip past another obsidian outcropping, Jenell pounced from the forest and slammed into it from the side, knocking its head into the rock.

It fell down, nonplussed, as Trisk's claws reached its throat and finished it off. He stopped to catch his breath. Something about the forest sapped his energy, or perhaps his flight over the lake had taken more out of him than he thought.

"Can you block the kill from view while I go back a second?" he asked her.

She spread her wings over the deer, imitating the screecher they'd seen here earlier. She did her best, but it was too large for her to cover all of it. "What're you looking for?"

"It was licking something off the crystal," he explained. "I want to see what it was so we can use it to lure more deer out."

He climbed back, looking for the doe's rock. When he located it, he was surprised at what he found. It was the same rock the screecher earlier had bashed the pheasant against.

He touched a paw pad to the stone. It came away red, and he licked it.

Pheasant blood.

He returned to Jenell and told her what he'd found as they dragged the deer back with them. Even if none of the other groups grabbed something to eat, they could feed all eight of them on a body this large.

His companion didn't see the deer's strange treat as anything sinister.

"Deer like salt," she explained. "It's humid and wet here, so all of us will find ourselves craving it. And blood is salty."

He shook his head in disbelief. Still, if all of the deer in the Blackwald were this big, they'd be done in no time.

Though if a doe is this size, how big is a stag? I should keep them in their groups of three for safety.

By the time Jenell and Trisk returned to the cabin, night had arrived, and the stars had come out.

The eight-legged, neon stars which crawled through the canopy, hiding behind their webs to lure in prey.

TRISK HELPED PULL THE LARGE DOE BACK INTO THE butchery. Together with Jenell, they cleaned the kill while the others talked about what they'd discovered.

Everyone was hungry—*peckish* was the word Yenni used, causing Trisk to roll his eyes—but Jenell insisted they cook the meat first. She explained she hadn't ruled out a sickness jumping from prey to gryphs as the cause of the disappearances. If the gryphons were salting and cooking the meat and the opinicus hunters were eating it raw, it might explain what had happened.

To ease the pain of waiting, Trisk told them they could open the spice crate and coat the meat in northistle oil. He imagined the previous occupants had been saving it for a celebration on Fracture night, but since they were gone, he didn't see the harm.

"So what did you find?" he asked.

The team that went west, towards Dire Naralin's border, announced that they'd hit a tangle of thick vines and brambles. That was unpleasant, but it was also promising—boars and wild hogs loved to snack on the prickly fare. Despite his order that they stay together, they'd split up and each watched a different section, keeping track of the prey animals.

"There are a few types of shaggy birds, all different heights, who feed on different plants nearby," an orange opinicus explained. "They have spurs on their legs. I know you said to mind the trees for spiders, so we looked around. There's a berry patch near a rocky overhang we can use to ambush them from above without dealing with the canopy."

Jenell looked up from the stone gryphon basin, where she was washing off her claws and beak. "I'll go with you tomorrow. I have a good memory for what's edible here.

It's probably better to use the sour berries as bait, but they'd make a good treat when they're fully ripe."

"I found a bunch of parchment in storage, behind the rain barrels," Trisk added. "I'd like it if we could write these things down to help future teams that come in here. So long as the Blackwald is full of prey, Dire Haynil will keep sending opinici here. We take one copy with us, leave the other for the next set of opinicus hunters."

Spirits willing, he would never find *himself* back here again. He wanted to keep track of the prey and peculiarities, however, and especially the dangers they encountered.

By the time they were done processing the kill, the initial strips of meat were done cooking, and everyone gathered around to eat.

The venison was good. Heavenly, even. Trisk didn't know if that was the chef, the northistle oil, or the deer itself, but everyone was singing his and Jenell's praises by the time sleep came.

As a precaution, a gryph was chosen to watch the door and keep the fire going. He'd alternate with another at midnight. On Trisk's list of things to do, he added in, *Find a way to secure the door closed.*

He curled up, beak over tail, and looked at some of the decorations on the wall. Next to his nest was a carved charm. It had antlers and some strange glyphs he recognized but couldn't quite place. The craftsmanship was impressive, and he wondered if these had been gifts from gryphons. Surely no opinicus had such impressive knifework.

Just as his full belly convinced his brain to turn off, he remembered where he'd seen the glyph before—carved into the ice earlier that same day.

7

POND
COLDBRIGHT

While Jenell took two opinici west to locate berry bushes and ambush points for the long-legged birds, Trisk brought the other five hunters with him south to see what he'd find.

There wasn't a road or even anything as official as a trail, really, heading south, but the forest in this direction had seen more paw traffic. The kinds of prickly plants that coated the ground with organic caltrops were absent, a clear sign that gryphs were tending an area. The branches had been cleared higher here than in other sections, meaning that a gryph in a hurry could just barely fly towards the lodge if they were mindful of their wingspan and altitude.

He even saw some markers on trees hinting at prime hunting spots. Sadly, they weren't the same hunting glyphs he was used to, meaning each would have to be explored and added to their information book.

Every half-mark, he stopped and checked he had everyone with him and changed who was in the lead.

They went slowly, so two marks had passed before they located fresh water.

Yenni was in the lead, so it was less a discovery and more of a misstep that sent her plunging ten feet into the rapids. The path they followed hit a ledge and dropped down precipitously. Beneath them, a cave opened up and spewed out a fast-moving river.

Trisk shouted after her, taking advantage of the drop and clearance to fly above the water as she was washed away. Visions of losing an opinicus on his second day in charge flashed through his head, but he heard a loud splash and the river opened into a pond.

"Hey, a swimming hole!" Yenni shouted back. "And the water is warm!"

Trisk had not forgotten what the previous lake housed. "Out of the water, Yenni. We don't know what's in it yet."

She ignored him, using the opportunity to wash. Her feathers puffed up like a wet pigeon, and she shook them a little as she preened.

Only when Trisk shouted, "Rampaging dires, do you see the size of that leech?!" did she quickly move back onto land and return to his side.

Together, they worked their way back up the river back to find the other opinici. Torn between chasing after their leader or staying put so they didn't get lost, they'd made the right choice.

He reached the cave entrance and chirped up for the rest to glide down. When he realized they couldn't hear him over the constant forest noise, he shouted and waved his wings and forepaws wildly until they got the hint.

While the hunting marks and plant pruning had been subtle indicators of gryph involvement, the cave entrance had more overt indicators. Clay trinkets hung from roots that had pierced the top of the cave. Some had chimes that jingled in the cool air coming out with the river.

With the constant avian chatter of the forest, Trisk had to stick his head inside the cave to hear their song. Remembering Yenni's comment about the pond being warm, he put a paw in the water and felt the heat coming off of it. This wasn't scalding like a mountain hot spring, but it was warm for the bottom of a valley. It felt like the layer of water atop the pridelands' lake on the hottest day of the fracture.

As tempted as he was to explore it, he didn't have a lantern with him, and a lot of dangerous things hid in caves, so they continued onwards, searching out the pond. Long reeds grew along the pools of trapped water beside the rapids, but the trampled foliage suggested previous opinici had steered clear of them, so they did the same.

Every so often, a water bug leapt down from a reed, distracting Trisk from his thoughts of the cave. Considering the water for the stone gryphon fountain was coming from somewhere, he wondered if the creek bed was dry because the water table was underground now.

His head was in the clouds—mist?—when Yenni shouted that they'd reached the pond, warning the others to watch for leeches. Cascading tiers of pools softened the rapids before dripping them down into the pond, keeping most of the water crystal clear.

Bass darted in and out of the aquatic plants, catching minnows. The song of waterbugs and amphibians was just audible here. Across the pond, wary of the opinici, egrets and cranes stood above the flora. Thankfully, his hunters knew to give them room. The birds' beaks were spears, and they always aimed for the eyes.

He watched the bass near the surface, trying to see

what was beneath them. A small water scorpion dove to avoid being caught by an egret, swimming past the fish who would happily have made a meal of it, only to be caught in a deepwater current and whisked away.

"What do you see?" Yenni asked him.

He pointed to the southern side of the pond. "There's another cave there, and the water flows out of it. I see some catfish hiding in the depths. But there's also two more currents feeding into the pond. I think we're likely to find small lakes and creeks throughout the valley, probably interconnected."

"What makes you think the water leaves the pond?" she asked.

He looked at her. Her green plumage, dull compared to the vibrancy of a gryphon, made her blend into the moss and tall grasses of the wald.

"Water gets stagnant if it can't move," he explained. "Fish like these, bass and catfish, need moving water. Even the large swamps other prides have tend to be less like a stagnant lake and more like a wide, very slow river."

Because they were twisted like heartwood, Trisk had missed that the trees around the pond were some sort of cypress. Their gnarled knees didn't look out of place, and cypress wasn't his favorite wood, but if they started running low on firewood, he didn't want to risk cutting down a heartwood and bringing spider eggs into the lodge.

The cypress roots hid small fish in the water and allowed frogs and toads to perch on top, and his stomach rumbled. The toads, yellow-green monsters as big as his head, had a lot of meat on them. The trouble with amphibians was that you never knew which ones would make you sick.

The mist above swirled, and Trisk braced himself. It wasn't a screecher, however—it was a dragonfly. Three dragonflies, actually.

Dragonflies had been named after the extinct hexapodal ancestor to wyverns, but most didn't live up to their etymological heritage. The dragonflies in the Blackwald came as close as any, stretching about three feet long, and the first of the trio managed to snatch a large toad off the cypress knees and pull it into the air above Trisk.

The second missed its frog and was nearly snatched by a heron, who clipped its wing. The dragonfly tried to fly over Trisk's head, but this time he was ready. With a quick leap, he caught its wings and brought it down.

Yenni outdid even Trisk. The final dragonfly had a fish in its claspers when she snatched it out of the air, two treats for the price of one.

Well, now I know where to go if we run out of other things to eat.

He let his hunters stay a little longer until everyone had caught a dragonfly. While the bugs were large, they were light enough once the legs, head, and wings were snipped off to fit into a beak.

With mouths stuffed full, today felt like a victory. The hunters had food. They had water. And now that they knew the way here and that the lower branches had been cleared, they had a straight shot flying from the lodge to the pond. Any prey larger than a dragonfly would still need to be dragged back, but it was good news.

The opinici were so excited to find bugs big enough to eat that when he shouted, "Okay, it's time to head back," there were a few groans. He rolled his eyes.

Let's see how they feel after a few days of coming out here.

He let Yenni lead again so he could keep track of

everyone. It was easy to fool himself into thinking that they'd covered several marks of territory today, but they'd only explored a very narrow slice of it.

He also hadn't seen any sign of deer or moose. That could mean nothing. The herds could have found better, more defensible drinking water. Maybe they knew opinici had watched this pond in the past. Perhaps there were other predators Trisk had missed, like screechers, who nested in the mist where he couldn't see them.

Here's hoping the screechers don't grow big enough to eat moose. Thankfully, nobody is going anywhere alone on this trip, so everyone should be relatively safe.

Had the previous opinici been careless? He didn't know. Even two days in, the din of birdsong that rendered his ears useless for hunting was starting to grow on him. In any other environment, being told he couldn't use sound to hunt would have made him leave immediately. Down here, it felt natural.

He spared one last look for the pond. A large, moss-covered log floating in the middle of it suddenly submerged. He blinked, but the ripples in the water told him what he'd seen was real.

He turned and followed the rest of his hunters back to camp, giving the reeds along the rapids a wide berth.

SOMEHOW, DESPITE EXPECTING TO HAVE A FEW MARKS OF time to hunt near the lodge, dusk arrived before Trisk's team made it back.

His first warning that his internal sense of time was off was a large moth. Its wide, dark blue wings flew overhead, and when he looked up, he saw the 'stars' starting to come out.

"Let's pick up the pace a little." He thought back to Jenell's reminder not to spook the other opinici and amended his statement. "I don't want Nell worrying about us. I told her we'd have dinner ready by the time she finished with the berries."

Yenni snorted. "Oh, she's going to kill you if you get back and there's no food."

"Well, let's make sure I get killed as little as possible." It was too hard to set the pace from the back of the pack, so he pushed to the front. "If you don't want Yenni to stab *you* in the butt, too, you'd better hurry!"

Overhead, moths crashed into webs, attracted to the neon lights. Sometimes, Trisk would hit a large stretch where all of the spiders were the same color, a sea of light blue for a quarter mark at a time. In other places, the blues, reds, and greens mixed together.

To his relief, they reached the lodge without any spider bites. He'd seen a few opinicus wings twitch when the moths fluttered overhead, but with their beaks already full of dragonfly, they kept their paws on the ground.

Still, the way back felt endless up until the moment where it ended. His paws stepped onto the soft grass and Jenell called out to him from the darkness.

"There's our fearless leader!" she shouted from the door. "I thought for a moment you'd disappeared into the mist."

His clever retort was muffled behind the bug meat. Jenell opened the door and ushered everyone inside, closing it behind them so nothing took note of the lantern light inside.

"Yenni, what are you eating?" Jenell asked. "What are all of you eating?"

Trisk waited to answer until he'd reached the butchery in the back and spit his out. "Dragonfly."

"That's... not something I would have thought to hunt," Jenell admitted. "It's pretty meaty, though. I'm not sure how to prepare or preserve it."

He filled her in, even mentioning Temperance's comment that most of the opinici down here ate them and sent the red meat and fish back top to the gryphons.

"We did find some spices nobody recognized." Jenell searched through the crates by the salt. "They don't taste like they'd work for fish or venison, and there were a lot of them. Let's give it a go."

While dragonflies weren't as thrilling a meal as the previous night's venison, catching them made for an exciting story as the group ate together and chatted.

"Did you end up finding your berries?" Trisk asked.

She nodded. "Blueberries, several varieties. The nice thing about wild blueberries is that they all mature at different rates. If we keep track of where the different types are at, we could have fresh blueberries for months."

He considered what it might take to turn the berries into a jam or preserves. They were expected to provide a certain weight's worth of food for the aeries and pride-lands, and meat was easier to do that with than berries.

Maybe we keep them down here as opinicus treats. The gryphons don't need to know.

"There was one thing, though." Jenell tapped her beak with a claw. "We came across some broken pottery. We'd found a few small boars, but where we found the pottery, something large had broken through the brambles."

"Ooooh," Yenni sing-songed. She was sharing her fish-

and-bug meal with the orange opinicus who had gone with Jenell. "A large boar means a lot of meat when we catch it!"

Jenell looked around the room. "When I say a large boar, I mean a *large* boar. We'd need Lord Njorn's help to take this one down safely."

Trisk looked up. Everyone was staring at him. "I don't think he'll fit down the tower."

Nobody laughed.

He sighed. "The thing about hunting boar is that there *is no* completely safe way to do it once they're above a certain size. I know you'd all like to kill the weird, forest god boar and have enough meat to go home, but boars are... crafty. Mean."

"That's probably for the best," Jenell conceded. "I was thinking with my stomach."

Yenni deflated. "I really wanted to try boar. Can we still kill the small ones?"

"Yes, if you stay in groups of four to do it," Trisk commanded. "And make sure the large one isn't in view. I don't want anyone bringing angry boars to our front door."

That appeased the group, and as they finished eating, grooming, and turned in for the night, Trisk caught up with Jenell alone in the mender room.

"I thought you'd come," she said. "You want to know about the pottery?"

He bowed his head. "It's hard to pick berries with paws. Carrying around a clay pot isn't an unreasonable way to go about it, but it's also unexpected for opinici like us. Was it old? Perhaps from when gryphons were still coming down here?"

Jenell pulled out a few bottles of antivenom from the

batch and set them aside. "No, the grass around it had been trampled down and hadn't recovered yet. It's also hard to tell, but I think it had blood on it."

Trisk thought back. "Hippogryphs, then. Wilders. We knew they were probably out here. The weird, circular marks on the burned lodge could have been their rear hooves. And if they're gathering berries that close to the lodge, and if they're responsible for the other disappearances, they're going to figure out we're here pretty quickly."

She finished separating the medicines, adding one of the vials in her satchel, a common treatment to keep cuts and scrapes from getting infected. "What're you thinking?"

"Yenni's plumage."

Jenell smirked. "I didn't realize you were attracted to female gryphs. I wouldn't have put my wing over you while you slept."

"What?" He realized she was teasing him, and shook his head. "I mean her coloring makes her nearly invisible in the wald. I think I'd like to assign her to watch a different area each day. The pond. The berry patches near the bramble. I want to see who we're dealing with."

Jenell nodded. "How'd your adventure go? Anything out of sorts?"

"Not that I remember." He thought back. "No, that's not right. We found a cave where the underground river comes out, and someone had filled it with trinkets like the ones hanging in the nest quarters and some wind chimes."

"I've been thinking about the trinkets," she began. "I assumed they were from the aerie, but I had a look around while you were with Lord Njorn, and the gryphons weren't making anything like that up there."

Trisk and Jenell walked out into the hall, now empty except for a single gryph tending the fire.

He reached up on the wall and tapped one with a claw. "Could be a wilder thing. Hippogryphs have talons, too."

"That's true. Some wilder camps are like small aeries." She lowered her voice. "Though what the trinkets are doing *inside* the lodge has disturbing implications."

He shrugged. "Previous hunters probably stole them. The spoils of victory."

"What victory?" she countered. "*Every* opinicus sent down here disappeared."

Trisk looked at the door. Perhaps tomorrow's task should be reinforcing the front door against boar.

Or, you know, anything else that may just happen to come our way.

8

YENNI
COLDBRIGHT

After the excitement of the first two days, Trisk and his opinici took some time to hunt and relax without exploring further. Teams worked in groups, filling up baskets with berries, catching some of the tall, flightless birds, and even pouncing an adventurous pheasant who peeked out of the bramble patch at just the wrong moment.

The hunters loved the spongy river of moss with its obsidian monoliths. They were horrified when he smeared the bird's blood on a spire, but true to form, salt-starved deer sought it out. No bucks were tempted, only does again, but they brought down three with the same strategy he and Jenell had used.

The last deer bucked Trisk off as he pounced, leaving him behind in a pile of soft moss. The deer's run took it about twenty yards before it slipped, hitting its head on the way down.

The two hunters waiting to ambush it were still hidden when a screecher the size of a hippogryph slipped down from the mists. It mantled its meal, wings spread to hide it from view, not realizing it was blocking its own vision of the hiding opinici while it ate.

Despite Trisk's orders not to harass the screechers—there was no way of knowing how many could be circling overhead, out of view—the orange opinicus took advantage of the opportunity and struck it from behind, catching its neck and killing it before it could make a sound.

"Three kills is enough for now," Trisk decided. "Let's head back. Try to keep the screecher hidden."

He considered scolding them, but there didn't seem to be a point. If they kept up this rate of hunting, they'd be done soon and could go home.

When he wasn't using blood to hunt deer, he checked on Yenni. Without getting close to where she was hiding, birdsong allowing, he'd let out a whistle and wait for her response. They'd make this exchange a few times a day. She seemed well concealed, but he wasn't taking chances. Not when he was increasingly certain there were wilders nearby.

He didn't believe the tales of hippogryphs as bloodthirsty monsters. The hippogryphs he'd seen were mostly tired, sad, and just trying to live their lives. If push came to shove, he suspected his team of opinici could beat an equal number of hippogryphs in a fight. Opinici were small, but they were bigger than a hippogryph, and the ones who hunted were all muscle.

During the evenings, he took time to talk privately with each opinicus in his pack. Jenell and Yenni he spoke with every day, the third opinicus was just whoever sought him out.

"I worry I'm not pulling my weight," Yenni said one

evening. "I feel like you're punishing me for stabbing you in the butt."

He laughed, then saw she was serious. A large part of being a leader, he'd found, was anticipating the anxieties of his underlings and reassuring them before they felt the need to voice them—something he'd failed at with Yenni, it seemed.

"You have the perfect plumage to hide here," he explained. "That's all there is to it. There's no hard feelings from earlier."

She toyed with the berry tart Jenell had given her. There was no bread, so no one asked what the crust was made of. "But I'm not *doing* anything. I just sit in the tree."

"You're keeping everyone safe." He licked blueberry goo from a paw. When he wasn't hunting, he'd forget to eat for days. But on trips like this, spending all day searching for prey left him famished to the point where he could out-eat Njorn. "It's my job to figure out how to hunt enough meat. It's also my job to make certain all eight of us get home. In my judgement, what you're doing is more important than hunting."

"Could I take a day off to hunt?" she asked. "One of the orange opinici could take over."

Most herbivores were orange-green colorblind, so an orange opinicus blended into the foliage as well as a green one might. That's why red wolves or foxes didn't have trouble getting spotted.

"Yenni, you're not out there searching for prey," Trisk explained. "It's the predators I'm worried about. Now, tell me what you've seen."

She deflated under his admonishment, but hopefully, that meant she'd remember the danger. "I found an old hunting mark near the start of the bramble, and Jenell was right, there's a large boar hiding in there. It's only a little smaller than Lord Njorn. I caught a glimpse of it devouring an entire berry bush on its own, and when large beavers try to gnaw on the trees bordering its home, it kills and eats them."

"Boars are omnivorous, I suppose." He'd never heard of a boar eating a beaver before. "I'll pull back the hunters a bit. Sounds like it might consider us a snack."

The complaints from the other opinici were more mundane. Mostly, they were scared. But with each shipment they sent up the tower, they came closer to leaving.

Unfortunately, Trisk hadn't been able to talk to Njorn. It was usually Temperance and the aerie gryphons who picked up the meat, and they waited for Trisk to leave before landing.

His responsibility was to his hunting pack, but he felt like the families of the lost opinici deserved answers, so he decided it was time to get creative.

"Hey Jenell," he called into the great hall. "Do we have a crate small enough to fit up the ramp to the tower but large enough to fit three deer and a screecher?"

She looked up from tending to the fire, twisting a turquoise bracelet on her wrist. "Sure, we have a few. But a gryphon won't be able to carry those on its own. You'd need a dire."

He grinned.

JUST BEFORE DAWN, TRISK AND A TEAM OF OPINICI PUSHED the large crate up the tower. It was too big to move with the meat inside of it, so the deer from the previous day were brought up separately. The hunters closed the crate, then retreated downstairs.

Several other boxes of goods were nearby, along with a smaller crate. This one was splattered in dragonfly blood, a dead screecher posed on top of it. Trisk used its large, wyvern-like wings draped over his small form.

He waited in the shadows while Temperance and her escort flew down. He stifled his laughter when, even working together, they couldn't lift the crate. They finally grabbed some of the smaller boxes, ignoring the dead screecher, and disappeared into the morning sky, some going north and others going west.

It didn't take long before Njorn, the Golden Dawn, descended alone—and let out a squeak unbefitting a dire when Trisk jumped out from his hiding spot.

"Njorn!" the opinicus shouted. "I've missed you. Are you safe? Is everything okay?"

"I... don't know. Something is strange up there," Njorn admitted. "The gryphons are always dragging their paws when I ask something of them. The numbers don't add up, either. I think they're hiding food, which is weird because there's so much of it. I did some searching, and I don't think it's at the aerie. I checked the crates at the back of the cave and they're all empty."

Trisk's ears perked up. He was certain they'd smelled full of food when he'd checked them. Where had it gone?

"Maybe they're using it for trade?" Njorn ventured. "The aeries sometimes interact with each other across pride territory lines. Four missing shipments is too much for a few gryphons to eat. Oh, and the aerie seems to have a bug problem."

Trisk shivered. "I'm sure Grumpy the Cannibal will be back any moment, but I wanted to ask you about something we found all over the place. Does this symbol mean anything to you?"

He pulled out Jenell's tracing of the glyph and showed it to Njorn.

The dire looked confused. "I can't translate our words for you. It's forbidden. No undired know the language."

"All of the missing opinici down there were writing it on the walls." Trisk had expected this challenge and suspected Njorn's curiosity would win out. "I think the wilders were scratching it into the ice, too."

A few moments passed. He worried that Njorn wouldn't tell him and the gryphons would return before he could slip back into the tower, but the dire finally caved.

"It's a compound word. Cold-bright." Njorn hesitated, but seeing Trisk's confusion, he said a little more. "Some of the old words for gryphons, opinici, hippogryphs, and wyverns use compounds like that. Some of the, er, less flattering things you may have been called by dires are commonifications of the old terms."

Trisk went through his mental catalogue of sapient creatures. "I don't get it. This was marked over some of the missing opinici. What killed them? I can't think of any gryph type that sounds cold and bright."

"Killed?" Njorn laughed. "They weren't killed by it. The word is for kirin. They were the opposite of dragons, who were black-flame, in some of the old tales." Njorn used both the common and dire forms of black-flame. "If dragons were creatures who created change through destruction, kirin were beasts who killed in order to try to return things to an ideal primordial state. Someone prob- ably saw the word somewhere and repeated it. You know how superstitious hippogryphs are. It's not like they have dires to read the script."

Trisk's patience was wearing thin at Njorn's laughter. "The opinici's names marked with that term are still dead."

Njorn stopped his laugh. "You're right. I'm sorry. Maybe that's what the wilders call themselves. I need to get going, but I have something for you, a gift."

The dire rifled through his packs, pulling out a small, triangular bit of pottery with several holes in it. Trisk couldn't figure out what he was supposed to do with it.

"It goes in your beak," Njorn explained. "You cover holes with your talons, or the one on the bottom with your tongue, and it makes music when you exhale."

Trisk blinked.

"It's not a love pebble," Njorn assured him. "Cerris' predecessor was certain that if he covered all of the holes and blew, the sound would reach from the bottom of the Blackwald up to the aerie itself. Temperance found it where he disappeared."

It had a leather strap tied to the tip, so Trisk put it over his head and let it hang from his neck, but when it rested on the ground, he rewrapped it twice. He'd have to practice with it later. With Njorn's comment about talons, Trisk would need to see if his paws could cover the right holes. "Did it work?"

"Don't know." Njorn shrugged. "If it did, no one came to rescue him. If it didn't..."

The dire's ears perked up. "Go on, get out of here. Only use it if there's an emergency. And please be careful down there, okay? I've had a lot of time to think, and... I miss you."

Trisk froze. His feelings for Njorn were strong, but the

more time he spent with opinici, the more he realized how dangerous this dynamic was for him.

Of course, not having the relationship, especially out here, also put him in danger.

"I miss you, too," he said, and disappeared back into the tower.

9

BRAMBLE
COLDBRIGHT

In the days that followed, Trisk practiced with the beak instrument. Yenni wanted to call it the beakirana, but the orange opinicus she was so keen on suggested 'songbird' and the term caught on.

Trisk's natural speech had a bit of a scratch and soft growl to it. He liked his voice. Others obeyed him, he'd never had trouble finding love, but it wasn't anything he'd call melodic.

When translated through the songbird, though, it came out haunting and musical. To the chagrin of others, he wouldn't let them use it. Part of that was him trying to practice during the evenings, but an even larger part was him not wanting their dragonfly breath on his musical instrument.

Jenell adjusted the leather strap so he could wear it around his neck. Even with his best attempts, however, paw pads were not equipped to cover all of the holes on the side. Despite Yenni's protests that he was just getting good at using it, he asked her to find some gum-trees so they could plug a few of the holes.

"Do you think it'll reach beyond the Blackwald?" Jenell asked one night when they were cleaning up in the butchery. "Do you think Njorn will really hear it?"

"No, not really," Trisk said. "But I'm hoping if I get into trouble, you'll hear it and come save me."

She grinned. "Oh, are you serious? Well, you'd better hope you're not being chased by anything big."

"Yeah, just how big is a kirin?" he asked.

She rolled her eyes, then saw he was still serious. "From my song, you mean? *Little kirin, little kirin, don't eat me?* They were supposed to be the largest of the undireds after dragons. They had deadly horns to put a moose to shame and were known for their cruelty and solitude, if the old tales are right. Why do you ask? Do you think a kirin left my song and ate our friends?"

"The word on the opinicus paws upstairs," he began, "it means cold-bright in dire. They use compound words. I guess kirins and dragons didn't get along."

"What's the compound for dragon?" Jenell asked. "Leggy-wyvern? Tall-screecher?"

"Black-flame." He didn't repeat the word in the old speech for her. "Njorn thinks the wilders here saw the word on an old dire tablet or ruins and use it for themselves. I don't know, that doesn't sound right to me."

"The alternative is that a dire gave it to them." She finished curing the last of the jerky and got the stone gryphon fountain going to wash her paws, pulling her bracelet back so it didn't get wet. "Don't look at me like that. A wilder camp this remote could have started out as a pride we don't know about, then became wilders after their dires died off. It's not the craziest thing we've heard about the Blackwald."

"A hidden pridelands, full of wilders." He played with

the idea in his head. If that were the case, Dire Haynil's gryphs were the real intruders. "I still think the markings in the snow the first night were hippogryphs, though, not gryphons. I'm sure I saw hoofprints."

That didn't mean he thought the hippogryphs had burned down the lodge, but he was certain they'd been there that night, whoever the real culprit was.

"The old prides weren't as concerned about those sorts of things." She moved over so Trisk could finish washing his own paws and went to douse the kitchen fire.

"Guess that's why they went extinct," he said. "Too many hippogryphs in the mix, not enough dires."

DAYS PASSED, THEN WEEKS. GAME BECAME HARD TO CATCH in their stretch of the Blackwald, sending the hunters farther north. The twisting vines planted at the base of the lodge finally reached the heartwood trees past the grass. The deer learned to avoid obsidian stones covered in blood. And even the dragonflies were becoming scarce.

Trisk had gone through the list of hunting marks on trees, trying to figure out what they signified. Near some, he found specific animals, shards of pottery, and antlered charms hanging from trees.

All antlers under the mist, all antler-free above. That can't be a coincidence.

One mark was near an empty forest glen. He'd sworn with annoyance and the mists above had erupted into shrieks, so he assumed the triangle meant 'screecher nesting ground.' Which was unfortunate, because the blueberry bushes in that section of the Blackwald were ripe, and they'd had to abandon most of the area near the bramble. The boar god was on the move, and Trisk didn't want his hunters caught unaware.

Many of the marks also heralded water. The combination of rocky soil and high water table meant he could be anywhere in the Blackwald and stumble across a waterfall coming out of a cave and disappearing down into an abyss with no sign as to where it went from there.

He wandered down to the pond searching for more marks left by his predecessors. The disappearing log had turned out to be a type of small crocodile, and while they usually left gryphs alone, pulling kills along the river path was a harrowing experience. The hunters had accomplished a little fishing, but once the crocodiles associated opinici with food, it became a dangerous endeavor. The best Trisk managed was a brief wash on the shore while someone else kept watch every few days.

He wore the songbird in his mouth, practicing as he explored. Some notes disappeared into the cacophony of Blackwald sounds, but he'd found a couple that cut through. Oddly enough, Jenell's kirin tune had many of those notes, and he filled his non-hunting times creating new versions of that song to take his mind off of the noise. He played one now for the crocodiles in the reeds along the rapids.

They were unimpressed.

But as he passed by the cave where the river spilled out of the earth, he thought he heard a familiar melody echoing back to him.

That's funny. I must have made my song thinking about the chimes.

He checked on the cave—the only place other than the inside of the lodge where the sound of the birds disappeared—and was surprised to see the chimes and trinkets were gone. None of his hunters would do this; the Black-wald had made them all superstitious.

At the moment, they were hunting moose in the north, having finally tracked down the herd. But they wouldn't get near the water after Jenell told them about the fish under the ice.

Yet for all that, the chimes were gone. And the trinkets, too. Had the hippogryphs taken them? They'd been up for weeks. Why now?

A strange feeling passed over Trisk, and his feathers stood on end. Inside the cave, he saw light glinting off of two bright green eyes. Opinici tended to slink down, but even at his tallest, he would not have been able to reach eye level with the pair staring at him now.

He slowly backed out, then flew above the cave. He'd told everyone to stay in groups, yet he'd almost become crocodile bait checking on wind chimes.

Okay, the river cave is off limits. We know the wilders are checking there.

Yenni hadn't seen any sign of the wilders, but Trisk held onto that as the best theory for the disappearances. It was why he'd stuck so close to the lodge. He didn't want to provoke them. With any luck, he'd be leaving soon. Unfortunately, somehow all of the food they brought up the tower was never enough. Temperance had met him up top a few times, telling him that they needed more.

No gryphs can eat that much.

He played his songbird a little more, but hit the wrong note, one that shouldn't be audible over the sounds of the wald.

And he heard it.

When he'd slipped into the cave, the cacophony had disappeared. When he slipped out, it was still gone. Or was it when he'd heard the sounds from inside the cave? When *had* the wald gone silent.

If the ceaseless noise unsettled him, this new silence was worse. Jenell was leading the moose-hunting expedition where the river froze over, but Yenni was supposed to be watching the bramble.

He dropped the songbird, letting it hang around his neck, and ran faster, breaking into flight. It was a shorter distance to cut northeast through the forest, but he couldn't fly that route, so he went north to the lodge, then east to find her.

He almost whistled his usual greeting to her when he reached the blueberry overhang but stopped himself. Silence was a sign of predators, and the loudest prey was the first caught.

This is just some noisy hippogryphs, he reassured himself. *They probably startled a screecher nest or something.*

Yet that didn't feel right. His hunters had killed deer, giant birds, screechers, and moose, and never once did the deafening song of the forest stop. There were so many different birds that made up the noise that he didn't know how you'd silence all of them. It would take something the size of Njorn.

He climbed the rocks to find Yenni's perch, but put his paw over her beak to tell her to be silent. She pointed down at the edge of the bramble patch.

Near where Jenell had found the broken pottery, there were three bodies. Or what remained of them, at least. Trisk's eyesight was pretty good, but it took him a moment to pick out what he was seeing. Something had trampled them into pieces.

The first body he made out, based on plumage colors, was an opinicus. He could tell because it had a pair of forepaws. The other two had hooves, suggesting they were hippogryphs. There was more smashed pottery, a few trinkets, and a few pair of...

Are those antlers? Were they part of the chimes and trinkets they've been hanging up? I wonder if they moved the ones from the cave here.

He wanted to ask Yenni if she'd seen it happen, but he couldn't figure out how to convey his meaning without speaking. Finally, he moved his beak next to her ear, and just before he spoke, the cacophony returned, deafening them both.

"It's so much louder after the silence," Yenni complained. She scratched at her ear with a back paw.

Trisk pointed to the remains. "Did the birds stop when the boar attacked? Did you see it happen?"

"No, they were already dead when it stopped." She looked sheepish before admitting, "I'd dozed off. I woke up and suddenly there were bodies everywhere. I screamed, but it was loud then. Actually, when it got quiet, the only thing I heard was you playing your songbird."

"That would have been right when I put my head inside the cave." He felt uneasy. That was also when he'd heard the strange sounds coming out of the cave, before he discovered the chimes were missing.

Do crocodiles sing?

Yenni stood and stretched her paw, then glided down to the berry patch and began to prowl closer.

He joined her, uneasy being on the ground with a killer boar on the loose. "Is this wise?"

"Boar's too big to sneak up on us," she said. "When it goes through the bramble, I can see the whole section shake around it."

Trisk hadn't thought much about the boar being in the

bramble patch, but with its size, its skin must be thick to survive the prickles and thorns. As they came closer, he could see a huge opening in the wall of northistle.

"Stay back," he told Yenni, and he crawled towards the remains. He didn't want boars returning to eat the dead gryphs: they could develop a taste for opinicus. Beyond safety concerns, he didn't know what the wilder death rites were like, and he didn't want their spirits to linger in the Blackwald. Even if it was their home, it felt like a cruel place.

His instincts told him to run away, but there was a part of his brain that sensed something was off. He moved closer to the entrance of the bramble, and he found the first dead boar.

Do boar kill their own? Or did the wilders do this?

He backtracked and looked at the pieces of pottery. They were full of fruits he'd seen around the wald and some he hadn't—green cherries, red blackberries, something pink and green. It looked like they were bringing an offering to the boar.

"Yenni, take the songbird and go back to watching the bramble." He tried to wipe his spit from the device before pulling the strap off of his neck and putting it around hers. "If you see any movement, warn me."

She waited patiently while he showed her which holes to cover to pierce the forest noise, then climbed back to her observation post.

Trisk took a deep breath, fought back memories of getting tangled in northistle as a kit, and entered the break in the brambles.

TRISK'S JOURNEY INTO THE THORNY DARKNESS WAS ILL-fated from his first step. He jerked his paw back, removing several prickles before continuing.

The body of the boar in front of him made his stomach rumble. He'd have to borrow Yenni to try to drag at least this boar back to the lodge. It would make a nice meal. He checked the carcass to see how it had died, and he found himself at a loss.

It didn't look trampled. But it also didn't look like it had been taken down by the two hippogryphs and opinicus outside. The claw marks on its stomach were thick, almost dire-like. He felt a sinking sensation in his own stomach. The kind of creature with claws this big who could go toe-to-toe with a boar was a wyvern.

He sniffed. No burning smell.

Would a wyvern use fire inside the bramble? Or would the northistle dissuade them?

The thought that he was crawling through a location that was one spark away from becoming the world's largest cooking fire did little to alleviate his anxiety. Despite the boar's taste for beaver, they'd succeeded in stealing enough trees that there were a few spots that gave a view of the entire bramble, or so Trisk had assumed when he was on the outside. Now that he was in the bramble, either it went much deeper and farther than it looked from above, or his mind was playing tricks on him.

He thought back to the old tales. It was said a gryph should never fight a wyvern in its own warren. It was best to lure them out. He practiced turning around, making sure he *could* get back out, then continued deeper.

The diffused light of the mist sprinkled through the gaps in the brambles, casting shadows of spikes on all surfaces, making it hard to tell where it was safe to step.

He was so busy watching his paws that he missed that the path had opened up until the scent of blood overwhelmed his nares.

He looked up into the face of a boar that dwarfed him, one Njorn would have been proud to kill, one that would have definitely been too big to drag up the tower. Trisk's breathing turned ragged, but the boar's eyes, while open, were lifeless.

He reached a trembling paw up to the side of the beast and extended his claws to get a look at the other side. He scaled the boar, paws shaking, traveling from its back to its side and looking down at its stomach. Its thick hide resisted his claws, making it slow going.

The boar's ribs were visible. The stomach and soft tissue was gone, eaten. The bite marks were large, almost crocodilian.

Wyvern? Would a crocodile travel this far from water?

He thought back to the green eyes in the river cave. They hadn't been right against the water. They'd been up high, higher than his head.

His nares adjusted to the scent of blood, and he thought his mind was playing tricks on him when he smelled water. With the brambles dampening the noise outside, he could just make out the sound of running water.

Maybe it was a crocodile.

He looked around the nest, seeing several blood stains. If there had been more boars in here, they'd also been eaten—or dragged into the mysterious stream by crocodiles.

All it took was one muffled splash, and he turned and crawled as silently and quickly as he could manage out of the passage. Thorns caught on his wings and hide, tracing long lines in his skin. His blood mixed with the boar's. All he could think of were those green eyes.

By the time he made it back to Yenni, he was shaking. He knew they should take the boar in the entryway back to the lodge. He knew they should handle the death rites for the wilders.

But all he could manage was to go back inside, past the fireplace, into the butchery, and wash himself in the stone gryphon basin.

Yenni didn't ask him what was wrong. She just pulled spikes and brambles out of his skin where she found them until Jenell returned to the lodge.

10

HIPPOGRYPHS
COLDBRIGHT

"We didn't find any dead wilders," Jenell said the next morning. "We left the large, half-eaten boar, but we pulled out the small one."

Trisk winced as she tended to his cuts and scrapes. He wasn't superstitious, but the thought of the bodies being carried away by animals gnawed at him. The description *half-eaten* suggested that whatever he heard coming out of the water had fed upon the dead boar. "Did the forest go silent for you up north about midday-ish?"

"It did. Was that when the boar died?" She used a bit of the same sticky resin they'd plugged some of the song-bird's holes with to bind his wounds closed. "You're going to have some new scars. Don't fly if you can help it. You're good to go out, but maybe let someone else do the pouncing."

He instinctively started to lick at the wound, only stopping when she smacked him on the beak. "Sorry. And no, Yenni says the boar and wilders were dead long before the silence. It happened when I was singing songs for the crocodiles."

"That was a good use of your time?" She put away the bottle of medicine and slung her bag around her neck. Her bag, much like her light blue bracelet, carried a myriad of medicine and bloodstains on it. It was too bad Dire Haynil hadn't made her a mender, but Trisk appreciated whoever had added her name to the expedition list despite her being a kitcarer.

Trisk shrugged. "I was practicing already, and I noticed the antler trinkets and chimes were missing from the river cave. I thought I heard them, the chimes, but it was just the crocodiles singing. By the time I'd stuck my head in there to see the bright green eyes staring back at me in the darkness, the birds had gone silent, and I went to find Yenni to make sure she was okay."

"Melodic, green-eyed crocodile?" Jenell laughed. "Sounds like my mate when she's in a bad mood. Croc eyes shine red or orange, yellow at best. And I wouldn't call their little chirps and growls melodic. Must have been something else in that cave. A magical, musical bear. Or perhaps an amorous heron that took a fancy to your stripes."

"Whatever it was, it was big." Now that he thought about it, he was certain the non-crocodile's song had heralded the forest's silence.

She made her way to the hide separator, pausing to note the antler trinkets. "If the wilders took their charms from the cave, do you think they'll come for the ones here? Maybe we should pack them up and leave'em somewhere for the wilders to take. Starting with the thirty they hung in the butchery. They must get more arts and crafts time than the kits back home do."

"Let's hold off on that." He slipped past Jenell and into the main hall where the others were finishing a bugs-and-berries breakfast. "Until we know what the trinkets mean to them, we're just as likely to make them mad. If they keep to themselves a little longer, we can get out of here."

She stopped him. "There will be other expeditions after us. We won't be the last Dire Haynil sends here."

"You saw the dead boar. Something big was eating it." He'd assumed discovering the fate of the other opinici was his own pet project, but there was a look of desperation in her eyes. "When we get back, we tell them there's a wyvern warren near here, and Dire Haynil will show up personally to clear out the wald. Problem solved. It probably *was* a wyvern."

"And what happens to the wilders if Dire Haynil shows up here?" she pressed.

He frowned. "We can't fight wyverns. Eight little opinici aren't going to save the aerie or the wilders."

"Are you or are you not Undired Lord of the Mists?" Her tone, while jokingly, was also pleading. "You know Lord Njorn. What happens to the hippogryphs if he shows up? He's a blunt instrument, and this is a wound that requires precision."

Trisk hated that she was right and hated that he wished he could wash his paws of this whole mess. There were seven other opinici here he wanted to safely see home. "Fine. I'll go south tomorrow and warn the hippogryphs. Hand me one of their trinkets. I'll ask what this whole thing is about, too. I promise."

Trisk was regretting his promise by the time his first paw stepped outside the lodge. While the Blackwald was brighter than he had ever seen it, the mist was nearly touching the ground, and the ground had a layer of frost on it.

Jenell had suggested he take several hunters with him south, but in the end, he'd decided just to bring Yenni. She was shaken up by the dead wilders, particularly the lone dead opinicus, and didn't want to sit alone in the trees in case whatever killed the boar came back.

When Jenell claimed the northern wald would be frozen and the moose would be holed up until it melted, Trisk allowed her to escort them as far south as the pond. That seemed to make her feel a little better, and she even let Yenni grab the portable lantern.

He wasn't sure why Jenell was so invested in this, but he suspected she was following along to see if he'd try to fly despite her warnings about the resin holding his bramble scratches closed.

I would have, if the mist wasn't so low.

Soon into their trek south, the canopy disappeared into the white. Every so often, a screecher would come so close that they could see its feet poking out from the bottom of the mist.

"Want me to reach up and catch one for you?" Jenell asked Yenni, who kept looking up. "I can hold it down so you can tickle its belly and toss it back into the air."

Yenni laughed. "No, I'm fine."

Trisk led this time, remembering Yenni's initial fall at the rapids, and when they arrived there, a surprise was waiting for them.

Mist spilled out of the river cave, covering the rapids and freezing them solid. Despite memories of the strange song and green eyes, he couldn't resist taking advantage of the ice to look inside the cave again.

Several small snouts were poking through the ice,

which Jenell assured him was normal for crocodiles so they could breathe during the cold season.

"Want me to tickle one for you?" he asked her, but she'd turned serious once they were in the cave mouth.

"Only if you think fresh ice will keep the crocs imprisoned," she replied.

The mist deeper in the cave swirled, and the opinici beat a hasty retreat, not wanting to discover that the ice had missed a reptile or two.

This water was so warm when I put my paw in it a few days ago. How did it get so cold so fast?

The pond had a layer of ice that obscured the water, and both he and Jenell stepped back when a bass swam up to the surface, earning them both a weird look from Yenni.

"Where are you taking the hunters while we go south?" he asked while Jenell performed a final check on his cuts and bruises.

"Beaver hunting," she explained. "Now's a good time to scout out their dams while they're hiding from the cold, figure out the best places to ambush them after things warm up. And if we can find some fresh snow, I can figure out what predators are around by their paw prints."

Yenni's ears perked up. "Beavers? I saw them trying to steal trees near the bramble. Are there a lot of beaver dams?"

"You didn't see them when we flew in?" Jenell asked. "Mountain snowmelt and spring storms are hitting their peak right now, pun intended, and beavers are flooding the highlands to keep the water from spilling down here."

"Oh, well, thank them for me on behalf of my dry paws!" Yenni chirped.

Jenell turned to go, leading the hunting troupe west

from the pond. They only had to go a few steps before they disappeared into the mist.

Yenni opened her beak. "Nell's not going to—"

"—no, she's not going to thank a beaver for you," Trisk confirmed, though he wondered if Jenell was exaggerating or not. Part of what seemed to be keeping the large lake frozen was that moving water wasn't reaching it. If that was the beaver's fault, would destroying their dams help melt the ice?

Do I really want a lake with a dragon-sturgeon swimming around in it, attacking gryphs?

If the lake melted, he'd never find out what was at the bottom of the frozen sinkhole. There'd definitely been something down there, something causing the mists. If he were right and the underground river was fed by the lake, it would explain why it was spewing out mist.

I could always ask the wilders. I assume those are their runes around the sinkhole.

WITH THE MIST OBSCURING THEIR VISION, TRISK AND YENNI were forced to depend on their feet to find the hidden path south. Whenever one of them stepped on something sharp, they readjusted their heading. It was slow going, but the longer they walked, the more he warmed up.

At first, he attributed this to his muscles. He was always warmer once he got moving. But they passed by a new spring, unfrozen by the cold snap, and he could feel the heat coming off of it.

Yenni nearly put two paws in before he reminded her of the crocodiles. She returned back behind him.

"I wonder if it's safe to drink?" she asked, as many

springs this hot were not. Their question was answered sooner than they expected.

At an oxbow offshoot of the stream, a small purple creature dipped its beak into the river and drank, unaware of Trisk and Yenni, who slipped into the reeds to watch.

The creature was a gryph of some sort. Seeing it from the front, all Trisk could make out through the mist was a beak, foretalons, wings, and... antlers.

"Is it a kirin?" Yenni whispered.

He thought back to Jenell's words about how kirin were the largest undired sapient creatures. The drinking beast was barely opinicus sized. In fact, without the antlers, Trisk thought he might be a little taller than it was.

The non-kirin turned, giving Trisk a better look at him, and showing where the antlers attached to a kind of circlet-style helmet he wore. He had hooves, a horse's tail, and a violet mane.

"Hippogryphs. Wilders?" Yenni asked, this time a little too loud.

The horned gryph turned and looked at the reeds.

Trisk took a gamble and called out to him. "Hello! We don't mean you any harm. We just wanted to ask—" but the hippogryph disappeared into the forest.

"Skittish dears." Yenni walked to where the hippogryph had vanished and took a drink. "Water seems fine."

Trisk joined her. "It's possible the previous hunters attacked them. They don't really have any reason to trust us."

Yenni sniffed. "They're wilders in Dire Haynil's territory. They know the rules. All unprided gryphs do."

What Trisk had taken to be mist here was actually

steam coming off of the river. If the oxbow was this warm, the river itself must be too hot to swim in.

While both were wet and white, the steam pushed back the mist, revealing large, stone pillars. In the middle of the billabong, a statue of a hippogryph rose up. It looked down its beak at them in judgement. Despite its age, it was in good condition. Someone had been keeping the vines from taking root.

"I don't know that I've ever seen a hippogryph tall enough to look down its beak at me," Yenni chided, but Jenell's words about the old days were coming back to Trisk.

"I don't know that they are unprided," he said at last. "I think Nell's right. That this was once a pride of some sort that lost its dires. Wilders who don't know they're wilders. They probably ignored the lodge for years until something happened."

Yenni finished looking around to where the hippogryph had disappeared. "So the Blackwald is their pride territory, and when the aerie took more than it needed to eat, they burned the lodge on the other side of the mountains and took the food back?"

How do the aerie gryphons fit into this? They're so weird. Maybe they return the food to the wilders as a bribe. An aerie caught between two prides, trying to keep both happy.

He didn't know if that made sense, but this did change how he would approach them. If he had been dealing with normal wilders, he'd approach them from a place of power, as a prided gryph in his rightful lands. But these may not be Dire Haynil's lands.

Not that any direlord would allow the undired to claim territory or the name of *pride*. Perhaps Njorn could negotiate with them, turn them into an aerie. It would be tricky since hippogryphs weren't normally afforded that honor. Still, maybe they could work something out. All undired craved the protection of a dire. That was gryph nature if the teachings were to be believed.

Thoughts of Njorn's warm embrace filled Trisk's thoughts, but he pushed them aside. There was another, very real possibility. That boar had been killed by something large and unconventional.

What if they *did* have a dire helping them?

THE BLACKWALD DIDN'T APPEAR ANY DIFFERENT THIS FAR south, but Trisk and Yenni were making better time, and he knew what that meant—someone was tending the forest here, making it easier for gryphs to live in.

They were getting close to the pridelands.

Pridelands, not wilder camp.

He was sure of it now. At some point, mixed in with the trees on either side, they began to see stone columns set into regular intervals. Some were still topped with small hippogryph statues.

Yenni looked up. "Always hippogryphs. Never gryphons or opinici."

"Weird." Trisk's word undersold it. There was a hierarchy that a pride enforced. Dires over undired. Gryphons over opinici. Opinici over hippogryphs. No pride he'd heard of would keep hippogryph statues around. The gryphons would be offended.

Where did dragons and kirin fit into that mix? Or were they outside the cycle, like wyverns? I've never seen a dragon or kirin statue, if they ever existed.

"Do you think they're all hippogryphs?" she asked.

"No, that's not right, there was a dead opinicus by the boar, too. But maybe that was one of the aerie's missing hunters who joined them. Oh, am I talking too much?"

He shook his head. "Their lookouts know we're here. If we'd snuck up on them, they'd probably have killed us. Being loud shows we're not here to do them harm. It lets them count us. You don't sneak up on anyone you want to talk to."

"You're very good at this," she said. Before he could thank her, she continued, "Which is strange, considering how bad you are at other things."

He blinked. "What other things?"

"Relationships. Making friends," she replied. "Anything social. Obeying rules. You should see if they're recruiting. You belong in a place like this, not the pridelands. I'll bet they're all rude like you."

He wasn't expecting to be critiqued by Yenni. In the future, he'd bring Jenell along, instead. But her chatter was having the effect he intended, and they started catching glimpses of hippogryphs in the forest around them.

While the steam had died down, allowing the mist to return, he could make out antlered gryphs following along behind them now, too.

He interrupted Yenni's unsolicited advice on how to make friends. "Okay, enough of that. Be respectful. We're now diplomats here on behalf of Dire Haynil. What we do reflects upon our pride."

That changed her demeanor. She stood taller. Her tail, which sometimes drooped during long walks, was held a little higher. She even managed to lick a paw and adjust her ears as they walked.

None of the antlered gryphs around them spoke, so

Trisk didn't speak to them. He thought of warning Yenni about what to do if they were separated, but it was too late now. They were herded towards an arch, presumably the entrance to their pridelands.

Beyond the arch, a stone bridge over bubbling water led into an open area surrounded by columns and an aqueduct system. Steaming water crashed down from a waterfall, feeding into little stone canals that formed a barrier around an artificial island. The steam kept the mist at bay, and for the first time since his journey to the lake, Trisk could make out the clouds above them.

Small pools collected and cooled runoff, and brightly-colored fish swam in them. Several had all fish of the same color, reminding Trisk of how some sections of wald seemed to have all blue star-spiders. Someone was curating the nature of the Blackwald. And once he had that thought, he realized that the pottery meant that someone wanted the large boar in the brambles, had been bringing it food like a pet.

Had the boar offended the hippogryphs? Is that why they'd killed it, if they had?

Trinkets and chimes hung from the tree branches. Some bore the *coldbright* rune of the kirin. Others had different words in the dire script. One he thought he'd seen on the letter of Dire Haynil's winguard.

So are they the Kirin Guard, then? It explains their silly headwear.

"Follow my lead," he whispered to Yenni. Once they were in the center of the island, he put his front paws down and mantled his wings.

"We've come to pay our respects," Trisk shouted. "We would like an opportunity to speak and learn about each other."

While he kept his beak down out of respect, he saw the edges of the island fill with antlered gryphs. There were thirty in total, but about ten of them had paws and not talons. The talons all belonged to hippogryphs—he saw no sign of gryphons in their ranks.

A hippogryph stepped forward. Where the others all wore antlers taken from animals hunted in the Blackwald, this hippogryph wore a pair made of obsidian and black heartwood. His plumage was a dark, smoky grey; his beak, hooves, and tail were colored a fiery red.

There were red dots on his flank, resembling the star spiders. This was clearly the hippogryph Temperance had referenced back at the aerie.

I'll have to look closer at the spiders. I wonder if his spots glow, too. Maybe that's how the hippogryphs hide at night. Nobody gets close enough to look twice at an arachnid.

The hippogryph descended from a stone platform above the waterfall. Behind the curtain of boiling water, Trisk saw another hippogryph statue, this time wearing antlers too large to have come from a real, living creature.

I wonder if the other statues had antlers that fell off or if they added antlers to that one?

Trisk stood, still mantling. The gryphs around the edge were all staring up at the statue, not at the black-and-red hippogryph.

"I'm Trisk, and this is Yenni," he began. "We're hunters at the lodge. We've come to—"

"We know who you are and why you've come," the hippogryph said. "These are not Dire Haynil's land. If he wishes to keep his aerie on the peaks, we will allow it. If his gryphs are starving, they may eat what they hunt here. But they must not interfere, and the dires must remain above the mist for their own safety. They must not take the wood from the forest, or it will spread."

Trisk thought of the carvings and decorations at the aerie and the strange mist full of spiders up there. If he hadn't seen it, he wouldn't have believed it. Did the trees produce the mist, or did they attract the spiders who did? Perhaps there was a third option.

I am not going back in that cave if the answer is the spiders.

A wind blew in from the north, pushing the mist over the heated river and causing the chimes to ring.

"Why are your trinkets hanging in the lodge?" Trisk asked, but the hippogryph had already turned and was walking back towards the waterfall.

The leader's hooves were coated in something that resonated when he stepped on the white stone. "I'm not here to answer your questions. You can go."

Trisk looked at the designs on the hippogryph's flank and tried to remember the word Njorn had used.

Black-flame. The opposite of cold-bright, the word for kirin.

Trisk spoke in his best imitation of Njorn's dire speech when he said, "Black-flame." When the hippogryph responded to the name, Trisk continued. "What happened to the hunters who came before me?"

One of the antlered opinici shifted uncomfortably, a bracelet of turquoise beads and pretty green eyes catching Trisk's attention. Past her, he could see wooden cages wrapped in northistle like the kind from the bramble near the lodge.

The cages, at least the ones he could see, were empty.

Blackflame's eyes were sad, and he looked through the waterfall at the statue while he spoke. "The *cold-bright* gets us all, one way or another. Leave up the wards. Consider them a gift. She says they're linked to the kirin. She says to depart soon, while you still can."

Trisk didn't know statues could have a gender. He backed away slowly, Yenni following suit, and they waited to unmantle their wings until they were on the other side of the bridge. Several antlered shapes tailed them, but only to the oxbow in the hot river. Once Trisk and Yenni passed it, they were left on their own.

11

OPINICUS
COLDBRIGHT

Night descended upon Trisk and Yenni long before they reached the lodge. The sound of the birds shifted, became deeper, but didn't relent even in the dark of night. Trisk was so used to having four walls around him and being inside before sundown that he hadn't considered the noise never let up.

His mind drifted as they walked. When the stars came out, Yenni had her first experience seeing them for what they were when a moth came too close.

The shadow behind some vibrant, almost-neon blue stars wrapped itself around the moth, paralyzing it with a bite and wrapping it into the web.

Yenni's squeak of alarm and profanity earned a laugh from Trisk.

"That's why we're not flying." He was sympathetic. He remembered his first experience with the arachnids. In the weeks that had passed, however, he'd stopped seeing them as sinister. He wasn't ready to start naming them Cuddles, but as long as the stars remained in the sky, he would give them a pass.

To calm Yenni, however, he began to play basic tunes on the songbird as they walked. At first, it was just little bits of tales he remembered as a kid. As they passed the pond and frozen rapids, the mist picked up.

Almost against his will, he found himself singing Jenell's kirin song.

Keep walking. Stop singing. Move past the cave.

Every opinicus, or at least every opinicus hunter, had an instinct inside of them. No matter how afraid he was, Trisk didn't increase his pace. Prey fled. It drew attention to itself as vulnerable. And that attracted predators.

"Enough with the song, please," Yenni said. "At least until we get past the cave."

Instead of running past the cave, he kept going slowly, keeping his eyes on the rapids. In the darkness, they may not see the cave, but they'd see the cliff they needed to scale to move past it, assuming they didn't walk right into it.

Yet the cave *was* visible. And audible. At first, Trisk thought he was singing again out of habit. But when he reached up a paw, the songbird instrument hung loose around his neck.

Mist poured out of the cave, illuminated by a dull, white light. They slowed, reaching the cliffs illuminated in the strange glow at a crawl.

He and Yenni still wore two of the trinkets from the lodge he'd intended to return to the hippogryphs. He asked her for hers now.

"Why?" she asked. He didn't respond because he didn't know.

To ward off a glowing white crocodile with green eyes? The wilder's hidden god? Maybe just for luck?

He listened to the song from the cave. There were no

words, not that he'd been able to create words with the songbird, but it was definitely the same kind of sound. Were there new chimes inside? Glowing fungus? He hadn't come out at night to know if the cave always made these sounds. Once he was aware of it, he realized the birds had gone silent again, suggesting that it had begun as they approached.

Without entering the cave proper, he stood on the ice outside it, mindful of the crocodile snouts, and hung both of their charms at its entrance.

Perhaps it was a trick of the light, but the glow seemed to dull, as though retreating.

Trisk and Yenni pulled themselves up the cliff face, reaching the most spider-infested section of the Blackwald. They went four steps before the noise of the forest returned, deafening them.

Both opinici broke into a sprint north.

Only prey runs, but it runs because it doesn't want to be eaten.

THE OTHER HUNTERS HAD GONE TO SLEEP WHEN TRISK AND Yenni hit the lodge door, but Jenell was still awake.

Which was a good thing, as they hit the door in the literal sense. They smashed into it, falling back as it didn't give way, then pounded to be let in.

The sound of a barrier being moved slowly came from the other side, then Jenell slid the door open.

"What was that?!" Yenni shouted. "Why did you lock us out?"

Jenell held up her paws to say sorry, her bracelet sliding up past her ankle when she did so. "I apologize.

When you two didn't return, I thought the wilders got you and might be coming for us next."

Trisk would have done the same. He was upset for an entirely different reason. "Jenell, how does a kitcarer get assigned to a hunting mission?"

She shifted uncomfortably. "Really, you're going to degrade my profession because I secured a door? You said you'd been meaning to for weeks and kept forgetting. You didn't complain when I patched up your thistle wounds."

"Nell, the door barrier was a good idea," he said slowly. "But we came out here knowing we'd have to hunt. How did you convince Dire Haynil to assign you to this group?"

Yenni's mind hadn't quite caught up with his. "Why does the *how* matter? Isn't the *why* more important?"

"I know why." Trisk reached out slowly, not grabbing at Jenell's paw, but just lifting it so the bracelet hung limp. "Your mate isn't back at the pridelands. I'd assumed she was a kitcarer like you, but considering that you met out here, I think it's likely she was a hunter. Probably one of the hunters who went missing from the last batch."

Jenell pulled her paw back. "No, she was due to rotate back before then. It just took a while to bribe my way into being sent out here."

"Nobody questioned your name on the list?" Trisk asked. "I would have."

Jenell laughed. "Lord Njorn was the only one who saw the list. He doesn't know opinici. He just assumed it was right."

Njorn, you dumb moose. Why didn't you let me look over the list before we came? Anyone smart would have asked why we had a kitcarer with us.

Trisk sat in silence for a hundred heartbeats, debating

whether or not he should tell her. Finally, he decided that it would be wrong not to.

"An opinicus wearing the matching bracelet is among the wilders," he said at last. "She had brown fur, green markings, and bright green eyes."

No response came. The fire started to die out, and Yenni went to rekindle it. Eventually, Jenell asked what their options were.

"We can rescue her!" Yenni responded.

Trisk shook his head. "Only if she leaves the southern ruins. There were at least thirty wilders, mostly hippogryphs. We can't get in there. And I can't ask any of our hunters to risk their lives. It would be better if we finished hunting and let the others leave first, then the two of us can try to get your mate back."

"Three," Yenni appended. "And did you count the ones on top of the columns? There were another five hippogryphs up there where the statues were missing."

"What happens if she comes with us?" Jenell asked.

Trisk didn't know and said as much. "I guess it depends on what she says and if Njorn will back her up. If we say wilders took her prisoner, it'll go better. But I know you were worried about Dire Haynil wiping out the hippogryphs here, and that will definitely happen if we say she was taken prisoner."

"Did she look mistreated?" Jenell twisted her bracelet.

He couldn't imagine what she was going through, wondering if her mate were alive, finding out she had been here all along. "Not that I saw, other than having to wear some fancy hats."

"There were cages," Yenni protested. "They must have locked up the opinici and brainwashed them into worshipping their weird kirin god. They kept talking to a wet statue."

When the pressure of silence descended upon them again, Yenni pushed a little. "What would you do, Trisk? If you were Nell?"

"I'd find a way to get my mate alone, convince her to come with me, and flee back to the pridelands," he said. "Leave a warning for the hippogryphs and pray they flee before the direlord's wrath comes."

"Do you think they will?" Jenell looked up from her bracelet to see both Yenni and him shaking their heads. "I'm sorry, Trisk. I don't trust Njorn, and I don't want the wilders' blood on my paws, even if they're weird. I'll help you finish up the meat quotas for the aerie gryphons, then I'll talk to my mate. If she's happy, though, I'm going to stay."

"I bow to your wishes. One more missing opinicus isn't going to seem strange." He thought through their options. "We should save up some meat. The quota numbers keep changing, and I think the aerie wants to keep us down here as long as they can. Let's give it a week, stock the butchery full, and put a full shipment's worth on the tower so they have to let us go."

"...Thank you, Trisk. You're not as bad as they say," Jenell replied.

He laughed, then turned serious. "I need to warn you, though, that any group of gryphs who base their lives around something that's not true are going to be danger- ous. Maybe not today, maybe not tomorrow, but I think Blackflame is using the legend of the kirin to keep his fake pride in a state of fear."

"We all believe a lie or two," Jenell said. "That our

dires care about us. That our spirits live on. That the God's Tear created dires."

Yenni sniffed. "Show me a dire who doesn't think they came from the God's Tear and maybe I'll stop believing that one."

"What're you going to tell the other hunters?" Jenell asked Trisk.

He shook his head. "I don't know, but I'll tell them in the morning so you can hear it, too. They need to know about the hippogryphs and the plan to get out of here, but I don't want to spook them, either."

"What'd they say about the boar? Do they think we killed the wilders there?" she asked.

Trisk shrugged. "They weren't really answering my questions. But I didn't get the impression they thought we'd done them harm. They even recommended we keep the trinkets hung."

"What for?" Jenell checked the fire one last time. It was about time for the fire tender change.

"For whatever killed the boar, I guess," Trisk replied, and the three of them climbed up to the attic to sleep.

12

MOOSE
COLDBRIGHT

The next morning, Trisk told his hunters a heavily-edited version of the truth and then a lie.

When it came to the wilders, he told the truth, for the most part—they lived in some lost pride ruins, they wore antlers because they worshipped the kirin, and there were a few opinici among the hippogryph ranks but no dires or gryphons. He also said the wilders were okay with them hunting as long as they didn't go south of the pond.

The lie he told was that the reason he wanted a log kept of the plants and animals here was because they were supposed to leave behind a caretaker to mind the place before the next set of hunters came.

"You've probably been wondering why we brought along a kitcarer," he said while projecting a false confidence. "It's not because you're a bunch of babies, though I see now that all hunting groups need someone to hold their paws and tell them they're special."

There were a few genuine chuckles this time. Despite his terrible leadership, the hunters here had finally started to like him.

Miracles do happen. Praise the kirin. Notify the spirits. Fetch me a fancy hat.

"We're going to leave behind supplies for Kitcarer Jenell, and she's going to finish the log and train the next set of hunters who arrive, then she'll return home. So be sure to thank her before we leave."

Several hunters thanked her immediately. They may chuckle at his jokes, but they genuinely liked her.

She stood and bowed. "Thank you for the well-wishes. Now that you're all feeling so kindly towards me, allow me to sour the mood a little. In order to reach Trisk's goals and force the aerie gryphons to admit their bellies are full, we're going to have to take down the big moose."

Trisk's brain went straight to Njorn, but it turned out while he and Yenni were playing diplomats in the south, Jenell and the hunters had located several moose herds, including one with a bull moose large enough to rival the boar god.

"Hey, fearless leader," Jenell chided him. "Get your head out of the clouds. You and Yenni are a big part of my plan. Go fetch some resin for your paws."

He stood up straight, then his brain caught up with her orders. "Resin... for my paws?"

Jenell grinned. "If you think that part's crazy, wait until you hear the rest of my plan."

THE REASON MOOSE HAD BEEN SO DIFFICULT TO HUNT, Trisk discovered, was because they lived north of the frozen lake in the mountains and only came down to graze in the Blackwald every few days. There was a mark near their favorite grazing patch, but the brook near it had frozen solid.

With some practice, all of the hunters had grown used to flying low along the dry creek, staying below the mist where the screechers awaited them, moving between the sharp shards of obsidian sticking out of the ground.

They'd still have to drag the dead moose back through here, fending off the leathery, noisy birds, but that was a problem for the afternoon. The first step was to take down the bull moose that protected the herd and kept chasing off the hunters.

And that last part was the key to Jenell's plan. The bull, whom Trisk had nicknamed Njorn the Second to the amusement of the others, was dumb and hated opinici. It would chase them for great lengths.

Which was why the hunters had become adept at flying along the dry creek. The beast was too fast to escape by paw.

Jenell led them along the bank of the frozen lake to the trees lining the other forest, stopping right on the edge. "Here, sit down and rub the resin on your paws until you don't slide on the ice. I want you to be able to run and jump, so don't make it too sticky. You need to be able to get airborne."

While Trisk rubbed the nasty, gritty resin on his paws, Jenell continued her plan.

"The bull usually shows up after we've killed two or three of the smaller moose. When that happens, I want you here to shake your tail at Njorn II to get his attention. Then lead him onto the ice."

Trisk looked out at the frozen lake. "Is that wise, considering our... friend? Won't he mess up your plan?"

"Our fish friend IS the plan," Jenell grinned. "Let the

dragon-fish wear out the moose, then go in for the kill. Once he's down, I'll lure the fish away from the kill while you drag it to shore. He seems to like my plumage."

To prove her point, she flew over the lake until a dark shape appeared beneath it, and she lured the fish to the northern edge of the lake. Trisk made a mental note of where the fish stopped. Presumably the last stretch of ice from there to the shore was solid, and that was the end of the liquid water.

"Okay. Let's do this. Yenni, don't go near the center of the lake. The ice is... thin." Trisk didn't know why he lied. Maybe he didn't want opinici inspecting the frozen sink-hole. Maybe he had just had enough weirdness and wanted to leave. He wondered if Jenell had told the other hunters. Nothing on their faces suggested they knew.

Trisk let Yenni chase him around the ice, making sure they both had traction. Once they were good, they gave the signal, and Jenell led the hunters into the mountain forest to hunt moose.

It only took sitting down to realize they'd forgotten something in their plan. Running across ice was fun. Sitting on ice was very cold.

He called to Yenni, and they pulled a downed log onto the ice. It was from the mountains and wasn't black heart-wood—he didn't want spiders crawling on him—and they watched the shore.

For all their teasing about Jenell being a kitcarer, she was incredibly adept at organizing other gryphs. The first dead moose had been dragged out of the forest by half-mark, and by the full mark, they'd killed four young bulls.

Blackflame said to only kill what we could eat. I wonder how far north he can see.

By the time the fourth bull touched the edge of the ice,

a cry unlike anything Trisk had ever heard emitted from the tree line. It looked like one of the trees had taken a step forward, and Trisk's brain needed a moment to realize he was seeing a moose.

Jenell's hunters fled into the sky south, leaving just Yenni and Trisk on the ice in front of the beast.

"Well, shake your tail!" Yenni said as she pushed him off the log and towards Njorn II.

While Trisk's tail did swish to and fro, he mostly stood on his back paws and spread his wings to get the beast's attention.

Just as he worried his grey plumage and black markings might make him hard to see or that the moose might be wary of the ice, Njorn II lowered its head and charged.

Trisk turned and ran—*only prey run*—and made a break for where he'd last seen the fish.

Despite the resin, his paws kept losing traction. When Njorn II first caught up with him, he was barely able to leap into the air, pushing off of the giant antlers and getting behind the moose.

While Njorn II's hooves gave it surprisingly good traction while charging, they didn't do much to let it turn or slow down, and it went sliding past Trisk.

Yenni caught its attention and kept it running after her while Trisk caught his breath. She flew into the air much earlier than he had, and the moose didn't slip this time, instead altering its course slightly to come at Trisk.

Trisk fled, wishing he'd put twice the coating on his paws. To his relief, the dark shape under the ice was coming straight at him from the front. Unfortunately, Njorn II was coming at him from the rear, and he didn't know which would reach him first.

Against his smarter judgement, Trisk held his course,

charging the fish's shadow. It disappeared for a moment, diving down, and Trisk had visions of the sturgeon knocking him *into* the moose.

Here lies Trisk. He died like he lived, shaking his tail at a dumb moose named Njorn.

Just before the bull caught Trisk, the dark shape rose up and slammed into the icy surface.

If the fish had just bounced Jenell towards the sink-hole, what it did to the moose was complete destruction.

A moose large enough to make a dire feel insecure about their height flew twenty feet through the air back towards shore, landing on the sitting log and splitting it in two.

Trisk and Yenni were both too stunned to do anything. Only the disappearance of the dark shape under the ice reminded them to get airborne so they didn't repeat 'The Last Flight of Njorn II.'

Jenell and her hunters were ready, and they descended upon the bull moose before it recovered from its fall. Its neck was massive, and four different opinici all went straight for the jugular with a series of surgical strikes, then backed off while it bled out.

From the end of the liquid water under the ice, the fish watched, seething as the opinici stole its meal.

Jenell and the other hunters flew north and began to drag the four smaller moose carcasses along the bank towards the Blackwald.

Trisk found a safe, warm spot to sit and watched as Njorn II's blood blossomed across the lake's surface. He couldn't believe opinici so small had killed something so large. It would take them a day to process the meat, because the other moose weren't small, either. This would finish off their quota.

"Do you mind watching the bull?" Jenell asked, seeing him already doing so. "This works better if four of us drag a moose carcass while three defend it from screechers, and we go one at a time. I just don't want wolves stealing the other kills, so it would be nice to have someone watching."

Trisk blinked. "Wolves?"

"Timber wolves," she confirmed. "Small things that are too skittish to enter the Blackwald, but happy enough to chew on a dead moose. We'll be back in two marks."

"Sure. I'll stand guard," Trisk said. But once the hunters disappeared from view, he took a look at the center of the frozen lake. This might be his last chance to get a look at the frozen runes.

He found Jenell's bag on the log and took out a healthy dose of the resin, coating his paw pads until they stuck to the ice.

No slipping this time.

TRISK WANDERED THE LAKE EDGE, OUT OF SIGHT OF THE sturgeon, then approached the frozen sinkhole from the north. While the resin on his paws felt terrible, it finally gave him an opportunity to land by the runes and look them over.

He circled the pit first, but the mist obscured his vision, and he wasn't willing to fly down into it. He had more sense than that.

The sun away from the Blackwald was brighter, though still fuzzy under the mist, but it turned the scratched ice around the pit into one white glare. He had trouble sticking his landing, the ground arriving faster than his paws expected. He crawled to the edge and began to inspect the rune.

And it was just one, single rune repeated several times, the same one he'd seen on the wilder trinkets: *coldbright.* Kirin.

Something about seeing it naked without the antlers or other adornments the wilders used raised his hackles, but he wasn't sure why that would be. It was just a word.

Words can be dangerous.

He thought back to Yenni's admission that she'd seen a lot of the old language as a messenger, and how nervous that made the other hunters. Dires killed the undired who tried to learn their secrets. The fact that Njorn had told him both the words for kirin and dragon was a testament to how much he trusted Trisk.

The opinicus looked up at the aerie. Was Njorn the First okay? Trisk missed him.

Several dark shapes were gliding down from the aerie to the frozen lake.

Gryphons.

Trisk swore. He had no chance to get back to the shoreline to hide. Nor was he about to hop down the giant hole.

He decided to trust his plumage. He tucked his legs and tail in, kept his wings close to his side, and prayed the glare would keep anyone from seeing him.

The gryphons seemed more interested in using ropes to carry crates towards the sinkhole. If Trisk was curious what was in those crates, he didn't have to wonder long. The one that flew right over him still had dragonfly stains. It was the same one he'd hid under to get a word with Njorn. It didn't look like they'd opened it, either, just removed the dead screecher off the top.

It was a genius solution, which is why he was so surprised a gryphon had thought of it. The frozen water would keep even the perishable foods from going bad, and the mist hid the supplies from anyone from the pridelands who came snooping.

Five gryphons flew the crate in, led by Cerris. Trisk sat still, waiting until they exited. Once they'd flown past his position, he counted to make sure all of them had left.

Time to sneak.

Now that he knew it was just some dishonest aerie gryphons hiding food, he wasn't afraid to go down into the darkness. He'd never seen a gryphon half as brave as an opinicus. And he should still have half a mark before Jenell got back.

With a quick flight to check that nothing was sniffing at his moose, he slowly glided down past the mist.

WHILE THE ENTIRE IDEA OF A SINKHOLE WAS THAT IT WENT deep, it didn't occur to Trisk that this flash-frozen abyss might reach to the bottom of the lake. Especially considering what he knew about there being some liquid water around.

And yet, when he set his paws on the damp ground, he felt rocks and not ice. He picked up one of the lake stones, feeling its smooth texture against his paws. The light through the mist, the light through the ice, made shadows dance across the depths. The pattern of the shadows so closely matched the fossilized coral pattern he'd seen on other lake rocks that he didn't realize at first that what he was holding was a bright, patternless white.

He looked through a few of them at his feet, trying to

find the perfect stone to add to his collection. He slipped a paw-sized lake stone into his pouch before exploring further.

Hopefully, it turns out to be valuable.

Frozen caves had been carved into the ice in several directions, giving Trisk an uneasy feeling. If he knew one thing about staying dry, it's that you didn't start carving into the ice walls. That seemed like a great way to drown and freeze to death at the same time.

He couldn't get a good look at where the ice tunnels went because each one had a crate blocking the view. Down at the bottom, several boxes had broken open.

Must not be easy to fly one of those down a hole in the ice. You think they'd clean up after themselves, though.

He located the dragonfly-stained crate and sniffed at it, confirming it smelled like the salt and spices Jenell had used to preserve the meat. This was definitely where the missing crates were going. He even found a few with star patterns in red, blue, and green paint—likely relocated out of the dire cave when Njorn arrived.

The only thing he didn't know was why they were hiding so much food. They had to know the dires would come asking questions. What was their endgame?

His time before Jenell returned was running out, but Trisk flew over to the crates on the ground and found the remains of several smashed to bits after their food was eaten, which felt like a waste considering how hard it was to get good crates out in the aeries.

If someone were eating the food, though, it raised a possibility he couldn't ignore. He knew the wilders had a few cages, but it was possible the missing opinici were held here, too.

The bottom of the sinkhole had a large passage that went south.

Trisk did not go in that passage. He was not about to go under the liquid water of the lake. It could go straight back to the lodge, and he would not walk it.

Instead, he found a slightly higher passage where the ice looked solid and the crate didn't fully block his way in. He crawled over the box, and in the dimmest light he could see in, he walked back and looked for signs that someone was being held here.

It quickly became too dark to see anything, but he made a few chirps and nothing responded. He reached up and tapped the ice. To his reassurance, it was frozen so solid, he couldn't scratch any of it away with his claws.

Most likely a trick of his imagination, the cave grew brighter when he tapped. Several massive lake stones practically seemed to glow white. When he crawled back over the crate to the sinkhole proper, the caverns were clear as day. The mist, too, was slightly luminescent.

Guess the sun finally came out, or that dark passage let my eyes adjust.

With his newfound vision, he saw something glinting on the lake bottom. Against his better judgement, he flew down and picked it up. It was some sort of aerie medal. He didn't know the name, but the style denoted the leader of an aerie—and under it, he saw several bones.

The top bones seemed to belong to the aerie's previous gryphon leader, but the others had feline forepaws like his own. Suddenly, the frozen sinkhole in the ground where Cerris and Temperance were dumping their bodies didn't seem quite as safe as it had a minute ago.

Trisk pocketed the medal, then got a running start by

going around in a circle and kicking off the crates, beating his aching wings to get out of the hole and pausing on the ledge. He didn't see any gryphons, so he made his way back to the moose just in time to shoo away a lone timber wolf that had started gnawing on Njorn II's ankles.

Tomorrow, we leave. Tomorrow, I tell Njorn, and he comes back with an army to stop these murderers. I just need to make it one more day.

13

DEPARTURE
COLDBRIGHT

Processing so many dead moose was a chore none of them would forget. While Jenell's plan was to take a few days to clean them, it turned out that the earlier moose kills filled the butchery, forcing them to leave the bull outside while they hurried to make room for more.

Trisk and Yenni took turns standing guard. The idea was to keep the screechers off of it, because with the song of the forest, no one inside would hear if the moose guard outside called for help.

And, in fact, Trisk finally received confirmation that there were screechers in the mist above the lodge when a pale one swooped down, trying to nibble on the bull moose.

Trisk leapt out from under the overhang and killed the screecher. Then he used its impressive wingspan to cover most of Njorn II.

It took two more screechers coming down to nibble before he could create a white, leathery umbrella atop the moose comprehensive enough to keep others from spotting it.

How do the screechers see out of the mist? I was blind in it.

Questions for another time. With all of this meat brought up at once, Njorn the First would declare the hunt over, they could evacuate, and they could send in reinforcements to arrest Cerris and Temperance.

He'd explain to Njorn that Jenell had wanted to stay to document some sightings. She'd disappear to be with her wilder wife, so she'd be away from the reach of the aerie gryphons. The next batch of hunters would assume she'd just disappeared. And, hopefully, Trisk could convince Njorn about the bones in the frozen lake without Njorn requiring them to actually *go there*.

Trisk pulled out the badge from the lake and gave it a look over. He wished he knew the name of the aerie's old leader. The fancy metalwork told him all he needed, however. It must have belonged to someone important. He put it away and went back to watching the moose.

Were his plans great? No. They were mediocre at best. But they made Jenell happy, and they got Trisk and the other hunters out of here alive and unmurdered.

The boredom of watching a moose covered in dead screechers gave his mind a lot of time to consider how things could go wrong. If the wilders saw the hunters had taken months worth of moose carcasses out of the Blackwald, they might get angry. The aerie gryphons could decide they were better off killing Njorn and the opinici immediately and then fleeing into the night, though that seemed unlikely when Njorn and Trisk wanted to leave more than anything, and a gryph would have to be completely insane to challenge a dire.

Then, of course, there was the Blackwald itself, whose mysteries and horrors seemed to complicate the most simple of Trisk's plans with green-eyed monsters, boars, or vampiric deer.

The dull, afternoon light played across the soft grass, a stark contrast to his nerves. He had grown complacent here. The constellation spiders, the screechers, even the hate-fish large enough to devour gryphs. He felt... not *at ease*, but more *at ease with his unease,* if that made sense.

It does not.

He reached into his pack and pushed past the medal, looking for a soft lake stone to worry his paws against. Now that he had it out in the daylight, he thought he might be wrong about its origins. It didn't look at all like the fossilized coral Kristel's pride often wanted to trade to Dire Haynil.

Its grey-white texture came off in his resin-soaked paws. It felt softer than most rocks he knew, except perhaps calcium. Trisk didn't know much about minerals, but it was easier to steal a few valuable gemstones than most other things he could trade, so he had some hidden away in his packs to sell later.

The lodge door opened, and Yenni came out.

"Time to switch moose guards?" he asked, pretending not to be panicking.

Can we lock the tower doors to keep the gryphons from sneaking down them? Would that raise suspicions?

She shook her head. "I don't think we have energy to finish the last moose tonight, but we've made enough room to bring it inside. Are those... dead screechers?"

"Sure are!" He stood and stretched his paws, slipping the lake stone into his pack. "Seems they like the taste of moose. Alright, let's get this one inside."

ONCE THEY WERE SURE NO ONE WOULD STEAL THEIR KILL, Jenell gave the hunters some time off to relax. With their departure in sight, the orange opinicus took each gryph to leave their paw prints behind on the wall, and Yenni decided to take the last of their plant and berry supplies to roast the screecher wings as a final treat.

With everything in order, Trisk met Jenell outside the lodge door. "It's time to see if the wilders will take you."

"Or if they'll let my mate go," Jenell added. "I've always known wilders to be reasonable when there aren't gryphons around."

"I don't think these are normal wilders." When he reached the edge of the grass and took his first step onto the hard, compacted leaves caused by the hunters, the extra resin coating he'd put on before going into the sink-hole stuck his feet stuck to them. He shook a paw, trying to dislodge a leaf.

Jenell laughed. "Do you want to go back and wash your paws at the fountain?"

"No, I'm fine." He gritted his beak and kept walking, ignoring the things sticking to him. "It's going to be dark before we get back anyways. Let's just... see if we can fly to the pond."

Perhaps as a kindness for their final days, the mist was high enough that the bottom of the canopy was visible, and they were able to reach the pond before they had to return to walking.

"Now that we're away from the camp, is there a reason you wanted me to leave early?" she asked. Whether she was a mind reader or just noticed his nervous tics, he couldn't say, but he explained what he'd seen at the bottom of the lake interspersed with Njorn's comments on the old aerie leader's journal.

Jenell's eyes grew ever wider. "So the old leader went to find out what was killing the opinicus hunters, and Cerris killed him and dumped his body, then they started stealing food and hiding it? But... why?"

"I have no idea," Trisk admitted. "Maybe they planned to leave before now, or they're waiting on another pride to attack. Caslir or Caranel could hide an army in the wald."

Jenell snorted. "Njorn's arrival tossed a rabid ferret on those plans. When we reach the wilders, I can ask my mate what happened. She might be able to fill in some gaps before you return."

They continued on a while longer in silence, the weight of their situation settling in. When they passed by some old hunting marks, Trisk changed the subject by wondering aloud what their purpose had been and asking Jenell about it.

"Water, maybe?" she suggested when they stopped to drink. "We found water by most of them, which led us to prey."

"Could be prey. I don't remember water near the screecher nests, but they were clearly marked." He thought back to the broken pottery and the boar. The hippogryphs had been feeding it, up until something had taken a fatal bite out of the beast. "Did you find pottery at the other sites?"

She tapped her beak. "At a few of them. And the water was marked with trinkets once we knew to look for them. The deer herd had a favorite watering hole; we found pottery there. Same with the moose and screechers. You think the wilders were encouraging the meaner animals to set up camp where there was water? That seems silly."

He shrugged. Without going deep into the bramble to find out if his nares were right about there being water there, he had no way of testing his theory. He didn't think the wilders would give him a straight answer.

Though when he remembered the stone gryphon statue had been covered in antler trinkets when they first arrived, it helped reinforced his water theory. He wondered what had happened to those trinkets after Yenni pulled the lever.

Down the drain, I suppose.

Already familiar with the correct path, they made better time going to the southern wald than the previous time he'd come here with Yenni. There were even a few spots where he and Jenell could glide, though twice on their journey, the Blackwald turned silent, and they stepped off the path to hide until the sound resumed.

"I wish I knew why that happened," Jenell said. "It wasn't like this when we first got here."

He tossed his head, catching the birdsong instrument in his mouth to play a few notes. "It all started when I played your kirin song for the crocs. I thought it sounded like the chimes, but the chimes were smashed."

"And you call the wilders superstitious." She rolled her eyes.

He grinned. "Do you think I'd look good with a pair of antlers? I mean, we have all of those moose... no sense letting their horns go to waste, right?"

"I think deer antlers are more your size," she started to say, but she paused when they saw more hunting marks on the trees. Or, rather, a hunting mark that had been scratched out. "What do you think this means?"

"They scratched out the boar glyph when it died. Do you think they're hunting down the large beasts?" He put his paw on the glyph. "I know we're short on time, but can we look now, while we have a little light?"

She nodded, and they stalked through the woods, checking for indications of animals or wilders. They'd only gone thirty feet when they discovered signs of a struggle. Branches had been snapped, heartwood saplings broken into pieces, and dried blood decorated the glade.

A chunk of obsidian as thick as the lodge's tower stuck out of a small pond. A nest of moose and deer bones had been smashed to the ground nearby, leaving Trisk to wonder if the mess had fallen from atop the obsidian.

The nest had belonged to a screecher. At least, that's what he assumed. His evidence was a detached wing leaking blood into the water. The rest of the screecher, which could have eaten a hippogryph in one bite, seemed to have disappeared into a hole spewing out misty water.

The ground had been torn up around the area where the river came out of the ground and spilled into the glade, as though something monstrous had clawed its way into the cave.

Or out of it, Trisk thought with a nod to the large green eyes near the crocodile rapids.

"Did the wilders do this?" Jenell asked. "Did hippogryphs do this?"

Trisk looked at the nest. In addition to bones, antlers of all sorts had been used like twigs to construct it. Congealed yolk filled in the gaps.

Without thinking, he pulled the lake stone from his pouch and began worrying it with his claws and paw pads. It was oddly relaxing amid the chaos.

"We need to get back on the trail south," he said at last. "It'll be dark soon, and I don't want to be in the thick forest when the spiders come out."

The branches above them rustled, and both opinici crouched. It wasn't more screechers, however. It was hippogryphs wearing antlers who dove down and landed before the hunters.

"I asked you to leave." Blackflame stomped a hoof against a shard of broken obsidian, a sound that cut through the din almost as well as Trisk's instrument had. In the trees around them, at least twenty hunters came out of hiding in a circle around the screecher's wing.

Jenell held up her paw with the bracelet. "I've come to speak to my wife, and I'd like to ask about joining if she isn't willing to leave."

The hippogryph leader considered her. As the sun descended, his smoky fur disappeared into the darkness while his fiery reds shone.

"She's here of her own free will," Blackflame said. "She hoped you would not come, but since you are here, you may see her. Your friend, however, must leave."

Trisk started to protest, but Jenell cut him off. "I'll be fine. Go back to the lodge; get everyone home."

He frowned, but if this was what she wanted, that was her choice. He started to try to get some answers from Blackflame before they forced him north when he realized that it wasn't just the hippogryphs who were glowing. He was emitting a dull, grey light as well, or at least his pack was.

He opened it and pulled out the stone fragment. Then he looked back and could see where he'd tracked dust from the soft stone everywhere he'd stepped, courtesy of the resin.

Blackflame reared back, kicking the stone out of Trisk's paws and into the stone obelisk, where it broke. Two more hippogryphs grabbed him and shoved his paw into the water, nearly drowning him and scrubbing his paw pads off trying to remove the white glow. He recognized the purple-maned hippogryph holding his head underwater from the oxbow.

"Where did you find that?" Blackflame shouted at Trisk. "Where did you get the kirin egg?"

Trisk splashed to keep his head above water. "It's not a kirin egg, you superstitious wilder. It's just a rock from the lake."

He could see where they'd get that impression. The soft calcium probably tasted a little like eggshell. But he hadn't stolen their silly kirin's eggs.

The mountains blocked the last of the sun, and the effect was like an eclipse. The canopy lit up with spiders, and the markings on the flanks of the hippogryphs made it look like the entire world was a web.

The screecher wing sat on the ground, forgotten, but the mist rolled out of the churned ground and left a white glow along the water's edge.

"Go," Blackflame said. "Leave!"

Trisk tensed. "May I get a guide back to the trail?"

Their leader turned and walked away, but one of the spider-patterned wilder opinici spoke out. "Follow your paw prints."

Sure enough, Trisk's resin-and-eggshell paw prints showed the path he'd taken through the woods.

He thanked the wilder and backtracked. While the canopy stars trapped moths, he resisted the urge to panic when he saw a star pattern on the ground. Wilders were gathering at the obsidian nest, and he now put their numbers closer to fifty.

It's like a real pride here.

14

FRIENDSHIP
COLDBRIGHT

T risk followed his steps home, reassuring himself that Jenell would be fine with the wilders, perhaps even safer than he was going to be tomorrow around the aerie gryphons. He wished he knew what her wife was telling her, but once he and the rest of his hunters were under Njorn's protection, they should be safe.

His glowing paw path stretched ahead, disappearing in the mists, guiding him home. Occasionally, he'd find long stretches where he and Jenell had been able to glide, but he remembered the route well enough to find his way again.

He dared not repeat the flight in the dark. He could see now how low some spiders built their webs, and he wondered how he hadn't smashed into any on his way down.

The path back began to look better-traveled, and he knew he was approaching the pond. Still, he was surprised when he broke through a tangle of blueberry bushes and was greeted with the white glow of mist on the water and several dead crocodiles.

He gave the glowing water a wide berth. While it had been the smaller crocodiles who had hidden in the reeds and harassed his hunters dragging kills back to the lodge, the bodies left floating in the pond were large enough to eat gryphons.

Were those always just beneath the surface, waiting? I'm surprised we didn't lose anyone. Those must be what the wilders are calling kirin.

Unlike the mist in the air, the fog floating on the river was thicker and it wasn't cool, it was downright frigid. Against his better judgement, he passed a paw through it and came back with a coating of rime.

As he approached the climb and the river cave, he slunk down, belly brushing the forest floor. The light coming out of the cave was bright, and staring at it messed with his night vision, turning the rest of the forest an unpierceable black.

He didn't look away, but he crawled around to the side so he wasn't facing directly into the cave. On the ground on either side of the entrance, below where he and Yenni had hung them on their way back from seeing the wilders the first time, were two smashed trinkets.

He climbed around and above the cave and looked back, seeing the glowing river snake its way through the middle of the Blackwald. He continued on the path, pausing a few times when a dull glow spilled out from the woods, always near the hunting marks left by their predecessors. Each denoted a place where water burst through the surface, but it unnerved him that all of them were glowing.

There were no paw prints from the lodge to the cliffs, but neither were there the carefully-curated blue spiders. He saw a few glistening as they hid, and in the light of the mist near a side trail, he could see tattered and torn webs drifting in the cool night air, as though something large had flown through them.

Just when Trisk'd had enough of the oppressive darkness, he saw his paw prints in the springy grass ahead, along with where he'd tried to wipe his paw on a tree. Something had come by and scratched it off, possibly wilders angry at his 'egg' theft.

He hastened to the cabin, alarmed his glowing paw prints continued all the way north to where they killed the moose, and smacked the door with his paw harder than he'd intended. Nobody opened up, so he hit a few more times, then started shouting that it was him.

The door opened a crack and Yenni peeked out. "Oh! It really is him! Let him in!"

Three pairs of paws pulled him inside, whereupon they closed the door and began to secure it shut again according to Jenell's recommendations.

"Where's Nell?" the orange opinicus asked, worry tracing strange patterns in his facial feathers.

Trisk was too tired to lie. "She found out her wife was with the wilders and asked them if she could stay. They said yes."

The hunters looked amongst themselves.

"Is that... safe?" Yenni asked.

He looked around and saw just how spooked the hunters were, worse than their first day here. "Why wouldn't it be? Did something happen?"

The orange opinicus cleared his throat. "Something tried to break in."

"A boar?" Trisk suggested, hoping they weren't going to say gryphons, but they shook their heads. "Bigger?"

Yenni pointed to the door. Trisk turned, but he didn't see what they were getting at. The door itself seemed solid. Really, it was a testament to the skill of craftsgryphs across the pridelands.

Then he noticed the damaged walls. Something had hit the front door so hard that the walls around it had cracked. That didn't seem like murderous aerie gryphons, which only made him feel a little better.

Still, we are definitely barricading the tower door tonight.

He stood on Yenni and the orange opinicus to get a better look at the cracks, and he discovered something else surprising—there was evidence the support beams had been destroyed several times before now. Places where they'd been broken, fixed, and now hung broken again. But also places where clearly the structure had been smashed in the past but had been reinforced and held this time.

His mind made the calculations. The other lodge had burned, so if he was wrong about that being wilders and it had been Temperance, his group of hunters were in trouble. It could also have been an actual wyvern, though the only evidence he had of that was the toothy bite marks in the large boar, which his instincts said weren't made by a beak.

Though now that I know how big the crocodiles grow, maybe they were the culprit. Wyverns aren't exactly subtle, either. We'd have found their warrens by now if it was them.

"Two opinici watch the door. Find hides or blankets, let the fire in the main fireplace die out, it's producing too much smoke," he ordered. "Everyone else, grab your nests and move them to the butchery. Barricade the tower door, but not so much that we can't get it open in an emergency.

Nothing is going to get in here, but if it does, we're going out the tower."

Yenni raised a wing, waiting for him to call on her before speaking. "The butchery is full of crates of moose meat. There isn't room for us to sleep there."

"Right, the moose. We left it outside for marks." Trisk relaxed, only now realizing he'd been worried that if aerie gryphons were coming for him, that meant something had happened to Njorn. "No wonder you had predators banging on the door. We should have cleaned up outside, covered the scent."

"So it's not spirits?" Yenni asked.

Trisk blinked. "Did you think it was ghosts? That smashed into the door? I thought ghosts could walk through walls."

"Wyvern ghosts can't pass through walls," a blue opinicus explained. "Only opinicus ghosts can do that."

Ah, that was my mistake. Only living wyverns need warrens. It all makes sense.

Trisk leapt atop a pile of cushions so everyone could see him. "I don't know what tried to get in here to steal our moose, but it wasn't a ghost. That said, because I know that wyvern ghosts are a concern, we're going to drag the crates of sealed moose up the tower, then sleep in the butchery. Sound good?"

The orange opinicus took a cue from Yenni and raised a wing and waited to be called on. "Are the crates going to keep screechers from stealing the food? I don't want to have to stay and hunt more."

"Check the lids, then use the last of Jenell's resin to seal them shut if we need to." Trisk picked out which two opinici were on door duty and went to fetch his nest and fly it down, then he led the efforts to pull the crates up the tower.

It took them several marks to finish because they had to process the bull moose first, but five sweaty opinici collapsed on the empty stone floor, panting.

"Can we light the kitchen fire?" Yenni asked. "It's going to get cold in here after I bathe."

The blue opinicus looked up from his panting. "How do you have energy to wash? I'm going to drag my nest in here, fall asleep, and just deal with being sticky in the morning."

"Have you been bathing in the fountain?" Trisk asked. He'd been using the pond, though had he known how big the crocodiles got, he would have looked into other options.

"Sure, the basin is bigger than it looks." Yenni reached up for the lever and everyone tensed, only relaxing when she pulled it into the top location and not all the way down.

The aqueduct made its angry, stuttering groan, and water filled the basin. From the same place as the liquid, however, came a freezing mist.

"Shut it off!" Trisk swore, but it was too late. Even with the lever pushed back to the closed position, the mist filled the room.

He shoved the opinici back to the main hall, grabbing the few nests they'd pulled into the butchery, and shut the door.

"Everything okay?" one of the two guards asked.

"Did something happen in the kitchen?" the other said upon seeing Yenni coated in frost.

Trisk sighed. "New plan. We're all sleeping in the main

hall. We'll watch the door together. And someone relight the fire before Yenni freezes to death."

Well, Trisk thought, *at least tonight can't get any worse.*

TRISK HAD A COMMON BELIEF ABOUT WEIRD THINGS ON hunting trips. He believed that, for each weird happenstance, it was allowed to occur exactly once.

If he went to catch a squirrel who had fled into a den, reached inside, and that den was actually full of writhing snakes, that was weird. And he would, of course, be very careful about reaching into random holes in trees after squirrels in the future, but he wouldn't expect to have the exact same thing happen on that same hunting trip.

Once a hunting trip was done, then it became okay for snakes to happen again, because the hunters could go, "Oh, haha, that happened to me, too, a few fractures back! What a coincidence."

That is to say that when Trisk went to sleep in the great hall of the lodge surrounded by six other opinici, when he put rotating groups of two to watch the door, he was not expecting anything to actually try to break in. It had already happened once while he was out walking back from the wilders. For it to happen twice would upgrade its status from *weird* to *unbelievable,* and unbelievable things did not generally happen to him.

Thus, when something pounded on the door in the marks between the middle of the night and morning, he did not share the panic of his fellow opinici, several of which screamed and two of which leapt into a nest together to hide—their differently-colored plumage would have appeared the same to a prey animal.

No, for whatever had attacked the lodge earlier to return was unbelievable. And he doubted Temperance would come from the forest and not the tower. So while his hunters panicked, he walked towards the door and listened, and what he heard was...

Jenell.

"Don't open it!" Yenni shouted.

Part of Trisk's brain knew she could be giving him the correct advice, but he opened it anyways, allowing Jenell and twenty hippogryphs entry.

Weird, he thought. He'd originally suggested the barriers to keep out wilders, yet with the sound of Jenell's voice, he had opened the door and let them all inside.

It was a tight fit with the antlers. His hunters were afraid even though they were relieved to see Jenell.

"You need to get out of here tonight," she commanded them. "Don't go by the aerie. Head straight back."

Trisk tensed, and his veil slipped ever so slightly. "I'm not going without Njorn."

"Then circle back once the hunters in your charge are past the mountains." Jenell wove through the bodies to the door to the butchery. "But the gryphons are going to kill you and feed you to the kirin's brood. And they've probably already done the same to Njorn."

Trisk had never seen Jenell like this, and he didn't trust any of kirin talk. "Brood? Now it's lots of tiny monsters? The kirin isn't real, you said so yourself. And no aerie would kill a dire. That's insane."

"I don't think it is." Jenell had trouble opening the door, which was stuck. "It's been bothering me. Why do any of this knowing that eventually, Haynil would send a dire to investigate? I think that *is* their plan. I think they knew if enough hunters disappeared, eventually a lone dire would be sent here. And if they sent his escort down into the Blackwald, they could find a way to poison or kill him while he slept. Killing a dire and feeding him to the kirin has been their goal from the start, and Njorn has been alone up there for weeks with them."

Trisk's decision would have been very different if there were not thirty hippogryphs staring him down. "Fine. I'll get the hunters past the mountains, but then I'm going to check on Njorn."

He moved next to Jenell, and together they pulled, snapping the door free from the ice on the other side holding it shut.

Cold, wet mist flooded into the great hall. Before it extinguished the fire, Trisk got a good look at the stone gryphon fountain. Rather, he got a good look at the hole in the wall where the statue had been. Something had tried to burrow out of it, reducing it to rubble. The stone floor of the room was flooded, but the water had turned to ice.

A sound came from the hole in the wall. Not the huffing of a boar. Not the growl-chirp of a crocodile. No, it was a song.

Jenell swore. "We're going to the wilder camp. That's the only safe place."

The hunters, having spent years listening to Njorn tell them that wilders and especially hippogryphs were brutes, protested. Yenni the loudest.

The hippogryphs, content to let Jenell do the talking before now, hit their limit.

"Then you're our prisoners," the purple hippogryph said, and to make his point he pulled out some rope. "I'm sorry, Jenell, we don't have time for this."

Within moments, each opinicus hunter had a rope

tied around their neck and was led out of the lodge and into the night. The hippogryphs didn't bother closing the kitchen door. They didn't bother closing the lodge door, either, and the glowing mist seeped out into the night, illuminating the grove.

15

WATERFALL
COLDBRIGHT

Trisk's paws did not appreciate making the walk down the Blackwald a second time. The slack on the rope was long enough that they were able to glide through several sections. When the hippogryphs reached the drop off to the glowing river, they backtracked and took a path invisible to Trisk that bypassed it.

In fact, there were many detours. Sections of the forest were full of glowing mist, and it was like walking from day to night to day again as they passed the brightness.

Rarely, they reached a marker and the hippogryphs would call out for more of their own kind. It seemed the wilders were in retreat, and whatever their plan had been at the obsidian screecher nest, it had been abandoned marks ago.

During one of these side trips, Trisk managed to work the songbird's leather strap up through the ropes and give the instrument to Yenni. It was a long shot—Yenni liked Jenell, she might betray him—but he knew once they reached the wilder camp, Jenell would take the instrument from him.

Every so often, they came across the body of a dead wilder. Most looked like they'd been killed by frightened wildlife, but two had clearly been taken apart slowly.

Trisk shivered. Jenell may think this had been monsters, but he saw the cruelty of gryphons in the carnage.

Did any of the bones in the pit belong to hippogryphs?

Despite knowing that a small cage awaited him at the end of the Blackwald, he felt a sense of relief when they reached the heated river and its oxbow hippogryph statue. Right now, he'd rather be with wilders than gryphons. For many of the hunters, this was their first time seeing the ruins, and they were impressed. While they watched the columns, Trisk looked at the mist.

It was closer to the ground than previous nights, but the steam held it back.

They finally crossed the stone bridge into the wilder camp. The canals and aqueducts around the refuge boiled. Trisk winced as a drop of hot water splattered against his fur.

It's a good thing we had a nice, long walk first. Going from the mist in the lodge to this place's heat could stop even a dire's heart.

Blackflame stood in front of the waterfall, the statue of the giant hippogryph behind him loomed even larger than Trisk remembered from their previous visit. Small hippogryphs carefully adjusted the stones around the aqueduct to make sure the water kept flowing.

"I thought you didn't want me here," Trisk snapped as he was led into the circle.

Blackflame looked down at him. "It's not personal, except that I'm trying to save your life. You're going in the cage until morning, then we'll help you find a way out of the Blackwald. But be warned: the kirin has your scent now."

Trisk didn't appreciate being stuffed into a small cage, but at least his cage was next to Yenni's. She curled up, paws under her body, and sat very still. Only hippogryphs were allowed to guard the cages, and the few wilder opinici gathered on the other side of the camp. Next to Jenell was her green-and-brown mate with her matching bracelet, and they talked back and forth quietly.

I suppose it's too much to hope they're planning to unlock our cages after the hippogryphs go to sleep.

Dawn came both slower and faster than Trisk expected. A false dawn came quickly as the mists consumed the rest of the Blackwald, their blinding incandescence breaking through the steam where the cold could not. The hippogryphs, while not friendly towards the hunters, were unfazed by the brightness.

The heat from the boiling waterfall wore on Trisk, preventing him from sleeping. He entered a dream-like state where he heard the song of the kirin. He begged for cool water, but the guards shook their heads.

He only saw their resolve soften once, when the forest went silent, and the shadow of a long, antlered shape wove around the outside of their camp. It opened a snout full of teeth before the hippogryphs increased the waterflow, then disappeared.

I must be hallucinating, he thought. *That can't have been real.*

Yenni looked over to Trisk in a panic, but he shook his head.

Not yet. Save it for the real monsters.

When true dawn came, he didn't notice at first. The air around them was so bright, he didn't realize it was day until he looked up and saw that the mist above was refracting the light of a blue sky now.

Tentatively, the mists retreated, the hippogryphs closed off portions of the hot springs feeding the wall of steam, the temperature in the cages became tolerable, and birds began to sing again. For the first time since Trisk had set paw in the Blackwald, the birds sounded like normal birds. Their chirps were ever-present but not overwhelming.

"So do we get to leave the cage now?" Trisk coughed out when Blackflame walked by. "You said we could go once your monster left."

The black-and-red hippogryph looked down at Trisk. Before he could reply, more of the hippogryph wilders took the opportunity to speak their minds.

"We should kill them and leave them for the kirin."

"You heard Jenell's warnings. If they leave, they'll bring back the gryphon dires to wipe us out."

"She said the dire who circles the skies above the wald is searching for the grey opinicus. Keep him as a hostage, let the others leave."

Several more condemned him in the language of dires, alarming the hunters who had never heard it spoken by undired before.

Blackflame looked down at Trisk. "Is there something you'd like to say to the Kirin Guard asking for your death?"

Trisk stood as best he could in his tiny cage. "I think you know it's wrong to keep us here, and you'll do the moral thing."

The lead hippogryph stared into his eyes. While his fur and feathers were painted, his eyes were naturally a smoky grey. "We do what is right. Not what is *moral*. That has been our charge since the dragons died off. To keep the kirin in check."

"Even if I did think there's a kirin out there, which I don't, what does that have to do with me?" Trisk asked. "I'm not in Pride Kirin or whatever. I'm just an opinicus who wants to get these gryphs home. Jenell will vouch for that."

Blackflame circled his cage. "You hunt the food that your gryphon overlords feed to the kirin's hatchlings. A kirin we had kept locked under the ice for generations, trying to starve it out. Then you show up, killing the moose, culling the boars, murdering the screechers, and now the kirin has grown so strong it has laid eggs. And when the gryphons who worship it toss your dire's dead body down there, the eggs will hatch and it'll feed on his corpse."

Trisk blinked. Their weird kirin mythology was much more elaborate than he'd initially thought. "If the kirin is real, how come it doesn't fly away from here? I saw you guarding the hole where it ate the screecher, but the mist is light over the frozen lake where you seem to think it lives."

The hippogryphs laughed, and one with a vibrant, purple mane replied. "The kirin's nest generates the mist, but it can't breathe past them. The dragons' fire once kept them in check, burning away the mist and suffocating them. But when the kirin were thought extinct, the other gryphs turned on the dragons, killing them all. But they were wrong, the kirin weren't extinct. They hid in the mountains where their mist was contained beneath the frozen lakes, waiting for their chance."

Blackflame picked up the story. "Only the hippogryph herds remembered the danger. We guard the mist, cultivating animals too large for the starving kirin to fight. But your gryphons made it strong again, falling prey to the kirin's lies and promises of power.

"I thought... perhaps it isn't so bad. For the kirin to spread out of this valley, it would find itself facing off against Naralin and Haynil. Dire gryphons and opinici are not so grand as a dire hippogryph, but they get the job done. But then you brought me the kirin egg fragment, and we knew the danger was greater than that. They will be full grown in a year, too many for even your dires to fight. Be warned, the kirin will hunt and kill any gryph who touches their eggs. Whether or not you die today, you would have died last night had we not brought you out of the mist. Your life is ours to do as we wish with."

Dire hippogryphs? They really are batty.

"It's a good story," Trisk said. "It's not the lie I'll tell Njorn and Dire Haynil when we get back. All you have to do is lie low when Haynil checks the Blackwald, then come back out after he's left. Problem solved. Just tuck yourselves behind your waterfall with your pretty hippogryph statues for a couple of days and nobody has to get hurt. Then you can go back to guarding a frozen lake full of magical crocodiles with minty breath or whatever you were saying."

"I wish I could trust you," Blackflame said to Trisk before turning to his new ally. "Jenell, you said he had a musical instrument around his neck, but it's gone. He's not as resourceful as you think he is."

The lead hippogryph checked the necks of the other hunters, but all were bare. Since they'd all been sleeping before getting kidnapped, none of them even had time to put on their packs. All of Trisk's stolen wealth was in a nest frozen solid by mist back at the lodge.

He listened as the hippogryphs and Jenell argued back and forth, but his mind drifted to the shape in the mists. Something large, with antlers and sharp teeth. He was willing to accept that there were some weird animals out there, but he refused to believe it was a kirin until he saw it for himself.

During the Jenell and hippogryphs' arguments, it was of small comfort to Trisk that nobody really wanted to kill them all, but compelling cases were made that the gryphons in the aerie had planned to feed them to the kirin anyways, so the wilders were just speeding up the process the slightest amount while also keeping their secrecy intact.

Trisk thought of himself as a reasonable opinicus. He held out hope that the wilders would do the right thing. For a group of weird cultists, they were fairly level-headed. Jenell's wife had even brought over some cool water and berries for them to snack on while waiting to see if they were about to be murdered. And there was something out in the mists, maybe that thing with green eyes who loved songs, so they weren't as crazy as he'd initially thought. Or perhaps he'd grown as crazy as them. It was hard to tell.

Regardless, when it came to the strange beasts of the world, he would always pick a fight where he had the dires on his side. Thirty hippogryphs may have captured eight opinici, but the full might of Dire Haynil's pride would scourge the aerie and the Blackwald into nothing. They could burn away the mist with plain old fire of the non-draconic kind, break the beaver dams, and turn the lake back into water.

Let that abyssal hellfish eat the imaginary kirin eggs.

The more he thought about it, the less he could leave

things to chance. He *needed* to warn Dire Haynil about both the wilders and the aerie gryphons.

And yet.

Overhead, where the steam pushed back the mist, a small screecher with a long tail chased a dragonfly. Across the bridge, he saw a family of long-legged birds roam around, picking boiled fish off the surface of the canal. And the spotted patterns on the wilders reminded him of how the forest canopy had its own set of stars in the night. And the antlers on the wilders spoke to the diversity of game in here, game that didn't deserve to be overhunted.

It would be a shame if the Blackwald disappeared. He was surprised to find himself thinking that, but it was true.

He was about to ask that the other hunters be allowed to go, and he'd stay behind to see if that helped sway the wilders to do the right thing, but an argument had broken out in the old speech.

The purple hippogryph with the long mane turned to Trisk and shouted, "Enough talk! It's not for us to decide. Let their fate be left up to the gods!"

All of the hippogryphs turned to the scalding, boiling waterfall with the creepy hippogryph statue behind it.

Rather than wait to see if he were about to be boiled alive, he decided he'd given these wilders the benefit of the doubt for long enough.

"Yenni," Trisk said quietly. "It's time."

16

DIRE
COLDBRIGHT

T risk watched Yenni with curiosity. She stood, her fluffy underside having concealed the songbird instrument. She batted it with a paw, sending it flying at him.

He didn't know what her plan was. Perhaps she thought he'd catch it in his mouth. If so, she greatly over-estimated his reflexes.

The instrument clipped a bar, ricocheted off of his beak, hit the top of the cage, and landed at his paws.

"Trisk, NO!" Jenell screamed, but she was too late. The songbird was already in his paws and headed towards his open maw.

He covered all of the holes and blew as hard as he could. The shrill sound cut through the cry of the birds. If they'd been at their full din, perhaps the sound wouldn't have reached as far as it did. As things stood, he had blown like his life depended on it, like the lives of the other hunters depended upon it.

The hippogryphs covered their ears. Jenell took her

mate and fled for the forest. The waterfall seemed to shimmer, the statue coming nearly into focus.

When nothing happened, several of the hippogryphs, led by the purple one, started shouting at Trisk and approached his cage.

Trisk, however, never lost faith.

"Whatever we do with the others, *this* one is going in the cauldron," the violet beak said.

Something white and red fell to the ground with a splat—the remains of a large screecher. Their high-pitched squeals filled the mists, and a dozen more crashed down around the hippogryphs in a rain of body parts, then silence.

The wilders' anger changed to confusion. The purple one turned to threaten Trisk, but he never got his chance.

The mists above swirled and parted, and Njorn, the Golden Dawn, crashed like a meteorite into the wilder camp, reducing the hippogryphs near Trisk's cage to a bloody mess on impact.

With one swipe of his talons, Njorn smashed the tops of the cages, letting out the hunters.

Trisk could hear Jenell swearing at him from somewhere beyond the trees. She got as far as "Damn it, Trisk!" before her mate pulled her away. He knew what she was going to say. Njorn was a blunt instrument for a job that needed precision.

They were going to boil me alive, Nell. The time for subtlety has passed.

Some of the wilders fled. Every opinicus who had abandoned Dire Haynil's pride knew what happened to traitors and vanished into the forest, risking the kirin's mist over Njorn's blind rage.

Smart move. The kirin may be a tale to frighten kits, but Njorn is a waking nightmare, a true monster.

My monster.

Most of the hippogryphs lowered their horns and charged Njorn, attacking as a group. They were surprisingly good at taking on a creature much larger than themselves. Hippogryph hooves, talons, and beaks were all sharp beyond what would be allowed in a pridelands setting. Safety meant nothing for them.

Trisk didn't have to give the word. Yenni had already gathered the hunters. Where the hippogryphs went straight for Njorn's eyes—which widened at the audacity of an undired thinking it could fight *him*—Yenni knocked them out of the sky and killed them like she was hunting screechers.

I guess when you're training to kill a beast as large as a kirin, you don't stop to consider what someone small can do.

Trisk didn't join Yenni. Though many of the hippogryphs fled out of fear, Blackflame fled with a sense of purpose, and *that* concerned Trisk.

There was a small arch at the bottom of the waterfall Trisk had missed in his previous visit here. Going through it would still lead to a few burns, but the stone would keep most of the hot water off. Beyond the arch, beyond the wall of fire and water, Blackflame was arguing with someone.

Trisk chased after him. Most wilder camps would disperse if their leader died, and this one was likely no different.

He made it to the entrance of the arch before Blackflame reappeared, his talons dripping red paint.

Nobody gets their talons done in the middle of fighting. That has to be poison.

Blackflame tried to charge past Trisk, but the opinicus pounced, getting a paw's set of claws into the hippogryph's flank. The hippogryph stumbled but managed to buck Trisk off.

Trisk tumbled, but his paws held traction on the moss growing out of the stones, and he was back on his feet before Blackflame and quickly interposed himself between Njorn and the red-taloned assassin.

The clueless dire continued fighting and killing hippogryphs, a living shield of opinicus hunters watching for any wilders going after his eyes, stirin, or other weak spots.

Blackflame changed tactics, leaping into the air. Trisk followed after, coming close but missing catching the hippogryph's tail. Blackflame flew high, past the columns and into the mist.

Trisk swore but followed him up there. Inside the mist, sound disappeared, as did sight. It was a wall of white. Every so often, he could feel the way the moisture-laden air moved, but he didn't know if it had been a screecher or hippogryph who slipped past him.

By the time he felt the mist displace from a dive, he was too late, and Blackflame was nearly to Njorn.

Rather than follow, Trisk trusted in his hunters. He glided down, searching for a spot on the bottom of the mist where he could see below it while his grey and black feathers made him invisible from below—in theory.

One of the hunters, Yenni's favorite orange one, leapt off of Njorn's haunch and knocked Blackflame out of the way. Yet when the red on Blackflame's talons scratched the orange opinicus, the hunter fell limp.

Blackflame flew back up to try to dive again, but Trisk was ready. He flew down from the mist and caught Blackflame when the hippogryph was most vulnerable, right before he got up into the mist.

The force knocked Blackflame down, into the rocks atop the waterfall. While he was still stunned, Trisk caught the hippogryph's talons and shoved them into the scalding water just like Blackflame had done to wash off Trisk's glowing paws.

Grabbing hold of someone as a gryphon or hippogryph was fairly easy, courtesy of the talons. For Trisk, it was a more brutal affair, even with his dewclaw. He shoved all of his claws into Blackflame's wrist, only pulling them out when the poison was gone.

"Stay down and Njorn will let you live," Trisk said, praying he wasn't telling a lie.

But Blackflame wasn't having it, and the moment Trisk's back was turned the hippogryph attacked.

Trisk felt long scratches along his back. As much as he'd only wanted Njorn to save them from the cages, as much as he hadn't wanted any wilders to die, instinct kicked in and he rolled, slamming the hippogryph into the ground and sending him sprawling off the ledge and into the waterfall.

Trisk let out a cry of grief the moment he saw what he'd done. His only mercy was that it looked like the fall and stone had killed Blackflame and not the water. The hippogryph's reds and blacks washed into the aqueducts, staining them.

The hippogryphs down below stopped fighting. They turned and fled into the Blackwald, just as a gargantuan scream sounded from behind the waterfall.

THE ANTLERS BROKE THROUGH THE WATERFALL FIRST. THEY were not moose antlers, nor were they deer or caribou. They were unlike any configuration Trisk had seen. They were, if he had to describe them succinctly, the antlers of a predator.

His first thought was that the kirin was real. Even Njorn, down below, looked afraid and confused. Then a face covered in glistening, silver armor broke through. Its wings and feathers were adorned in a style lost to prehistory and were far too thick for the waterfall to do it any harm.

The creature that passed through the waterfall looked down at Njorn.

It looked *down* at Njorn.

"A d-dire hippogryph!" Yenni shouted. Her hunters stepped back.

The rival dire's armor protected her stirin and made it hard to reach her eyes. Her feathers, a light grey that Trisk envied, glistened like mercury as the water passed over her.

She was still steaming when she opened her beak. Her words sounded like poetry chiseled in crystal. When she spoke, the steam and her bright beak created prismatic diamonds in the air around her.

Trisk recognized a few words. *Cold-bright* and *black-flame* appeared several times from both Njorn and the dire hippogryph.

Trisk had never seen Njorn mantle to anyone except his fire, but his lover's wings were half open, and Njorn crouched a little, keeping his eyes from meeting the other dire's.

"What's she saying?" Trisk shouted down. His impetuousness caught both dires off guard. The hippogryph made a few remarks, clearly angry despite how beautiful they sounded to Trisk's feline ears. Whatever she said must have been particularly insulting, because Njorn's hackles rose and his mane puffed up.

"In common, for your gryphs and mine," Njorn ordered. "She says her name is *diamond-beak*," he spoke in the language of the dires before translating it.

Diamondbeak turned from Njorn to Trisk, giving the undired the full fury of her gaze. "The wyverns, the gryphons, and the opinici have all forgotten their promise to keep the kirin and dragons at bay. The hippogryph herds do not forget."

"With all due respect," Trisk began, "you put us in cages first. Njorn came to save me. If you'd let us go, none of this would have happened. You would still be holding your sacred charge."

Trisk didn't know that for certain. Even if she were the only hippogryph dire to have ever set hoof upon the ground, her existence was a threat to the sovereignty of the prides. Dire Haynil would kill all of them to keep her existence a secret if he found out.

"And so you killed my little dragon, *black-flame*?" she asked, pointing to the body of Blackflame, now drained of color. "My herd has hunted kirin for generations, hidden beneath their mist. That will not end this day."

Diamondbeak charged Njorn, and for the first time, the golden dire felt what it was like to be weak before a larger opponent. He fought valiantly, but she threw him into a pillar, collapsing it into a canal, sending scalding water all over the wilder camp.

Herd camp, I suppose. But that gives me an idea.

The monstrous hippogryph charged, and Njorn grabbed her horned headdress, several spikes going into his forelegs, but it was no use. She used her own talons to lash out, leaving long red marks across his stomach. Without armor, he was at a disadvantage, and this was a fight neither Yenni nor any of her hunters were stupid enough to get involved in.

Trisk, however, was *exactly* that stupid. He would become the advantage Njorn needed, better than armor or talons. The small grey-black opinicus glided down from the waterfall, finding the small arch Blackflame had used. The water burned Trisk's wings and back as it splashed around him, but he got behind the waterfall.

The space beyond the arch was massive and empty. That made sense—what he'd assumed was a massive statue turned out to be a dire who had watched them all through the water on his previous visits—but it still surprised him. He looked up and thought he saw a few screechers chasing moths near the stalactites.

He remembered that he was looking for something of Blackflame's, and moved his gaze to the wet floor, where he found a turned over pot and red paint pooling around it.

That can't be good for the environment.

He licked his paw and checked the pads. While his body had its fair share of cuts, his paws seemed to be free of lacerations. He would find out in a moment if that were true or not.

He dipped a paw into the poison. His favorite paw. His lucky paw. He didn't dare do two in case one had scratches, but when he slipped back through the archway, his best paw was a bright, vibrant red.

Diamondbeak had Njorn on his back. One hoof was pressing down hard on his stirin, and he had lost the will to fight. Trisk couldn't tell what was said as she spoke in the language of the dires, but the more of that language he heard, the less beautiful and more vicious it sounded.

As a kit, he'd once asked his mom what the difference between a rabid wolf and a cruel dire was. She'd boxed his ears, told him never to speak ill of the dires if he wanted to live, but he'd never forgotten her answer.

The difference between sentience and sapience is malevolence.

Diamondbeak's bragging was so grand and large, her desire to inflict pain upon Njorn so strong, that she did not see a small, grey opinicus hopping along on three legs so his red paw didn't wash away in the cooling puddles.

A lifetime ago, Njorn had once asked Trisk why opinici were better hunters. Trisk had given a lot of reasons—they were smarter than gryphons, more attractive, stealthier, and just generally better at everything that mattered in life.

The real answer was a mix of a couple things on that list related to stealth and cunning. But the real trick that made opinici better than gryphons and hippogryphs was their retractable claws, which meant their deadliest weapons never dulled.

Trisk placed his paw on Diamondbeak's side without her noticing, then his claws sprang out, driving the venom past her thick hide. He pushed deeper, trying to drive the red poison into her wounds.

With one swat, he went flying across the grounds, across the stone bridge, even.

Diamondbeak swore. That particular word appeared to be the same in common and dire. She reflexively licked at her wound, tasting the bitter poison.

Trisk's own paw was beginning to burn from having the poison on it. He didn't know what the effect would be on someone so large, but he knew Blackflame believed it would bring down Njorn.

I forgot about Njorn.

"Do your job, you dumb moose!" he shouted with the last of his strength. While a cut on his paw would have killed him by now, he was still starting to feel funny, and his motor control was fading.

"My job?" Njorn blinked. "Oh, to protect the hunters."

Diamondbeak was so concerned with her poisoned wound that she didn't see Njorn coming. He pushed her hoof off his stirin, then latched onto both straps holding her armor in place and tore it off.

What came next was violence.

In Trisk's mind, he'd killed Diamondbeak, and Njorn, at best, got credit for the assist. However, seeing a giant, golden dire kill the only dire hippogryph in the world would probably be the image painted on pridelands walls.

Not that Dire Haynil would let anything that happened here be known.

A green-and-brown opinicus shape with a blue bracelet on her paw dashed out from the forest and shouted, "I found him, Jenell. Get the antidote."

Jenell, good 'ole Nell, appeared a moment later and shoved something fruity-tasting down his throat from a glass vial. He felt his paw get shoved into the hot, black water to wash off the poison, then someone carried him back to Njorn before both braceleted-shapes disappeared back into the Blackwald to avoid punishment.

The last thing Trisk saw before he lost consciousness was Njorn's mane covering him to keep him warm.

17

LOVE NEST
COLDBRIGHT

T risk woke up to find himself cuddled by something much, much larger than he was. Instinctively, he reached up and petted the golden beak with his paw. He'd missed this feeling of being enveloped by someone he loved.

It was only when he opened his eyes that he realized he wasn't curled up in a private cave somewhere, away from prying eyes, but instead they were still in the center of the wilder camp.

He jerked awake, pushing Njorn away. "Stop, don't let them see."

Njorn chuckled. "They're all gone. It's just us."

"But we're outside," Trisk mumbled. Yet the mist blocked sight above the wald, and so he relaxed, melting into Njorn again. His whole body ached, and he just wanted to sleep, but he had one more question. "Where did they go?"

Njorn shifted. His back paw had fallen asleep, making Trisk wonder how long they'd been like this. Once Njorn had feeling again, he spoke. "Yenni's mate was poisoned. I carried him myself, escorting them through the mist to the snowfields. He should be okay. They're going to walk him home. Then I came back here. Jenell said the orange opinicus was taking to the antivenom better than you, so we shouldn't move you back to the lodge just yet."

Yenni's... mate? I suppose there's nothing like nearly dying to cement a relationship. I wonder if he asked or if Yenni did?

"We sure showed Diamondbeak. I'm like those spiders. Poisonous if you're trying to eat me, but venomous when I—" a coughing fit muffled the last of Trisk's words. He cleared his throat. "What's going to happen to Jenell and her mate? And what are the hunters going to tell Haynil?"

For once, Njorn didn't correct his slip-up to *Dire* Haynil. "Jenell is going to take the other wilders and leave here. I'll tell my father she died. Yenni and the others are going to say they were kidnapped and I saved them, then I went to confront the wilders. That way, they won't have been around when I killed the dire hippogryph."

Nearby, Diamondbeak's limp body sparkled in the spray of the waterfall.

"You're going to tell your father about her?" Trisk looked up at the sky. He didn't want to spend the night here, but he wasn't sure how long he'd been allowed to rest. "And what happened at the aerie?"

Njorn stiffened. "Yenni told me about the wilders' accusations. I... need to go see if there's any truth there. Food has definitely gone missing, but feeding opinici to a monster? Murdering all those gryphs? It seems ridiculous."

"We have gone from weird to unbelievable." Trisk

thought back to the shape in the mist. The antlers had been the same as the pair on Diamondbeak's headdress: a predator's antlers. And Trisk didn't see a beak, he'd definitely seen a toothy snout, though he'd admit he had been through a lot, including being poisoned.

Well, poisoning myself. But that came later. Was the kirin real?

He tested his wings. "Please be careful. I did find the missing crates. They were at the bottom of the lake. There were also the bodies of a dozen opinici and one gryphon. I took the gryphon's aerie medal with me before I left. I put it in my pack to see if you recognized the name, but I'm certain Cerris was behind all of those killings. I don't think his predecessor went into the mists. I think Cerris and Temperance killed him and tossed his body down into the lake."

Njorn shook his head in confusion, his mane drifting back and forth, and Trisk realized Njorn didn't know about the kirin's supposed nest.

"There's a sinkhole at the center, flash frozen like that. It goes all the way down to the ground. That's where the wilders said the kirin lived. That's where they said the aerie gryphons were providing food for its eggs. I don't know about that, but there are bodies down there, and I saw Temperance bring the food crates there."

Trisk looked down at his paw, the one that had left behind the glowing paw prints, the one that had killed a dire with a small amount of help from Njorn. It hurt like hell. Jenell had wrapped it before she left, but he knew his vanity would take a hit when he saw what it looked like underneath.

Blackflame said the kirin killed all who touched its eggs.

Trisk's paw print had led from the lake to the lodge

down to the screecher nest. He'd left his blood on the thorns in the boar's bramble.

Funny to think the kirin might be hunting me. Well, if you're real, little kirin, good luck finding me now.

He reached reflexively for his missing pack, forgetting everything he owned was up north in the great hall. He thought of asking if he could ride on Njorn's back to get to the lodge. Seeing how big Njorn was next to the black heartwood trees, there was no way Njorn could make it all the way from here to there by paw. Honestly, Trisk had no idea how Diamondbeak had managed to go anywhere in here. Maybe that's why she stayed behind her waterfall.

Instead, he just offered, "I need to get some gryphs' things from the lodge. Why don't you... take care of the aerie and then meet me there?"

Njorn looked concerned. "I'd rather bring you with me. Or drop you off on the other side of the mountains."

"I'll be fine," Trisk said. "The aerie gryphons are definitely going to ambush you, though. Please be careful."

Njorn laughed. "Jenell said the same thing. When she said the hippogryph's poison was made from spider venom, the living quarters at the aerie made a lot more sense. She said they'd learned it from torturing hippogryphs to ask them about the kirin, then she gave me a vial of antivenom."

Trisk felt relieved, but there was a part of him that still resented the decision Jenell had forced him to make: to use the songbird. "If she'd just stayed with the wilders, we'd all be fine. She was just so certain you were already dead."

"She also seemed sure the kirin is real," Njorn countered. "So I suppose she's not as smart as she looks."

Trisk took a few steps towards the bridge. "I... saw

something in the mist. It was so hot, I was so tired, that I can't be sure it's real. But I'm sure it had antlers. Did Nell describe the kirin to you? Had she seen it?"

Njorn shook his head. "She just said she trusted her mate."

"Well, keep your eyes open if you go to get the supplies from the lake, I guess." In the back of Trisk's mind, the kirin's song played, and he could see the green eyes from the river. "I'm going to gather my things so we can leave tomorrow. The lodge has enough room for both of us. Just knock when you want in. Not too hard, though. The front wall is one stiff breeze from collapse. If I had to guess, a certain dire hippogryph broke through it a few times."

Njorn hesitated, perhaps wondering if the word of his opinicus lover was good enough to pick a fight with an entire aerie over, and then leapt into the sky.

Trisk limped north. He'd had enough of adventure, enough of death and disappointment. Maybe some hippogryphs had stayed around and held a grudge. If so, he couldn't blame them.

Hell, maybe the mythical kirin would hunt him down. If not, he'd leave here soon enough, but at least he'd get one last night in the Blackwald with Njorn all to himself.

TRISK WALKED FOR MARKS, IGNORING THE PAIN IN HIS PAW. The mist seemed clearer, as though it had retreated from the southern Blackwald. Limping through a forest, any forest, had the potential to attract predators, but he made it to the pond unscathed. The dead crocodiles were gone, probably carried away by industrious herons to eat elsewhere, though the fading light showed some small orange eyes staring out from the reeds.

Nature heals itself, given the chance. We were the over-hunting wolves, and now we've been culled.

He paused in front of the river cave. The water flowed freely again; the ice was long gone. The slight haze inside didn't look misty, nor did it glow.

Not entirely sure why he was doing it, perhaps because there were no wilders around to do it themselves, he scratched the word *coldbright* into the soft stone with his unbandaged forepaw.

Was the kirin in the mist real?

He saw its toothy snout lurking around every corner. Someone—probably Jenell—had draped the songbird's strap around his neck while he slept. He lifted it into his beak, but with the bandaged paw, he couldn't cover the right holes to re-create the kirin's music.

He used his wings to buffet himself as he climbed with three paws, reaching the final path to the lodge. The stars above repaired their nests. The constellations grew more blue the closer he came to his resting place these past weeks, with a single red spider looking out of place as he neared his destination.

The grass and vines around the front door were still frozen. He slipped, forgetting his paws lacked their resin coating now, and in his spin he hit his flank on the door. As he preened his fur back in place, he saw the scar left by Yenni's beak on their first day here.

He sighed. At least Yenni and the other hunters were safe.

Not Jenell.

He shook his head. She'd find her way to another wilder camp. Or perhaps the remaining Kirin Guard would head into the caves below the river and find out if there was any truth to their myths.

A thin layer of frost covered everything inside the lodge, so he got to work lighting the fireplace in the great hall. He left the front door open to let the moisture out. This was the closest thing to a dry night the Blackwald offered, and the creatures of the darkness seemed to be taking tonight off.

A wall of ice sealed off the butchery. He considered leaving it, but when he discovered an abandoned pack full of heavy obsidian, he flung it at the ice and broke through.

The kitchen and butchery were slippery, so he started up the cooking fire. With any luck, the crates of salt and spices wouldn't be ruined. Once both fires were going, he returned to the other room and flew up to the ceiling in the great hall, catching the platform with his good paw and pulling himself into the attic. The eight nests his troupe had used were still downstairs, and he didn't feel nimble enough to get them all back up here, but the nests of past hunters sat along the edges.

It took a little searching to find the vials of paw ink, but he sat down next to the paw prints of his hunters and marked what had happened to each. For Jenell he put *coldbright*, but for Yenni and the other five, he wrote *safe* in common. And he drew a little heart between Yenni's paw and the pawprint of the orange opinicus she'd taken a fancy to.

He paused when he reached his own. He was neither kirin food nor Kirin Guard, neither missing nor safe.

It is up to whoever comes after me to record my fate.

He left it blank, returning downstairs to clean his paw in the melting ice by the drain. It would be nice to wash himself in clean water. He poked at the rubble of the smashed gryphon fountain. Then, despite his better judgement, he pulled down the lever.

To his surprise, the mechanism groaned to life, and water flowed down, pooling on the ground. He pulled it down once more, and a flood came out, spilling onto the ground.

I guess it's fixable.

He picked through the rubble, removing the basin and bits of gryphon fountain, and piled them outside in the icy grass. There were still several large blocks of stone that prevented him from crawling back and taking a closer look at where the water was coming from. Once he was done clearing out what he could in the butchery and unbarricading the tower door, he returned to the great hall to disassemble several small nests to create one that would fit Njorn and himself, then finagled the last two back up to the attic.

When he rediscovered the light barrel for collecting rainwater stashed away in storage, he filled it with water and washed himself, keeping his bandaged paw in the air so it didn't get wet. Once he was done, he pushed the barrel over and watched the water spill down the drain. As an afterthought, he brought the remaining antler trinkets from around the lodge and hung them over the fountain rubble. He debated putting some over the front door, but he'd never known monsters to knock, and something had, in fact, burst through the plumbing.

Though my bet is on crocodiles and not kirin.

Several marks of cleaning with the fires going had dried out most of the lodge, and he decided he was safe to close the door. He rifled through the hunter's packs, finding a lot of moose jerky, charred screecher feet, and in Yenni's pack, some blueberry tarts.

He ate those first.

Fed, watered, and cleaned, he tended to both fires one last time, giving them as much fuel as he could fit, and curled up in a nest far too large for just himself to sleep until Njorn arrived.

18

REUNIFICATION
COLDBRIGHT

The haunting melody of the kirin permeated Trisk's dreams like a soft mist. Several times in the night, he jerked awake, his vision filled with a strange brightness before he opened his eyes to see the dying firelight.

The third time he awoke, however, it was to the sound of someone knocking on the door. It took him a moment to remember that he was waiting for Njorn. It had taken so long, Trisk just assumed his big moose had decided to sleep at the aerie with Cuddles the Spider.

He scratched idly at the back of an ear, then got up to open the door. He hadn't bothered with the barricade.

The door swung open, but Njorn was nowhere to be found. The fire crackled behind Trisk. He pushed the door all the way open.

"Njorn?" he called out. His voice traveled through the silent night, echoing back at him. He tried another name. "Jenell?"

As his eyes adjusted to the night, he saw a large, golden shape in the grass. Njorn's body was limp, but

Trisk chalked it up to exhaustion. He took a step forwards before his danger sense kicked in.

"N...jorn?"

Mist flowed from behind the dire gryphon, covering the glen. Njorn's eyes were closed, and Trisk stared at his lover's chest until he saw it rise and fall slightly.

Trisk froze, afraid to move closer or to leave. He stood there, staring at the limp body of Njorn, until a breeze dislodged some of the mist. Njorn's talons and paws, stained chalk-white from the frozen lake, were limp. He floated an inch above the ground.

Trisk took a step back, but Njorn moved closer. As he breached the mist, speckles of blood were visible on his coat. Njorn moved two more 'steps' closer, and Trisk could now see that the golden dire was being held up by a giant pair of antlers. Whatever was behind them remained concealed in the bright whiteness that enveloped the forest.

Trisk swore, scrabbling for purchase on the wet ground outside the door so he could flee back inside the lodge. He slid inside and tried to shut the door, but the kirin moved with preternatural speed, using Njorn's body to hold it open.

The strange beast of the Blackwald roared, a sound unlike gryph or wyvern, a hybrid of fish, bird, reptile, and mammal. It twisted its horns, and through the gap by Njorn's shoulder, Trisk watched the overhang above the door fly into the air, could practically hear Diamondbeak teasing him about his disbelief in the back of his mind. The kirin continued to ram the entrance, Njorn's body appearing in the open door, but the monstrous antlers on either side slammed into the lodge, and the wall began to crack and crumble.

Staring into Njorn's eyes, trying to figure out if he was still alive, Trisk froze. It was only when the entrance to the lodge crashed into rubble and the kirin threw the golden dire's limp body into the great hall that Trisk's reflexes kicked in.

The opinicus leapt straight up, dodging Njorn, and glided towards the door to the kitchen. The stone wall between the halves of the building had survived in the other lodge, so he took a gamble it would buy him at least a little time.

In the firelight, the kirin looked like nothing he had ever seen before. Or, rather, it looked like everything he had ever seen—its mouth had a wildcat look with reptile fangs. Silver nictitating membranes rolled back, revealing eyes that shone green with the light of the flames. It had both scales and a furry mane, and its folded wingfeathers looked like green metal plates.

Its body snaked out into the yard, tail tufted on the end, but with all of the writhing, Trisk couldn't get a good look at how long the creature was, precisely. He was too busy scrambling into the kitchen as the kirin's icy breath extinguished the great hall's fireplace, plunging that room into a white glow.

Shutting the door to the kitchen felt petty and, in other circumstances, hilariously ineffective, but Trisk did it anyways. He looked around the kitchen. The tower was too wide. The kirin, large but lithe, would slither up it.

Or would it? Its antlers are so wide, it might get stuck. But... it got through the underground river somehow.

He didn't bother to think further on that plan. He'd already cleared away the rubble he could move by the stone fountain before going to bed, and the large blocks that were left wouldn't give him enough space to follow that path, even if he wanted to crawl through the water to try to find an exit. For all he knew, the kirin could breathe underwater and there wouldn't be air in there.

Which left him with one alternative. The trick would be to keep the kirin from realizing what he'd done.

He grabbed a piece of unlit firewood in his beak and used it to smash the lit pieces and knock them into the cool, damp ground. Then he ran to the salt crate and worked it open.

When the kirin smashed through the kitchen door, Trisk got a surprising glimpse of its antlers. The same way fanged deer often had long incisors they could force back, the kirin was able to do the same with its impressive horns.

The kirin didn't get a good glimpse at Trisk, because he threw a pawful of salt in its eyes as soon as it broke through.

While the monster roared, Trisk forced himself into the fireplace and began to crawl up the chimney.

It was a good plan. It was an *excellent* plan, even. Trisk would have liked to think that against most opponents, it would have worked. And when he heard the kirin tearing up the drain to see if he'd crawled down there, he thought it might have.

Unfortunately for him, the kirin's hearing was well-tuned to detect sounds underground, and he hadn't made it past the top of the room when things went wrong.

From below, a blast of mist froze his tail and hindquarters. Like a kit tongue stuck to an icicle, his body, already pressed tight against the sides of the chimney, seemed frozen to them.

With claws that had dug through the icy lake bottom and rocky soil of the Blackwald, the kirin began to break apart the chimney, revealing its prey. Before the ash-covered Trisk could get away, it wrapped one of its taloned, reptilian paws around him.

While the kirin was large, Trisk could see that the kitchen doorframe had forced it to squeeze its size smaller, like a field mouse squeezing through a trap.

Or a rat snake squeezing into a trap to eat the mouse.

He stared into the eyes of the kirin, and for the first time, it occurred to him that this wasn't an 'it,' it wasn't a 'monster,' except in the sense that wyverns felt like monsters to gryphs.

The eyes that looked at him now, the green, shining eyes in the mist from the hippogryph camp, showed a malevolence to them. It didn't seem to be personal, just that the kirin wanted one more thing to play with.

Did the other wilders flee in time? Did Jenell get away? Or did it hunt them down?

Trisk squirmed, the mouse in the vise, but the kirin tightened its grip. Then it opened its mouth wide, its fangs coming out, the rat snake with its meal.

Before it could close its jaws, a loud crash shook the center wall, and Njorn's roar deafened all three of them. Part of the door frame collapsed, and the kirin squealed in pain. Trisk couldn't see what was happening on the other side of the wall, but he heard the sound of a long, leathery whip-like tail thudding against the body of a dire, then silence.

But during the kirin's squeal of pain, it lightened its grip slightly, and Trisk slipped out in a puff of ash and made a dash up the tower.

EVEN WITH HIS BURNED FOOT, TRISK MOVED LIKE A mongoose, weaving up the tower as fast as he could go. His claws tore apart the wooden ramps, but he didn't dare look back. Cool air blasted after him, but this wasn't the chimney, and he had enough of a lead that he didn't get frozen.

Survival instincts and sass were stored in different parts of the brain, and despite one part of his brain telling his beak to stay shut, he shouted something inappropriate back at the kirin, thanking it for the refreshing breeze on his nethers.

The kirin roared furiously, confirming that somewhere in its time hiding in a lake waiting to end the world, it had picked up common.

Trisk was expecting to hit the door with its weird opening mechanism at the top of the tower, but he'd forgotten they'd filled it with moose meat for tomorrow. When he reached the first of the smaller crates, he saw Yenni's handiwork: a small wedge had been used to keep the crates from sliding back down.

He pulled out the first wedge and kicked the crate down towards the kirin. Then he pulled out two more wedges and scrambled over the larger boxes.

A roar followed by a crash came from below. Trisk fumbled with the device, but even the easier version on the opinicus side required two strong paws, and he was down one bandaged forepaw. He ended up using his back legs to get it open, then squeezed through and shut it behind him.

He lay on the platform, panting, trying to figure out his next move. The kirin had wings, so it could surely fly. Whatever direction Trisk fled to, it would be right behind him. He'd never get to safety in time, if there even was a safe place. Njorn was supposed to have gone to the aerie first, but what if he hadn't? Cerris and Temperance could be waiting up there.

Can I work the steam at the wilder camp? Will the water-fall keep me safe?

The kirin had finally managed to contort itself between the heavy crates of moose meat and rammed the door. Had there been room for it to have used its antlers, the door would have broken in a few hits. With only its snout and forehead, the door was doing an admirable job of holding its own—for now.

What now? Where do I go? Is Njorn okay? If I run away, does it go back down and finish him off?

The door started to creak. The wooden tower, however, began to shake and splinter on its own, which gave Trisk an idea.

That's right, the tower was starting to rot from the outside.

He used his beak to rip off the bandages on his favorite paw, revealing the burn marks. He didn't take the time to wince, instead putting the songbird in his beak, covering the holes, and blowing as hard as he could.

The shrieking sound echoed across the wald. Several screechers, hidden in the mist, shouted their protests, but no response came from below.

Come on Njorn, I need your might now, you big moose.

Trisk pushed some empty crates the gryphons had returned against the door, but there was no weight to them. The crates packed heavy with moose meat were all in the corridor, the kirin's body pressed between them.

Just as the door started to give way, a golden shape appeared in the mist below, climbing its way up talon-over-claw.

"Njorn!" Trisk cried. "You're alive!"

The only reply he got back was coughing. Njorn pulled himself onto the platform, panting. "Killed the gryphons... at the aerie. Thought... you were lying... about the kirin. Caught me off guard at the lake."

A reptilian claw wedged itself through a hole in the tower door and began trying to pull it down.

"We have to work fast!" Trisk pointed to the tower, which looked to be on its last legs. "One good hit and it should go down. The kirin has wound itself through the heavy crates. With any luck... it'll just snap under their weight when the tower falls."

Njorn didn't look like he was in any shape to fly, but he didn't hesitate. He stood on the far edge of the platform, ran, and flung himself down at where the tower looked weakest.

Trisk was so busy looking over the side of the platform that he forgot what it was connected to.

Njorn hit the tower, cracking the supports and sending it falling before the golden dire disappeared into the mist.

Trisk managed a prayer that his friend had enough strength to glide away before the collapsing tower flung Trisk into the sky-sea of mist at an alarming speed.

The kirin cried out in fear as the tower fell.

Trisk bounced off of a large screecher in the mist, spread his wings, and tried to fly down where he thought the cabin was located, hoping he didn't find tree branches first.

The sound of the tower falling had an organic, meaty crushing feel to it. And when he landed—crashed, really —he searched for the tower remains.

The kirin had managed to get its head out through the hole in the tower. Its silver nictitating membrane covered its eyes, and Trisk forced them open to make sure the creature was dead. He cut its throat to be sure, then collapsed in the spongy moss, panting.

He stayed there, cool night air covering him, for half a mark before he heard a voice calling out for him.

"Triiiisk!" the voice came. "Triiiisk, where are you?"

He coughed, tried to make words form at an appropriate volume, and finally gave up and used the songbird to play a few notes.

Njorn lumbered into view, his golden form a welcome site. The kirin's dead body seemed to emit mist, and the world around them was fading into a lightless white.

"Is it dead?" Njorn asked.

Trisk nodded. "I suppose I should give you the assist on this one, too, since you helped a little."

Njorn laughed, a genuine sound Trisk had missed, and helped the opinicus to his feet.

Trisk padded over to the collapsed tower. The center of the kirin's body had been crushed beneath the largest crate. "I guess Njorn killed the kirin."

"Of course I did," Njorn the Gryphon began, but Trisk pointed to the crate. One of the opinici had scratched *Njorn the Second* into the wood.

Njorn sniffed at the box. "Who's Njorn the Second?"

"A moose," Trisk laughed. "A very big moose."

Njorn shook his head, but when Trisk kept laughing, he finally joined in.

Trisk only stopped when the cool of the mist sent him into another coughing fit.

"I think we're going to have to walk," Njorn said. "My wings gave out on the glide. They're not going to let me fly again for a while."

Trisk stared into the green eyes of the kirin. "I'm not going back. I thought the wilders were crazy, but they were right, even if they went about things in a rather murderous way. I'm going to find Jenell and as many hippogryphs as stuck around, and we're going to see if it had a mate and eggs."

Njorn bristled, condensation dripping off of his mane when he did so. "You can't become a wilder. You'll never be allowed back at the pridelands. If you stay here and anyone from my dad's pride recognizes you, they'll kill you."

"Njorn, I love you, but I can't worry about what everyone else does." Trisk put an ash-covered foreleg on Njorn's mane, leaving behind a paw print. "I'm not going to spend my days waiting to see if we get caught together and Dire Haynil has me killed. I'm going to stay here and do what the wilders couldn't. I'm going to keep the Blackwald safe."

Njorn scratched at the ground, a nervous habit he usually kept in check around strangers because it didn't project a dire's strength. "Please, don't do this. You can't stop the pride from sending in dires to cull the Blackwald. There's too much food here."

"But you can." Trisk reached up and pulled Njorn down to eye level. "You might catch up to Yenni and the others, you might not. But what *you* say as a dire gryphon has a lot more weight than what *I* say as an undired opinicus.

"Tell them that the Blackwald is flooded and the prey animals are all dead. That the gryphons here killed the opinicus hunters, stole the remaining food, and were too ashamed to admit this land was ruined. You have the entire way home to think up what to say, and you have a voice gryphs will listen to. So do it. Lie if you have to."

Njorn remained silent. Trisk didn't blame him. He was

often unaware of the power he had, often didn't use it unless his temper got the better of him.

"I don't see how to tell a story of a kirin and a dire hippogryph that doesn't include a lie," the golden gryphon said at last. "I just don't want you to be out of my life."

The cold around the kirin was too much for Trisk, and he had to move away, following the wreckage of the tower back to the lodge ruins. "It doesn't have to be. You can slip your escort, come visit me here. Enough of that, though. Come help me scavenge a nest. We'll sleep under the stars."

"Under the stars?" Njorn sounded excited until he looked up and saw the blue glow of the spiders. "Oh."

Trisk grinned. "They're not so bad once you get to know them. See that shy red one among the blues? I call her Snuggles."

Njorn sighed but helped Trisk drag the ragged nest out of the broken entrance of the lodge. Between Njorn's giant gryphon talons and Trisk's tiny opinicus paws, they managed to patch each other up as best they could before sleeping the last few marks of the night under the creeping cosmos.

EPILOGUE
BEAVERS

Trisk stood on a branch overlooking the remains of the severely-pruned bramble patch. Teams of hippogryphs had come through, tracing the river from the boar god's den through the northistle to where it disappeared beneath the earth. Sharpened stakes were placed around the entrance.

Everyone's paws glistened with sweat. With the kirin's death, the sun burned off the mists by midday, and they only returned after the sun disappeared behind the mountains. Disposing of the kirin's body, a task thought impossible, turned out to be fairly easy. As his expedition months ago had joked about on the original flight to this godforsaken place, there was only one dire dumb enough to purchase the hide of a creature that did not exist.

Thus, hanging on Rada's wall, no other dire had questioned whether or not the kirin's hide was real. They all assumed he'd been duped. And in exchange, Trisk had received enough wealth to redesign Blackwald Aerie, drain the flooded hippogryph herdgrounds, and repair the lodge in the glen. All places he was now in charge of.

When I told Njorn to make up a lie to save the Blackwald, I didn't think he'd blame it all on me.

By all accounts, Njorn's speech had been dramatic. He'd gone on in great length about Trisk's failures and the things Njorn had been forced to do to salvage what he could. As punishment for Trisk's incompetence, Dire Haynil had made Trisk the leader of the worst aerie in the pride. They still had a small quota of goods to send back from time to time but not enough to put a strain on the local moose population.

And, except when pride gryphons were spotted flying in to pick up tithes, hippogryphs were allowed at the aerie. In time, perhaps Njorn would convince his father to allow them membership, even if just for the aerie and not the pride as a whole. It was the least Njorn and Trisk could do after killing their dire.

In my defense, her herd tried to poison Njorn, tear him apart, and boil me alive.

Trisk didn't know if he'd see another dire hippogryph. Jenell's wife claimed the herds here produced one every other generation. If that happened, they'd need to find a way to hide the foal.

The sound of the songbird instrument cut across the Blackwald, followed by echoing sounds from several others they'd crafted in its likeness.

"That's everyone except the lake gryphs," Yenni said. Most of Trisk's original hunters had come back to the Blackwald to form the new aerie. Yenni in particular had grown fond of this bramble patch from having to watch it and was happy to be in charge of keeping the boar population in check.

A longer, musical song came from the north. Trisk recognized it as coming from the orange opinicus. "He's getting pretty good at this. Maybe we should have him come up with a few songs to teach the others. What's he say?"

Yenni traced the notes into a branch and translated them. "He says they're all in place, but your *guest* from the pridelands won't wear his hat."

"That dumb moose is going to regret it if he goes head-to-antlers with a kirin bareheaded," Trisk grumbled. "I'll go handle Njorn. You signal Jenell and tell her it's time."

Yenni's piercing notes echoed across the forest. Several screechers shouted back at them. The leathery creatures had adapted well to the additional sunlight, hunting in the morning mist and shouting at anyone who flew by them during the day, as they did to Trisk now. He shouted back at them playfully, then looked at the lodge, now missing its tower. Beyond it, spongy moss filled the dry creek bed as it ran towards the frozen lake, resembling a vein of gold.

He'd waited all summer for this opportunity. His aerie had mapped all of the river or creek exits from the aqueduct beneath the Blackwald. They'd left trinkets and runes at each exit. Then he'd waited for the rains to come. The beavers had done their work, and every plateau on the mountains had been flooded, new lakes springing up and old lakes growing larger.

Neither the lack of mist nor the rains nor even the summer sun had melted the frozen lake. Despite Trisk's hopes that it was over, something had taken the body of Diamondbeak and dragged it underground after the kirin's death in the tower.

And it's time to find out what that is.

He landed on an outcropping of obsidian where Njorn was arguing with an orange opinicus.

When Njorn saw that Trisk was wearing Blackflame's old obsidian heartwood antlers and had both ash and red clay staining his fur, the dire sighed. "Well, if I'd known we were going to dress up as a couple, I wouldn't have put up a fight."

Trisk and the orange opinicus got the antlers— Diamondbeak's old pair, which caught on the cave when something dragged her body into it—secured to Njorn's head just in time.

The beavers' grand architecture collapsed under the attack of teams of opinici and hippogryphs, and all of the warm, summer lakes drained into the frozen sinkhole.

The gryphs around the cave entrances stood next to their pikes, claws or talons out. Each hole had one hippogryph wearing a pair of wooden talons dipped in spider venom, decorated in smoke and flame paint.

A whirlpool formed in the lake, and for a long time, nothing happened. Then, with both a roar and a song, the lake lit up brighter than the sun and Trisk flew to meet whatever came out of the abyss.

YOUR DIRE ADVENTURE

GLENN BIRMINGHAM

INTRODUCTION
PAGE 293

Y ou are a wyvern, and you are having a very bad day. You've really messed things up. You let that deformed gryphon escape, and Lady General is so angry. She's always growly and shouty, but she's never been *this* shouty before.

You want to sink into the ground as she calls you *runt* and *stupid*. Lady General likes smart wyverns. She really, really doesn't like stupid wyverns. So when she calls you stupid, and idiot, and useless, you know she's serious.

You know she'll report this when the wing returns home. That doesn't bother you as much as knowing she'll never want to work with you again. For all the shouting, Lady General is like you — small, picked on, *useless*. You admire her for having acquired her own wing, even if she was assigned the wyverns no one else wanted to command. You can't help that *they* don't see your value, but you thought Lady General would.

Hearing her lump you in with the others makes your stomach feel sick. You want Lady General to succeed. You want to help her do it! But she sees you the same way she sees the other two brutes.

You realize you've been too caught up in your own thoughts to pay attention to what she's saying. You refocus just in time to hear her command everyone back into the cave with orders to *wait and do nothing*. While she goes and fixes things.

She stalks off into the forest.

You can't let her leave and fix your mistakes or she'll never respect you. She'll never *see* you. You chase after her.

The laughter of the rest of the wing of wyverns follows you.

YOU CATCH UP TO LADY GENERAL AND CONVINCE HER TO give you a second chance. She tells you to go scout the smaller gryphon camp while she goes to *fix this mess*.

She warns you to eat or disguise any kills to make it look like they've been done by gryphons. She has a plan and doesn't want you to ruin it. Use your tail and your wing claws. But *no fire*. She makes you repeat her instructions seven times before she lets you go.

You're definitely not going to mess things up this time! You use your best stealth to slip through the dense forest, skirting around Rada's village with enough distance you don't expect to run into anyone. You're headed into the hilly area, where Lady General says she thinks a second village is located. You were spotted in the hills, so that makes sense.

A smell tickles your nose — feathers and sweat and a bit of blood. You creep closer, investigating the scent.

It's a gryphon, or at least something gryphon-adjacent. It's crouching in a bush, staring at an acorn on some leaves. You wonder if gryphons eat acorns, and if so, why this gryphon is watching it like the acorn is going to attack. The gryphon is so still and intent, you worry it'll hear you if you move away, so you wait for it to kill the acorn, making enough sound for you to ease away.

When it does attack, though, it's to catch a rat that has come to investigate the acorn. That...makes more sense, but the gryphon doesn't eat the rat, just throws it into a pile in her bush.

What could anyone want with a pile of rats? They must be ingredients in some kind of dark ritual.

You shudder at the eerie behavior. Unfortunately, your shudder transfers through your wing to a bush, and the foliage shakes, betraying your position.

You hold your curses and your breath as you crouch low, hoping the gryphon doesn't notice.

But it's looking your way now, squinting as it searches, its eyes skimming over you. It hasn't seen you yet, but its expression is suspicious.

If you let it go and it reports hearing or seeing you, you'll be in big trouble. You promised Lady General you wouldn't let another one slip past you. This time, you should strike fast and kill the gryphon before it can escape.

But maybe it didn't see you. If you attack it, you might draw more notice. You're not too far from Rada's village; other gryphons might be out in the forest.

You could follow it and see if it raises an alarm on its way back. This means you might have to attack a larger group if it does alert someone on the way, but you might observe something strategic for Lady General, too.

You need to decide quickly. The gryphon is scooping up its dead rats and growing increasingly nervous.

- Page 297: Let her go and continue with your mission

- Page 301: Attack her and fix your past mistake

- Page 306: Follow her and see what happens

LET EURAIYA GO
PAGE 297

Y ou let her go. You wait for the gryphon to get out of
hearing range before you move on. You make your
way deeper into the hills and find the second gryphon
camp. You observe it and report your findings back.

Lady General sends you out on several other missions
that you also complete successfully.

Everything is on target. Things are going well. The
extra intelligence you've gathered in observing the camps
has helped set the time of the attack for optimal success.
Lady General no longer scowls when she says your name.

A week later, your wing is in the forest planning the
main attack. Lady General wants to wait for night: it's the
night of the Fracture, and the gryphs will be relaxed, not
expecting danger.

A gryph stumbles upon the wing — you kill it, not
about to let one escape right in front of the Lady General!

The wing is arguing about whether the gryph's calls
raised an alarm. Lady General decides it's too risky. If
everyone stops arguing and flies there now, you'll beat

anyone on the ground and catch anyone in the air, retaining the element of surprise.

She gives the order: attack now. She takes flight, but you're still suspicious about gryphons in the area.

You smell something. A gryphon. Lady General snarls at your delay.

- Page 299: Investigate the smell

- Page 300: Ignore it and join the attack

INVESTIGATE EURAIYA

PAGE 299

You recognize the scent of the gryphon in the woods you'd previously let go. Clearly she had suspicions and has somehow managed to follow you!

You attack the gryphon, killing her quickly before she can squawk anything that might alert Lady General that you've encountered each other previously. You've saved your skin and also the raid! If she'd gotten away... Well, best not to dwell on that.

- Turn to page 350

IGNORE EURAIYA
PAGE 300

The scent suddenly is not important as Lady General calls for attack.

- Turn to page 352

ATTACK EURAIYA

PAGE 301

The gryphon hastily gathers a surprising number of rat corpses together in some kind of pack. Its movements are jerky, and it keeps glancing over to where you're flattened on the forest floor.

You're distracted for a moment, alarmed and repulsed, wondering why it could possibly want a pack full of rodents.

You give yourself a stern shake. You can't let it get away. Lady General has declared the attack will take place on the night of the Fracture. If the gryphon escapes, it'll alert its dire. And if the dire doesn't kill you, Lady General just might.

No, you *definitely* can't afford to risk the gryphon slipping away.

You leap out, crashing through brush and low-hanging branches, your large body working in your favor for once on this infernal mission.

The gryphon's eyes go wide, and it freezes like good prey as it sees you. It's just a small thing.

. . .

YOU CAN SNAP THE GRYPHON IN HALF WITH A STRONG BITE. But it's twitchy and fast, making it more agile in this verdant hellscape than you are. If your bite misses, you might not get a second chance.

A tiny blast of fire will *definitely* kill it, but the Lady General won't like that. She's said over and over again: *no fire.*

No one has to *tell* the Lady General, though, and slogging through all this dense growth has made the morning meal a distant memory...

Your stomach rumbles in anticipation.

- Page 303: Breathe fire and be certain

- Page 304: A fast strike with teeth and claws

TOAST EURAIYA

PAGE 303

The gryphon turns and flees, fast as a rabbit. It's a good thing you've got a mouthful of fire prepared, because the gryphon is already out of range of your teeth.

You open your jaws and allow a small jet of fire escape.

Or that's what you planned to do. It's been too long since you last let the fire out. Instead of a targeted stream, a torrent of flames escapes. It consumes the gryphon before it can even cry out.

It also consumes all of the underbrush in a twenty-foot cone in front of you. And now the bark of the trees is catching fire. And sparks have dropped to the forest floor. The decomposing leaves are smouldering — no, they're properly on fire now.

You gulp down the rest of your flames.

Lady General is going to be so angry...

- Turn to page 341

BITE EURAIYA
PAGE 304

Your leap takes you to the gryphon, your claws are out, your wings pointed like spears as you reach for her. Her eyes widen then contract in fear, and she lets loose a truncated scream. You grin, feeling that familiar rush as your claws reach for the kill.

A rat hits you in the face, its whip-like tail scoring your eye. You blink and move your head a fraction to toss the dead rodent free. But the distraction has done its job. Your claws close on empty air.

Another rat sails towards you as you gather to leap again. You blink and duck this time, avoiding the projectile. The gryphon has annoyingly good aim. And her beak is whipping those rats out of her pack and at your face faster than you'd have believed possible.

She slings more rats even as she scuttles and flutters away, keeping you at bay, until she squiggles through a narrow hole in a briar patch where you can't follow.

You smash your way around the briars, using your size and strength to force a path. But by the time you spot her again on the other side, she's too far ahead to catch. You try anyway, racing through branches and vines that tear at your wings and eyes.

But it's too late. She's made it back to the village. And she's chattering away. The gryphs around her are puffing up and starting to look your way.

You flee.

- Turn to page 343

FOLLOW EURAIYA

PAGE 306

You slither through the underbrush, trailing the gryphon as she returns to Rada's village. She doesn't hear you over the sound of her own passage, and she starts to relax the closer to home she gets. You can still smell the rats in her bag and occasionally see it swaying and bumping at her side. You suppress more shivers and try not to imagine the rituals she will use them in.

You finally reach the village. While the gryphon proceeds along, you crouch low and small, peering through a bush to watch her progress. It's quiet. The gryphs are either still asleep or away right now. You file that tidbit away for Lady General: *village empty near dawn.*

There's another gryphon approaching yours. You tense, tucking your tail tip under your chest so it doesn't twitch and betray you. This is it — will she raise the alarm? Did she actually see you?

There's a moment where the two gryphs squabble, and you tense, preparing to either attack or flee. But they clam down and walk away together. No alarm is raised.

You wait a few more minutes, just to make sure, but all remains quiet.

You breathe a sigh of relief, then congratulate yourself. It was *smart* of you to let her go! If you'd killed her, she might have been missed. And someone eccentric enough to pick rats out of the forest is clearly a witch of some kind. Unlike the hunters your team has killed before, the death of a witch might lure the dire out of its den.

You edge away from the village, back into the infernal forest. You make your way to the hilled area to complete your scouting assignment for Lady General.

Late in the afternoon, after *ages* of endless grasping trees and prickling, tangling vines, you take a moment to rest and clean some of the sap off your chest and shoulders. You curse the violent foliage around you.

Fortunately your curse is silent, because otherwise you wouldn't have heard the sound of several chirpy voices raised. Gryphons.

You swivel your head, locating the source of the sound, then start easing your way in that direction. It's a good thing, you tell yourself, that you're still sticky with sap and covered in leaf shreds. It will help cover your scent.

As you approach, you identify more and more voices. This isn't two or three gryphons, it sounds like a whole village. Your tail wiggles in excitement. *Finally!*

You wonder why you haven't seen anyone flying between the two villages. You've been skulking about all day searching for this den of pests because there hasn't been anyone to follow home. You're hungry and irritated and your snout is sticky with sap. Now that the gryphons are within your grasp, you feel a strong urge to crush them and vent your anger.

You remind yourself that a *smart* wyvern gets answers to their questions before jumping in and eating things.

You get close enough to see (and smell) that this is, indeed, a second village. It's even shabbier than the main village, but it's larger than you expect. It's large enough that you wonder if there's another dire out here. Lady General will definitely want to know *that*. Why else would Rada allow this village in his territory unless it had a dire defending it?

You watch for the rest of the day, circling around the smelly village to determine its size and topography. You kill a few of its inhabitants that are in your path, scavenging up a meal in the process.

You realize, when you're scrubbing your tongue against a tree — finally, a use for the foul things — after killing a denizen, that these gryphons are sick or deformed. They smell worse than a days old corpse, they're dirty and unkempt, and many of them have some kind of genetic condition making their back legs stick-like.

These must be the dire's cast-offs. You certainly haven't seen or heard anything of a dire all day. And dires aren't known for being quiet and hidden. So these must be the rejects from Rada.

You realize you have an opportunity. You can attack the village — a motley group like that stands no chance against you, even alone. This will reduce the number of gryphons prowling the forest, making it safer for your group to scout. It also will likely get rid of some of the dire's healers, who surely live here to care for these sad specimens. And if you wipe out this village using the Lady General's techniques, it will look like there's a large number of hostile gryphons in the area, making the dire spread his warriors even thinner.

Alternatively, you could leave the village intact and start laying the trail to point to this village as the hostile force Lady General is trying to conjure. The deformed and neglected rising up, demanding more food and better living conditions makes sense, right? If this works, the gryphs might start attacking each other. It might even draw the dire out early!

But which one is the *smart* choice?

- Page 310 Destroy the village to increase success of the main attack

- Page 331: Turn the gryphs against each other

ATTACK WILDERS

PAGE 310

You sneak into position. You know the gray one with the stick-leg deformity is one of the leaders here. If you kill him, the others will be less likely to coordinate an attack against you.

You wait, fire tickling your tongue in anticipation. You swallow it down, remembering Lady General's plans. *No fire.*

Finally, the gray one comes close enough. There are two others with him, but you have eyes only for the gray. He's the healthiest of the bunch. Definitely him first.

You launch yourself out of the forest, defying the bushes and tree limbs that try to drag you back. The gray doesn't react in time. He's under your claws, your wing spike is descending to stab him through the eye and ensure his death.

But you took your eyes off the others. Your singular focus was a mistake. The other two gryphs are at your sides. You feel their beaks close around your wing spars. They pierce the membrane with pincer-like grips on each wing and haul backwards, pulling your wings away from your body, spreading them wide and sending you sprawling forwards.

You thrash your tail and neck, trying to reach one of them, but they're fast, out of range. And the gray has jumped away while you thrashed after the others. He's shrieking something. Some kind of alarm.

You roar in frustration and pull on your wings. The pain in them increases, and you can feel the bones bruise. If the gryphs were much heavier or their bites stronger, you'd be nursing two broken wings right now. As it is, you succeed in pulling them off their feet and regain your balance.

Before you can sideswipe them with your tail, a whole horde of gryphons descends upon you. Their sharp little beaks hook into your wing spars, your tail, your flanks. Some of them land on your wings, forcing them flat. They're hissing and cawing at you from all sides, their eyes bright with bloodlust.

You're overwhelmed. Between the weight on your wings and the vicious hooks in your appendages, there aren't many options.

Clearly these gryphs have encountered your kind before. Another wave is coming at you with ropes. The gray one stares down at you in triumph.

This is what happens when wyverns fight like gryphons, you seethe, staring up at the leader of the vermin.

The fire builds in your throat. They only think they've won — your fire is your most powerful weapon. You can still roast the leader and probably enough of the ones on your wings to shake yourself free. But you have to do it before they bind you with the ropes and cut off your fire.

You know Lady General will be angry, though. She is

adamant no one use fire until the main attack. And this would be a *lot* of fire...

You realize there's another option. When the rope-bearers get here, the ones pinning you down will have to move. There will be a window where you'll be able to overpower them, if you can seize it, and if they don't have another trick under their feathers.

Or you could get out of here. If you use all your strength, you can tear yourself away from them. Literally tear. Your wings will be useless once the adrenaline wears off, but you'll be able to outpace them by air before then.

The rope-bearers are approaching. You're worried more about getting out of this alive than anything else. What's your best option?

- Page 313: Fight with fire

- Page 315: Fight without fire

- Page 328: Flee

TOAST WILDERS

F ire is the great equalizer. It's the power that wyverns have always had over gryphons, the power that keeps the gryphons in check.

And these gryphons need to learn their place.

You let the fire swell in your chest until it fills your throat and mouth. Until you let it erupt from you.

Flames engulf the gray gryph, charring him into nothing. You sweep your head around, fire streaking down in sweeps of molten death. The gryphons on your left wing fall with shrieks of pain and the scent of charred feather and hair. The gryphons on your right jump back instinctively, some releasing their clamp on your wing, some not. You melt the ones still attached to you and singe the others.

You use your newfound freedom to sweep around and eliminate those too slow to let go of your flanks and tail. And now you're completely unencumbered by the pests.

You chase down each of the escapees and pour fire over them until they crumble apart. Then you turn your sights to the village...

Once they're all dead, you return to the gray leader and bathe his corpse in your hottest fire, melting his bones until he is nothing but a shadow on the ground.

You look up. The flames have spread around you, their warmth a comforting presence. Smoke and ash billow up into the sky as the flames spread. The trees are succumbing now, flames licking up their trunks, climbing to the skies.

You gape your teeth in a grin, a fierce joy bubbling up in you. You are a *wyvern!*

- Turn to page 341

FIGHT WILDERS WITHOUT FIRE

PAGE 315

N*o fire.* You have to fight, there's no question about that, but you need to salvage the situation. You have size and strength on your side. They have numbers.

You lie still, like you've given up. The gray one, though, is watching you. He knows you're dangerous and doesn't let his people slack.

When the rope-bearers arrive, it takes all you have to remain quiet and feign calmness. You let them stand on your neck, let them rope your mouth closed. You struggle, but just enough to keep their attention focused on your head and the fire you let lick your teeth.

As the gryphs at your head slip the ropes around your snout, you feel the attention of those around you stutter. This is your opportunity. Eyes locked on the gray one, you allow yourself a small grin of victory.

You whip your tail, yanking it out of the mouths and claws of your captors. With a writhe of your spine, you send it smashing into the gryphons on your right wing. They crash into each other, letting you go with squawks of surprise.

You're pulling your wings to you, coiling your tail to thrash to the other side, when the gray one shrieks something. Beaks descend towards your eyes, but you squint them closed. That doesn't deter you from regaining your feet.

The two boulders that crash down onto your wings do, though. You roar and thrash with pain, but the ropes around your maw are secured and the beaks pecking at your squinted eyes are persistent.

There's nothing you can do as the pests crawl over you, trussing you up until you can't move. When they roll the boulders off your wings one at a time and tie them back, you can't even take advantage of the opportunity. Your wings hurt like they've never hurt before. You wonder if they're broken. And they're tied up behind you so you can't relax them.

You can't even see what's going on because of the infernal pecking.

When they finally pile off of you and start dragging you into the village, the severity of your situation really sets in.

You're well and truly captured. You can barely move, and the pain in your wings is unbearable. You don't know why they're keeping you alive, but you're pretty sure you don't want to be here to find out.

Which means you have two options. You can wait for someone from your wing to miss you and come after you. Or you can try to escape.

They're both terrible options. Your day can't get much worse.

• Page 318: Wait for rescue

- Page 320: Try to escape

WAIT FOR RESCUE
PAGE 318

You don't have the energy to try and escape. Even if you could manage it, your wings are in no condition to get you in the air, and you're losing blood from all the chunks the stupid gryphons ripped from your flesh in the fight.

Lady General will come looking for you at some point. She knows where you are. And she'll tear this village apart when she sees what they've done.

You get as comfortable as you can with your snout tucked into your chest and your wings hyper-extended behind you. You fall asleep fantasizing of the destruction Lady General will wreak when she gets here...

You don't sleep well. The night stretches on forever. Lady General doesn't come. When the sun rises, the gryphons start waking up and chattering. They come and stare at you with fear and anger. Some shriek things at you. You have no difficulty imaging what they're saying.

You nap fitfully when the pain allows.

You're awoken by a hush and tenseness that has spread over the village. A brute of a gryphon approaches with the cursed gray leader. He's no dire, but he's one of the largest gryphons you've seen and an eye-watering red. Beside him walks the rat-gathering witch from the forest. You shiver, then immediately regret it as pain spikes through your wings.

The gray brings them over. They study you, the red with bravado, the witch with fear. The fire is trapped inside you by the severe bend in your neck, and you're too drained to make a threatening display. You imagine Lady General descending upon them right now, crushing them down like insects. It helps cut the shame.

The three gryphs walk around you, examining you, as they talk in urgent tones. The witch and the red brute confer then, with a final piercing glance back at you, take flight. Your hope sinks as you notice their course is a direct line to the dire's village.

- Turn to page 344

ESCAPE!

PAGE 320

They take you back to their shabby village, which smells even worse once you're inside it. If you're going to have any chance at escape, you need them to think you're not a threat.

You allow yourself to enter the recuperating meditative state that allows you to accelerate your healing by shutting down all other unnecessary processes. You can still hear what's going on around you, but you lie unmoving and are otherwise insensate to the world. Even what you hear comes as from a distance and is processed in a woolly haze.

Over the course of the remaining day, your wounds slowly close. Your torn muscles and bruised wings swell and ache, then gradually ease. It would take several days in this trance to heal fully, and you know you don't have that kind of time. You can only hope you will have healed enough by nightfall to effect your escape.

The sounds that filter to you reveal two guards are stationed nearby. You hear the villagers come, gawk, and leave. You hear the village activity increase as gryphons come home in the evening, then quiet again as they settle for the night. You hear one guard leave. The other rests nearby but is no longer shifting and twitching, made nervous by your nearness. Instead, it is sighing and huffing.

When the guard's noises turn to the soft breathing and slight whistling that indicates sleep, you rouse yourself from your trance. It's difficult, your body wants longer to heal, but you force yourself back into awareness and examine your situation.

Silently, you test your injuries and your bonds. Your wounds hurt but not in a way that indicates structural damage. You can fight through pain, so that's good news. Your wings aren't broken, but they're heavily bruised — the meditation helped significantly, but you'll only be able to fly a short ways before you risk permanent damage.

Your bonds are the more immediate problem. They have you trussed up so tightly you can barely move. Your head is tucked against your chest, forcing your throat into a tight bend you can barely breathe through. Your tail and claws are bound together, and your tail is further bound to your wings, which are pulled up behind you almost the point of dislocation.

If you can get your head free, you can untruss yourself. You spend the next few marks flexing against the ropes and knots, forcing your snout into your chest. You stretch them until there's no give left, then reassess.

You have enough slack to turn your head a bit. You think you can reach some of the vine-ropes binding you if you really strain. If you can get them near your teeth, you can chew through them and free yourself. It's not going to be a silent effort, though, and you don't know how long you can count on the guard to sleep. If he catches you before you're done, they'll just truss you up again and bind you even tighter this time.

But the slack also means you can get a nice curve in your neck if you angle your head just right. Your fire is accessible. And fire is the bane of all ropes.

Small problem: you're not actually fireproof. Your hide is fire-resistant, but you're going to have to send the flames straight into your shoulder and let them lick around you to reach the ropes. Wyvern fire, even at its lowest intensity, is made to kill. And you're going to be as close to the source as a thing can get. You'll probably survive. But it's going to hurt. A *lot*. And you'll have burns from it that can kill you if they get infected. You'll have a nasty, melted trophy of this on your skin for the rest of your life, if you survive that long.

But at least it will be over quickly.

You need to make your decision and act before your guard wakes up.

- Page 321: Burn through your ropes

- Page 325: Chew through your ropes

BURN THE ROPES
PAGE 321

Go out like a wyvern! The thought tickles at you, sending your tail tip twitching against your wings (though only the smallest wiggle). Another voice reminds you that Lady General said no fire, but you're committed now.

You take a deep breath, both to kindle your fire and to brace yourself for the pain. But there's no bracing that will be sufficient, you know. Before you can think about it, you let the flames free.

Your shoulder is on fire. Literally, for a few moments. Then with pain for much longer. The ropes wilt away, freeing your head. You twist your neck around, whipping the fire across the ropes binding your wings. The bindings whither to ash, and your wings fall heavily at your sides. Another wave of pain hits you as your flight muscles, cramped from being forced into an awkward position for so long, tear as gravity proves too strong for your stiff, weakened muscles to overcome.

Your flames cut off with a gasp. You can't move your wings. They're frozen, half-spread at your sides, as inanimate as saplings. Between your shoulder and your wings, you've reached a level of pain where it's all you can do not to scream. Instead, you're panting through your mouth to hold the scream in.

Not that it matters. The guard is awake now. He's screeching for others. You can't manage to care. You find that you're rocking as you pant, your head bobbing forward and back in time with your breath.

The world beyond you almost doesn't exist. You barely mark when the gryphons gather or when they flee. Their sounds are background crackling, all you can hear is the scream of pain inside as your shoulder burns and invisible fire burns your wings from within.

No, the gryphons are gone. But the crackling remains. You blink and your eyes refocus, only now noticing you've been staring at nothing. For how long? The crackle and hiss around you swells.

Fire.

A fan of fire stretches out in front of you, stretching up into the trees. It's already consumed debris on the ground and undergrowth and dwellings. Now it's clawing up the trees. Spreading as wind picks up burning needles and leaves and carries them farther afield.

You don't know how long you've been bathing the area in fire, but the gryphons have evacuated, leaving you there alone. Free.

A laugh bubbles up inside you, but what erupts from you is the scream you've been holding back.

- Turn to page 341

CHEW ROPES

PAGE 325

No *fire,* Lady General said. You've followed those rules so far, and that's what got you into this mess.

But as tempting as the fire is, you know it's not worth it. You'll be too badly injured by the burn to get away. Besides, how will you ever attract Lady General if your side is melted away? Wyverns are supposed *to* burn, not *be* burned.

As quietly as you can, you strain for the vine, twisting your neck into a position you didn't realize you could achieve before. It takes some lingual gymnastics, but you manage to get the rope to your teeth.

Your mouth is dry. That's fortunate because it means you're not making moist noises as you chew and shred, which would surely wake the guard. But it's unfortunate because now you have woody bits of vine sticking into your gums and tongue, fine splinters you can't possibly remove.

You manage to saw through the rope holding your neck down. It breaks with a quiet snap. You freeze and listen for the guard.

Only soft whistles meet your ears.

It takes too long to get your neck uncramped. Once you can move it again, you immediately go for the vines around your wings. If your neck was that bad, you know it's going to take a while for your wings to recover enough to get you out of here.

You have to roll on your side to get enough leverage to reach the wing ropes. Which turns out to be fortunate, because once they snap, your wings are worse than useless. As you gnaw at the remaining rope strands, you stretch and flex your wings with silent urgency.

You can taste your blood in your mouth and the nasty sappy/woody vines. And the gryphon guard has stopped whistling and is taking deeper breaths. Is it waking? You gnaw faster, your teeth cutting into your skin even more than when you were being careful.

The last bindings slither away. You quickly shake feeling back into your legs and roll to your feet. Your wings are recovered enough to tuck into your sides, but you're not going to be flying on them just yet.

And the guard is snorting, its ears twitching.

Time to go!

Since flying is out, you'll need to leave by foot. You cast around, looking for the direction that takes you past the fewest dwellings. Fortunately, you're over in a refuse area, so there aren't too many gryph nests nearby.

You find what you're looking for behind you. It's the wrong direction from the warren, but once you're in the forest, you can circle around.

You crouch low and use all your powers of stealth to sneak towards the trees. It feels a bit silly, sneaking when you're in the open, but you don't want to wake the guard with a rustling misstep. You probably look ridiculous, and you're glad no one else from your wing is here to see you.

Behind you, the guard has awakened. You hear his squawk of alarm. Others take up the squawk just as you pass into the underboughs of the forest.

You can't breathe a sigh of relief just yet. You put a bit more distance between you and the foul village, but then wait and listen. When it seems no one wants to risk coming to search for you in the dark, you allow yourself a grin.

It takes the rest of the night to find your way back to the warren. The cursed forest is even more difficult to navigate at night, and plants that you could swear don't exist during the day keep reaching out to grab and bind you.

• Turn to page 343

FLEE THE WILDERS

This was a mistake. And there's nothing you can do about it now except get back to the warren and let Lady General know. These gryphons know you're here now, and clearly you can't fight them alone. You need to live to fight another day.

Which, unfortunately, means sacrificing yourself right now.

The gray gryphon is staring you down, waiting for you to make your move. So you indulge him.

You take a deep breath. The gryphons holding your head and neck down tense, their little claws prickling into your skin. The nooses around your snout and neck tighten, tightening off your fire. But that's fine.

You let out a roar through your clenched teeth, lips pulled back and tongue down to let sparks spray free. You're not trying to breathe fire, just frighten them a bit. And it works.

The gryphs in front of you leap back as the sparks approach them. Unlike wyverns, gryphons are quite inflammable. The sparks also catch the attention of the other gryphons holding you down.

In that moment of distraction, you act. You surge upwards, bucking the gryphons off your back and neck, then spin in a rapid circle. Some of the gryphons let go as you spin. More do not. You feel the sting as chunks of your flesh are left in their beaks. Some chunks more than sting — like those in your wings.

You know your wings are bleeding and in bad shape, but you don't look at them. If you see them, the pain will register, and you'll be grounded. Instead, you whip your tail around, throwing back a few gryphs who recovered from your surge, and throw yourself into the air.

Your wingbeats are off, apparently they're damaged more than you thought. But your legs are still plenty strong. They get you high enough that your faltering wings can sort themselves out. And you're flying.

You don't risk a glance back until you're well above the trees and have found a rhythm in the air. You're only a fraction of your normal speed, but you're still faster than the gryphs. They're just now clearing the trees, and every slightly-wobbly beat of your wings is lurching you farther ahead.

They don't chase you very far before giving up. The gray leader lasts the longest, but even he gives up as it becomes clear he has no hope of catching you.

Once he gives up, you find a spot to land. You're not a stupid wyvern, so you weren't flying straight back to the warren. You'll make your way back afoot.

You decided to stop just in time, it seems, because as you're landing, your worst-damaged wing gives out. You tuck your wings to your sides, still ignoring them. It's going to be a long trek back, especially now that you've sprained your ankle in that rough landing. You don't want to be distracted by awareness of your wounds.

Instead, you end up distracted by thoughts of how Lady General will react to you mucking things up a second time.

- Turn to page 343

DISCREDIT WILDERS

PAGE 331

The Lady General will be so excited. You're taking *initative!* You're being *smart.* You take some of the cloth off the dead gryphon at your feet. It's dirty and smelly, but it seems to be a kind of badge to mark these sick ones. You'll tear it up and leave it on the claws or beaks of the next gryphons you kill.

That will *definitely* turn the dire's gryphs against the sick ones. And while they're fighting each other, your team will swoop in to victory!

Now, you just have to find some victims...

YOU CLIMB THE NEARBY TALL HILL AND FIND A POSITION TO look out over land. You have to bite some tree limbs off, which turns out to be a strangely satisfying activity. You get distracted, gnawing on the limbs, splintering offending bark between your teeth, until thoughts of the Lady General's disapproval snap you back to the mission. What would she think, finding you clinging to trees with your wings, sap and splinters in your teeth? You make a mental note to wash your face and mouth before returning to her.

Once more on task, you survey the area. You're exposed up here, so you need to make your observations and get back down before anyone sees you.

Your eyes are drawn to the left and an especially thick and verdant patch of trees. There are two small groups of gryphons leaving, hunters by the looks of it, carrying their kills back to the main village. And there's another group arrowing towards it.

There's some bright movement in the corner of your eye. You swivel your head. To your right, equally far away, is a waterfall. There are rocky cliffs over that way, and what looks to be a lake at the base of the falls. It looks lovely and peaceful, and you can easily imagine couples going there for a romantic interlude. Unless gryphons didn't do that sort of thing. But surely the fresh moving water would attract them if nothing else.

Then there's a flash of movement in the middle. A lone red gryphon flying away from Rada's village. Flying low and fast. With purpose. It dives down into the trees and disappears. It's the closest to you, and either the gryphon is alone or it's going to a location of interest.

You're conflicted. What would please the Lady General more?

Taking down lots of hunters in the forest sounds appealing both to your own inner hunter and because it would deliver a bigger blow to the dire. But your size and bulk will make discovery riskier. You also don't know how many gryphon packs are there right now. Surely not too many or they would get in each other's way...

Picking off gryphons by couples or singles at the romantic waterfall isn't quite as brave and dashing a choice. But it might be the *smarter* one, since there's less risk of being caught.

You only have enough time left before you have to report back to go in one direction.

And then there's the lone gryphon — what was it up to? You could go there first then make your decision, but if you run into trouble, you might not have time to make the kills and plant your evidence.

- Page 334: Hunting grounds

- Page 336: Romantic Waterfall

- Page 338: The Lone Guard

HUNTING GROUNDS
PAGE 334

You sneak into the hunting grounds, the epitome of stealth. You imagine yourself getting the drop on group after group of hunters, picking them off one by one, building a mountain of corpses from which you will rule.

You shake the fantasy from your head. Who would *want* to rule this awful place, you remind yourself, disentangling from a persistent vine.

Rada, you suppose.

Well, that will soon be fixed. Really, you're doing all these fluff-brains a favor. Surely even death is preferable to these horrible conditions.

You sigh silently and press onwards. Eventually, you make it to the hunting grounds. Where, to your shock and amazement, everything is exactly the same. Trees. Vines. Brambles. Thorny things. Mud. Snakes. The attack can't come soon enough.

You slink around, scouting for hunters. You catch a few scents, but nothing fresh. By the time you come across a group, you're irritated and hungry.

Your stomach rumbles and makes the decision for you. A quick strike instead of a stealth attack.

The gryphon is in your stomach and another lying at your feet before you could even summon flames. You bolt the gryphon down, then immediately regret it as your stomach complains.

While your guts are sorting themselves out and giving you what-for, you discover gryphons have surrounded you. You discover this when they descend upon you with beaks and claws, as you watch your fire-filled drool dribble down to coat the regurgitated remains of gryphon.

You put up a good fight, killing several in the process, but your stomach is still roiling, and your fire keeps coming out as sprays of mucus-coated sparks. The gryphons overwhelm you and pin you down.

- Turn to page 344

ROMANTIC WATERFALL

PAGE 336

You fight your way through the possessed foliage to the little waterfall. It's prettier than you expected. The water rushes and tumbles in a gentle melody that would make a perfect counterpoint to a fire. The air is a tad cool; there's a slight breeze. The water is fresh and clear. Even the demonic jungle recedes nearby, giving way to rocky ground.

The rocky ground is a kink in your attack plan. You'll have to lure the gryphons off the rock and near the forest or risk them taking flight before you can overpower them. You come up with several plans and decide on a place to settle in for the wait.

It doesn't take long for a gryphon to come by. And it turns out, the rocks aren't much of a problem. Over the next few marks, you catch several gryphons by ones and twos. They tend to avoid the rocks and stick near the forest, putting you in a prime spot.

You puzzle the rock-avoidance out as you wait, the pile of bodies behind you ever-growing. When one of the gryphs is swept onto the rocks by a gust of wind and yelps as it prances off, you realize the rocks must be hot, warmed by the direct sunlight. Your thick, fire-retardant skin didn't register that, but these thin-skinned gryphons must get burned.

Once the sun starts to set, you decide you have enough bodies. You pull them out of the forest and scatter them around the waterfall, careful to leave bits of the fabric on their claws or in their beaks. All told, you have ten victims. There *were* eleven, but then lunch happened.

Feeling satisfied with your work, you slip back into the trees and return to the warren.

• Turn to page 348

THE LONE GUARD

You follow the lone guard. You find a cave with a camp of gryphs in cages. The guard is shouting at them, and they're afraid.

The only thing you hate more than gryphs is bullies.

You kill the bully.

Having done your good deed, you don't feel guilt when you eat the gryphs in the cages.

Satiated, but with no bodies to plant, you need to revisit your other options.

But there's a coldness and light coming from the depths of the cave. You wonder what could be causing it. Lady General might appreciate if you investigated. You still have time to plant your evidence but only if you don't delve deeper into the cave.

- Page 334: Huntings Grounds

- Page 336: Romantic Waterfall

- Page 339: Investigate Cave

INVESTIGATE CAVE
PAGE 339

The mysterious, cool mist makes you reconsider your choices. What's even stranger is the way it seems to ooze out of the ground. There's an air current pushing against you, leaching the heat from your body, and it seems to want you to leave.

Still, you push on. It's just a cave, what's the worse that could happen? You're a wyvern! Wyverns are what other species are afraid of meeting in caves. You fear nothing!

...Except Lady General's disappointment.

You continue on for some time, and when you look back, all you can see is a wall of white.

That's strange, you think, *but at least I can touch the walls to find my way back.*

You settle on your hind legs for a moment and reach out with your wings, but you cannot feel stone. It's like you're in the sky, in a cloud that never ends. You can hear the faint sound of music, and you decide to follow it. After all, someone has to be making that sound, and they'll know where the exit is.

In the distance, you see flashes of green light. You

follow the lights, creeping low to the ground. They lead you deeper and deeper into the cave, then they vanish.

You reach around with your wings and snout, searching for the cave wall again. This time, you can feel the shape of stone and moss in front of you.

At least, you think it's stone and moss. All you can see is white. And a pair of green eyes.

• Turn to Page 346

FIRE ENDING

PAGE 341

All around you, your flames take on their own life. Released from your will, they spread and grow. They writhe along the ground, spreading like vines of light. Others jump to the sky, clawing up trees, pulling leaves and bark in to feed their bid for the heavens.

Smoke, white and thick, the escaped spirits of millions of tiny, expired flamelets, billows away, lifts above the trees, a warning to all denizens — *we come.*

The sound of a billion fiery mouths snapping up life roars and crackles around you. Sparks spit as they jump towards new, untouched horizons. Heat buffets you, bathes your skin, dries you out, bakes down into your bones.

Your flames live, grow, reproduce. Their lives and the lives of their children play out around you, entrancing you with their beauty and strife. Some smother themselves, some dance on the winds, some burn like a flash and expire, some smoulder and seethe. Each has a voice which rises in supplication. You are their creator. Their every gyration, leap, death is a worship to you.

You bask in their reverence. Your soul quiets and absorbs the catastrophic tribute of your flames, filling with a sense of rightness. You are a wyvern. This is your purpose. All is right within you.

Even when the spirits of your children are spun away on the wingbeats of a dire, you feel nothing but peace. The dire descends. In its eyes you see not death but the reflections of your legacy. You call the flames to you, rouse them to fight for you. To avenge you.

Dire Rada claims your death, even as your spawn close around him.

- Page 293: Return to the start of Your Dire Adventure

- Page 355: Move on to the next story in the anthology

LADY GENERAL ENDING

PAGE 343

You arrive back at the warren, exhausted and anxious. Lady General is there.

You tell her what happened.

You've screwed up. Again. You knew she was going to be unhappy. You thought she would snarl and shout. You expected she might pummel you a bit to vent her displeasure.

You never really expected her to kill you.

- Page 293: Return to the start of Your Dire Adventure

- Page 355: Move on to the next story in the anthology

Just when things couldn't get any bleaker, a huge shape descends upon you, falling from the sky like a stone to land in front of your snout.

The ground shakes from the impact. This can only be Dire Rada.

Not only is he enormous, but he has that look of the dired. You had erroneously thought gryphon dires would be less terrifying than wyvern dires. But Rada is just as feral and twice as mean. He bristles with rage and doesn't look on the best side of sane.

And that look is being directed squarely at you.

He says something. It's not the shrill, chirpy language of the gryphons but another language. You don't understand either way.

He doesn't seem to mind. When he breaks your wings, it's as dispassionately as if he were flicking a bone aside.

He takes off again directly, leaving you behind with some gryphons you would describe as hulking had Rada not been nearby to make them appear like skinny hatchlings.

These new gryphons are your guard. They cut off your fire, binding your neck and head with ropes, and take you back to Rada's village, where they position you in the middle of some sort of arena.

You have failed.

You don't realize how much until Rada returns and drops two bloody objects in front of you. He kicks them until they roll enough to reveal the faces of the two fighters of your wing. Your stomach twists and heaves.

You hope Lady General is smart enough to avoid Rada. You hope she's smart enough to abort the mission and return home.

You hold that hope until Rada returns with a third object.

Lady General's empty eyes stare at you, her jaw slack and loose.

You have failed everyone.

You don't have long to feel despair over that as Rada turns his mad gaze on you, and you learn exactly what the final moments of your wingmates were like.

- Page 293: Return to the start of Your Dire Adventure

- Page 355: Move on to the next story in the anthology

COLDBRIGHT ENDING

PAGE 346

The green eyes, the singing, the mist that is at once bright, impenetrable, and freezing cold—you have wandered into a kirin den.

Do the gryphs know there's one so close, you wonder? Do they know the danger they're in?

At once, you open your mouth to breathe fire. A stream of pyroclastic destruction cuts through the mist in front of you, but the beast of legend is already gone. In the song that echoes throughout the cavern, you can hear a laugh.

Desperate, you begin to breathe fire in all directions, looking for a path out. Every time the flames cease, the mist encloses you again. You see what looks like a side tunnel, and you hurry in there to escape.

You let a little fire escape from your lips, just enough to light up the room, and you're alarmed by what you see. Wyverns, gryphs—rows of each are frozen in ice and placed next to an egg that has begun to illuminate and rock in response to your presence.

You open your mouth to destroy it all, but the mist

seeps into your throat, and you begin to cough. By the time you finish your coughing fit, there are two green eyes in front of you.

The kirin speaks in the ancient language, musical and bitter, and then opens its own mouth. The mist around you turns to ice, and you're frozen solid. Before you enter a deep sleep, the kirin drags you next to a large egg.

Inside the egg, you see two green eyes staring out at you.

Your last thoughts are: *Maybe the Lady General will find me in time.*

- Page 293: Return to the start of Your Dire Adventure

- Page 355: Move on to the next story in the anthology

EXTERNAL PRAISE ENDING
PAGE 348

L ady General is pleased when you recount your day. Her eyes light up with that special look she gets when she's scheming. She calls you *smart*.

You don't know how things can get any better. You've definitely redeemed yourself for your previous mistake. And Lady General is muttering away about plans to further discredit the sickly village and turn the gryphons against one another.

You settle in the for the night, content to listen. As you wait for her to come up with her next plan and issue you more orders, your mind drifts back to the waterfall.

Maybe once this is all done and the pesky gryphons are eradicated, you'll ask Lady General to the waterfall for a drink and to warm yourselves on the rocks one evening. You might even venture to use her name. Would she mind that?

You spend a happy evening imagining the future.

- Page 293: Return to the start of Your Dire Adventure

- Page 355: Move on to the next story in the anthology

INTERNAL PRAISE ENDING
PAGE 350

You were smart to kill the spy. If she'd gotten away, she would have alerted the gryphs and foiled Lady General's plans.

Lady General calls for you and your wing to take to the air.

Once this is all over, you'll remind her how *smart* your quick action was. And maybe you'll ask her to come bathe her wounds at that romantic little waterfall you spotted earlier.

Puzzling over how to broach that invitation keeps your mind occupied until the gryphon village appears under you.

As one, your wing descends upon the hapless gryphons, and Lady General calls for fire.

Your fire leaps free at last, and you pour it out upon the denizens and their dwellings. Roars of delight, your own and those of your wing, resonate through the air as the fires rage and stampede through the village.

This is what you were made for. Fire and flight. The purging of the world with flame.

You are a wyvern, and you are having a very good day.

- Page 293: Return to the start of Your Dire Adventure

- Page 355: Move on to the next story in the anthology

Your wing is a thing of beauty. The four of you descend upon the unsuspecting gryphon village and bathe it in flames. It's almost as though you're a single organism in four bodies, so perfectly do you work together.

Lady General had always worried whether she would be able to get everyone to work together. You'd heard her muttering to herself about it in the night. But this attack puts all those doubts to rest. Even the headstrong brutes in the wing fall into formation and follow orders.

Dire Rada joins the battle during your second pass of slathering flames over his village. He is a terrible sight. Massive, crackling with rage, and roaring loud enough to leave your ears ringing. It takes all four of you to bring him down. One of the brutes falls before Lady General's strategy pays off but through no fault of hers — he was too slow to evade the dire's wicked claws.

The attack is over too soon. The Lady General declares it a success and orders the wing away. You want to stay longer, to dance in the sky with the flames, to pour out still more, but Lady General recalls you to your senses. Flying above fire is risky, even for a wyvern.

Chagrined, you suggest going to a waterfall you'd spotted on one of your previous scouting missions to bathe the wounds Rada has inflicted (no one escaped unscathed). Fortunately, Lady General agrees and seems to forget about you being an idiot about the fire.

You lead the remainder of your wing to the waterfall. Once the battle high has passed, you find a quiet moment to sidle up to Lady General. The brute is sulking downstream. Maybe he misses his comrade. You certainly don't.

You praise the attack and compliment the Lady General on her victory.

"No thanks to the idiots I'm saddled with," she mutters.

You deflate. Clearly she *did* remember you being an idiot about the fire. And that mistake with letting the gryphon get away. How are you ever going to be good enough for her?

You see a pole stuck in the bank with a string going into the water. The pole is bending and the string is sending out ripples as it jerks around.

You mumble an excuse to Lady General and shuffle over to investigate the pole. Peering into the clear water, you see a big fish attached to other end of the string.

You pluck it from the water and take it to Lady General as a peace offering.

She sighs, but you get a thank you. She even says your name. That's progress!

- Page 293: Return to the start of Your Dire Adventure

- Page 355: Move on to the next story in the anthology

RELWEN

SAYLOR FERGUSON

From the time she was a young gryph, half-grown and fresh out of the nursery, Relwen had wanted to be a Hunter. She could remember well the first day she strode up to the hunters, hoping to accompany them into the mountain forests in search of deer, or turkeys, or rabbits or any of the other prey items with which Relwen had familiarized herself for this moment specifically.

She'd stood only half as tall as the gryphon leading the hunt: Kasper, the silver-feathered son of Direlord Maylar. Relwen swallowed back her nerves and approached him carefully, tapping him on the flank with a gentle paw.

"Excuse me, sir," she said, chastising herself for the smallness of her voice. Kasper turned around, casting his gaze much higher in search of another gryph before looking down on Relwen. Surprise lit in his eyes.

"Shouldn't you be back in the nursery, little one?" he asked far too kindly.

Relwen, not entirely familiar with the proper ways to

address a higher-up, had bristled. "I'm not a kit! I moved out of the nursery today!"

Kasper's amusement was edging on annoyance, Relwen could tell. His eyes narrowed slightly as he tilted his head to study Relwen. "You're one of the half-breed kits, aren't you? Jessen's son?"

"Daughter," Relwen clarified, puffing herself up. "And I don't know who Jessen is."

"I guess you wouldn't," Kasper said. "But fact of the matter is that you can't join us today. This is a hunt for initiated Hunters only. We might come across some dangerous things out there."

Relwen stared across the stream that bordered the pridegrounds, gazed into the dark trees rising on the opposite side. No matter how hard she tried to imagine terrifying things lurking in the forest, all she could summon was a sense of wonder and a deep longing to be there under the canopy, breathing in the scent of pine and fern and moss.

"I'm not afraid," she said with confidence. "And besides, I'm going to be a Hunter someday."

A couple of the other gryphs in the hunting group chuckled lightly to themselves, but none of them made eye contact with Relwen when she stared their way. Kasper pulled Relwen's attention back to him by placing a patronizing talon on her shoulder.

"Listen, kid," he said softly. "Maybe nobody's told you about this before, and if that's the case then I'm sorry. But pride law says that half-breed gryphs can never hold titles. You can come hunting with us someday, sure. But you can't be a Hunter."

Relwen, tears prickling the corners of her eyes, pulled away from Kasper. "Well that sounds like a pile of wolf scat gone moldy!" she shouted before running away, desperate not to let the hunters see her cry.

She ran back to the nursery and collapsed in a heap, gulping back tears. Relwen hoped that the hunters hadn't seen her destination. After all, she might not have been telling the whole truth about having moved out that morning.

Stell, Relwen's closest friend and fellow half-breed, rushed over and began making worried noises, ever the little kitcarer.

I'll have to tell her, Relwen realized. *I'll have to tell her that no matter how hard we try, we'll never be enough.*

RELWEN WAS HAPPY FOR STELL. OVERJOYED, EVEN. WHO wouldn't be happy to see their best friend doing so well in life? Stell had become Wolfslayer and Kitcarer in one fell swoop, and now she was mates with the direlord's daughter. The unlucky little kit Relwen had grown up with was now one of the pride's biggest celebrities.

Relwen would never let Stell see it—she'd never let *anyone* see how she was feeling, after adopting the carefree persona she'd worn ever since her first great disappointment—but she was restless. Stell didn't need Relwen anymore, as far as she could see. She'd walked in on Stell and Lila giggling together in their nest enough times to realize her company wasn't needed in the nursery anymore. And she didn't think there was any great upcoming opportunity to rise above her half-breed status like Stell and become an initiated Hunter. Really, what was left for her in Maylar's pride?

"Relwen, pay attention!" a voice whispered harshly,

pulling Relwen from her thoughts. She glanced over at the gryph who'd spoken—Hunter Nylah, one of the few opinicus Hunters—and ticked her ears back apologetically. Nylah simply pointed her beak at the deer they'd been hunting.

About two marks north of the pridegrounds was a meadow. It broke up the endless tree line of the mountain forests, allowing sunlight to touch the ground and coax grass into existence. In the shadowed forest interior, there were few places where herbivores like the deer Relwen and Nylah were stalking could find such an easy meal. For that reason, the meadow was an excellent place to hunt, although the hunters were careful not to visit too often, in fear of scaring off all the prey.

It was also a pretty nice place for a romantic getaway, as Relwen knew. In the summer evenings, fireflies danced over the grass in a synchronous display of light. Relwen had come to the meadow in the summertime with several gryphs, laughing and tumbling among the fireflies and dandelions. Of course, that was neither here nor there, but all the same Relwen felt herself grow hot with the summer memories of this place.

Distracted, Relwen glanced over at Nylah with a raised eye ridge. "You remember that evening last summer when we came here and you got so scared by the killdeer you nearly stepped on?"

Nylah glared at Relwen humorlessly. "Shut up. We came here to hunt."

Relwen sighed. "It's too early for the fireflies anyway."

Nylah huffed, clearly annoyed now, and Relwen allowed herself a small smile. Yeah, she really must be bored if bothering her past romantic flings while they were trying to feed the pride was her entertainment for the day. She resumed staring across the meadow, at the grass turned brown and brittle after the long winter.

While Nylah's feathers were sort of like a humming-bird's, with green feathers on her wings and head and white feathers on her chest, Relwen, with her brown feathers, was much better suited for stalking unseen across the field in the cold months. Nylah was a better tracker, anyway, and Relwen was more skilled in taking down prey.

"You'd better pounce before it goes back under the trees." Nylah nodded at the deer, which was casually perusing the edge of the meadow, unaware of the two gryphs watching its every move. "If you want the pride to eat tonight, you need to…"

Relwen, beginning to tire of Nylah's annoying voice, interrupted her by charging at the deer.

With three flaps of her wings to boost her speed, Relwen caught up to the deer right before it could get back to the safety of the trees. The deer bleated piteously —but only once—before Relwen took its neck in her powerful beak and killed it.

A bloodless kill, Relwen thought with pride.

But if that was the case, what then was *that,* dotting a small tumble of granite rocks at the edge of the forest? Relwen stepped off her prey, moving cautiously toward the spattering of red upon the stones. She leaned down to take a sniff, confirmed it was blood. *Gryph* blood.

Alarm shot down Relwen's spine, making her feathers stand on end. She reached out, touching the blood with the sensitive pad of her paw. It wasn't warm, but that didn't mean much considering the cold weather that came with the end of winter. Far as Relwen knew, she and Nylah were the only gryphs to visit the meadow in over a month.

And there weren't any injuries in Maylar's pride right now. Relwen stared into the forest, spooked by its dark depths for the first time in her life.

Once again, Nylah's irritated voice cut through Relwen's thoughts. "Relwen! What are you doing over there?"

Relwen forced her feathers flat, taking several calming breaths. "Sorry," she called back. "Get over here and help me carry this deer."

The two gryphs dragged the deer carcass into the middle of the field, where it would be easiest to take off. Nylah never noticed the bloody stones.

But Relwen couldn't think of anything else as she and Nylah hefted the deer into the air and began their journey home.

FREEZING MIST COATED THE VALLEY OF MAYLAR'S pridegrounds the following morning. After tossing and turning in her nest all night, Relwen was more than ready to start the day. Fluffing her feathers against the cold fog as she left her lean-to nest, Relwen cast a glance around to see who was awake.

The mist blurred colors and shapes, and Relwen knew that nobody would see her sneak across the stream and into the woods. So that's exactly what she did. Besides, who here would miss the hunters' annoying shadow?

The flight to the meadow took a bit longer than it had the day before, primarily because Relwen found herself stuck in one fog bank after the other. The forest itself was clear of mist; very little ever permeated the thick tree line, but it hovered over the trees like a kitcarer over a flock of kits, forcing Relwen to fly haphazardly in the small clear space between the canopy and the fog.

Finally, she arrived at the meadow, which was coated in mist without the trees to chase away the moisture. She landed blindly among the fog, accidentally stabbing her paw on a pointy rock. "Ow," she muttered, shaking away the hurt. Being more careful now, Relwen crept across the field to the blood-covered granite stones.

And found herself promptly kicked in the chest by a well-aimed hoof.

Suddenly, Relwen was surrounded. It was difficult to make out how many there were through the fog, but Relwen knew immediately that she'd just been attacked by wilders.

"Wait!" she wheezed, still breathless and crumpled on the ground from the kick to her chest. "Please! I'm alone. I'm not here to hurt anyone!"

A hippogryph stepped forward, his feathers as gray as the mist over the meadow. Probably how he'd managed to sneak up on Relwen without her noticing, she figured. Though he cut an intimidating figure against the hazy sky, when he spoke, his voice was young. Younger than Relwen by a fracture or so.

"Check the field," he commanded. "Make sure this one is telling the truth."

The shadowy figures surrounding Relwen slipped away into the fog, leaving Relwen alone with the gray hippogryph. Her eyes still watered in pain, but at least her breath was returning.

"Who are you?" she rasped.

The hippogryph snorted in a way that was much more equine than a gryphon or opinicus. "I don't think you're in a situation to be questioning me." His voice was arrogant, but Relwen heard an undercurrent of nerves. She knew it well, had worn that voice herself for most of her life.

"All clear," called another gryph, returning to the hippogryph's side. "She's telling the truth: she's alone."

The gray hippogryph narrowed his eyes. Relwen could sense his confusion.

He has no idea what he's doing. I thought he was their leader.

"Who are you?" the young hippogryph finally settled on asking.

Relwen didn't see any good reason to lie. Not yet, at least. "Relwen," she answered. "From Direlord Maylar's pride."

This perhaps was the wrong thing to say. The gray hippogryph—and the small opinicus who'd reported back to him—both hackled.

"Did Maylar send you?" the opinicus growled. "If she thinks she's getting Jessen back, she's got another thing coming."

Relwen raised her paws to prove her innocence. "I have no idea who that is," she said as calmly as she could. "But I don't think Maylar wants them. I'm here for my own reasons."

"And those reasons are...?" the opinicus, a white-feathered variety, prompted. Relwen was almost too confused to respond. She'd thought the hippogryph was the leader here; why then was this opinicus questioning her?

"I was hunting here yesterday," Relwen answered once the fog had cleared from her head. "I noticed gryph blood. I wanted to find out what's up."

Something that looked very much like grief darkened both the hippogryph and opinicus's faces. "That's none of your concern," the hippogryph bit out through his beak, voice strained.

"If one of your gryphs is hurt, I could help," Relwen offered earnestly. "There's medicine in my pride; I could get you some..."

"No!" the opinicus snapped. "You need to get out of here and leave us alone."

"Shouldn't we take her prisoner?" the hippogryph muttered to his partner. Once again, Relwen found herself baffled. *Huh. Maybe she's the leader here. She does look older than the hippogryph, after all.*

The opinicus shook her head. "It would be more trouble than it's worth. Besides, Maylar knows there are wilder camps outside her pridegrounds. She's never caused us trouble before."

"But what about Jessen?" the hippogryph asked.

"Do you really think I'm not considering Jessen?" the opinicus growled at her partner. "I will keep Jessen safe. You don't need to worry your pretty hindquarters about it."

Relwen felt that this conversation was *definitely* something not meant for her ears. Rising back to her feet, she drew the wilders' attention. Two sets of angry eyes met hers.

"You're not going to take me prisoner?" she settled on asking. It seemed like the safest course of action, to draw their attention away from whatever the wilders feared she'd repeat to Maylar.

The hippogryph ground his beak. The opinicus spoke. "You just forget you ever saw us. Don't come looking again. And say nothing to Maylar. If you do, we'll find out, and we'll kill you."

The hippogryph shifted his feet. Relwen wondered how serious the opinicus's threat actually was.

"Got it," she said, forcing her characteristic lightness into her voice. "I never saw you."

"Good," the opinicus said. "Now get out of here."

Enough violence flashed in the opinicus's eyes that Relwen obeyed immediately, sore chest be damned, and flew like a pack of wolves pursued her.

But even under threat of death, Relwen couldn't quite chase her questions from her mind. *Whose blood was on those rocks?*

And who is Jessen?

THE MIST HAD BURNED OFF BY THE AFTERNOON, AND Relwen found herself spending some time with Stell and Lila in a patch of warm sunlight outside the nursery. Both of her friends had one ear ticked back to listen to the kits inside the building, but otherwise, they were wholly absorbed in Relwen's whispered story.

After all, the wilders had said not to tell *Maylar* anything. They hadn't said Relwen couldn't tell her friends.

"I don't know," Stell said, ever the worried kitcarer. "It sounds like nothing you need to be tangled up in."

Lila, holding Stell's paw in an almost-nauseating display of affection, nodded along with her mate. "The wilders around here don't mess with us, and we leave them alone. It's been like that ever since my mother became direlord."

"But it sounds like this Jessen has connections with the Maylar pride," Relwen argued. "I want to find out what that's all about. And I want to know what happened to the gryph whose blood was on those rocks. Neither of the wilders I talked to had any injuries, and they sounded really upset when I brought it up."

"Again, it sounds like none of your business," Stell said, shrugging her wings with a wince. The cold air must be bothering her old injury. Relwen frowned sympathetically, thinking again of the gryph who'd left the blood— another gryph with an injury, one who quite possibly didn't have access to the medicine they needed.

"It might not be my business," Relwen said with the characteristic flaunt to her voice. "But I'm bored and I want to find out those wilders' story."

I'm nobody in this pride, she wanted to say. *If I could help these gryphs, solve their mystery, maybe I'd feel valuable for once.*

"Please just don't get yourself hurt," Stell said. "I need you too much."

Relwen smiled halfheartedly. Maybe that had been the case before, but now Relwen was just a chatterbox who interrupted Stell's mated bliss with occasional hunting stories. Stories of a gryph who would never truly mean anything to the pride. Relwen loved Stell, but she knew the truth.

Nobody needs me.

RELWEN RETURNED TO THE MEADOW THE NEXT MORNING, landing right next to the blood-soaked rocks. She tapped the granite with a claw. "What happened to you?" she murmured.

"Tell me why I'm not surprised to see you here," a

gryph said, making Relwen jump about two feet into the air. Spinning around, she saw the gray hippogryph standing in the meadow behind her. His tone was nonthreatening, his posture relaxed. Maybe Relwen wasn't about to die.

"How did you sneak up on me like that?" she asked.

The hippogryph offered Relwen a small smile, surprising her. "My name's Mist. I've got serrated feathers, like an owl. Helps me stay silent. Hence my name."

If Relwen didn't know any better, she'd say this awkward hippogryph was flirting with her. Did wilders have romantic flings in this meadow too?

Despite Mist's charm, Relwen didn't want to be caught off guard. She hadn't forgotten the opinicus's death threat. *Stupid. You were so stupid to come back here.* Oh, well. Low self-worth would do that to a gryph.

"Where's your opinicus friend?" Relwen asked, scanning the field and surrounding forest.

"Bryn? I don't know that we're really friends, per se."

"Is she your leader?" Relwen figured she'd make the most of this conversation.

"More like... a co-leader, I'd say," Mist responded after some thought.

Relwen's eye ridges furrowed. "Gryphs don't have co-leaders."

"Well, she's the diplomat"—at this, Relwen bit back a laugh— "and I'm more the big scary fighter."

"I don't find you all that scary," Relwen said with a slight chuckle. She hoped this was casual banter, a friendly conversation that wasn't about to go south.

"You seemed to think I was pretty scary yesterday," Mist said. "Sorry about kicking you in the chest, by the way."

At this, Relwen's confusion overflowed, rushing out of her beak in a jumble of words. "Why are you sorry? Aren't I *the enemy*—a gryph from Maylar's pride? And whose blood is on those rocks?"

Mist stared at her wide-eyed.

"And who's Jessen?" Relwen asked, a bit of an afterthought.

"Are you trying to join our camp or something?" Mist asked after several more moments of confused silence.

A camp. A wilder camp run by some sort of... co-leadership between a hippogryph and an opinicus.

Are you trying to join our camp?

"Maybe," Relwen said, surprising herself. "I want to find out more about your people. I wouldn't have expected kindness from a bunch of wilders, but I'd like to see if I can return it in any way."

"Kicking you in the chest and threatening death aren't particularly kind actions," Mist suggested. "How do I know you aren't a spy?"

"I'm here alone; you know that because you probably already scouted this entire field before you spoke to me. And you let me go yesterday. And you're being kind now." Relwen shrugged. "Not many others have spoken to me like an equal before."

"We're all equals in our camp," Mist assured.

"Because you don't have a leader?" Relwen asked. Mist tensed, and Relwen knew she'd hit on a sensitive subject.

"Follow me," Mist said, ignoring Relwen's question. "But be careful; there are wolves in these woods."

Relwen laughed, trotting into the forest after the silent hippogryph. "Believe me, I know."

Relwen could've sworn Mist stared down at the blood-covered rocks as they passed, a shudder traveling the length of his body. Something was very wrong here. And Relwen was about to learn just what it was.

RELWEN FOLLOWED MIST FOR CLOSE TO A MARK, WINDING past familiar hunting areas into an unknown part of the mountains. They walked along the edge of a gorge, a river crashing over half-submerged boulders several hundred feet below.

"How come I've never known this river was here?" Relwen asked, shouting to be heard over the roar of the water.

"It goes underground a mile south of here," Mist yelled back. "The gorge used to keep the wolves away, but..." he choked on his words, swallowing hard. Relwen narrowed her eyes.

The blood, the wolves, and Jessen? Relwen was no closer to understanding the wilders' situation.

Finally, they broke away from the gorge and trotted another mile or so north before coming across a thick tangle of rhododendron bushes. Mist let out a songbird whistle, waited a minute, and received a similar call from within the rhododendron.

"I'll go first," he said, ducking under a small arch in the tangled plants. "It's a bit of a squeeze."

Relwen couldn't agree more, scraping underneath the branches on her belly. At one point, hair from Mist's equine tail got stuck in her beak and she spluttered.

"Move faster," she hissed. "This tunnel sucks."

They emerged from the thick tangle of rhododendron, and Relwen rose to her feet within a sort of rhododendron dome. Gentle sunlight penetrated the canopy of bushes and soft ferns coated the ground. Able to stand up properly, Relwen noted the size of the wilders' camp was about twice that of her pride's nursery. Around twenty wilders of all shapes and colors milled around their home.

Relwen didn't have long to enjoy it. A familiar white-feathered opinicus was striding through the ferns toward Relwen and Mist, a stormy expression on her face.

"What is *she* doing here?" Bryn growled. "If she's come for Jessen, well she can take Maylar's orders and shove them up her—"

"I'm not here for Jessen," Relwen said, exasperated. "All spirits, please believe me when I say I don't know who Jessen is, and I don't know why Maylar would want them—"

Relwen was cut off, as she so often had been of late, by another gryph speaking. "Relken? Is that you?"

Relwen stiffened. Who here knew her birth name, the name she had changed to reflect her true self?

A gryphon with dark brown feathers made her way over to Bryn's side, staring at Relwen with such hope in her eyes that it made Relwen's feathers prickle.

"It's Relwen," she said curtly. "And who's asking?"

"Are you a half-breed?" the brown gryphon asked, continuing to pry. "From the Maylar pride?"

Relwen narrowed her eyes. Bryn was shifting her feet awkwardly, evidently privy to something Relwen didn't yet know.

"Who are you to ask me these questions?" Relwen's tone was still cold. This had nothing to do with her quest, with the blood or the wolves or Jessen.

"I'm Jessen," the brown gryphon said. "And I think I may be your mother."

Well. Maybe this *was* relevant.

The next several moments were a blur. Jessen leapt forward to embrace her daughter—which Relwen accepted, albeit stiffly—while Mist gawked and Bryn apologized heartily for her poor treatment. When Jessen finally pulled away from Relwen, talons still resting on her daughter's shoulders, Relwen made one request.

"Tell me."

And Jessen told Relwen her story. She'd been a highly valued Hunter in Maylar's pride, favored by Maylar herself, although Jessen never returned the direlord's affections. When she found herself falling for an opinicus Hunter, she thought she'd be able to keep their love secret. She certainly didn't plan on having a kit. And when that kit was born an opinicus—well, that was all the evidence Maylar needed to know that her prized Hunter had broken pride law. Jessen and her lover were exiled immediately.

Relwen's father died shortly after, killed in a nasty lightning storm. Jessen had wandered the mountains for some time, mourning the loss of her child and mate, before stumbling upon this group of wilders. She'd lived with them ever since.

"You thought because she was one of Maylar's best Hunters, that Maylar wanted her back? After all this time?" Relwen asked Bryn. Relwen, Bryn, Jessen—and Mist, for whatever reason—were relaxing on the far side of the wilders' camp, lying in the soft grass.

Bryn nodded. "After what she did to Jessen, Maylar doesn't deserve to have her back." She fixed Jessen with a fiercely protective stare. If she could guess, Relwen would say they were mates.

"Well, I've never heard Maylar mention Jessen," Relwen reassured the anxious opinicus. "I think she assumes you're dead," she said, glancing apologetically at her mother.

"It had best stay that way," Bryn said firmly.

"Bryn, please," Jessen said, grasping Bryn's paw in her talon. "I'm not going anywhere."

Remembering that Mist was there, Relwen spoke up again. "Jessen, are you a co-leader of this camp too?" She thought her mother might be more forthcoming in her answers than the hippogryph and opinicus who had led her in circles with their half-answers.

"We don't... we don't have a leader right now," Jessen said, blinking back tears.

Relwen gazed openly at her mother. "Is that whose blood is at the meadow?"

To her surprise, it was Mist who answered. "We were ambushed," he said, his voice low, haunted. "A pack of those cursed blue-eyed wolves caught us in the middle of our hunt. There were only three of us and six of them. Half as big as a dire gryphon, I swear." He swallowed, staring down at the ground. "It was the middle of winter. We were hungry. So were the wolves, I guess. But Toark wasn't going to let them take our prey. He told us to take our catch and flee." Tears were openly cascading down Mist's face at this point.

"We ran, because he was our leader, and because he told us to. He stayed to fight the wolves and keep them off our trail. Soon as we'd dropped off the food, I flew back to the meadow. And the wolves were... they were..." Mist gulped, clearly unable to finish his sentence.

Relwen didn't have to ask. She knew what the wolves had done to Toark, why there wasn't a body.

"I'm sorry," Relwen said, and she meant it from the bottom of her heart. Because she knew why those wolves were plaguing the wilders' woods, woods they used to avoid.

It all went back to a day fractures ago, when a hunting party had returned to Maylar's pridegrounds after being attacked by wolves. There had been a curfew, two kits rescued by a gryph with wolf eyes, and a forced removal of the wolves from Maylar's land.

Relwen hadn't cared at the time where the displaced pack went. Now she did.

And though she hadn't had anything to do with the wolves, she felt it was her responsibility to help these gryphs.

THE EVENING ARRIVED FASTER THAN RELWEN WAS expecting after spending the day socializing with the wilders. She was quickly learning everything she'd been taught about wilders was wrong; they didn't smell and they weren't scavengers. Rather, they had more honor than many of the gryphs in Maylar's pride and cared deeply about one another.

It also helped that Relwen's mother belonged to the wilder camp. She'd never imagined meeting her parents —she'd thought they were dead, as did the rest of Maylar's pride—but it was nice to have someone who loved her without question. Sure, they'd just met that day, but Relwen already knew she was going to be close with her mother.

"Do you want to stay the night?" Jessen asked her, hope alight in her eyes.

"No, I've got to go back to Maylar's pridegrounds." Strange, that it was no longer *home*.

"But you'll be back?" Jessen stared earnestly at Relwen.

She answered without thinking. "Yes, I'll be back."

Mist insisted on escorting Relwen to the meadow, since she might not know her way back from the wilder camp. They walked companionably in the afternoon light, no longer jogging as they had that morning. Relwen knew they could probably fly, but this was fine, too.

"Is it really true that your friend killed a wolf?" Mist asked. "It sounded like a bit of a tall tale when you said it earlier."

Relwen smiled at the awkward, charming hippogryph. "Stell tells it better than I do. But yes, it's true. And..." she swallowed, staring down at her feet. "And I'm afraid it's the reason the wolves are attacking you. Because we ran them off Maylar's land."

Mist brushed a gentle wing against Relwen's shoulder. "Hey, that's not your fault."

"Maybe not," Relwen admitted. "But they're my people, and they should've considered that there might be consequences to their actions."

"Direlords don't care about consequences," Mist said.

"But I do." They'd reached the meadow, the granite stones stained with the blood of the wilder leader Toark.

Relwen was spreading her wings when Mist blurted, "I want to see you again."

For the first time in her life, Relwen felt a fluttering in her belly, something more than just physical attraction.

"You will," she promised, and took flight from the meadow.

UPON RETURNING TO THE PRIDEGROUNDS, RELWEN SOUGHT out Stell. The black-feathered opinicus was, as Relwen predicted, in the nursery. Her friend's blue wolf eyes narrowed on Relwen as soon as she walked in the door.

"Where have you been?" Stell asked, striding over to preen her friend. "You've had me worried all day; you usually stop by the nursery at least once to say hi."

Jessen may love Relwen unconditionally, but she remembered that Stell loved her just the same. Which was why Relwen already knew this conversation would be difficult.

"Stell, can we talk in private?" she asked softly, leaning into her friend's preening. It was a tone of voice she rarely used outside of serious conversations with Stell, although she was hoping that now, with a purpose in her life, she might be able to shed the carefree persona she'd worn for so long.

"Absolutely," Stell replied. Asking Lila to keep an eye on the kits, Stell led Relwen out of the tent.

"How would you like an evening flight?" Relwen asked with a smile at her closest friend.

"I'd like it very much," Stell said.

The two gryphs took flight, riding the day's dying thermals high above camp as they had countless times throughout their lives. With the shadows cast over the mountains by the setting sun, half of the pridegrounds lay in shadow while the rest glowed golden. Once they were at a safe altitude to talk privately, Stell set her wings to glide and fixed an anxious stare on Relwen. "You looked for the wilders again, didn't you." It wasn't a question.

Relwen flushed. Stell knew her too well. "I found them."

"Relwen, you—" Stell began, but Relwen cut her off.

"My mother was with them," she said. "She isn't dead. And she wants to build a relationship with me, and I think I want that, too." Once she started, the words fell out of her beak one after another. "And they lost their leader to a wolf attack. The wolves *we* chased away from here last fracture moved into the wilders' land, and they're suffering. They don't know how to fight wolves."

Stell processed all this carefully, tears forming in her eyes. "And you do," she said finally. "You've learned how to fight wolves from all the hunts you've accompanied."

Relwen smiled weakly, brushing her wing against Stell's. "After I learned I couldn't be a Hunter, I thought those hunts would never be anything more than a fun pastime. Turns out they were useful all along."

The two friends soared in companionable silence, circling the valley twice before Stell spoke up again. "You're leaving," she said, matter of fact.

"Yes," Relwen said, and she heard her dear friend begin to weep softly. "Oh, Stell," she murmured, reaching out a paw.

"Is there anything I can do to make you stay?" Stell asked around her tears.

"Stell, you know there's nobody aside from you who needs me in this pride. And even then, you have Lila. You have the kits. You're valuable and you're wonderful and you'll be okay without me. But I want to be valuable, too. And I think this might be how I do that."

Stell snorted back tears gracelessly, giving Relwen a watery smile. "Those wilders are going to be so lucky to have you, camp leader Relwen."

Relwen chuckled damply. "I'm nobody's leader."

"No, but you will be," Stell said with confidence.

Moved by her friend's belief in her, Relwen reached

over and grasped Stell's paw in her own. "I love you, Wolf Eyes."

"I love you, too. And I'm going to miss you so much." Stell squeezed Relwen's paw before letting it fall away.

"Tell Lila I said good-bye," Relwen requested. "I don't want a big to-do in the pride about me running away."

"I'll never tell them where you went," Stell promised.

Relwen waved a paw dismissively. "They probably won't even notice I'm gone."

Just like that, they'd slipped into their easy give-and-take banter, and Relwen knew she would be alright to leave. Stell was going to have a wonderful life—a peaceful life—with her mate, and Relwen was going to lead a life of adventure, battling wolves alongside her wilder family.

The two lifelong friends gazed at one another for a few moments longer before turning to go their respective ways. But before she'd beat her wings more than a few times, Relwen spun around in the air. "Oh! Stell!"

Stell turned around, hovering in place.

"If you ever want to meet, I'll visit the firefly meadow every other full moon."

Stell smiled. "I'll see you there."

And so they separated, Stell descending to the nursery and her mate while Relwen set her wings north. To the wilders, to adventure, to her mother and her crush. To a place where she'd be valued.

Relwen flew home.

CONTRIBUTORS

Glenn Birmingham is a fantasy author, fountain pen aficionado, and ink enthusiast. When he's not filling his endless supply of journals with dragon stories, he's publishing them as the Reunification series, starting with *Dragon Source*. He lives in Colorado with his two cats, yard of native plants, and spouse.

He can be found at GlennBirmingham.com or on Patreon/BirminghamGlenn

Author of The Gryphon Generation series, Alex resides in Chattanooga, Tennessee, where he was born and raised. He started out in pizza delivery and now works in industrial maintenance at a car manufacturing plant. His love of reading took him from Larry Dixon to Jess Owen and into his own writing.

Alex enjoys spending his free time socializing and writing. He is obsessed with car culture, practicing falconry with his red-tailed hawk named Ranger, and playing video games. He also likes to travel to other countries and experience new cultures. He plans to write many more gryphon-themed books and hopes you'll join him for the journey.

J.F.R. Coates is a speculative fiction author, focusing in fantasy and science fiction. His work tends to focus away from the human characters of the setting, instead giving life to the creatures that dwell alongside the familiar. From dragons and gryphons, to creatures of his own creation - like the ailur or starat - these story worlds are full of fascinating creatures to get to know.

You can find his stories on his website at jfrcoates.com, or follow him on twitter @jfrcoates.

Saylor Ferguson is a writer who would much rather be a gryphon. When not reading or writing tales of gryphons, dragons, birds, or wolves (or some combination of all four), she can be found hiking, fishing, or hawking.

Author of the upcoming Dragons of Time series, Saylor lives in the Appalachian Mountains of North Carolina.

K. Vale Nagle is alarmingly hard to kill.

After surviving several pulmonary embolisms and multiple organ failure, he kicked his writing into high gear and saw his first short story and novel publications. When he's not writing creature fantasy or fighting for his life, he enjoys reading, archery, and exploring the Rocky Mountains with a tabby cat by his side.

He can be found writing the Gryphon Insurrection series, also about gryphons and opinici! Pick up *Eyrie* and give it a try.

Dustin Porta is an artist and writer from rural Pennsylvania who moved to the Gulf Coast to live and work on the ocean. His art and writing is available at dustinporta.com.

Anna Marie "Paws" Privitere cut her teeth editing articles at RPGamer.com before moving on to being a social media manager and copy editor. Find her on Twitter @amprivitere.

Fleeks is a dragon-hearted creator from Europe who specializes in vectors and linework illustrations. www.fleeks.art

M. H. Wolfe is the prolific author of fantasy books that blur the line between creature and human. His writing introduces us to animals and monsters alike that have lives as emotionally and philosophically complex as any human. Beyond that, his works feature engaging characters and stories that won't let you stop turning pages.

C. "Kitt" Gafford is a graphic design artist who adores animals and fantasy creatures. Their small menagerie of spoiled pets — from chickens to cats — keeps them inspired.

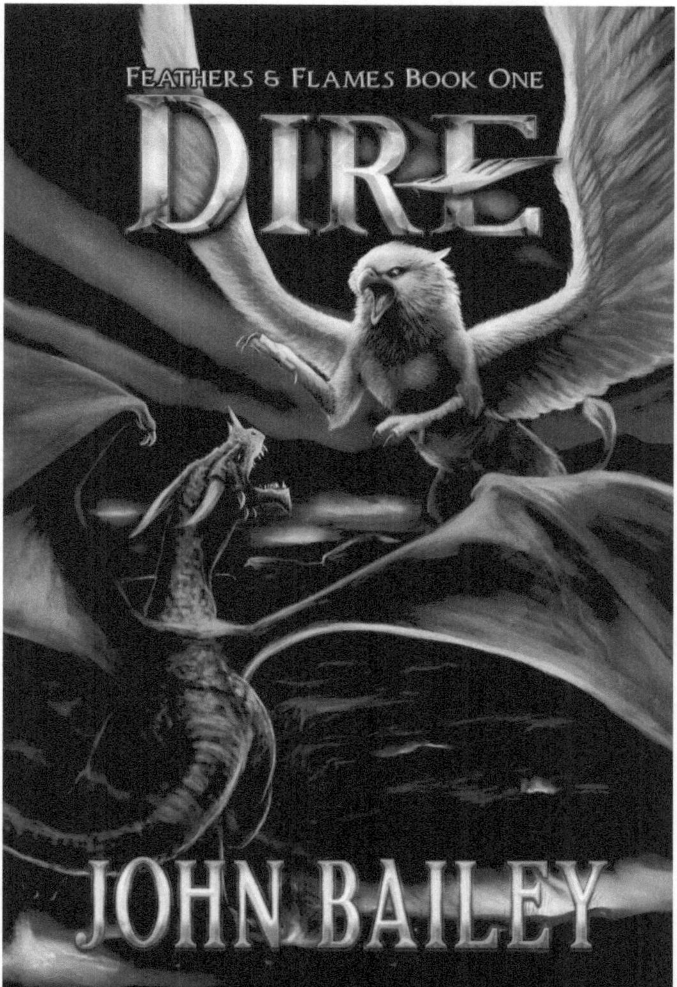
FEATHERS & FLAMES BOOK ONE
DIRE
JOHN BAILEY